"Strube has a powerful way of dr
her characters' head. What is par
skill in *The Barking Dog* is that we desperately do not
experience what Greer experiences, yet the story is told with such humour and suspense that it's hard to put down . . . Urgent rather than erudite, hyper-realist rather than lyrical, *The Barking Dog* is a plea for awareness. The carnage that is Greer's life exists just around the corner, and we are Greer, living in the repulsive middle of a dangerous social and environmental soup of human construction. *The Barking Dog* is a rare achievement, unstintingly honest, hilarious and dreadful delight."

—*The Globe and Mail*

"As usual in Strube's work, the characterization is lively and the snappy writing is full of caustic zingers on contemporary urban life and the absurdities of pop culture, especially television and advertising . . . *The Barking Dog* confronts and affronts, but it's not easy to forget." —*Toronto Star*

"Strube peels back the fast-food, tabloid cynicism that shrink-wraps urban life and show us the dark matter beneath . . . a compelling ride [that] acquires a depth of horror reminiscent of Greek tragedy." —*National Post*

"A novel is more than an argument, if it's a good one, and this one is. It's an engaging and genuinely affecting narrative. Greer Pentland is perhaps Strube's most sympathetic protagonist, a stubborn cynic who's hard on herself but soft and warm as custard to the bruised people around her." —*Vancouver Sun*

"*The Barking Dog* absolutely must go down in the canons of literature as a great tragedy. There is more truth in this novel than in so many others." —*Kitchener-Waterloo Record*

"A classically tragic plot that shatters under the weight of its cathartic climax." —*Georgia Straight*

"Her portraits of characters caught in urban angst are riddled with laugh-out loud humour . . . Strube's rueful insistence on contemplating human darkness is tempered by a certain wistfulness, a yearning for something finer, a flicker of hope that is never quite extinguished . . . a book that crackles with anger, righteousness and a strange kind of passion for living. Strube's mandate has always been to unsettle, not merely entertain, and in *The Barking Dog* she has succeeded admirably."

—*Edmonton Journal*

THE BARKING DOG

a Novel

CORDELIA STRUBE

ALSO BY CORDELIA STRUBE

NOVELS

Alex & Zee
Milton's Elements
Teaching Pigs to Sing
Dr. Kalbfleisch & the Chicken Restaurant
The Barking Dog
Blind Night
Lemon
Planet Reese
Milosz
On the Shores of Darkness, There Is Light

STAGE AND RADIO PLAYS

Fine
Mortal
Shape
Caught in the Intersection
Marshmallow
Mid-Air
Absconder
On the Beach
Scar Tissue
Attached
Past Due

For Carson

One

It started with me thinking there was a man in the house. I'd wake Jerry. "There is no man," he'd say.

It was around this time he started screwing what's-her-face.

So I'd tell myself I was imagining things, that maybe I wanted there to be a man, that maybe my man-phobia was what Jerry would call an attention-getting device. But suspecting that the man was inside my head didn't make me feel any better. Because I started to fear that he was embodying something hideous in my makeup, something I couldn't face. I would've preferred to have been robbed. I could've called somebody, dialled 911. I've always wanted to dial 911. The thugs-in-blue could've come with guns.

I don't know what I imagined the man was doing in my house because in the morning nothing was out of place; the stereo was intact, the TV, the VCR—objects I hated and would've liked to have had stolen. Objects that absorbed my beautiful son and transformed him into an unresponsive, twitching blob.

The man stayed in my consciousness for a couple of years. I dreaded going to bed because he'd be lurking downstairs, fingering my belongings, sneering at the wedding photo and Jerry's phallic golf trophy (another object I would've liked to have had stolen). I'd knocked the stupid thing over at least five times, and once threw it at Jerry. It was unbreakable.

I never went to look for the man myself. I don't know what I was afraid of: that he didn't exist?

The prosecution's been trying to sniff out "dysfunction" in my family: personality disorders, anti-social behaviour. Something that would constitute conditioning for a psychopath. I worry that on the stand my dysfunction will show. Which would be bad for Sam. I'm supposed to appear normal, just as he's supposed to appear normal.

The point about the man business is that it occurred just before I realized that Jerry was screwing what's-her-face. Not the one he married, but the first one—my neighbour—who borrowed things from me: garden tools, blankets, roasting pans. She had her own husband. They played golf together, went to Florida and Arizona to try different courses. So I don't understand what she was doing with my husband. But then I've never understood what's so great about golf.

Now I know that "the man" was the cancer stalking me. The cancer was embodying the hideousness in my makeup.

The joke is that Jerry was diagnosed with it first. I'd told him to go to the doctor because he was chronically fatigued, beyond his regular Jerry-not-wanting-to-do-anything-with-his-family fatigue. He went for tests, then more tests. I took the doctor's call because Jerry was too scared to talk to him. He stood watching me, his face flaccid, waiting for the verdict. I decided that even if the news was good, I'd appear grim, just to rattle Jerry.

"Yes," I said sombrely to the doctor. "I understand . . . unhunh . . . unhunh . . . yes . . . I see." Something like that. I was simply absorbing his diagnosis, not repeating it. But Jerry panicked before I even got off the phone. He walked into the closet and closed the door.

It was thyroid cancer in the early stages. There was to be minor surgery and radiation. Small stuff compared to what I would have to go through.

I stared at the closet. "Come out, Jerry."

No response.

I considered my options. I could've pleaded with him to come out, assumed the womanly role of nurturing and assured him that everything was going to be just fine, not to worry, poochy woochy. Or I could've lit a match, slipped it under the closet door and made a run for it. Or I could've blockaded him in there. Fed him occasionally.

I did none of this because I didn't understand yet that life is the very second you're in. You don't dick around wasting seconds.

I went downstairs and finished the birthday cake I'd baked for Sam which he hadn't touched. I yanked out the ten candles that hours before I'd carefully arranged. Consuming slice after slice, I felt sorry for myself for being a mother so wronged, so misunderstood. Then I found myself hoping my husband would die from the cancer, that it would spread up his throat into his brain because this would mean I could sell the house and move to Hawaii. I imagined tropical breezes, ocean spray, rum cocktails. I imagined my boy, rejuvenated by the salt air, running towards me calling "Mummy."

He never hugs me anymore. Never. To think I once had the freedom to hold him whenever I wanted. To think I was that lucky and didn't know it.

Eventually, Jerry came out of the closet and shuffled downstairs. I took my time telling him, only at the end admitting that the oncologist wasn't terribly worried about it.

It was after his course of treatment, when he was considered to be in the clear, that he started "playing nine holes" with the first one, the neighbour who borrowed the pots and pans. I had the impression he was living life with relish, now that he'd been faced with his own mortality.

Which I can understand. It's sneaking around I can't stand. Don't lie. I hate lies. Politicians who lie should be thrown out of government. Or failing that, shot.

I asked him how he thought Sam felt about his dad screwing the neighbour. He said Sam didn't know. I said of course he does. He asked if I told him. I said of course not. Children know. They always know. Then I told him to get out. Shouted at him, threatened him with lawyers. We didn't actually throw things that time. At one point I considered hurling the phallic golf trophy. But he left with little resistance. I think he was relieved. They shacked up for a bit, then she went back to her husband. Maybe he was a better golfer.

I was hurt, of course, self-esteem impaired. It seemed important at the time. Now it's impossible to comprehend how brain-dead Jerr could've had such an effect on me. But life's like that. You go through these things that seem to tear you apart. Years later you wonder why. Years later you're going through some other thing that seems to be tearing you apart.

I told Jerry that it was *his* job to explain *his* side of the divorce to Sam. He never did. At first, I said lame things like we don't love each other anymore. But during the divorce proceedings I found myself referring to Sam's absentee father as anal-retentive, emotionally retarded, small-minded, dick-driven, cheap.

Anyway, this is all ancient history. The point is my son. What happened to my son?

In the courtroom, everybody stares at me. How could she give birth to such a monster? How can she stand it? What did she do to drive him to it?

Well, you know what? I wasn't even around. I'd actually won a raffle, a weekend pass to a spa. I never win anything, and spas give me the willies—strangers slapping oil all over you and squeezing your zits. But I thought, I've got to try it, it's in the country, it's free, maybe aromatherapy will change my life. I hated it; at one point a taut Chinese woman was rubbing me with rocks. Anyway, I had no idea what my boy was up to, didn't even hear about it until I came home greased. By this time, Sam had been in an adult jail for twenty-four hours. He'd lied about his age, possibly to protect me but more likely to protect his part-time job as a security guard at my brother-in-law's hospital. Jerry got the job for him, told him to lie about his age because Jerry got a paper route when he was three or something and believes that all enterprising young men should get jobs and become millionaires by the time they're twelve. It used to drive him wild when Sam would *spend* his allowance rather than stash it in his piggy bank.

So I think about that often: *If I'd been home, would he have done it?* Probably. I don't keep tabs on him anymore; it's futile. Which made the whole bail issue terrifying. When the schlep of a duty counsel advised me that we could apply for bail—meaning write a huge cheque or post the house—I thought, You must be joking, take the killer home? But then he was there, my lost son, looking at his hands, tapping his feet, trembling even though the room wasn't cold. The duty counsel, awash in sweat, kept removing his lawyer duds, first his jacket, then his vest, tie. Of course we must try for bail, I said. The Crown will oppose it, he advised me. No, really? It was then I called Jerry who contacted the hot-shot criminal lawyer. I was rattling within during the proceeding. We had to sit through what felt like several hundred requests for bail before it was our turn. The whole time I was thinking, *Please* don't lock him up, *please* lock him up. I couldn't believe any of it was happening, had happened. I didn't know who my son was anymore, what he could do. Our lawyer was worth his hundreds of dollars, a Houdini eluding the Criminal Code. He made it sound like boys kill people every day, no big whoop, and the poor kid has no criminal record, no motive and no memory of the incident which suggests, *if* in fact he did commit the crime, he may have been unconscious of his actions and therefore not responsible because he had no knowledge or appreciation of what he was doing. I think the judge let Sam off because he wanted the lawyer to button it so His Honour could proceed to lunch. Then there were papers to sign, a recognizance and a document registered against the title of the house, which was the surety payable should Sam skip town.

But the conditions caused me some sleep deprivation. Every couple of hours, I'd wake and check his room to make sure he hadn't made a run for it. Days should have been easier as he was expected to attend school, but it was June, exam time, meaning not his regular schedule. I had no way of tracking his movements. I'd ask feebly, "Do you have an exam today?" and he would mutter something unintelligible. I'd phone the school, talk to voicemail knowing my call would not be returned because the staff were busy planning their summer vacations. He was subject to a curfew, supposed to be home between 10 p.m. and 7 a.m., but usually he'd show up those few minutes late; just enough time to cause my heart rate to zoom to three hundred beats per minute. And he was ordered to report to the police every forty-eight hours, which he did, but it was weeks before I stopped phoning the division to ascertain that he'd checked in. Now I never call. He's a good boy. I think. Or anyway understands that jumping bail is a bad idea.

The thugs-in-blue advised me that I could have him rearrested at any time if I felt it was necessary. They've been itching to get their hands on him, the "rich kid" with the fancy lawyer.

After the remand hearing, driving home, I asked Sam if he had any idea why he'd done it. He repeated that he didn't know if he'd done it since he had no memory of the incident. We were in the car, stopped in traffic. There'd been an accident, sirens wailed, a blood-thirsty crowd gathered. We sat in silence although his foot kept tapping.

"I have difficulty believing that," I said finally.

"What?" His foot stopped.

"That you can't remember anything."

He shrugged, resumed tapping, turned on the radio, fiddled with the tuner until he found something obnoxious. He told me if I'd been there, he probably would've killed me. He said this without malice. As though killing people was normal, to be expected. Why? He wouldn't tell me. Over the months since he was charged, we've had different versions of this conversation. He shrugs, avoids my eyes, stares at the TV. Is that shame? Remorse? What is it? He won't tell me.

So I stare back at the excuses-for-human-beings who line up early outside the courtroom to get a front-row seat. I don't understand why we're so popular; have there been no child abuse/murder/sex crimes lately? Is the press so starved of ecological disasters, stock market crashes and savage warmongers that we've been upgraded to page three?

The gawkers have big appetites. During recesses, they munch potato chips and chew on Kit Kat bars. They have already condemned my son and are titillated by my despair. I have no answers for them. I am ashamed and distraught and enraged. I grieve for the little boy I knew. He did exist once. I've got the photographs.

Two

The judge appears to be drowsy today. Too many cocktails last night, or maybe he was at a cross-dressing party. I can see him in gold lamé and garters, fishnet stockings, glittery pumps, doing the mashed potato. I hate the old fart because he doesn't listen. During the preliminary hearing he spent most of his time grumbling and telling the defence to "get on with it." The defence irritates him, and the dull jury take their cues from him. Particularly the winner of the Sonny Bono look-alike contest who also happens to be the foreman. I think of O.J., and all his entertaining, expensive lawyers strutting about in their pink shirts and silk ties. Our lawyer, though expensive, is not entertaining. His robe sags from his shoulders as he shuffles about, wiping his nose every three minutes. Why? myself and the jury wonder. Is there snot on his moustache? He's also balding and has some kind of scalp condition. The Crown, on the other hand, is a tall, blond and handsome football-player type. During his predictable opening statements, the female jurors eyed him lustily. As he expounded upon the overwhelming physical evidence, they sat with legs crossed, tightening the walls of their vaginas. He has been gleeful while calling forensic witnesses to the stand and almost peed himself when his top cop presented the jury with gory photographs of the murder victims. As the jurors' faces paled, the football player swelled with self-satisfaction. An open-and-shut case, he was thinking.

Yesterday, a mentally ill man was shot to death by a cop. Two bullets landed in his head and one in his throat. A woman who witnessed the slaughter described the victim as surprised to be shot. The cop is claiming he acted in self-defence because the man, yards away from him, pulled a hammer from his coat. Now there's a reason to shoot somebody. I always say, if he's got a hammer, whack him. Before he became mentally ill, the dead man was in medical school.

I wonder what my jury would feel about the photos of the dead medical student's head. What's left of it.

The football player regularly reminds us that Sam rinsed the blood from his clothes before returning home. This would suggest knowledge and appreciation of the act. On the other hand, I know Sam. He hates dirt. He washes his hands frequently, showers twice a day. He will not wear a shirt twice before laundering it. He bleaches his whites. I'd say he's borderline OCD. The fact that he cleaned up the mess doesn't surprise me.

Baldy with the snotty moustache has to prove that Sam is not guilty by reason of non-insane automatism because he was sleepwalking when he committed the murders. Therefore he was rendered incapable of appreciating the nature and quality of his act, or knowing that his act was wrong. I'm trying to believe this. Baldy has rounded up hired-gun shrinks and psychologists who have attached electrodes to Sam's head to measure his brain activity during sleep. They believe it is possible to snooze while clubbing people to death.

Jerry's father used to sleepwalk. It was a family joke. In the morning, there would be food left over from his night's foraging. Once, he started mowing the lawn, waking the neighbourhood. Less amusing was his habit of urinating in the closet.

But as far as I know, he never killed anybody.

When Sam started sleepwalking, we didn't worry about it. Sometimes, before he got out of bed, he'd scream, in which case I'd go to him and try to offer comfort. But he'd stare at me glassily. His pupils would be dilated and his muscles tense. When I tried to console him, he'd be unresponsive or unintelligible. If he did wake up, he would have no recollection of what he'd been doing or dreaming. He peed on chairs a few times, but other than that he never caused harm. I told myself it was nothing to fret about, just a family trait, like receding hairlines and varicose veins. Besides, he's always been an anxious kid. Anxious kids have nightmares. Fortunately, in his teens, the sleepwalking episodes became less frequent. I was hoping he'd outgrown them. But the security job at the hospital required that he work nights. It's never been easy for him to fall asleep at night, never mind during the day. But it paid better than McDonald's so we figured it was worth doing. The theory was that he would adjust. Besides, it was only for the summer, until he went back to school. And it kept us apart, providing me with an excuse for the complete lack of communication between us. Sometimes he'd fall asleep on the couch while watching soap operas. I'd turn the TV off and cover him with a blanket, then sit on the armchair and watch him; listen to his breathing. When he's back to a normal schedule, I told myself, when I've finished being Hiroshimaed, things will get better. Like it could be that simple.

Only a year ago he sliced off the tips of two of his fingers trying to use Jerry's tile cutter. I heard shrieks from the basement and found him staring down at the meat of his fingers on the floor. I tried to staunch the blood pouring from his hand with paper towels, but it was useless. He'd always become faint at the sight of blood and dissolved into the little boy I'd known. "Help me, Mum," he whimpered. I drove him to a walk-in clinic, sat beside him in the waiting room, made him hold his hand over his head to reduce the flow to the wounds. At one point, he rested his head on my shoulder. I cling to this memory as if he were dead.

How does someone squeamish about blood beat people to death? Didn't it gush, spurt, splat? The cross-eyed forensic expert testified that Sam must've made repeated wild swings with the shovel dripping in blood. Did he vomit before he rinsed it from his clothes?

The prosecution's shrink experts state that Sam is barely out of a troubled childhood, a victim of an ugly divorce. We were neglectful parents, I in particular have been an unsupportive mother, sacrificing family for career. All this deduced from "psychological assessments" of Sam that took hours long. I get the impression that the more I'm made to look like a self-centred bitch, the better it is for the prosecution because self-centred bitches produce cold-blooded psychopaths. The experts are convincing and I'm beginning to agree with them. It *is* all my fault. Suddenly, a need to protect my son overwhelms me. I want to rush over to him, wrap my arms around his stiff shoulders, tell him everything's going to be all right, Mummy's here.

He'd probably spit in my face. He wants me to take no part in his war. If that's what this is. Who are his enemies? Two golden agers watching TV on a Sunday afternoon?

I guess the divorce was ugly. I can hardly remember it, don't want to remember it. The biggest problem was the fucker wouldn't let me sell the house. The market was down, he insisted, we'd lose money. So Sam and I continued to live in the house of horrors, imagining the sounds of smashing dishes and hostile voices, robotic sex.

That was the tipoff, when Jerry didn't want to boink me anymore. Not that I wanted to boink him, but sex is compulsory in marriage. You don't have to talk to each other, just fornicate a couple of times a month and you'll know you're normal.

I cough loudly in an attempt to wake the judge. It doesn't work. The excuses-for-human-beings gawk at me. Is that a smoker's cough? they titter. Maybe she smoked when he was in the womb and that's why he kills people. Maybe she drank and he's suffering from fetal alcohol syndrome. Maybe she was a junkie, injected and snorted substances, smoked jangs, chewed mushrooms.

The prosecution refuses to believe that Sam didn't know the old couple. They lived seven houses away, the football player points out, how could he not know them? I guess Blondie doesn't live in the city where you can go for years without knowing your neighbours while inhaling the stench from their barbecues.

I cough again. The clerk looks at me. As does the victims' only daughter who has come to court every day seething with hatred for my son. Sometimes I try to imagine being her, sitting motionless, visualizing what her defenceless parents must have had to endure. Did they scream, plead, weep? Did they lose control of their bowels before or after they lost consciousness? Apparently there was "excessive fecal matter" at the scene of the crime. I picture the blood and shit and busted skulls with the TV still going, a televised sermon. "Jesus said, 'I am the light of the world,'" a coiffed preacher intones. "'Whoever follows me will never walk in darkness.'"

The blood begins to congeal around the bodies.

"Praise the Lord!"

What were heads are now swollen, pulpy masses. The blood darkens, the corpses stiffen.

The only daughter must want to see my only son burned alive.

I still haven't figured out how to present myself as the mother of the murderer. As I'm under scrutiny doubtless my behaviour could influence the outcome of the trial. Should I convey remorse, since he isn't? Should I cower in shame? Let the tears flow freely? How can I help my son?

The isolation I feel is not unlike what I felt during radiation therapy. Stripped of my paper smock, partially covered with a lead apron, my neck and mutilated chest positioned by a technician who said, "You must keep still," then quickly fled, closing a heavy steel door behind her, provided me with an aloneness I'd never felt before. Isolated in the sealed chamber, my only company was the high buzzing as the radiation began, which soon mellowed into a low chant. While the laser beams ricocheted around the room, burning holes through me, the technicians, comfortable behind glass, discussed their babies and mortgages and SUVs; the lives they believed they controlled. I can never be that ignorant again, I realized.

Periodically memories jolt me. That day in the bakery, its shelves lined with doughnuts and pastries, cookies, cakes; a child's paradise. "What do you want, sweetie?" I ask him.

"A whole wheat roll," he replies.

"You have a choice of all these yummy things and you want a whole wheat roll?"

"Yes."

A normal eight-year-old does not ask for a whole wheat roll when faced with butter tarts.

As the football player maligns my son, I feel the jury looking to me for argument. Again, I don't know what expression to wear. The gawkers whisper, snicker and snort. As much as I realize that they're low-lifes, I fear I will break under the burden of their disdain. During sleepless nights, I sense them outside, still watching, judging, wanting to see my son crucified. I lie in the darkness wondering if *he* is lying awake, feeling their disdain, or if he's sleeping and about to get up and kill me. I wouldn't mind this, if it were over quickly. In fact, I would've preferred he kill me in the first place. It would have freed me from the guilt I feel for having been a bad mother who put her baby in daycare, who felt defeated and therefore did nothing. And he could've scored my life insurance and headed for Hawaii to enjoy tropical breezes, ocean spray, rum cocktails.

Sometimes I ran away because I was afraid I'd hit him. I felt that impulse, that bolt of electricity in my arm. Is this what he felt when he started swinging the shovel? Is it genetic? Could *I* kill someone? Certainly there are obituaries I wouldn't be saddened to read.

Seeing him all dressed up in his court clothes reminds me of his brief career as a child actor. A squash buddy of Jerry's was in advertising and hired Sam for a few commercials. I thought Sam enjoyed the work, the attention, the money which he knew was being kept in trust for him until he turned eighteen. But one day he cut his face with an X-Acto knife. And hacked off his hair. I discovered the blood in the bathroom sink and his hair on the floor. I cleaned up the mess, my tears transforming his golden locks into clumps. I tried to talk to him about it. "Why did you do this?" I asked. He shrugged. "How could you do this?" I asked. He shrugged.

I put the hair in a plastic bag and showed it to Jerry. "Maybe he should see a shrink," I said. "He doesn't need to see a shrink," Jerry said, "he's just acting his age." Which was what I wanted to hear. So what if my son slices his face with an X-Acto knife? Boys do that. It's a hormonal thing.

The scars are still there, faint white lines, almost imperceptible to anyone but the mother. The hair's in my dresser, its lustre gone. It looks like a dead mouse.

My point is he's not a psychopath. I've read about psychopaths, they're big news, you can't help but read about them; psychopaths don't *deliberately* self harm. And Sam has been known to be kind. Last year he volunteered at an old folks' home, wheeled them out into the sun and listened to their boring stories. I had no idea why he was doing this. Because he missed my parents? He'd been the son they'd never had.

Baldy has recruited staff from the old folks' home to testify to Sam's niceness. Although I'm grateful for their testimony, I find it hard to believe that my foul-mouthed son is capable of such compassion.

He began wetting his bed when he was nine. In the morning, I'd find him curled up in piss with his hands over his head. "You'll be late for school," I'd warn and he'd respond with "Fuck off, you cunt-shitting bitch."

I must not tell this to the football player.

Jerry excused Sam's bedwetting and language by saying *he* hated his mother when he was that age.

Oh. So it's okay then.

The spookiest, creepiest thing is that Sam has never admitted that, if he did kill these people, he is sorry. I fear that he's incapable of "feeling sorry," that he's incapable of understanding what he has done. He thinks it's a movie. He thinks it's a murder mystery and he's the star.

Baldy intends to push the fact that he was an exemplary student. He's summoned two of Sam's high-school teachers to testify. I have been privy to Sam's teacher bashing, particularly of the teachers in question: Warty Morty and head-too-small-for-her-tits Miss Dubejsky. I am amazed that he was able to hide his true feelings from them. But then what are his true feelings?

Watching his profile, I can't believe he did it. He has the face of an angel. Tears bubble up again and I feel the phantom pain in my missing breast. Sam found the cancer on me. He's the reason I'm alive today. We were arguing, I was trying to stop him from going out with Jackie-the-slut. He pushed me, inadvertently bumping my breast. It remained tender for days, the lump became prominent. Maybe I should tell this to Baldy. He could make up a touching story about it. This child *saved* his mother's life.

What would the gawkers think if they found out I only have one breast? That I got what I deserved? Raising a boy like that, they'd conclude, it's no wonder she got cancer. What would they think if they'd seen me scrambling around the house this morning looking for my prosthesis? I take it out as soon as I get home because it rubs against the scar. The problem is, I can never remember where I put it. Once I found it in the fridge, behind the lettuce.

In the courthouse washroom, the excuses-for-human-beings ogle me in the mirror as they freshen their lipstick and powder their noses. They listen to me urinate. How can she pee? What kind of mother *pees* when her son is on trial for murder? Their gasps are audible when they spot me outside buying a hot dog.

Jerry arrives. He can't always make it because he's busy raping and pillaging small businesses on the verge of bankruptcy. Natasha's on his arm wearing a hat that looks like a constipated parrot. I wonder if *she* has the hots for the football player. Jerry just bought her an Audi for their anniversary which she doesn't know how to drive. She has a kind of job, consumer reporting on a morning talk show. She gets her hair done and reports back on it. "It was almost a sexual experience," I heard her say of a pedicure.

Now Jerry wants to sell the house to pay the legal bills. I don't argue. But nobody's buying. They know whose house it is.

Three

I'm showing a listing to a couple for the third time. *I* know they'll buy the house, but they don't. Or anyway, Hubby doesn't. Wifey's keen. The stained-glass windows and hardwood floors have mesmerized her. I smell foundation problems. This is why I hate residential real estate. I'm selling broken homes to people who'll break their backs to pay for them. Commercial real estate was easier: better money and it was always just business. But commercial real estate isn't what it used to be.

"It's *so* sunny," Wifey remarks. "We've never been here when it's been sunny."

"Great southern exposure," I point out. "Fabulous for plants."

So now I sell defective houses, making comments like, "It has a newer roof," or "It's very clean," or "It's certainly an original paint job." I don't like myself for this. I keep telling myself the residential stuff is just temporary. Right. As "temporary" as cancer.

The wife asks me about the fireplace. "It can probably be opened up," I tell her, while being completely ignorant of the inner condition of the chimney. I always encourage buyers to hire a house inspector. But the house inspectors don't look very hard. And anyway, if the buyers have their hearts set on the house, nothing short of a termite infestation will dissuade them from closing the deal.

"Honey . . ." Wifey calls. She's eager to show him something, but he's preoccupied with the sliding-glass doors to the deck which stick.

"It's a realistic price for the location," I say, in an effort to distract him. "Even so, I think we can get them down a bit."

"Honey . . ." She points out some detail in the woodwork above the dud of a fireplace. "Isn't that sweet?" She's imagining Christmas here. Chestnuts roasting over the open fire. Will *she* give birth to a son who will murder? She doesn't think so. She believes they will produce glorious children who will produce glorious lives. It will all begin in the house with the leaky basement. And she's probably right. What are the chances of giving birth to a murderer? One in a thousand? One in a million?

Yet I was apprehensive when he was kicking around in my womb. Other mothers worried that their children might be born mentally or physically impaired. I worried about giving birth to a sociopath. Because I believe they are born, not made. I was relieved when Sam grew into a fragile little boy with a constantly running nose. He didn't poke the eyes out of cats or stick pins into rodents. He collected caterpillars in jars and hammered holes into the lids, enabling them to breathe. Then he waited patiently for them to turn into butterflies. I emptied the jars while he was sleeping so he wouldn't wake up to dead caterpillars. "They must've turned into butterflies," I'd say when he presented me with the empty jar. "They must've squeezed through the holes and flown away." He'd collect more, watch them even more closely.

But when he was nine, he stopped crying. His grandparents died. He was supposed to go up to their cottage as he did every summer. He'd been looking forward to it, had planned renovations to his tree house. When I explained that they were no longer with us, he accused me of lying. After Jerry confirmed the news, Sam sat tearless in front of the TV for days. Years later, he accused me of wanting them to die, not caring that they were dead. He was right.

Last night I had the dream again. The attacker was swinging at my feet, beating them to a pulp, crushing my ankles. Then he moved to my shins. I heard them splinter, my kneecaps shatter.

The attacker is always faceless, bodiless. I'm only aware of the force behind his blows. He never tires and I know that within minutes he'll be battering my body, my arms, my head. I beg him to fracture my skull, to knock me unconscious. I plead to be struck dead. But he continues to bludgeon me in the same sequential manner and I can do nothing but wait.

I woke telling myself it wasn't that bad. Sam smashed their skulls. He did not assault their bodies. He only smashed their skulls. Only.

The surgeon tells me to lift my shirt but doesn't touch me while he examines the incision. He looks repulsed. I don't know why since it's his handiwork he's looking at. Unless he had an intern stitch me up while he dashed off to shtup a lab technician. He ambles back to his desk.

I fasten my bra, pull my shirt back down. "Did you know," I ask for openers, "that more women have died from breast cancer this century than soldiers in all the wars combined?"

"Who told you that?"

"I read it."

"You read too much." He has reprimanded me for reading before, because when I was first diagnosed I spent hours in the library perusing cancer books. I never actually borrowed the books because that would've meant I had cancer, and I was still pretending that I just had a little hyperplasia, no big deal. Besides, I didn't want the snooty librarians to know I was sick; signing out breast cancer books suggests you have breast cancer. Instead, I'd sneak a chair into a corner and hunch over the books, always keeping my hands over the cover to obscure the title.

I tuck in my shirt. "A 36.6 percent increase since 1969, that's pretty scary."

"Increase in what?"

"Breast cancer. It kills fifteen Canadian women daily."

"Don't waste your time with statistics."

"So you don't buy that one-in-eight line?"

He starts scribbling in my file which is bulging with test results and surgical reports. "That's deceiving. It's over a lifetime. Lots of things can kill you over a lifetime."

"That's comforting." I watch him scribble, feeling like the naughty girl sent to the principal's office. The naughty girl who can do nothing but wait for the principal to pronounce his sentence. "I'd like to talk statistics," I venture, "specifically to do with me."

"I suggest you ignore statistics. For a few years you'll be convinced every ache and pain is cancer. That's normal."

"I'm worried about my bones, that it's spreading to my bones."

"Have you got pains in your bones?"

"I'm not sure."

"Your bone scan was negative."

"Yeah, but nothing shows up until it's advanced."

"We'll do another scan in a few months."

This is not a cheering prospect. "Bone scan" means incarceration in the nuclear medicine department. A technician injects bone-seeking, radioactive fluid into your arm which collects in any area of the bone where there is "abnormal" cell activity. It takes the phosphorous compound two hours before they can actually see anything. You have to wait around with nuclear waste in your body before they can look for more cancer in your body.

"What if I *do* feel pain in my bones?"

His eyebrow twitches, hysterical woman, he's thinking. "If the pain is constant, metastasis may be there. As I said, we'll do another bone scan." He fiddles with something in his lab coat pocket, takes it out, fondles it. It looks like a small aerosol container, maybe mouthspray. In seconds, he'll open wide and squirt. "Try not to be obsessed about this," he adds. "It doesn't help and it may harm."

The idea that I might be harming myself makes me start to dribble out of my left eye. He's advised me that the reason I only tear out of my left eye and sweat out of my left armpit is that he removed many lymph nodes.

"I'm still weak all the time," I whimper. "I want to sleep all the time." I know he wants to boot me out of his office, but I waited an hour and forty-five minutes to see him. I *need* him to listen to me. "Do you believe this stuff about stress causing cancer?"

He sighs wearily. Why is he in this business if he finds breast cancer patients so tedious? "I believe that stress can inhibit the immune system and should be avoided."

"What if you can't avoid it?" He must know about the murders. Everybody knows about the murders.

He shrugs. "A lot of women with breast cancer are under chronic stress. So it would seem there is a connection there. I suggest you set yourself up in an ideal environment for healing."

An ideal environment for healing? What planet is he on?

"Keep up your self-examinations," he advises. "Early detection is key."

"What if the lump's tiny? I read that they can be smaller than peas, snuggled deep in the tissue. Some women can't even feel their lumps. Dr. Love, that American surgeon, have you heard of her?"

He stares at me as though I've just crapped on his carpet. "Yes."

"She says," I persist, "if women find their lumps, it's in the shower, or rolling over in bed, not doing self-exams. She says most women are too scared to do them."

Both his eyebrows twitch. "Let me ask you something. Is this reading helping you?"

"I think I should stay informed."

"There's informed and then there's misguided."

"What I read about mammograms giving false positives and missing the real thing isn't misguided—it's fact. And pathologists being overworked, looking at slides till they can't see straight." I'm speaking really fast, like the little girl who's so excited about having the correct answer she blurts it out unintelligibly. "Mistakes are made," I sputter. "Did you read that story about the poor woman who underwent chemo and radiation for a brain tumour that turned out to be benign? She's never going to recover from that treatment. Her immune system's toast, she's in constant pain. There was a picture of her in the paper, she's brain-damaged, bloated and bald."

"Those stories are rare."

"But it happens."

"I'm not saying it doesn't. I'm saying, does it help you to read about it?"

"Probably not."

"Precisely." He closes my file and stands. "Why don't you try to forget about it for a while?"

"I'm missing a breast. I can't forget that."

He swiftly reaches behind me as if to grab me by the scruff of the neck and hurl me out of the room, but instead he snatches a sweater which is slung over my chair. "You're one of the lucky ones," he tells me.

As he propels me out the door, I hear him squirt.

In the waiting room a bald woman sits crying. She's young, too young. Other patients watch her fearfully. They have no comfort to give. They can't even comfort themselves.

I take Sam out for Chinese food, which he used to love. He sits across from me, vacant. Around us are tables of Chinese men all talking loudly at once.

If found guilty, Sam will live in a minimum security prison for young offenders until he is twenty-one. After that, he joins the hardened criminals. If sentenced for life, he could be eligible for parole in fifteen to twenty years. That's a huge chunk of a young life.

When he was arrested, he was kept in a holding cell until the bail hearing. To get to the visiting room, he had to walk past more experienced offenders. "Why don't you stay a while and see what kind of sentence we give you?" they'd shout. Some would whistle and call out "nice ass." I know this because a guard told me what Sam had to endure. He wanted to protect my son. He advised me that he shouldn't have been telling me this but he wanted me to know that my son was "a good boy." I have no doubt that the guard was gay.

Sam told me his cell had a steel sink and toilet and solid steel door. A vertical slot in the door allowed the guards to peer in at him. A knee-high horizontal slot was used for food trays, food that was cold and greasy. He told me this during our first meeting after the arrest. We were sitting in a cubicle, separated by a wall of plastic. Just like in the movies, we had to talk to each other by phone. He said the occupant in the cell next to him was a murderer and a necrophile and howled like a dog. He told me that in the morning the toilets backed up, causing raw sewage to gush from other cells into his.

I didn't know what to say about any of this. Does a murderer deserve better?

He would rather die than go back to prison. I've cleaned out the medicine cabinet of anything remotely lethal. But when I look around the house, many tools of death present themselves. I'm reminded of when he was two and I had to make the house "child safe."

I can no longer put the bleach and trisodium phosphate out of his reach. I can no longer save his life.

Discussion among the Chinese men heats up. One of them stands and gesticulates frantically as though he's trying to act out a syllable in charades. Beside us, chomping on an egg roll, sits a Caucasian with a peanut head who's lecturing another Caucasian about hockey sticks. "Norwegian wood's the best. They got to go to Norway to get the wood, then bring it back here to make the sticks."

His companion looks perturbed, as though he can't believe he's sharing noodles with a man with a peanut head. "What's wrong with the wood here?"

"It's not as good as Norwegian."

"So why don't they make the sticks in Norway?"

"They don't know how to make good sticks in Norway." Peanut-head drinks from a can of Coke.

"Seems an expensive way to go about doing things," the perturbed man offers.

"That's economics. Supply and demand. Nobody wants shitty sticks."

Sam has finished all the dishes except the beef, which he

doesn't touch because he doesn't eat anything with a face. "Do you want something else?" I ask.

He shakes his head. "When's Dad going to take me somewhere?"

"I don't know."

"He doesn't give a fuck."

"Sure he does."

"All he wants to do is fuck Natasha, in her slit, up her ass, down her fucking throat. I hope his cock rots."

Peanut-head looks at us a moment, then absently taps his Coke can against the table.

"Fucking cunt," Sam adds. He's using this language to upset me. I look at my watch.

"You want to go?" he asks me.

"Do you?"

"I'm bored."

"What wouldn't bore you?"

"Fucking Natasha."

"Okay, time to go. You talk like that and I leave. You know that."

"I'll walk home."

"Why?"

"I need air."

"Alright." I leave money for the bill, put on my coat.

When he was arrested, he was strip-searched, the body-cavity version. That I couldn't protect him from this dehumanizing experience destroyed me.

I kiss the top of his head because this I recognize: the way the hair swirls at his crown. I kiss the head of a murderer.

My geriatric aunt Sybil and her equally geriatric pal Betty sit in my kitchen arguing politics. Sybil's a devoted communist, even though she's never visited a communist country. She keeps a bust of Lenin in her room.

"We have to get rid of the deficit," Betty counters feebly.

"The only people concerned with the deficit," Sybil declares, "are the rich. The poor don't give a rodent's rectum about the deficit. The poor stay poor, deficit or no deficit." She points to a pot on the stove. "There's stew for you, baby," she tells me.

Sybil lives with me because her pension was cut, along with the deficit. Without me, she would be living in a rooming house, eating cat food. She has no possessions because she's always given them away. She loves cooking stews. I have difficulty enjoying them because she slips in kidneys or liver or some other organ she considers essential to human health. She's eighty-seven, smokes, drinks vodka straight and takes megadoses of vitamins. She also has a heart condition and blacks out on a regular basis. A heart monitor strapped to her chest has provided hard evidence that she requires a pacemaker. But she insists that the white-coats just want to make money by testing and testing and sticking gadgets into her.

"I think they're greedy pigs," Betty says.

"Who?" I ask.

"The strikers. A nasty mob, the lot of them."

"Much better they join the ranks of the working poor," Sybil interjects. "They should shut up and be grateful they've got jobs, feed their children macaroni for lunch, breakfast and dinner."

"Oh for heaven's sake." Betty shakes her head and reaches for her cane.

"Bring back child labour to North America," Sybil suggests. "That would be good for business. Kids are low maintenance and don't complain. If they get sick, buy another one." Sybil pours more vodka. "Two hundred and fifty million child workers worldwide *now*. In this world. *We* buy the products they make. And they die at fourteen."

Betty's starting to look worried. "I'd better get going. Joe'll be waiting for his dinner."

"Fucking brand names," Sybil adds. "For a dollar a day, they're keeping you in designer labels."

Betty hurriedly collects her purse and coat. "I'll call you in a couple of days."

"Wait a week, maybe I'll be dead."

I see Betty out. Back in the kitchen I find Sybil smoking, exhaling into the fan above the stove. She points to a magazine article showing photos of children in Calcutta working in a battery-recycling factory. For fifty cents a day, they smash used batteries with hammers and separate reusable heavy metals with their hands. Their faces and bodies, barely clothed, are covered with black grime. "Welcome to the twenty-first century," Sybil says. With her free hand, she ladles stew into a dish and hands it to me.

I shake my head. "I had Chinese with Sam. Is he back yet?"

"Not that I noticed." She pushes the plate at me. "Eat. You need protein."

I take it because I'm too tired to argue.

"How is he?" she asks.

"The same."

I sit at the table and poke at the stew in an attempt to locate the unwanted organs. "If he makes it through this, he'll be more damaged than before."

Sybil nods and smokes. She's had a hideous cough for forty years. Everybody thought she'd die years ago. She survives, I believe, from sheer force of will.

"That's horrible about the children," I offer, feeling like just another ineffectual liberal.

"Betty's baskets for her plants. Children go blind and burn their hands on her baskets. I tell her and she buys more baskets."

"She doesn't want to know."

"Who does?"

I fiddle with the stew.

She squints at me. "Weren't you supposed to be seeing doctors today?"

"Cheeseburger and his buddy the plastic surgeon who wants to reconstruct my tit."

"And . . . ?"

"I'm fine. The plastics guy seems to think I'm fat enough to do a good job on the boob. I said, 'What about a nipple?' He said, 'I create one.'"

"Man as God."

"Their egos crowd the room. Anyway, I'm not going to do it. It's more surgery, complicated. It takes twelve hours." I find a piece of kidney and push it to the side of my plate. "Besides, it doesn't matter to me anymore."

"What?"

"Looking like a woman. A tit made from flab cut off my stomach isn't going to make me feel more whole."

After the surgery, when I was still in the hospital and Cheeseburger removed the layers of bandages, I couldn't make myself look at the incision.

"Not bad," he remarked. "Not a lot of swelling."

Then I looked and was transfixed by its ugliness. It was not part of my body, this long diagonal gash running from the centre of my chest and continuing underneath my arm. It seemed to me that no care had been taken to minimize the scarring. They'd attacked the cancer, unfortunately my body had been in the way.

Cheeseburger removed a drainage tube and palpated the skin surrounding the incision. "We'll get you off the IV today."

The tumour had been large but "contained." We'd had to wait for a pathology report to find out if the cancer had metastasized.

"Chin up," he said. "Looks good." Then he sauntered off to mutilate more women.

Sybil coughs and stubs out her cigarette. "You might change your mind."

"No I won't. I don't want a fake tit. It's a joke, who am I trying to kid? Myself? Ross?" Ross is the man I'd been "dating" preoperatively when we'd both been desperate for human contact.

Divorced himself, he is as dysfunctional as I am.

"Wait and see," Sybil says. "You might change your mind."

It bugs me that she thinks she knows me better than I know myself.

"I won't change my mind," I insist. "What good did having tits do me? I fed a psychotic child. Pacified emotionally retarded men who wanted their mommies. Forget it. It's over."

"Whatever you say."

I reach into my bra, take out my prosthesis and slap it on the table, emphasizing my point. We watch it jiggle.

After Cheeseburger left, I gently placed my hand over the space where my breast had been. It felt like raw, gristly meat. I made it to the bathroom in time to puke. After rinsing my mouth, my face, the sink, I sat on the toilet waiting to cry, or something. There was nothing, just a weariness, and a feeling of powerlessness. Sweat poured down the left side of my face and armpit.

That night, the breast cancer patient in the next bed, who had two small children and a doting husband, choked to death on her own vomit.

Sybil lights another cigarette. "They took the old lady across the street out on a stretcher. There were flashing lights, fire trucks, ambulances, quite a show."

"Was she conscious?"

Sybil shakes her head. "Her face wasn't covered though. Don't they cover your head if you're dead?"

"I think so."

"Who's going to rake her leaves? It's going to drive her bananas to know the leaves are taking over her yard."

"Maybe her children will do it."

"Doubt it. They're probably waiting to sell the house."

"Probably."

"Eat your kidneys."

They smell like horse piss. I jab one and put it in my mouth. It's a demonstration of love.

In the bath I do my exercises, "walk the wall" with my fingers. I can still only raise my arm to half its normal range. The physiotherapist explained that there's scar tissue adhered to my chest wall, made worse by the radiation.

While towelling off, I catch sight of my chest in the mirror. Usually I avoid this, but tonight I eyeball the jagged, fibrous tissue.

I finger the ridge of skin but can't feel my touch, only numbness. Apparently nerves regenerate very slowly, if at all. The phantom pain, Cheeseburger told me, may never go away.

So what? I'm one of the lucky ones.

Why don't I feel lucky?

Four

My mother used to slap our heads with a fly swatter. Once she swatted my sister so hard her ears bled. I stood by, doing nothing. Or maybe I screamed, "Stop, Mummy!" What I should've done was hit my mother with a brick. But she was my mother. I wanted to love her and be loved in return. She could be nice. She liked Christmas, would always go to great lengths to make it special for us. We looked forward to Christmas.

She drove my bleeding sister to the hospital. I wanted to go with them, but my mother wouldn't let me. I'd be curious to know how she explained the bleeding ears to the doctor. Rachel remembers nothing. She was only four. Nobody reported child abuse in those days. I don't think anybody knew what "child abuse" was. If your kids were bad, you hit them.

It is impossible to be beaten at a young age and not believe you deserve it.

I decided to stop loving my mother when I was eleven. I came home after school one day with a girlfriend and discovered my mother sitting at the piano, masturbating. Unfazed, she pulled her hand out from under her skirt and resumed playing some Gilbert and Sullivan ditty. My friend stood mortified. On top of the piano were empty vinegar bottles collected by my mother for no discernible purpose. At her feet were hoarded newspapers and magazines which I knew she'd never read. Leftover chip packets and Coke bottles from the previous night's TV viewing lay undisturbed. Crumpled, dirty Kleenexes dotted the floor.

Standing beside my friend in her crisp pink dress, I observed the chaos of my home. I saw the strangeness of my mother and decided that I would never bring a friend home again. And that I would stop forgiving my mother and, in so doing, stop loving her.

She blamed my withdrawal on adolescence. Which was fine by me. When I asked her to buy me a bra, she slid her hand under my blouse and felt the weight of my breast in her hand. "They are getting bigger, aren't they?"

I don't know if she was insane. She was never diagnosed and treated. She may have just been eccentric. She collected bugs, stuck pins through their bodies and pinned them to the walls of the garage. I don't know why, if she thought they were beautiful and worthy of display, or if she was hanging them up like scalps. But that was my mother, inexplicable. She and my father could go for weeks without talking to one another. And yet they would still copulate. We'd hear them, bumping and grinding. But in the morning, the cold war would resume. We weren't always clear on what they were fighting about. Once they argued about whose car should be kept in the garage. He'd arrived home first, leaving her no choice but to park in the driveway. This infuriated my mother because she adored her car, and a big snowstorm was imminent. She insisted that her Lincoln was more deserving of protection than his Impala. But my father wouldn't budge. During the night, she went into the garage and drove nails through his tires. On discovering this the next morning, he said nothing, just changed the tires.

This all smells of mental illness and must not be revealed to the football player who ruts and scrapes while spouting words like "vicious" and "brutal" and "crazed." As the shrink wars continue, I try to maintain a benign expression. I think, *Nun,* pretend you're a nun. But I'm having difficulty keeping the "experts" straight. None of them know my son. I don't know my son and I live with him. These wizards have spent an hour or two with the boy. I watch helplessly as the men in bad suits squeeze him into a textbook psychiatric profile. Each seems equally confident with his diagnosis—more confident than I've ever been as a mother.

Baldy determinedly quashes any suggestions of insanity because the plea is non-insane automatism. He knows that the football player keeps raising the issue because, at the very least, showing that my boy suffers from a disease of the mind, or proving that somnambulism *stems* from a disease of the mind, will stop Sam from walking free if he's found not guilty. They'll toss him in the loony bin and throw away the key.

The football player's experts claim that internal causes—a combination of genetic susceptibility, lack of sleep, high stress levels—conjoined with Sam's psychological and emotional makeup pose a "recurring danger to the public" and should be treated as insanity.

I'm not sure I disagree with them. But according to the Criminal Code, the "impairment of mind" must be caused by illness, a disorder or an abnormal condition. Sam's encephalogram was normal. And sleep is a normal condition. According to Baldy's experts, Sam's mind and its functioning was impaired but not by sleepwalking. The impairment was caused by sleep, a natural condition. The act was done by the muscles without any control of the mind, similar to a spasm, reflex action or convulsion. Therefore, say Baldy's team, it was done involuntarily. While wiping snot from his moustache, he reminds the jury that only those who act voluntarily with the *requisite intent* to commit an offence should be punished by criminal sanction.

One of the football player's experts doesn't disagree with the sleepwalking business but claims it's a pathological condition and that such a violent episode could possibly recur. Another one of his team says Sam wasn't sleepwalking at all but was in a "hysterical dissociative state." This lack of harmony among the prosecution's experts could pose a problem for the football player.

I think of my mother swatting my sister and wonder if she was in a "hysterical dissociative state."

Leaving the courthouse, I'm approached by a severely disabled woman strapped into a motorized wheelchair. Her head lolls to one side, her hands jerk repeatedly. I'm afraid she's going to say something horrible about my son, she's going to curse him. And like the profanities of a hag oracle, her oaths will resonate with me forever. I start to cross the street, to flee.

"Please help!" she shouts.

I stop. "What?"

"Can you help?" She's almost unintelligible. Even her tongue has become an obstacle she must overcome.

"What?"

"Can you do me up?" She nods towards her chest and I realize that she's referring to her zipper.

"Of course." I lean over her and grip the ends of her windbreaker. I doubt my ability to perform this simple task. The zipper will stick and this poor woman will be forced to sit with me hanging over her, fumbling with her jacket. "It's chilly today, isn't it?" I comment, to distract her from my clumsiness. She emits a sound I interpret as a chuckle. She watches my hands intently, hands with motor control she no longer possesses. Amazingly, the zipper works. I slide it up to her collarbone. "High enough?"

She nods, smiling. "Thank you."

I am in flux, not only because her trust and geniality have disarmed me, but because the action of zipping up someone else's zipper has taken me back to Sam's childhood; the good old days, when I could help. My left eye is dribbling again. A drop lands on the woman's pink windbreaker, spreading red. She looks up at me, surprised. "It's okay," I mutter. "Will you be alright?" She says nothing, only stares, obviously concerned about my emotional well-being. Stunned that this stranger with enormous problems of her own is concerned about my emotional well-being, I smile stupidly. "It's okay," I repeat and scurry across the street to the underground parking lot where hopefully a psychopath is waiting for me with a tire iron.

It's only Jerry. Natasha must be in the car, reapplying her face.

"We have to talk," he says. Dialogue out of a bad movie. This happened often during our marriage. We'd be fighting and I would feel like an aging Farah Fawcett in a made-for-TV movie about an oppressed wife.

"Why?" I unlock my car door manually. Jerry's got the remote gizmo for his Merc.

"Over a drink, dinner, whatever suits you."

When I got breast cancer I felt even more like an aging Farah Fawcett in a made-for-TV movie. "I really don't feel it's necessary, Jerr."

"Our son's life is at stake."

More bad dialogue. I try to think of an expensive restaurant. "Okay, how about Lotus?"

"Fine. Tonight?"

"I've got plans."

"Tomorrow?"

"Seven." I rev my engine and consider backing into him, but he skitters out of the way.

Because I believe in exploring all possibilities, I'm attending a support group for cancer "survivors." We sit in a circle on bum-numbing chairs. Everyone reveals tragic stories about difficult childhoods, bad marriages, failed surgeries. I can't stand it, don't like to dwell on that stuff, don't see how it helps. How many people don't have troubled childhoods, bad marriages and failed surgeries? Human life involves suffering. I don't see how you can have a fully functioning brain and not suffer.

One of the survivors, sporting a bad wig, insists that He only puts obstacles in your path that you can handle. The more suffering, the more blessed you are. What a crock. In my experience, lethal blows don't make you stronger, they kill you.

The bad-wig zealot recounts the story of a fellow cancer survivor who swallowed many barbiturates and put a plastic bag over her head. I think efficient self-deliverance when life inside your body becomes untenable is to be admired. But the zealot is outraged. "She had no right!"

The group leader/yoga guru sensing a fundamentalist, serenely moves to another topic: talking to our cancers. "Show it your anger," he urges. "Anger is good if you let it out. Shout at your cancer, scream at your cancer."

We all look frightened by this prospect, as though our cancer is a boss we've been avoiding confronting for fear of losing our jobs.

In a way this makes sense. We don't want to disturb the cells. We want them to settle down, to stop proliferating. Shouting and screaming don't make things better.

Disappointed with our inability to show our anger, the leader changes tactics and inquires about our families, how we *feel* about them. Everyone, except me, insists that family has become more important to them than ever before. I think but don't admit that, faced with the possibility of imminent death, the idea of "family" seems absurd to me. What binds you to these people other than genetics? I consider the time and energy I've invested in "family" wasted. I was chasing after an ideal, something implanted in my brain by *The Partridge Family* and *The Brady Bunch*. Years of watching "family-oriented" television has permanently impaired my rational thought. That our marriage could never meet the Bradys' beehived housekeeper's standards (she was always wagging that disapproving finger at me) may be at the root of my problem. Like so many of my generation, I believed that I could have it all, that I could make it happen. And when I couldn't, I became enraged, mostly with myself. But because beating up on myself wasn't any fun, I'd vent my fury on Jerry. Once I'd incited him to rage, I had someone to rage at. I *needed* him to rage.

So where does the boy fit into all this?

I used to make excuses for his behaviour. With cancer in my face, I have no energy for this. You can choose to do either good or bad. Nobody forced him to kill. I have trouble (as I'm sure the Sonny Bono look-alike does) with the concept of an involuntary murder.

Our tranquil leader instructs us to close our eyes and imagine our cancers. "Picture your cancer," he says. "Now imagine beams of light shining down on it. The beams narrow and become laser sharp and begin to destroy your cancer. Feel the heat of the laser. Visualize the healthy tissue beneath the cancer." I do close my eyes but can't resist opening them again to peek at my comrades-in-suffering. *They* seem to be visualizing their cancers. Their foreheads crease with concentration. When the leader talks about healthy tissue, their foreheads relax. I wish I could do likewise. All my life I've wanted to be more like other people. But the more I try, the more I stand out as the misfit. Maybe my mother felt the same way but at some point stopped trying to fit in. What was it that made her stop trying? Madness, despair? Both?

Our group leader/yoga guru instructs us to hold hands. "We're going to help each other with healing hands." I feel the damp grip of a fierce woman who is defiantly not wearing a prosthesis. My other hand is clenched by a pale waif who smiles compulsively. She's pretty, one of those women who's been told all her life she has a pretty smile. In an effort to please, she constantly smiles. What happens to her face when she looks in the mirror at her scars?

"Close your eyes," the leader instructs. "*Trust* the touch. *Feel* the energy moving through your hands."

He soothingly explains that good killer cells are created when you express anger. Good killer cells zap the free radicals which lead to cancer. But depression produces no good killer cells. Cancer thrives on depression, therefore we must fight it and believe in our "wellness."

The smiling waif's grip is starting to hurt. I don't think this is helping me.

My parents were found dead in the woods not far from their cottage. They were mauled by a bear. My mother had always been fearless of wildlife. Animals were her pals. She'd chat with them, offer peanut butter sammies. But this bear was not her buddy. It had been a long cold winter; berries were scarce. A taste of human must've seemed inviting. Or my mother wouldn't stop yapping, irritating the bear, disturbing its peace. During her senior years, my mother became convinced we were all stealing from her. Maybe she accused the bear of stealing. Anyway, it must've been a gruesome scene. I've stood where it happened and tried to imagine it. Apparently my father put up a struggle. What was my mother doing? You'd think she'd have tried to belt it with a stick or something, or run for help. There was no evidence of this. It appeared that my mother prostrated herself in front of the bear.

When radiation started to bubble my skin and cause swelling in my remaining breast so painful I thought it would explode, I stood where the bear had its lunch. I shouted at it to come and get me. "I want my ticket punched," I kept telling it, waving a ham sandwich at the woods. "Come on, you big ugly lug, you chickenshit, you wussy!"

It has occurred to me that my mother wanted to die because she was losing her mind and body. She wanted my father terminated because she didn't want him having any fun without her. So she dragged him out to look for berries, having packed meaty sandwiches to attract large carnivorous animals, and waited for the opportune moment. She knew there was a danger because, weeks before, an inexperienced national park attendant had been attacked by wolves. The local cottagers, including my mother, were shocked and repeatedly uttered the chorus, "Animals don't kill unless provoked."

If my son is any example, the act of killing does not require provocation. The act of killing results from the distorted thoughts of the killer. The bear was having a bad day. Or maybe it was asleep.

One of the library books I furtively read associated breast cancer with loss. Suffering a "major loss" deprives the body of relaxation, rest, exercise and emotional expression. The resulting stress inhibits the immune system, allowing cell mutations to occur.

I thought about this while waiting for my first mammogram, trying to decide if the death of my parents qualified as a "major loss." A waiting-room magazine revealed that Oprah was fat again and I wondered why she'd let this happen. I blamed her for porking up. Then it occurred to me that "healthy" people blame sick people for their illness. It's because they're so negative, they say, so angry, so bitter. It's because they didn't eat right, drank alcohol, smoked cigarettes, screwed around, ate Twinkies, sunbathed, farted in public. The healthy want it to be that simple. This is how they convince themselves that they won't fall prey to a devastating illness. When I was "healthy," I assured myself that it had to be in the genes. Well, guess what? My family may be nuts, but nobody's had cancer.

The joke is nothing showed up on the mammogram. I was ecstatic, but Cheeseburger wasn't happy. He sent me for more blood tests, an ultrasound, a liver scan. He ordered a chest X-ray to determine whether or not cancer was in my lungs. He was determined to find something and he did. Did he celebrate when he was proven right?

"Worrisome cell changes," he told me, regarding the biopsy results. Worrisome isn't a word you want to hear from your surgeon. I felt my chair growing and me shrinking.

The book also linked breast cancer with dysfunctional childhoods and "mismanaged emotions later in adulthood." I never think of emotions as manageable. They manage me. I wondered why the book stressed mismanaged emotions *later* in adulthood. Was it okay to mismanage them *early* in adulthood?

"Positive thinking" was crucial to healing, the book emphasized, stress was to be avoided; even if it was occurring on an unconscious level, originating in crippling childhood psychological trauma.

How would you know if you were experiencing stress on an unconscious level unless you were conscious of your unconscious? This brings us back to Sam's state of mind during the killing. How conscious was his unconscious?

At home, I pull out my prosthesis and toss it on the coffee table. I have to search for the remote because Sam never leaves it on the TV. Relieved he's out, I still worry about him. Not that he'll get into trouble, because he doesn't. But just the thought of him drifting through the city, friendless, opens a pit in my gut.

I call Sybil but suspect she's out. We had a fight in the early hours this morning over the pacemaker issue. She'd blacked out. I found her in the bathroom with toothpaste in her mouth. After making sure she was still breathing, I checked her pulse. All seemed normal so I carried her to bed, which wasn't difficult because she's skin and bone. I wiped the toothpaste off her face and kissed her and decided that if she didn't regain consciousness in seconds I'd call 911.

"Did I fall?" she asked on waking.

"Yes."

She wiggled her arms and legs. "Nothing broken."

"You have to get that battery installed," I told her.

"Why? There's no harm done. I'm fine."

"This time. How stupid can you be?"

"Where are my smokes?"

"Are you mad? Or just incredibly selfish?"

"What's selfish got to do with the price of eggs?"

"I don't want to be left alone here," I told her loudly. "You can't leave me alone here."

"You're born alone and you die alone."

"I was born some time ago and I'm not dead yet. And anyway, you won't just die. It's never that easy. You'll have a stroke that will paralyze you or deaden your brain. You'll be a veggie that I will have to look after. I'll have to wipe your butt and force mush down your throat. Thank you, Auntie, but I've got enough problems."

"Now look who's being selfish."

"Oh please."

She discovered a cigarette in her cardigan pocket and headed downstairs to the kitchen fan.

"Don't forget to take your vitamins!" I quipped. I've often told her that no dose of vitamins can undo the damage that smoking has done her. But she believes in vitamins as she believes in Mr. Lenin.

I knew I wouldn't be able to get back to sleep and followed to make sure she was all right. She ignored me so I sulked in the living room. My hope was that she'd come to her senses and plead for forgiveness. All I heard was the fan.

I find the remote between two sofa cushions and flick on the news. A woman, eight months pregnant, shot her fetus with a pellet gun. The pellet lodged in the baby's brain. The puncturing of the uterus brought on labour. The baby survived but is in critical condition due to brain damage. Was this woman insane?

Should she be acquitted on the basis of insanity? Perhaps she experienced crippling childhood psychological trauma. Maybe she was hit on the head by her lover and will also plead non-insane automatism. Maybe she was asleep.

I experience a strong physical reaction to this story, imagining the woman pointing the gun at her belly and firing. How ignorant was she? Hadn't she heard about abortion? What about CONTRACEPTION? I want the woman holed up for life, far from any penises that might impregnate her. I could even tolerate her being executed with a pellet gun or, at the very least, sterilized with sharp instruments. As far as I'm concerned, no mercy should be shown this woman.

And yet I expect mercy for my son?

I see him at one and a half, a cherub playing with building blocks. Infuriated that he couldn't hold more than one in his hand at a time, he hurled them across the room and howled. From then on, I would limit the amount of blocks available to him. Was this wrong? Was I already limiting his options?

On the swing, swinging happily, then suddenly crying out, "Stop, Mummy!"

I slowed the swing down. "Stop! Stop!" he kept screaming while tears streamed down his face. What had frightened him? I looked around the deserted park. What was he seeing?

What's he seeing now, in the city that condemns him? What offers comfort? That *I* can't makes me feel worthless. Let the cancer cells blossom and burn, search and destroy. I deserve it.

I don't think these are positive thoughts.

Five

There's no question that since the murders, my associates at the real estate office have been keeping their distance. I'm rarely asked to help out with open houses anymore, but it's the weekend and Todd must be desperate because he asks me as soon as I get in. "Sure," I reply. Helping out Todd is always a good plan because he can sell anything. He has no qualms about leaky basements. And he's fair when it comes to sharing commissions. I watch him empty three packets of Sweet'N Low into his coffee.

"What do you think I should wear for my photo on my home page?" he asks. I'm not sure if he's speaking to me or to Estelle who's also by the coffee machine. "Should I wear a tank or go topless?" he clarifies. "I saw this French guy's home page. He was really built up. Like too much. He's obviously on steroids, which is seriously sick. Did you read about that kid, some kid, sixteen or something, hung himself with a belt because he was on steroids? They make you mental, right. It's pathetic. His parents were stinking rich. It just goes to show."

"What?" I inquire.

He seems to have forgotten my presence and I realize he wasn't talking to me. "What?"

"What does it go to show you?" I ask.

"That money isn't everything."

"Oh. Right." I stare into the steaming black hole of my coffee cup. Todd worships money. He plans to be rich by fifty and retire to a sunny clime.

"Anyway," he continues, "this French guy, he's on this rock in the Mediterranean, all greased up, right. I mean, top that."

I think about the steroid victim's mother. Did she find him hanging? Did she faint, scream, vomit, wrap her arms around his legs and beg him to come down?

I pour cream into my coffee. "Why do you have to top it?"

"For fun. It's just a joke. I'm not serious. I just want to top it."

The paramedics cut the boy down. The mother falls to her knees beside the mass of toxic muscle. "We're very sorry," the medics say.

"Do something," the mother orders, accustomed to being obeyed, to being able to buy her way out of anything. "Give him oxygen, blast his heart. Something."

"We're too late, ma'am."

Estelle offers Todd one of her chocolate-covered Oreos. He waves them away emphatically. I take one.

"Maybe you should go topless with your jeans a little unzipped," she suggests.

"No way," Todd responds. "That look grosses me right out."

"Why wear anything?" I offer as I head back to the front desk to check my messages. The husband of the perfect couple has called. This is a good sign.

After I return his call and am preparing what I consider to be too low an offer, Estelle fills me in on the latest regarding her sick cat. Estelle continues to associate with me (even though I'm the mother of a murderer) because I listen to her tales about Bunny whom her former vet labelled neurotic and anorexic. Her current vet is a surgeon and suggested that Bunny had inoperable cancer when he discovered little bumps around the cat's groin. Much blood was drawn from Bunny's furry legs. Meanwhile he continued to vomit yellowish fluid and refuse food.

"I offered him poached chicken breast last night," Estelle says sadly. "He wouldn't touch it. Not even the broth."

"What about salmon steak?" I ask.

"I tried that. He wouldn't touch it. Even pork roast. He used to *love* pork roast."

Estelle is a smoker and I suspect she'd like to go out for a butt but doesn't because she needs to talk about Bunny. "He's not even affectionate anymore. Never plays mouse. He used to wake me up in the morning by sitting on my chest. Now he doesn't even get up on the bed."

"Maybe he's too weak from not eating."

"He doesn't even purr anymore."

It's entirely possible that Bunny has decided it's time to die. He's sixteen. This must be ancient in cat years.

"They pumped fluids into him yesterday," she adds. "They're afraid he's going to dehydrate. They don't inject it into a vein like they do in humans—they just stick it under his skin. It makes this bubble." She grimaces, indicating the unsightliness of the bubble.

"Have you had any blood results yet?" I think of my own numerous blood tests—the waiting, calling Cheeseburger's office for results only to find the line busy, or voicemail.

Estelle nods. "There's too much calcium in his blood which is why they think he might have cancer." Just uttering the "C" word takes her breath away. She bows her head. "And something about white blood cells. I can't remember if there's too few or too many. Anyway, something's wrong. The vet wants to do exploratory surgery. He asked me . . . he asked me if I'd be willing to let Bunny go. If there's nothing to be done." Her chest begins to heave. If she dissolves into tears, I'll have to take her for a doughnut or something. "He said it might be best to let him go. That I should prepare myself. How can I prepare myself?"

No one at the office knows about my cancer. "I don't think you can prepare yourself," I tell her. "I think we spend too much time trying to prepare ourselves. If the worst happens, it still devastates us, regardless of preparation. If the best happens, we can't really appreciate it because we're burnt out from preparing for the worst."

In reading books about cancer, I've tried to prepare. Still, I find myself in the waiting room of a preoccupied surgeon who must refer to my chart to remember which breast he lopped off. Take control of your cancer, the books tell me. How? I was asleep when he cut into me. I'll be asleep if he cuts into me again. How can I take control? Get a second opinion? He *is* my second opinion. My first opinion looked like Harpo Marx and kept taking calls from his broker.

"I just feel so helpless," Estelle confides.

"What did he say the chances of it being cancer are?"

"He didn't say. But I could tell from his face he was worried. He wants to open him up right away."

I contemplate the vet bills for kitty surgery. How's Estelle going to pay for it? She rarely sells houses. Wouldn't it be better to let Bunny die rather than put him through the trauma of repeated tests and surgery? Cheeseburger tells me that my prognosis is good because the cancer hasn't spread to the lymph nodes. I wonder how many of the despondent women in the waiting room he once told were "one of the lucky ones." One of the lucky ones found out seven weeks after she'd been told her nodes were clear that she'd been given the wrong test results—that in fact her nodes tested positive. "Did they give a reason for the error?" I asked her. "Cutbacks," she responded. "Nobody even apologized."

Estelle shivers. "Somebody I thought was a friend," she continues, "told me I should have him destroyed." She starts to sob.

I hand her a Kleenex. "It's a tough one."

I'm meeting Mr. Perfect downtown in an hour. I don't have time to comfort Estelle.

She looks at me suspiciously. "*You* don't think I should have him destroyed?"

"No, not at all. It's just I'm not big on surgery."

"It's different when it's your cat."

"I'm sure."

Irritated with my lack of compassion, she skedaddles outside for a smoke. I finish the offer and arrange an appointment to present it to the vendor and agent.

The truth is nothing could've prepared me for radiation therapy, the killing of cells good and bad that induces inflammation, forming even more scar tissue. Fifteen to twenty-five years after being irradiated, the tissue still feels thick, hard, wooden. Nobody talks about this because we're supposed to consider ourselves lucky to live another fifteen to twenty-five years. To a cancer patient, fifteen to twenty-five years is a lifetime. What the books didn't tell me, what I read in a magazine the other day, is that the blast of radiation can create genetic damage that can lead to other types of cancer. "Worrisome evidence" suggests that radiation may promote lung cancer in the irradiated side of the body.

Oh joy.

I'd still have done it. When you have a malignant tumour in your body, you want it cut out and any remaining treacherous cells burned. You try not to think about what else gets destroyed. Kind of like nuclear war.

Although I did look at the bull's eye the radiologist tattooed on my chest to give the technicians a target, and think there has to be a better way.

The chemo cocktails I refused because, let's face it, the stuff is poison. I figured the side effects would kill me. Besides, it's still unproven that chemo on women whose nodes test negative improves their life expectancy. And I can't get excited about being chemically sterilized which is inevitable when your ovaries are being deadened by chemo drugs.

One of my waiting-room companions died from an aneurysm during chemotherapy. The lethal chemicals thinned the walls of her arteries. She was thirty.

I told my flabby oncologist about a study which indicated that of a hundred node-negative women with "favourable histological types of cancer" whose removed tumours were small, ninety will not have a recurrence, and of the remaining ten maybe three will benefit from chemo. He looked bored. He rarely moves, I keep expecting him to grow moss. "In other words," I persisted, "toxic chemotherapy with dire side effects, *death* for example, is given to a hundred women to prolong the life of three."

"Uh-hmm," he responded.

"Sounds a bit like senseless violence, don't you think?"

"It's a completely personal choice."

No kidding.

What puzzles me is that since tumours grow at different speeds—are as individual as the bodies they inhabit—and not all cancer cells multiply at the same rate, why are all breast cancer patients given the same recipe for survival? We're told treatments have improved, are less invasive, toxic. We're reminded of the bad old days when surgeons not only cut off breasts, but removed the ovaries and adrenal glands. Next they'd inject women with male hormones which would make their skin oily, pimply and hairy. We're supposed to feel lucky because now we're only disfigured, burned and poisoned.

I suspect that most of the time adjuvant therapy is offered because the white-coats are afraid of being sued.

Periodically, I see a newspaper headline proclaiming that a cure is in sight. I read the article and discover it's about new drugs being given to mice, or the same old drugs being administered differently to women "at risk" for breast cancer. Tamoxifen, an estrogen blocker, has been mainlined to breast cancer patients for decades. On postmenopausal women, it doubles their risk of developing uterine cancer and blood clots in major veins and the lungs. On premenopausal women, it brings on early menopause. Imagine being twenty- or thirty-something and being told that you might get cancer, therefore you should take a drug that'll make you menopausal, might give you uterine cancer or a stroke or a heart attack, but *might* prevent you from getting breast cancer.

Or you can have a prophylactic double mastectomy. Which still doesn't guarantee that you won't get breast cancer.

I know it's unfashionable (and negative) to be a feminist and demand equal opportunity and all that, but let's face it, guys would not be expected to take this shit. If there were a disease for which the only treatment was to cut off men's pee-pees and poison and burn their bodies, a cure would be found—or at least a cause which would lead to prevention. No amount of research funding would be denied the quest to save the penis.

I'm stopped at a light and a squeegee kid with pierced everything blades up to my car. I shake my head as he wields his squeegee menacingly. He slathers dirty water over my windshield anyway, risking prosecution. I will not give the little twerp money. While he hovers by my window, I stare straight ahead. He raps my windshield with his knuckles. "Have a nice day," he sneers as I step on the gas.

Cheeseburger tossed out tamoxifen as an option. I explained that blocking hormones that are natural to the female organism confuses me; don't we need hormones to be healthy? He was on hold with his travel agent because, that afternoon, he was to depart for a cancer convention in Las Vegas, of all places. He was very concerned about getting tickets to a show.

"And if hormones cause cancer," I persisted, "why are menopausal healthy women instructed to gobble hormone replacement pills?"

"Hi," he said to the phone, then scribbled something on a memo pad. "Are there dance numbers in that one?" He stared at me with a faraway look, already envisioning naked implanted girls dancing around with feathers. "Sinatra?" he asked. "An impersonator, right, of course. It's just him?" He pulled out his mouthspray and fondled it. "I'm more interested in dance numbers, you know, a show." The travel agent put him on hold again. "What was that?" he asked me.

"If hormone replacement therapy prevents osteoporosis and heart disease, and reduces menopausal symptoms, why is it okay to strip women with cancer of these very same hormones?"

He shrugged. "You don't have to take them." He opened wide and squirted. I wondered why he'd become so obsessed with halitosis, if he was on one of those high protein diets that give you animal-carcass breath.

"I mean," I forged on, "if the drug assured long life, it might be acceptable. But this just isn't the case with hormone blockers, they just make us sick."

"So don't take them." He held up a finger, silencing me. "Hi," he said to the phone. "Great, that sounds great. Good stuff." He hung up and stared at me. "Any other questions?"

"Well . . ." By this time my carefully written notes seemed ludicrous to me. I felt like the kid who has all the right answers to the wrong exam.

"Do the hormone-gobbling women get cancer?" I muttered in a last-ditch effort.

"The risk is slight, if there's no cancer in the family."

"That's another thing, not one breast cancer patient I've spoken with has cancer in the family, or even fits into the 'high-risk' category."

"Trust me, I've spoken to more patients than you have."

"What I mean is, this disease continues to have no clear cause. Or if there is one, like it's the hormones pumped into livestock that reach us via their milk and muscles"—by this time I was waving my hands around for emphasis—"or if it's the gases emitting from the plastics we use daily that are interpreted as estrogen in our bodies, nobody's owning up. It wouldn't be good for business."

He looked at me as a parent looks at a child who simply *will not* behave. A parent who is deliberating over which course of action to take: a spanking? Go to your room? No dessert? "You're too serious," he said finally, folding up my file and sliding his dance-number memo into his shirt pocket. "Do something fun for a change, relax."

Traffic halts because a preppy man, attempting to cross at a crosswalk with his dog, is nearly run down by a minivan. He bangs the rear window of the vehicle that nearly killed him. The van stops abruptly, the driver's door swings open and out charges a man with a head too big for his body and a snake tattooed around his leg. The preppy man, considerably shorter than the tattooed man, tries to explain with some vehemence that he and his dog were nearly killed on what *is* a crosswalk. But Tattoo Man doesn't want to hear about it and repeatedly shouts, "Move it, asshole, you're blocking traffic!" The rest of us cower in our cars, anticipating fisticuffs as the two men lean into one another, their faces almost touching, spewing their rage. "Move it, asshole, you're blocking traffic!" becomes an impenetrable refrain and the preppy man, sensing Tattoo Man's pent-up fury towards mankind in general, backs off with his doggy.

Where does all this hostility come from?

Tattoo Man, victorious, climbs back into his van and life goes on.

When I showed my sloth of an oncologist the newspaper article about a study revealing that girls are beginning menses on average at age nine, his expression remained unchanged and he looked to me more than ever like Henry Kissinger. Could this have something to do with our food supply? I asked. Are we not what we eat? Early menstruation puts girls at a greater risk of developing breast cancer later in life. *As* does late menopause. *Should* we be fighting menopause with hormone replacement therapy if late menopause puts us at a higher risk? And what about all those growth hormones thrown on the veggies which we eat to prevent cancer? Could these be interpreted as estrogen in our bodies? What about pesticides? What about all those genetically engineered Franken-foods? What about the air we breathe? I read that the salt and sundry chemicals we spread on our streets in winter are seeping into our water supply, causing cancer.

"Don't believe everything you read" was the oncologist's reply. "There is no scientific data that proves that eating meat, drinking milk . . . what was the other thing?"

"Environmental factors."

"Yes. There is no scientific evidence that proves any of these things increase your risk of developing breast cancer."

What he meant was conglomerates have no interest in examining the health risks of the chemicals that made them into conglomerates.

Gene therapy is in the news lately. So far it's only effective if your cancer involves the HER2 gene, roughly thirty percent of cases. Low dose chemo drugs that block the growth of the blood vessels that feed the tumours are being tested on mice. And DNA testing for women at high risk is supposed to become more widely available and affordable. That's swell. None of this means anything to us veterans in the waiting room who are already missing breasts and fearing that our doctor will tell us to get our affairs in order. These "advances" do not spare us undergoing ostensibly the same treatments breast cancer patients have had to endure for thirty years. And we, or I, resent propaganda that makes it sound as though breast cancer is being conquered.

Mr. Perfect has chosen to meet me in a bar so dark I can hardly see him. Surrounded by chocolate-coloured upholstery, he chats on his cell while perusing the offer. I gather he's in the food distribution business because he's becoming very excited about pies. "You won't believe it," he tells the phone, "it's like your grandma made it!" He drinks more beer, then starts tapping the nib of his pen against the offer. I look at my watch. He observes this and holds out a finger indicating that he'll get off the phone in a minute. The waitress presents him with another beer and I watch him ogle her breasts. Would he be eyeing them so intently if there were a tumour inside them? In a culture in which breasts are used to sell movies, cars, magazines, books, cosmetics, clothes, shoes, perfumes, alcohol, cigarettes—it's tough to think of a marketing strategy that doesn't involve breasts—it's astonishing how, once diseased, they're not worthy of the kind of funding available to look for life on Mars. Or sustain the arms race. Or retain baseball players. I mean, let's face it, they're irreplaceable. Women, well, they're not much use after fifty. Certainly no guy in his right mind wants to fondle their jugs when there's a twenty-year-old set available.

I wonder if the group leader/yoga guru would consider this healthy anger.

Mr. Perfect is phoning his wife, calling her "babe" while discussing the offer. "Don't get emotional about it, babe," he keeps telling her.

Behind me a young woman is complaining that she already has laugh-lines. "And my mother's hands," she adds, "look way younger than mine. So I guess I take after my dad. He looks really old and he's not even like forty-five. He works for Procter & Gamble and his hair's bleached white from all that Tide and stuff. He always smells of Tide or Bounce or something."

"Don't panic," Mr. Perfect tells Babe while reaching for his beer.

If Procter & Gamble turned Dad's hair white, what's it doing to the rest of him?

"You're panicking," Mr. Perfect admonishes.

"I've been seeing this naturopath," the man from Glad's daughter says. "He got me off gluten and refined sugar and has me taking all these drops. It's really helping. I still don't have that last ten percent, though. Most of the time I just feel ninety."

And this is a negative thing?

I want to tell Glad's daughter about the women her age in the waiting room who think of percentages only in as much as they offer prospects of survival.

"Let me handle it," Mr. Perfect tells Babe.

I am lucky that no metastasis was discovered. The problem is that that was then, this is now. What's happening in my body now? Cancer cells sloughed off the main tumour mass float through the bloodstream; they don't just party in the breast tissue. Which is what's so special about breast cancer. *It* doesn't kill. What kills is cancer in a different site that has metastasized from the original cancer. Which is why cutting off breasts, carving out lumps and digging out lymph nodes while thinking positive thoughts isn't making a shitload of difference to survival rates.

Mr. Perfect gets off the phone. "Want a bevie?"

"No thanks. I've got to keep moving."

"Alrighty."

He scribbles notes, demands for things he doesn't want like the chandelier in the dining room which the vendor specified wasn't included in the sale. Mr. Perfect's saying he wants these things so he can use them as a negotiating tool. He waves a twenty at the waitress whose breasts bounce authentically as she hurries towards us. Does he breastwatch with Babe around? It's great to be free of all that. Sometimes I feel invisible among men and I like it. I don't want them looking at my tit.

I've got the itches under my prosthesis and sneak a scratch while Mr. Perfect is signing. He hands me the papers. "Draw blood," he tells me. What a darling.

Maybe the Martians will find a cure. In the meantime the earthlings tell us we shouldn't eat fat, drink alcohol, smoke, take the pill (although now they're telling us we should take the pill), have multiple sex partners or experience stress. And we should have many babies starting in our teens that we breast feed until the next one comes along. Even as we are told these things we are cautioned that not eating fat or drinking or smoking or taking the pill (or not taking it), or having multiple sex partners or experiencing stress, or having many babies will ensure that we won't get breast cancer. We could live the life of a peasant, have sixteen children and still die of breast cancer, if we don't first die of exhaustion. Which might not be so bad. Obviously we're living too long.

Todd's open house is in a row built by a developer a year ago. It's tall and skinny, with tiny rooms, crappy carpet and cheap fixtures. I can hear the neighbour's stereo through the wall and suggest to the vendor that she turn on her stereo to block it out. She seems nervous and I wonder what it is about the house that's making her sell after living in it only a year. Best not to ask. She says "what have you" a lot. "Here's the bathroom and what have you. Here's the living/dining and what have you." While we're waiting to see if anybody shows up, she sponges the kitchen counter forty times. "I know this sounds silly," she says, "but I saw this dead bird and I'm really distraught. I mean, I don't know if it just dropped from the sky or if it was the victim of an attack." She squeezes her sponge again. "I don't know how to describe it but . . . it was like I was that bird."

I nod, listening for the doorbell, although I don't expect anyone to come. This house is what Todd would call "a real dog." I must remember to thank him for sharing it with me.

"It sounds silly," the birdlady says, "but I was crying and what have you. Do you happen to know if birds die in flight?"

"No idea. I suppose they can get sick and fall off trees."

She looks doubtful and starts sponging the counter again.

"Maybe they get heart disease," I add, "from pecking at junk food."

She shakes her head. "I suspect it was the victim of an assault. My neighbour poisons pigeons. He uses the same drug they feed birds in New York City. It causes nausea, convulsions, disorientation and slow death."

This is why she's moving.

"People can be so cruel," she adds.

I consider trying to cheer her up by saying, Things could be worse, my son kills people. But I suspect this might make her more nervous.

Driving home I hear about another crime, in America. A black man from Nigeria—who had come to make a life for himself in the land of the brave and free—happened to be standing at a bus stop when two skinheads approached. "Do you know that you're a nigger?" the one with a .22 calibre revolver tucked into his belt demanded. "Yes," the Nigerian responded, accustomed to eating shit to preserve his life, thinking only of his wife and child back home, his wife and child who needed the small amount of money he regularly sent them. "Are you ready to die a nigger?" the skinhead asked. "Yes," the Nigerian responded as bullets lacerated his body.

This is a worse crime than the one my son committed. I think. Does it make it better that there are worse crimes?

At home, I find him sprawled on the couch eating Doritos and watching *Goodfellas*. As more and more gangsters have their heads blown off, I watch him. While blood spurts out of "gun wounds" he seems unmoved. When the mortally wounded man starts knocking from inside the boot of the car, Sam laughs. When the gangsters open the trunk and stab and shoot the trapped man some more, Sam smiles. Is it all a joke to him? Did the old people look funny as their dentures loosened? Was it hilarious when they shit their pants?

I avoid violent movies because they mark my dreams. My sleep becomes disturbed by knifings, shootings, stranglings. Once I asked Sam if violent movies affected his nightmares. He shrugged.

Do the children of television have a greater tolerance for blood and horror than the rest of us? Does blood and horror, real or unreal, have any effect on them? Or has it become as blasé as commercials filled with cleavage?

I watch *Goodfellas* because I want to be with him. I want it to be like when he was little, when he would sing along with the commercial for Oscar Meyer wieners: "I wish I were an Oscar Meyer wiener . . ."

Sometimes, when I look at him, I contemplate cancer being the result of accidental changes in the genetic makeup of a cell—mutations. The cell reproduces, passing on its altered DNA. It reproduces independently, regardless of the body's needs. The cancer cells create their own network of blood vessels to secure the necessary nutrients to thrive. They don't need the host's network of blood vessels.

Sometimes, when I look at Sam, I think of my tumour, growing independently, robbing me of oxygen and nutrients. Unstopped, it would have outstripped its self-generated blood supply; portions of it would've died as the breast surface ulcerated. Infection would have followed, hemorrhaging and finally death. The tumour would have died with me.

Sometimes, when I look at Sam, I feel that he is the beginning and ending of my life; that I nourished him, that he mutated from me but still requires the shelter of my body. If I go, he goes.

I don't mean that he caused my cancer. I mean that we are as inexplicably linked as cancer is inexplicably caused.

Six

My hairdresser is a very busy woman. Today, an actress I recognize from TV commercials crosses and uncrosses her legs in the chair beside me. Anne separates strands of the actress's long hair and wraps it in foils. I notice her glancing at her watch, which means she's behind. The actress stresses that the blonde highlights must look natural on camera. She stares into the mirror, scrutinizing Anne's handiwork. I ponder if the bleach and peroxide is seeping into her pores, causing cell mutations.

Last night I dreamed I was dead. I was having dinner with Jerry who didn't know I was dead. He was telling me how to live my life. I considered telling him that I was dead, but I knew he'd argue with me. "You're not dead," he'd say. "Cut the crap."

I was so relieved to be dead.

I flip through a showbiz magazine featuring "inspiring stories" about showbiz types who have breast cancer. The "survivors" have layers of makeup on that make them look cadaverous. They're all smiling, revealing cosmetically perfected teeth. "They fought their toughest battle and won," the headline reads. This depiction of breast cancer as a battleground in which the strongest woman wins really irritates me. Does this mean that Linda McCartney was weak? Did she fail because she died? Is Olivia Newton John a stronger woman? I read on. Lovely stories all about love and positive attitudes and plastic surgery and putting it all behind you. This is news to me because according to my research breast cancer, unlike some cancers, is incurable. A "survivor" will never have the same life expectancy as others in the population of the same age and sex. A "survivor" has routine blood tests and bone scans and ultrasounds—to check for a recurrence—forever. You can't put breast cancer behind you. It marks you for life, what's left of it.

"I'd like to cut it off," the actress announces. "But it's not good for business." Anne nods sympathetically. "It's the guys," the actress explains. "They want it long."

"They think it's sexy," Anne offers.

"That's right. *They* don't have to take care of it. It's not like I can just get up and go in the morning. My boyfriend has long hair and just ties it in a ponytail. I hate it. I tell him to get a haircut. He says it's too much hassle. Oh, like me spending half an hour every morning blow-drying isn't a hassle."

"It's a double standard." Anne glances at her watch again.

"And then he complains that it takes me too long to get ready. He's the one who wants me to look great. If I went out looking like shit, I'd never hear the end of it."

"It's not easy being an attractive woman," Anne says, understanding that flattery will bring the actress back for more highlights, generating more income for Anne.

"Why don't you cut off his ponytail in his sleep?" I suggest.

The actress looks at me with distaste. I try to discern, without staring, if her boobs are real.

"You could snip it off," I elaborate, "like what's-her-face snipped off what's-his-face's pecker." I can see Anne restraining laughter. But the actress is not amused and resumes her stern surveillance of Anne.

I always hope to feel like a new person after a haircut and am always disappointed when the same old me stares back from the mirror. But I do feel slightly leaner and meaner, which is necessary when I'm about to face Jerry.

On the Friday before the murders, before I left for the spa, I was preoccupied with closing a deal on a house. Sam seemed normal to me, although he'd been sleeping off a night shift at the hospital, which meant he was cranky. And he was dreading the upcoming Saturday night because Emergency was always peopled with bleeding drunks, abused hookers and survivors of gunshot wounds. The previous Saturday, a homosexual had crawled in with a broken Coke bottle inserted in his rectum. Apparently he was howling like a wounded animal. Sam said it was the third homosexual in a month showing up with a Coke bottle up his ass. This seemed to upset Sam more than the plight of accident victims. In a rare confessional moment, he described to me a dream he'd had about someone forcing a rat up *his* rectum. He was able to fight the assailant off, pull out the rat and chase after the assailant with it. The rat had almost suffocated while up his anus so Sam had had to resuscitate it by pumping its ribs. Awake and free of the nightmare, he found this amusing—the idea of resuscitating the rat by pumping it. I don't know if he told me this dream to shock me, or simply because he was so disturbed by it he had to tell somebody. Either way it doesn't strike me as being the nightmare of a psychopath, because in the dream he plays the role of the victim *and* he saves the rat. When I asked him if he caught up with the assailant, he shook his head. When I asked if the assailant had a face, he said no.

Does this nightmare have anything to do with the killing?

I think he might have escaped the law had there not been an old man sitting on a neighbouring porch that Sunday afternoon. It seems to me the world is overpopulated with old men sitting on porches. I have one across the street. In ten years, he hasn't said a word to me but watches me steadily. I've tried staring him down, but it's impossible. His stare is so unwavering, I'm not sure that he realizes he's staring. Maybe he's gaga, and I'm just a bug on the windshield of his dementia.

Anyway, the man on the porch across from the senior citizens' house was cognizant enough to identify Sam and tell the police where he lived. When the thugs came to my door, I assumed I'd forgotten to pay parking tickets. Or that they were looking for a missing child. A few years ago, when we were digging around our foundation to fix a drainage problem, the cops came looking for a little girl. Our piles of dirt seemed to me to be the ideal hiding place for a dead child. "No, we haven't seen a little girl," I told them, worried that they'd start kicking through the dirt.

I have to park blocks from the restaurant, near the psychiatric hospital. As I get out, a mad man in a trench coat, galoshes and a touque limps towards me and points to a parked car. "Is that a Pontiac?" he asks urgently.

I look at the car in question.

"Is it a Pontiac?" he persists.

I can see no make on the car. "I don't know."

"Maybe it's a General Motors."

"Could be."

"Is a Pontiac a good car?"

"I don't know."

"My mother has a car. A Volkswagen Golf. Is that a good car? You should get a car. My mother has a car."

I lock my door and begin to flee.

"Suzie has a Toyota," he adds. "That's a good car. You should get a car. My mother has a car."

Is *he* capable of murder? Certainly if he did kill somebody the defence would have no problem getting him off on a plea of insanity. They'd just have to bring in a video featuring different models of cars with unclear makes. The jury could watch him go squirrelly. Someone should start a business offering crazy assassins for hire. You could book them, then forget about them. Let the judicial system grind over their abnormal minds, then let them loose on the condition that they take their medication and seek therapy.

I did try therapy once. My therapist had severe sciatica and was in constant pain. Occasionally, suffering would flash on his face and I would worry that I was upsetting him. I became preoccupied with his physical pain and would edit myself in attempts to distract him, make him laugh. I always felt it had been a good session if I'd been able to lighten him up a bit. When I told him I couldn't afford him anymore, he seemed crestfallen and insisted I still had a lot of "work" to do. I should probably try another therapist but there's something about sitting around telling a complete stranger about your fears, weaknesses and toilet-training history that just doesn't work for me.

Jerry sits with his back to the entrance. He's always done this. Most people wait facing the door, ready to welcome you. Not Jerr.

"Hi," I say.

"How are you?"

I don't tell him because he doesn't want to know. After my breast was severed, he asked me how I was and I made the mistake of telling him about the infection and the need for repeated aspirations of fluid. I had edema in my arm because, without lymph nodes, there's nowhere for stuff to drain. My arm was so swollen and heavy with fluid I had to wear a surgical stocking for support. I showed this to Jerry, thinking it was mildly amusing to have a surgical stocking on my arm. He looked revolted and I felt revolting.

"I'm swell," I tell him. "How are you?"

"You want a drink?"

"Sure." A Bloody Mary, a cancer cocktail. More than three drinks a week is supposed to pose a risk. I've cut back but this will be my fourth. There are so many things I'm not supposed to do or have. *Avoiding* these things stresses me out. The drinks arrive and Jerry asks my advice regarding a house Natasha wants him to buy. He describes its features and location, then tells me they want 2.5 million for it. I tell him this is reasonable although it isn't. At the table beside us, a young woman sits with her arms draped around the neck of a man who could pass for her father. But if he were her father, I don't think she'd be pushing her breasts up against him. Their clams arrive. I dread listening to them suck on their clams.

"It seems high to me," Jerry says.

"Any price seems high to you." The waiter brings my grilled goat cheese which I begin to devour. Jerry doesn't stub out his cigarette.

I'm not feeling good about the deal on the semi. The vendor was shocked by the low offer, and rightly so. Mr. Perfect is being an asshole. The vendor is newly widowed and vulnerable. She wants out of the house that contains her past. I wanted to tell her to be patient, that she could expect much better, even from this buyer, because Mrs. Perfect wants the house. But I'm not the vendor's agent. Her agent wears white loafers and is about to set sail on a Caribbean cruise. He's keen to close the deal at any price. The vendor doesn't know this. To justify my clients' low offer, I expressed concern about the leaky basement and blocked chimney. I also reminded her that railway tracks were not far off and certainly the trains were audible. My clients hadn't even noticed the tracks, couldn't care less about the noise. But in order to get the vendor to sign back, I had to make her feel that her house was a piece of shit.

"How's your health?" Jerry asks.

"Swell."

"Natasha thinks you look wonderful."

"How nice."

"She's seeing an alternative practitioner who she thinks is fabulous. He gives her herb teas and things. Homeopathic pills. She suggested you might want to see him."

"Does Natasha have cancer?"

"Of course not."

What do you mean, "of course not?" It can proliferate undetected for years. "Then how does she know this alternative practitioner would be fabulous for a cancer patient?"

"She's just trying to help."

"Well, do thank her for me. But I can't really afford alternative therapies at this point, what with legal bills and all."

He sighs. "I just thought I'd mention it."

"If she'd like to help, she could stop costing you money." I order salmon steak, vichyssoise and a green salad. The waiter looks hurried, although the restaurant isn't crowded. The clam eaters are slurping. Their shells pile up.

"He doesn't exactly possess a rapier wit," I hear Clam Man remark while Clam Babe daintily wipes grease off her chin.

Jerry wants me to ask why we need to talk. Instead I eat more garlic bread. I plan to breathe on him later.

"Sam's holding up quite well, I think," he comments. "All things considered." He starts to take out another cigarette, then remembers that I'm eating.

"Go ahead," I tell him.

"No. I should be cutting back anyway." He did for about a week, when he was diagnosed with cancer. "It infuriates Natasha. She won't let me smoke in the house, says she refuses to watch me kill myself."

"He has no balls," Clam Man insists. Is he referring to the man without the rapier wit, and if so, why is he denigrating the witless man? Because Clam Babe has expressed an interest in him? Is Clam Babe bringing up the witless man to make Clam Man jealous? Either way I think they're in for a romp tonight.

Sweat trickles down my left armpit. Jerry's getting to me. "Are we having wine?" I ask.

"If you want."

"Please. You choose."

The thing about Jerry is he always seems to be in control, even when he isn't. Except when he walks into closets because he's afraid he's got cancer.

He orders the wine as his steak arrives. He cuts into it and I watch it bleed. It makes me think of leaking breast implants. Anne, the hairdresser, told me about a politician's wife who consulted a plastic surgeon regarding breast augmentation. When she asked about leakage, he threw a sample implant on the floor to prove their durability. Then he told her to "lift her shirt." After assessing the situation, he advised her that her face looked like the curtains hanging in his office. They'd been hanging there for years. Old curtains sagged, he said, "Get the face done. Forget about the breasts." So the politician's wife had some collagen injected into her face which slid down to her chest and made her think she had breast cancer.

Clam Babe's boobs look real though, gelatinous. I'm not happy about my newly developed breast fetish. I'm always judging breasts: their size and tone, their authenticity. If one in eight women over a lifetime gets breast cancer, there's bound to be a lot of artificial bosoms out there. A tabloid headline I noticed recently at the checkout counter read, "Whose are fake?" Pictures of Hollywood starlets wearing low-cut gowns were featured. Is this like a witch hunt? Will they seek out the implanted and burn them at the stake?

"You've got to think positively," Clam Babe pronounces.

Another route to thinking positively suggested by the group leader/yoga master was to imagine a knight in shining armour attacking your cancer. I tried to picture the knight riding the white horse in that Ajax commercial from the sixties. He had a lance and was charging at something, dirt, I guess. I tried to imagine that the dirt was my cancer.

Jerry emits a low growl, which means he's annoyed with me for being inattentive.

"Have you seen any Betty Grable movies lately?" I inquire. He's always had this thing for Betty Grable, the airhead with the legs. I'm all for admiring prehistoric movie stars but choose somebody with some style.

"Let's not play games," he says.

"I was just making conversation."

"I'm concerned about how we're presenting ourselves in court."

"We?"

"You do realize that you look as though you think he's guilty?"

"Do you think he's not?"

"That's beside the point."

"Seriously, I'd like to know. Do you believe our son was unconscious when he killed two senior citizens?"

"I'm not ruling out anything."

The waiter brings my salmon, then the wine. Jerry pretends to taste it before nodding that it's fine. I take a couple of gulps and stare at him. "So what is it about *your* presentation that concerns you?" I know that nothing about his presentation concerns him.

"I'm more worried about you. Eyes are on you. Your testimony is going to be crucial."

"How would you like me to behave?"

"I'd like you to at least resemble a distraught mother, show some vulnerability. I don't think stoicism is going to work here."

"Do you think the divorced father showing up with a trophy wife half his age is going to work?" A piece of chocolate cake costs ten bucks here. I'll order it even if I can't eat it.

Clam Man, apparently getting worked up over the topic of the witless man and positive thinking, knocks over his wineglass, spilling wine onto his crotch. He and Clam Babe pat it with napkins, causing, I suspect, an erection. The hurried waiter stoops to the floor and collects the pieces of broken glass in a napkin. "I don't know how that happened," Clam Man keeps repeating.

"What is it with you?" Jerry says.

"What?"

"You seem completely preoccupied."

"Cancer does that."

"I'm very sorry that you have cancer. Nevertheless, we have a problem."

"You're not very sorry. You don't give a shit."

"Here we go."

"It doesn't matter, Jerr. I don't need you giving a shit. I do need you to stay out of my face."

"I would be more than happy to stay out of your face if you would pull yourself together in the courtroom."

I pour myself more wine, thinking about cigars. How I'd like to shove cigars up Jerry's nostrils, transforming him into a walrus. One of Sam's few friends pops into my lubricated stream of consciousness, a boy named Karl, who got run over by a car when he was eight. His older brother witnessed his death and was traumatized by it. The parents not only had to deal with the death of a son but the psychological damage of another. I conclude that it should have been Sam who was run over. Then he could have lived eternally as an eight-year-old in my mind, happily eating Zoodles.

"Maybe you should try talking to somebody," Jerry says.

Way back when, before we were married, I had an abortion because I knew we couldn't cope with a baby while trying to complete our degrees. Jerry never forgave me. He said I had castrated him. Years later, when Sam was three, I suggested we have another child. Jerry was barbecuing, smoke swirled around him. "Forget it," he said. "You can't even handle this one." He was getting his revenge for the abortion. He was castrating me. From then on, when we copulated, he always took precautions.

I look at him and try to figure out what Natasha sees—a paunchy businessman with an expensive haircut. Be still my heart.

Clam Man orders more wine. I'm certain he has a wife and kiddies cloistered in a house somewhere, watching violent television. The wife will smell Clam Babe on him, will dream of knifing Clam Babe, will dream of leaving Clam Man but will fear the consequences: delinquent children, financial ruin.

The weirdest thing is that after Jerry moved out he insisted on completing repairs on our house. He hired a contractor, but he himself could be found puttering about with a paintbrush or a screwdriver. More repairs were done to that house in those first weeks when he was shacking up with what's-her-face than had been done in the history of our marriage. I suppose he felt it was his last chance to protect his investment. Or maybe he did it out of guilt.

"What you do with your private life is a matter of indifference to me," he says. "What you do in the courtroom is something else entirely."

"I'll try to behave, Daddyo." I'm definitely bombed. I have to resist an urge to whip out my prosthesis and slap it on the table. "All those Raffi songs," I add.

"What?"

"All about love in the family and the more we get together, the happier we'll be. Sam used to sing them."

"I know what you're doing," Jerry tells me. "I can see through your crap."

Jerry has often insisted that he could not only "see through" my "crap," but the entire world's. He considers himself to be numero uno at bullshit detecting. Which is interesting considering what a bullshitter he is. Maybe it takes one to know one.

"You always do this," he says.

"And you always do this. That's why we got divorced. Cheers." I drink more. He's thinking I've turned into a souse. "Why don't you spend some time with him?" I ask. "Take him for a ride in the country or something. Look at the animals. He doesn't understand why you never want to see him."

"Is that what you tell him, that I don't want to see him?"

"Of course. I say you hate his guts and wish he were dead. That's why I'm surprised he misses you."

Jerry shakes his head, indicating that he can't believe my callousness and general demeanour. My mind drifts to Natasha's pierced nostril. When we were still speaking, she confided to me that her first husband had pierced it with a needle and a cork. It hardly hurt at all, she said perkily. I find it very difficult to talk to people with pierced nostrils. I keep thinking there's something stuck on their nose and have to resist an urge to pull it off.

I pick bones out of my salmon. "He blames us for his teeth."

"What are you talking about?"

"All that orthodontic work. He hated it, didn't think it was necessary."

"What's that got to do with anything?"

"Do *you* think it was necessary? I mean, after all, it was your idea or, should I say, obsession. Does he look all that different to you? Did having perfectly aligned teeth improve his quality of life? We should have spent the money on his head, not his teeth."

"Oh, don't start with that."

"Sometimes he was crying when I dropped him off. That's how much it hurt."

"Lots of kids get their teeth straightened and they don't kill people."

"So none of this has anything to do with you?"

"What?"

"His actions."

"Unlike you, I don't torture myself."

"Well, maybe you should, Jerr. Maybe if you got off the pot and took a look at your own shit, you'd learn something." I must be raising my voice because Jerry's looking edgy. In more secluded surroundings, he would've hurled something in my general direction. "Did you know," I continue, "that the male brain shrinks after twenty, which accounts for loss of memory and other decreased brain function?"

"Christ," he mutters.

I stuff more salad greens in my mouth even though I've lost my appetite. I've dripped salad dressing onto my blouse but try to appear unconcerned. Another recent dream comes into play: the dying plant. I was running around trying to shelter it from the icy rain. I pounded on the plate-glass doors of an apartment building, all the while trying to shield the plant with my body. When no one answered I cut the plastic pot containing the plant with a plastic knife. Water poured out of it. The roots had been rotting. I'd been watering it so much it was drowning. Natasha appeared behind the glass wearing her constipated parrot hat. "*I'm* the superintendent," she informed me, without opening the door. How could I let this happen? I was thinking, how could I leave the plant in a crappy plastic pot that I could have cut with a crappy plastic knife? Natasha strode away leaving me with my soon-to-be-dead plant. Okay, so the plant is Sam, but what's Parrot Hat got to do with it? I don't like it that she's the superintendent in my dreams.

"Did you know," I tell Jerry, "that a ten-year-old boy was left in a trailer home without gas or water for six months. He lived oh dog food. He didn't tell anyone he'd been abandoned because he didn't want to get his parents into trouble."

"What's that got to do with anything?"

"Children and parents. It makes you think."

"What?"

"See, that's what I mean, Jerr. Connect the dots. Your son, neglect. He stays loyal anyway, goes on believing in you, wants to believe in you. Eats dog food for you. Endures hideous teeth pain so that you won't think he's a wussy."

Jerry looks around the room as though waiting for reinforcements, the matron and the big orderly with a straitjacket who will haul me away.

"I snooped around his room the other night," I admit.

"What?"

"Sam's room. You know what he's reading, beyond the usual trash?"

"Is this going somewhere?"

"He's reading a book called *Winning Through Intimidation.* Do you think he might be trying to emulate somebody?"

Clam Babe leans back in her chair and folds her arms. "So are you going to stay bullish?"

Jerry pushes his plate away. "When are you going to stop resenting me for getting on with my life?" Ah, we're back to the bad movie dialogue.

"When you stay out of mine." The waiter offers the dessert menu. I shake my head sadly, knowing that I must leave now, before I smash the wine bottle over Jerry's head.

On his last day playing handyman, he stood before me in the garden. On my knees, with my hands in dirt, I looked up at him. "What are you doing?" he asked.

"Planting a rose."

"You don't want to put a rose there."

"I do want to put a rose here. I'm going to build a trellis."

"You don't know how to build a trellis." Then he started to tell me how to stain the deck, the same deck I'd stained without his assistance three years previously.

"Time to go, Jerr," I said.

Any qualms I'd had about being the abandoned wife left me. I just wanted him out. The next day, I changed the locks. When he found out, he was furious, insisting that it was still his house. From an upstairs window, I watched him fume on the front steps. I was surprised he didn't call the police and make a big ugly scene. Maybe he wanted to get back to stuffing what's-her-face. Or he was put off by the staring man sitting on the porch across the street.

Outside the restaurant, feeling weakened but determined, I head for my car. I remember Sam at almost two, flushing a toothbrush down the toilet, causing plumbing chaos which cost a fair sum to repair. Jerry was livid, but I just thought it was hilarious. Sam wasn't toilet trained yet. Flushing a toothbrush down the hole seemed a better idea than flushing his poop which he still valued. "It's not funny," Jerry said. "This is just the beginning. We have to watch him." Jerry proceeded to affix locks to cabinet doors, garbage cans, the toilet seat. Suddenly Sam couldn't get at anything. He couldn't explore. I let this happen. Because I didn't want to argue. And because a neighbour's one-year-old drowned in a toilet bowl.

We have to watch him.

Guess we blew that one, eh, Jerr?

Seven

I may not be the smartest person in the world, but it seems to me the football player's been spending way too much time blow-drying his hair and pumping iron while congratulating himself on the "overwhelming physical evidence" in this case. Meanwhile, Baldy, slow but steady, broods and schemes and digs up dirt that the football player attempts to dismiss. The latest surprise is that one of the prosecution's experts testified years ago for the defence in an automatism case. The defendant was acquitted and subsequently killed again. Baldy's suggesting that this expert's opinion is biased, that he might be unwilling to support a plea of non-insane automatism because he feels guilty about having helped this other killer get off. The expert becomes testy under Baldy's cross-examination which convinces me, and probably the jury, that Baldy's onto something. Blondie's other experts can't get it together either. Their testimonies are wordy and boring and even us plebs can figure out that they don't form the united front of Baldy's team. I wonder if this is because we're paying Baldy's guys more money. And if the football player is mediocre because he's a civil servant.

Climbing the courthouse steps this morning, I was spit upon by what must be a crazy person. I've noticed her before, darting behind pillars, muttering furiously, impersonating the Wicked Witch of the West. She must be short of cash because I've seen her snatch leftovers from trash cans. Presumably the courthouse offers her shelter and entertainment. So I don't know if she spat on me because I'm the mother of the killer, or if spitting at folk is just something she does; a kind of sport. In any case I've never been spit upon before. Spitting is something you see in movies, usually westerns. The saliva landed on my sleeve forming a sizable blob. Startled by the assault I hurried on, trying to locate a Kleenex in my purse to wipe off the spit. Of course I didn't have any and had to go to the washroom and face gawkers. Resisting an urge to soak wads of toilet paper to fling at them, I considered asking if they'd heard about the ten-year-old boy who was found hanging in a school washroom, strung up by two other ten-year-old boys. Children under twelve can't be charged with a crime, I felt compelled to explain to the excuses-for-humans, so you're going to have to boogie on down to the boys' homes to get in some good gawking.

I worry that the Wicked Witch of the West spat at Sam. I know he makes a point of arriving early at the courthouse to avoid harassment.

The testy expert's story is that Sam was not in a hysterical dissociative state, that he was a controlled young man who went into an extreme fit of rage and was fully aware of what he was doing during this rage. This does not concur with the previous expert's testimony (a giant with pointy eyebrows) who claimed that Sam was in a dissociative state, which is a subdivision of hysterical neurosis, which is a definite mental illness. The testy expert allows that Sam has a psychiatric problem that requires treatment to help him face up to what he has done. But this isn't the same as having a disease or a disorder of the mind—a definite mental illness as described by the giant. When the testy expert is asked if he thinks somnambulism can be feigned, he admits that this would be very difficult due to the precise symptoms and medical histories beyond the control of the accused that must be presented as evidence. Baldy reminds him, and the jury members who are still awake, that Sam has been subjected to numerous tests to determine that he does, in fact, experience somnambulism which, Baldy reiterates, does not stem from a *disease* of the mind. The testy expert asserts that he isn't saying Sam doesn't sleepwalk. He just doesn't think he was asleep when he bludgeoned the old people.

I glance at the jurors to see if they believe this guy. The old lady is definitely dozing. She's probably not that old, just hasn't had plastic surgery. I sympathize with her. Staying alert would be a problem for me as a juror. Not to mention the sore ass I'd get from the interminable sitting. Let's hope none of them have hemorrhoids. The other jurors appear to be listening, but are not particularly impressed. The Sonny Bono look-alike keeps twirling his moustache. The car salesman checks his watch and pulls on his nose hairs. The cheerleaders wait anxiously for the football player to flex his muscles again.

I suspect that each "expert's" testimony is only as effective as the expert is entertaining. If he mumbles or stutters or looks as if he'd rather be reading a book about brain transplants, he will lose the jury. They want action, entertainment, song-and-dance numbers.

Jerry and the trophy wife are whispering. Maybe she has to leave for a manicure. Why can he still make me feel powerless? What is it in me that lets him do that? The group leader/yoga guru would blame my low self-esteem. He'd tell me to imagine that I'm Snow White and Jerry's a dwarf. I don't understand why I forget what a wimpoid he is when he's confronting me in his big expensive clothes. The night I told him about the thyroid cancer—after he came out of the closet—he sat at the kitchen table and whimpered, "I wish I was dead" over and over again. Sam heard this because he was in the living room watching violent television. He was only eleven and didn't need to hear his father say he wished to be dead. To a kid this means: My child doesn't give me a good enough reason to live.

When I got home last night, Sam and Sybil were fighting again. He's never liked her, thinks she's a write-off because she's old and penniless. With the arrogance of youth on his side, he can't imagine a similar fate for himself. On his good days, he foresees making big capitalist bucks like his dad, although the means with which he will make the big bucks is unclear. Also, Sybil fed him his first hot dog when he was two and a half. He was obsessed with puppies. So when Sybil told him that the thing in the bun was a hot dog, he thought she meant it was made of dog or, worse still, puppy. He came home extremely upset, even after I sat him on my knee and explained that "hot dog" was just a name. Since then, he has never enjoyed meat and has become a staunch vegetarian.

So Sybil's stews are not popular with him. He says they stink up the house, which is true.

But last night I had no strength to referee their fight, which I knew concerned me. Sybil believes he drains me, that he's not helping my condition. She's still trying to change him, transform him into a young man with a social conscience.

As they didn't hear me come in, I crept upstairs, tried to brush the taste of garlic and salmon out of my mouth and crawled into bed. I turned the radio on hoping to be soothed, but it was eleven and I had to wait through the news. The woman who knifed her husband nine times but failed to kill him was acquitted on the basis of insanity, although, like Sam, she had tried for non-insane automatism because she'd received many blows to the head from her husband over the years. Now she would spend an indeterminate amount of time in a mental institution while her husband would marry her niece. "We're so happy for him," his sister said, "he deserves some happiness." After beating someone for twenty years? The "insane" woman's only regret must be that she didn't kill him. I see her blank-faced, in a room with a metal grid over the window. An attendant resembling a gorilla unlocks her door and hands her pills to swallow, which she does without resistance because she has no fight left in her. They had been fabulously rich and she had been a fabulous hostess. Why didn't she leave him? Low self-esteem? Fear of financial destitution? Children? I suspect she wasn't using visualization techniques. No knight in shining armour was attacking her fears.

Exhausted, I lay on the bed with my clothes on. I took out my prosthesis and put it on the night table. It made me think of one of those glass balls you shake to create a snowscape. I used to love those as a kid. The real world could be in chaos but life inside the globe remained tranquil. Maybe if they put snowscapes inside breast prosthetics, we'd cope better with stress.

I told myself I'd get up and change in a minute. Instead I fell asleep and dreamed that I still had my right breast. On waking I felt for it and was, as usual, jarred by the rigidity of the scar tissue. Tears dribbled out of my left eye. I thought, When am I going to stop crying about this? I've *got* to stop crying about this. A sign I'd seen on a store window floated past my mind's eye: Mastectomy Swimsuits 40% Off. What does a mastectomy swimsuit look like? What happens if you buy a mastectomy swimsuit, then find out you require a double mastectomy swimsuit? What's the return policy? I tried to imagine myself going into the store and asking to try on a mastectomy swimsuit and a matronly, blue-haired saleslady demanding, "A single or a double?"

I forced myself up and out of my clothes, but I couldn't sleep. The dog down the street was obviously disturbed by something because it wouldn't shut up. The barks came in threes, then there'd be a slight pause and I'd hope that maybe the mutt had zipped it. But then it would start up again.

I felt my remaining breast, which has become my enemy, a cancer ally I fear will betray me. I'm not thorough in my self-examinations anymore. I don't want to know, can't handle more treatment. Turning over my tear-dampened pillow, I tried to count sheep but instead some inane pop tune kept bopping through my head. I tried to distract myself, thought about garbage, how much there is, how insane it is that we're stuffing the earth with garbage. I thought about the packaging that becomes garbage, all the different forms of plastic. I thought about the chemicals used to produce the plastics, chemicals that are spewed into the air we breathe. I thought about the news that we shouldn't put hot food in plastic containers because the heat produces carcinogens. And "mercury rain" stealing the spotlight from "acid" because it gets into our water supply and mercury isn't something you want to drink; we're talking mad hatter's disease. And those extra hormones we're giving to cattle so they'll produce even more milk. I felt sorry for the cows with their swollen udders—the cows who are slaughtered when they can no longer produce milk, and therefore don't live long enough to develop cancer from all the hormones we're forcing into them. And I felt forlorn, not just about the cows but about the human race. Because we're willing to poison animals, fish, trees, ourselves, our children, all in the name of business.

Next I tried to come up with a good excuse for having stayed with Jerry for so long. Sam? Did I imagine it would be better for Sam? Did I not want to be alone with a son who was becoming increasingly remote? Did I still feel something for Jerry? Did I fear he would destroy me with the divorce proceedings? Did I fear being single? No clear answers to any of these questions presented themselves. Except lethargy. I had no energy to deal with any of it. Somewhere in my thirties the world became too menacing for me. I immersed myself in work, made money, hoping that money would make me feel safe. I bought us a king-size bed so that I could keep my distance. I was happiest in my car, going places, it didn't matter where. In my car, no one could get at me. I was free. Until cell phones became ubiquitous.

After court, I go to the bank. Someone's left their transaction record in the dispenser. I pull it out and check their balance. They're twenty-five hundred overdrawn. This improves my mood. At least I'm not overdrawn, yet.

Estelle is still at the office and hysterical because the vet couldn't locate a tumour in Bunny's belly. I suggest that this is good news.

"You don't understand," she tells me. "He knows there's a tumour somewhere—there *has* to be a tumour."

"Why?"

"Because of the calcium in his blood," she says as though I'm an idiot for having forgotten this important detail. "And there's something wrong with his liver."

"But no tumour on it?"

"No. But I have to give him extra vitamin E."

"That shouldn't be difficult."

"It is if he won't eat. They've left this tube in his stomach I'm supposed to pour liquid food into. He hates it. He keeps trying to pull it out."

"Can't you cover it with something?"

"I've put one of his sweaters on."

Bunny has sweaters?

"Now he wants to do a spinal tap to see if there's a tumour on his brain."

The vet's determination to find a tumour reminds me of Cheeseburger's determination to find a tumour.

"What about the lumps on his groin?" I ask.

"He says those are just dead fat cells. He doesn't want to tamper with those."

I have to meet the vendor and agent of the semi. Mr. Perfect has come up a fraction. I suspect that the widow is going to accept. The Caribbean-cruise-anticipating agent will tell her that they might be able to do better but he can't say when because it's a slow time.

"They have to shave his back," Estelle adds.

"What?"

"To do the spinal tap. They have to shave his back. They've already shaved his belly. He's going to be practically bald."

For some reason this upsets me more than all the other stuff: a kitty losing his fur, not understanding why. "It'll grow back," I offer. That's what they tell the chemo patients. As if this makes watching your hair fall out any easier. Sometimes all that grows back is fuzz, and it's always darker.

How do you tell Bunny that his fur will grow back?

"And he's been biting the staff," Estelle says. "He hates it there."

"I don't blame him." I've wanted to bite the staff, doctors and nurses with attitude. *They'll* never get cancer. *They* take care of themselves and think positively. I have no doubt that the hospital environment fosters illness. All you want to do is hide. You don't want to be seen with your wounds. You don't want to be pitied. You stay in your bed and stare at the colourless food in trays and marvel that they can possibly imagine you can eat it.

"They think he's a vicious cat, but he's not. He gave me three cuddles this morning."

"That's a good sign."

One of the women in my ward kept getting phone calls from the people in her "church." Over and over again she would relate the horrific complications of her double mastectomy, then say, "But God is merciful." I dreaded her phone ringing. I didn't bother with one. Who would call? Sybil, to tell me to eat liver. My sister Rachel to tell me my quality of life would improve if I sold Amway products. Ross, the dysfunctional man I'd been seeing before cancer, showed up with flowers. He stood by my bed looking like a man in disguise afraid of being recognized. "Relax," I told him. "I'm not going to show it to you."

"It's not that."

"Then what is it?"

"You being sick."

"That's my problem. You don't have a problem. You're free as a bird. Have you been line dancing lately?"

What I didn't know when we first started "dating" was that Ross secretly wanted to be a cowboy, had a collection of boots and hats and subscribed to western magazines all about ridin' and campin'. He wanted me to join him on an "adventure tour cattle drive"—a package deal offering accommodation "under the stars" and grits out of a chuckwagon and tea out of tin cups. In way of compromise I agreed to go line dancing. Country-western music wailed as we took anal little steps, do-si-doing and spinning round.

"I haven't much felt like dancing," he admitted, handing me some butterscotch candies. He knew I loved butterscotch.

"Thank you," I said.

"You're welcome. If there's anything else I can get you . . ."

"I'll call. Thanks a bunch, Ross." I saw no reason why he should have to hang around. He had his own concerns. His

A-plus daughter had fallen in love with an Italian who sculpted lawn ornaments. She no longer wanted to pursue nuclear physics. She wanted to have the Italian's baby.

After Ross left, the double mastectomy patient's phone rang again. "The blows only make you stronger," she told it. "God is merciful." I tried putting my pillow over my head but it didn't help. I thought of injured animals seeking solitude to die. How right this was and how wrong it was for humans to make such a big deal of the thing; drag relations in to look at your soon-to-be corpse. I turned on my TV, watched a sitcom about a bachelor who wanted to get laid but was worried about his body odour, then I watched a sitcom about two bachelors who wanted to get laid but by the same girl. It occurred to me that Sam might be watching this and that it was affecting his thinking, which would explain why he continued to yearn for Jackie-the-slut. Television was telling him that he must get laid. A movie came on about a bachelor who wanted to marry a good girl but desired a bad one. He kept breaking the good girl's heart by running around with the bad one. The good girl kept forgiving him because he kept insisting that he did want to marry her. But the bad girl had huge tits and lots of makeup and sang in nightclubs. What is this telling my son? I kept thinking. Follow your prick no matter what? Girls with big boobs and hair are more desirable than girls with small boobs and hair? What if you don't desire either? Does that mean there's something wrong with you? Do you screw Jackie-the-slut because you fear that if you don't, you won't be a real man? Why can't you just sit in your room and figure out who you are? Why do you have to do what everybody else does? Or what popular media is telling you everybody else does? How many people are sitting in their rooms trying to figure out who they are in the face of screens telling them who they should be?

The vendor signs away her house as though she is signing away her life. There must be circumstances compelling her to sell that I don't know about. Afterwards, beside his boat of an American car, the Caribbean-cruise-anticipating agent tells me that the vendor has Lou Gehrig's disease. "You know how that one goes," he whispers, "you end up a veggie, except your head's clear as a bell. There's nothing they can do, no drugs, nothing. They've given her two years. Terrible shame."

"Where's she going to live?" I inquire.

"One of her kids is taking her in. You know how it is, she won't be able to look after herself much longer." His beeper sounds. "Gotta run. If you can drop the purchasing agreement off at my office, that would be super. Give me a shout if you want to do an inspection."

What a repugnant little man, selling dying people's homes below market value so he can drink piña coladas and dance the mambo. He'll probably live to be a hundred.

Mr. and Mrs. Perfect dance a little jig when I deliver the news that the vendor has accepted their shitty offer. They ask me for business cards. They plan to tell their friends what a terrific agent I am. Their apartment is chrome and leather. Apparently it was his apartment before it became their apartment. She's wearing a sweater dress and a bulge indicates that she's already pregnant. The dream has begun. I wonder if she has felt it move yet. I remember watching my belly jiggle, placing my hand over a bump and wondering if it was a foot or an elbow. Sometimes his movements would concern me because they seemed so aggressive. Other times, when he rolled around inside me, I just felt an overwhelming affection for him. Who are we falling in love with when we fall in love with our babies in utero? A reflection of ourselves? Our vulnerabilities? Is that why we feel protective of them? Because we're anticipating the lives they will lead, the hurts they will suffer? Do we see them as ourselves before the abuses of time have toughened our skins and stiffened our joints?

One of the experts (resembling a Nazi interrogator) wanted to know every detail about the birth. I remember little except that I'd been dilated ten centimetres forever before the attending physician decided to finish his coffee break and deliver the baby. Coming out of the birth canal, Sam presented his hand first and got stuck. The doctor used forceps. When he finally made it out, Sam may have been slow to breathe, although nothing was documented by the latte-drinking physician. Nevertheless, the Nazi expert decided that it had not been a "normal delivery." He believed there was a loss of oxygen (possibly due to excessive anaesthesia) and prolonged reduction of blood sugar which endangered the "limbic sytem" and caused dysfunction. He cited Sam's bedwetting as evidence of such brain damage. He claimed that the damage had been diffuse, a condition caused by "antenatal and postnatal asphyxia," which is why it didn't show up on the encephalogram. The damage wasn't confined to a specific area. In court he rambled on about "control centres," located in the cortex where judgment and rational thinking are located. Sam's, according to the Nazi, had ceased to function. His violent action had been directed by impulse, without judgment or consideration or concern. Sam had no real conception of what had taken place. He'd been mindless at the time of the murder, at the mercy of his dysfunctional control centres.

Why did Sam present his hand first? Was he testing the waters, not sure he wanted to come out?

The lawyer of the woman who shot her fetus with a pellet gun is trying to get her case dismissed because the baby "wasn't human." According to the Criminal Code, a baby isn't human until it is born. However, had the woman succeeded in killing her baby, her action would've been considered homicidal. But because the newborn remains in stable condition—although brain-dead—the mother may get off so that she can get pregnant again and shoot another baby.

Forming intent continues to be the football player's problem, mine too. Sam didn't know these people. Maybe, when he was little, he batted a ball into their yard and they wouldn't give it back. Maybe he was angry with them for being alive while his grandparents were dead. One of the questions asked of Baldy's experts was, could a person formulate a plan while awake, then carry it out in sleep? The experts said absolutely not. What goes on in the mind during sleep is independent of waking mentation in terms of its objectives. There is no evidence that volition occurs during a sleepwalking episode. So again we're brought back to Sam's incapacity to intend or appreciate what he was doing.

I find Sybil sitting on the floor in the kitchen. "Did you fall?" I ask.

"Maybe."

"What do you mean 'maybe'?"

"I can't remember."

I help her onto a chair. "How long have you been down?"

"Don't know. A few minutes." She used to be able to get up. Now she just waits. I see the vodka bottle on the table, the "shatterproof" glass on the floor.

"Are you hurt?"

"No. Ross phoned for you. He sounded concerned."

I pour myself a small vodka which will probably have no soothing effect whatsoever.

"Are you going to call him?" Sybil asks.

"Probably not." I look around for Sam's Nikes, a signal that he's home. I spot them at the end of the hall, well worn, trustworthy. The shoes of a killer.

Sybil bends down to retrieve her glass, pulls the vodka bottle towards her. "Why not?"

"What?"

"Why won't you call Ross?"

"Because he's phoning because he feels guilty for not wanting to screw somebody with only one tit."

"I think he's a nice man."

"So, *you* phone him. Maybe you can be drinking buddies. He favours tequila."

She lights a cigarette, hobbles over to the fan above the stove and switches it on. "I don't think this is helping you."

"What?"

"Shutting people out."

"Don't start with me."

She exhales smoke into the fan. "You shut people out and dwell on your misfortune. It's not healthy."

Sybil believes that people don't live as long as they used to because they don't eat enough meat.

I drain my shatterproof glass and slap it on the table cowboy-style. "I'm going to bed."

"I told him you're busy, that he should keep calling."

"I don't want to talk to him."

"You have to talk to somebody."

"Why? Why do I have to talk to somebody? Is there some manual on cancer that says I'm supposed to talk to somebody? What else am I supposed to do? Stand on my head for ten minutes every morning?"

"Gerty did that and lived to be a hundred and three."

"I'm going to bed. Do you want help?"

"No."

"You sure?"

"Yes."

"You should get that frigging pacemaker installed. One day you're going to fall and I won't be there to pick you up."

When Jerry left, I bought new sheets, took the old ones outside and burned them, leaving a big black patch on my lawn. I felt that I'd torched Jerry. Eventually the grass grew back greener. But I went a little berserk on the replacement sheets: lots of colours and "designer" patterns. Tonight I'd prefer cream sheets. I'd like to be swaddled in cream. Instead, I languish in a jungle of green and purple.

Ross, what am I supposed to do about him? We went to Key West last year. It was his idea. I feared being swarmed by tourists and American consumer goods. During the entire drive from Miami, he played country-western music. He didn't take me seriously when I explained that this music made me want to scream and ram my head into the dash. He argued that country-western music was pure and honest, depicting primal emotions that we tend to suppress. I think he truly believed he was providing me with country-western therapy. Anyway, from that point on I knew we were just humouring each other by "dating"; using each other to fill that empty seat beside us. Which was fine, then. Now I don't have the patience.

My mother keeps butting into my mind in the same manner she used to butt into my bedroom. "What are you doing?"

"Nothing."

"You must be doing something."

"I'm not. Can you please knock?"

She'd sit on the bed and start playing with my hair. "Do you want me to set it for you?"

This from the woman who normally didn't notice me. But she had a thing about hair, mostly her own. She'd set it in big curlers, little curlers. She'd tease it, straighten it. Once she got a hairbrush caught in her beehive and became hysterical. My father and I tried to remove it but it was in a serious tangle. I'd never seen my mother cry before. Her face became puffy and blotched, eyeliner streaked her cheeks. My father drove her to a hairdresser. Not her usual hairdresser because she wasn't available. A stranger had to deal with my hysterical mother. On returning, my father rushed into the house to warn me that I must tell my mother that she looked beautiful; that it didn't look as though any hair had been cut off. I didn't have to lie, she did look good.

But my compliments only brought on more tears and she dashed up to the bedroom.

Over the years she spent more and more time in that bedroom. What was she hiding from? The stuff I fear? That Sam fears? Whatever that is?

I disentangle myself from the jungle, creep down the hall and stand outside his firmly closed door. I press my ear against it, trying to hear him breathe. When he was an infant I stood over his crib to verify that he was breathing. Sometimes it would seem that he wasn't. I'd place my hand gently over his ribs until I felt them move. After ascertaining that he was alive I would feel so incredibly lucky. So incredibly lucky.

I can hear nothing, and understand that it is absurd to expect to hear breathing through a door. I consider creaking it open and looking in. But what if he wakes "in an extreme fit of rage"? What if he doesn't wake but gets up and bludgeons me to death? What if he wakes in a hysterical dissociative state and strangles me just because I happen to be there?

I kiss the door, since I can't kiss him, then go back to my jungle. The left eye starts dribbling again. And the fucking dog barks.

Eight

"If," Baldy inquires of an expert as round as the Michelin Tire man, "when he bludgeoned Mr. and Mrs. Grundy, the cortex was not functioning, what was going on in his head?"

"A drive to act."

"Did he know the shovel was in his hand?"

"Possibly."

Baldy wipes snot from his moustache. "Did he know he was killing these people with the shovel?"

"There was no reason functioning."

"Did he know that killing people was against the law?"

"No."

"Do you mean that he didn't *intend* to kill or he didn't have the capacity to *form the intention* to kill?"

"I don't believe he had the capacity to form that intent."

And so the dance around "appreciation of the act" continues.

The crown has had another go at portraying the murders as sadistic, psychopathic killings. But sadism, the experts have explained, involves terrorizing victims before killing them. Sam didn't do any torturing. He just clubbed them.

"Did he know right from wrong when he was killing them?" Baldy persists.

"No." The Michelin Tire man pulls out a hanky and mops his brow.

"When did he regain cortical function?"

"Probably about an hour after the attack."

Which indicates temporary insanity, not non-insane automatism.

The Sonny Bono look-alike foreman must have a cold because he keeps sneezing and blowing his nose. The victims' only daughter glares at him, annoyed by the disturbance, then reverts back to staring at Sam. If eyes could burn, he would be toast.

I dreamed last night that I was trapped in a wooden shed with rats. Through a small hole I could see blue sky. I tore at the hole with my hands, bloodying my fingers, getting splinters under my nails. Okay so if the shed's my life, are the rats the cancer? Or is the shed the cancer and the rats my negative thoughts?

Jerry didn't show up today because Natasha's having gum surgery. He's sitting in a periodontist's waiting room while his son sits in court, listening to strangers postulate on his mental health. His son, the boy who bounced in the Jolly Jumper, remains motionless. This morning, he actually spoke to me, asked me if I thought it was going to rain. Accustomed to being ignored, I couldn't think, was suddenly tongue-tied. Losing patience, he grabbed an umbrella and was gone.

The murderer doesn't want to get his hair wet.

As I left the house, the five-year-old next door came charging at me on his tricycle. "You know what?" he asked me.

"What?"

"I just saw a vampire." He pronounced "saw" as *thaw.*

"In daylight?" I asked. "That's unusual."

It made me think of Sam on his trike questioning the three blind mice song. He couldn't understand how they could chase after the farmer's wife if they were blind. And he couldn't understand why she cut off their tails instead of their heads.

"Maybe she missed," I suggested.

A gawker standing outside the courtroom was wearing a T-shirt with the words "Quit looking at my ass!" printed on it. So of course I immediately looked at her butt to see what all the fuss was about. It seemed very ordinary to me. Maybe she wears the T-shirt to *make* people look at her ass. Because as soon as we tell someone not to do something, they want to do it. Was that how it was with Sam and the old people? Did they beg him not to harm them which only made him more determined to do so?

One of the "dissociative state" experts insisted that the dissociative state itself is an occurrence, not a mental illness or "disease of the mind." He explained that rarely does a severe dissociative state not caused by some underlying pathology recur. He suggested that there is only a slight possibility that Sam would experience a recurrence of this disorder of consciousness.

Slight possibility doesn't sound good to me.

Another one said that the sleepwalking was an abnormality of brain function and should therefore be regarded as a pathological condition which could recur if Sam were to experience all the same circumstances leading to the incident. He would have to relive that night shift at the hospital and experience the same stress levels, lack of sleep and emotional disturbances. I don't find this difficult to imagine. The boy is upset by the idea of homosexuals inserting Coke bottles up their rectums. He experiences anxiety if his whites aren't white, and he has never slept easily. But the sleepwalking experts insist that all he needs is "good sleep hygiene" to prevent a recurrence, i.e., going to bed at a regular hour, getting sufficient sleep and exercise, avoiding extreme weight gain, alcohol and medications that might lead to an attack.

This's all easier said than done. It's obvious that the sleep experts have never experienced insomnia or night terrors. I imagine them in their jammies, slipping between the sheets and blacking out. Tossing and turning is beyond their realm of experience. It would not be good sleep hygiene.

They have been unanimous in saying that sleepwalkers are very rarely violent. How fortunate that they don't live with one.

I meet the house inspector and Mr. Perfect outside the semi and hope that the vendor will be out. She isn't. Obviously weak, she languishes on a couch watching a talk show. "Don't mind me," she tells us. She pays no attention to either the buyer or the inspector. I attempt small talk with her while the two men prowl around the basement, but she isn't interested. She thinks I'm healthy. She thinks she will be long buried while I flit around offering dying people shitty money for their houses. I'd like to tell her otherwise but then she would deduce that the cruise-anticipating agent has told me about her illness. I hear grumbling downstairs and suspect that the Hardy Boys have discovered the leak. On the talk show they're discussing Ten Secrets for Great Sex. How can the vendor can stand to watch this, knowing that her nerves are dying, her muscles atrophying. Maybe she isn't absorbing what she's seeing. She's somewhere else entirely. Possibly with her dead husband, staking the peonies, cautioning her children to walk not run. Will they resent looking after her as she wastes away? Will her grandchildren fear her as they begin to understand that she's dying? Will she resent being wheeled out of her room because, even near death, her children will expect her to be "Mom," to care about their head colds and blisters, to offer Kleenexes and consoling words? She's probably tired of it. She probably wants to be left in peace with her diseased body, to relax into death, since she can't fight it. As her limbs distort and harden, as she is robbed of speech and breath, her "family" will seem even more remote. Perhaps it's easier to be offered no treatments; to be told simply that you will die, that you should get your affairs in order.

The Hardy Boys exit through the sliding doors, which still stick, and sniff around the outside the house.

"I don't need you to stand around and chat," the vendor tells me. "Go about your business."

"Of course, I'm sorry. I didn't realize I was disturbing you."

She turns up the volume on the talk show. Body-pierced women and men are debating the pros and cons of double-headed dildos and nipple clips. A tiny woman in revealing latex gear displays bondage beds, cages and full- or half-restraining racks. With quick, efficient movements, she demonstrates uses of a whip and a paddle.

After the inspection, Mr. Perfect wants to reduce his offer due to the problems with the house. I tell him to forget it, he's getting it dirt cheap *because* there are problems. He gets huffy but I am resolute. I am not causing this woman more suffering.

Early for my rendezvous with Ross, I order decaf because caffeine's supposed to be bad for me, although one alternative cancer treatment is caffeine enemas. Figure that one out—you can't put it in your mouth but, by all means, shove it up your backside.

I thumb through magazines provided by the café. "The Loneliness of a Sex Goddess" is a big story in one of them. It seems Raquel Welch hasn't had a man in years. Isn't she old by now and done with being a sex godess? She probably prefers to be left alone, practising yoga and drinking Taheebo tea. The magazine displays a candid photo of her in a trench coat on a bad hair day. She looks her age. How tragic.

Next I get to see inside Goldie Hawn's house. It's hideous, as is Goldie who refuses to stop wearing tight jeans and yellow hair. I study her face, guessing where the surgeon has been busy; probably around the jowls, the eyes, certainly the lips.

Beside me, two hairdressers complain about neck pains resulting from bending over people's heads, and shrinking dress sizes. They're sharing a cookie between them, breaking it into itsy-bitsy pieces. "Size six is getting smaller," one of them insists, "because there's no way I'm an eight."

I can't even remember being an eight. I turn a page in the magazine and see Liz Taylor looking fat and haggard. Her friends are worried about her, the article says, because she's killing herself campaigning for AIDS research. She has a cough now. A cough? Wow, that sounds serious. Maybe she swallowed a diamond.

"What's she doing with that idiot?" the size-six hairdresser abruptly asks.

"He *is* odd."

"He's got no pores on his face. I was up close and saw."

The other hairdresser nods while nibbling a fragment of cookie. "He does have beautiful skin."

"And some very feminine qualities."

"Clive says he's gay."

"He went out with a Chinese girl, didn't he? They're, like, size zero."

Ross approaches, looking miffed, and I worry that he's mad at me but it turns out he's annoyed with his daughter and the lawn-ornament boyfriend. "I even commissioned a doe and a fawn from the guy," he tells me. "I'm trying to be diplomatic."

"Are they nice?"

"Who?"

"The doe and fawn?"

"Of course not. I put them in the garage."

I express concern for his daughter, as he expresses concern for my son. But really we don't care about each other's offspring or each other. I don't understand why he insisted on this meeting. He feels guilty because he has two breasts while I have only one. This is understandable. The healthy always feel uncomfortable around the sick.

"Remember Mickey Matus?" he asks me.

"No."

"He's that South African guy who got a mole on his chest that turned out to be cancerous. He had a mastectomy and everything was going great. Well, guess what?"

"He's divorcing his wife and marrying a thirteen-year-old?"

Ross shakes his head. "He did that already." He leans over the table and says quietly, "The poor fucker has prostate cancer."

"Oh dear."

"I ran into him the other day. He'd just seen another specialist and wanted to get drunk. So we got drunk. He's an amazing guy."

"Because?"

"He's really researching this thing. He's talking to everybody before he lets anybody touch him. He's checking data, statistics. There's a ton of research being done."

"Prostate cancer, detected early, is usually curable."

"Yeah, if you don't mind them gelding you."

"Somehow I'd be willing to accept impotence in return for life."

"The thing is they don't have to do surgery now. They've got these radioactive seeds they can insert that nuke the tumour.

They're like smart bombs. They don't blast the whole area, meaning you don't get all the crummy side effects of regular radiation." He bites his low-fat muffin. "The guy has an amazing attitude. He's really fighting this thing."

"Ross, can I just point out that the reason 'tons' of research is being done on prostate cancer is because it involves men's pee-pees. Prostate cancer is not a leading killer of men. Breast cancer is *the* leading killer of women between thirty-five and fifty-five."

"There's research being done on breast cancer."

"Not tons. Research requires funding. Funding comes from organizations run by men. Breast cancer, unlike prostate cancer, has this nasty habit of sending out sentinel nodes, but nobody's developing techniques for tracing them. Testicular cancer, on the other hand, which is also prone to metastasize, being a guy thing, is being effectively treated by tracing nodes. Survival rates have improved dramatically. And by the way, those 'smart bombs' you're referring to still cause scatter radiation."

I can see I'm losing him, too much med talk. He shakes his head indicating that he's not going to argue with the negative ballbusting feminist. I'm trying to remember why I went out with him. Oh, right: his body. After his divorce he started working out and eating no carbs or dairy. His wife was a Swede and smeared cream sauces all over everything. Once free of her, he became a canola-oil man. I wonder if I should advise him that canola's genetically engineered, that mice gorging on the stuff are experiencing thickening of their stomach walls and other assorted internal mutations.

The size-six hairdresser fluffs her hair. "Mine takes *forever* to dry," she complains. "Not like yours."

Ross sips his decaf. "I only brought this up because I thought it might give you some hope."

"I appreciate that. The problem is, I don't have a penis so Mickey's news doesn't do much for me."

"The point is, new treatments are in the offing."

"Not for breast cancer, pal. Slash, poison and burn continues to rule the day."

"Fine. Forget I mentioned it."

I wonder if this is what Sybil had in mind when she said I had to "talk to somebody." If she were here, would she accuse me of "shutting Ross out"? Which is what I'm doing, because I don't want him in. When you think you're healthy it's easy to kid yourself that you're having a good time. It's easy to settle for less, fake orgasms and laugh at bad jokes. It's even possible to listen to country-western music, because it doesn't seem to cost anything. Tomorrow is another day, anything's possible.

"He's got the most gorgeous natural highlights," the size-six proclaims. "I hate him. It's always the guys that get the natural, have you noticed that?"

"Will you let me buy you dinner?" Ross asks.

"Why would you want to buy me dinner?"

"Because I'm glad to see you again. To see you looking so well."

This is another thing I've noticed about the healthy, they say you look well when you look sick.

"Put yoghourt and honey on your face," size-six advises. "It hydrates the skin."

I get up from the table, bumping it, of course, spilling some of Ross's coffee. "Sorry. Listen, I'm really tired. I'm going to pee, then I have to run."

He nods, looking relieved. Maybe I should have dinner with him, make him sit through it. Maybe he would learn something. What I don't know—not to call me anymore?

In the ladies' room, two sixty-something warhorses freshen their lipstick while discussing plastic surgery. "I have friends who've done it," the meatier one says. "It looks good but for how long?"

While widdling I notice that I'm sweating on my left side. Ross is making me tense. So much for a stress-free environment.

"I can't say I haven't thought about it," the stringier warhorse admits. "But I always think that if you need to do that kind of thing to yourself, there must be something lacking."

"In your life."

"Precisely."

Beside them at the sink, washing my hands, I observe their sags and bags and wonder how they'd look with a tuck here and there. And if their breasts are real. And if they seriously believe there is nothing lacking in their lives.

A fly buzzes around my kitchen. I detest flies—their sticky little feet, their twitchy little wings—and don't understand their function indoors. Outdoors they can at least feed birds. I search the broom closet for a fly swatter, finally unearth it behind buckets and mops, by which time the fly has flown into another room. I resume making my tuna sandwich, glad to be alone in the house, hoping that there will be something engrossing on TV. But the fly returns, lands on my sandwich, then flits about some more, bumping into walls, light fixtures. What pleasure can it derive from this erratic flying pattern? Why doesn't it find an open window and return to freedom? I grab the swatter and stand poised, waiting for it to land, but it doesn't. Watching it is making me dizzy. I sit down and look at my sandwich. Food has become uninteresting to me, particularly if it's been a doormat for flies. At the supermarket a young man with Down syndrome, carrying an armful of meat, stood ahead of me at the checkout, hugging his meat, with a blissful smile on his face. He was anticipating barbecues and roasts, fried chops and Shake 'N Bake. I miss hunger, the joy of satiating hunger.

I throw out the tuna sandwich. The fly is driving me nuts. I pick up the swatter again and try to be patient while waiting for it to land. But it continues to zoom in all directions. Panicking, I begin swiping at it in mid-air. It's as though all my woes are contained in this fly; if I can just kill it, all will be well. But my right arm's limited range of motion makes it impossible to swat above my shoulders. The fly seems to know this and adjusts its flight pattern to just below the ceiling. I stand on a chair close to the overhead light., breathing heavily, and knowing I shouldn't be doing this. It's absurd to be distressed by a fly. Finally, it lands, possibly within my range. I stand very still, holding my breath, and swing at it underhand. My arm betrays me, stopping short of the fly. I feel so helpless, so stupid, so completely out of control. Tears gush out of my left eye. The front door opens and abruptly Sam is at my feet.

"What are you doing?" he asks.

"I'm trying to swat a fly." I quickly wipe my cheek.

He looks around. "I don't see a fly."

"It was here. It's gone again."

"Are you going to stay on the chair?"

"No." I start to climb down and, to my amazement, he offers me his hand. The grip is strong, a man's grip. I hear the fly again. "It's back."

He takes the swatter from me, his eyes following the movement of the fly. He wastes no effort swatting. Admiring his slender figure, I marvel that such a physique could have originated in my body. The fly lands on the windowsill for what I know will only be a second. But Sam is there in an instant and, in one swift movement, kills the fly. I think of the shovel, the swing of the shovel, its impact on fragile bones. I can't believe those beautiful arms could do that.

The fly remains stuck to the swatter. Sam shakes it into the trash can, then looks at me. "You okay?"

The look of concern in his eyes completely disarms me. "Yes. Thank you."

"You should get some rest."

"Yeah." I want more of this gentleness between us, but I'm afraid to prolong it because I might say something that will provoke a sharp remark from him. At this moment, a sharp remark from him would knock me senseless. "There's pasta salad in the fridge," I tell him, "and fresh bread."

"Cool."

I climb the stairs feeling like the little girl who knows she has tried her parents' patience, that it's past her bedtime and that she has no choice but to surrender to the night.

Getting ready for bed, I avoid all mirrors. The TV drones downstairs. I turn on my radio and hear about a murderer in California who abducted, raped and killed a thirteen-year-old. His defence has been his upbringing; his mother neglected him, held his hands over gas burners, under hot taps. His father wasn't even around. How can someone who has been so abused not be expected to abuse? is the defence's question. Ninety-five percent of violent criminals in prison come from similarly dysfunctional backgrounds. Society is to blame for not looking after its children. Prison terms only make violent criminals more violent. I believe all this. I don't know how a severely abused child can recover.

But the American jury wants him dead. I can understand this. The girl's parents want to see him suffer as the only daughter wants to see my only son suffer.

Try to think of something else: what the vendor is up to, if she's asleep or watching late-night television-infomercials for guaranteed weight-loss products. I tell myself I'm lucky not to be the vendor. I think of Ross fretting over his daughter. Children are dying of leukemia daily and he's kvetching because his daughter has fallen in love. I think of the news story about the man who tormented his pit bulls so much they tore his throat out. And the woman who wanted to teach her red setter a lesson because he wouldn't stay in her yard so she tied him to her car and dragged him along a road until he was bloodied and broken. The man who shook his baby so hard he broke her neck. The woman who fed her sixteen-month-old son vodka and acted surprised when he crawled off a sixth floor balcony. The two men who tossed a twelve-kilogram rock off a highway overpass onto a passing car causing the eighteen-year-old driver to become blind and bedridden. The pregnant glue sniffer who refuses to stop sniffing glue even though she's already brain-damaged two children in utero through glue sniffing. The Children's Aid Society has taken the children away from her. Now they want to stop her from brain-damaging another by forcing her into a rehab centre for the duration of the pregnancy. Civil rights activists are outraged.

How did we get this stupid? Or were we always this stupid?

This is the second night I've noticed a car parked outside with a woman in it. I've pulled out the binoculars and deduced that it's the murdered old people's only daughter stalking Sam. I wonder if he realizes this. And if she's got a plan B, should he be acquitted, if she's stashed a gun in her glove compartment.

Probably not. Women don't usually do that sort of thing, not unless they've been beaten for twenty years. I suspect she watches our house because she doesn't know what else to do. Immobilized by grief, all she can do is stare. And hate.

I force my eyes closed, cautioning myself about the importance of good sleep hygiene. I close my eyes in an attempt to close out thought.

But the dog's barking again.

Nine

I was woken this morning by the rending of a chainsaw. So unusual was this for an urban neighbourhood that I immediately got up to look out my window. There was a man crawling on my tree. Actually it wasn't my tree, but the neighbour's, but it has sheltered me, shaded me, whispered leafy music to me for ten years. An oak so strong, so generous in its reach and tolerance of people digging around its feet and hanging swings from its branches that I had come to think of it as a kind of mother figure. The kind of mother I would like to have been or had—calm, patient, always there.

She stood two storeys high, must've lived two hundred years. Now she's dead. Shredded. Sawdust remains, and a few broken limbs whose leaves don't yet understand that their mother is dead. They dangle perkily from their stems awaiting further nourishment. By this afternoon, they will be starving. Tomorrow they will be shrivelled and lifeless.

As the saw whirred, I phoned the city, only to be put on hold for twenty minutes. Finally, a civil servant picked up. "A tree is being cut down in my neighbour's yard," I told him.

"Yeah."

"As we speak. It's coming down. Isn't there a bylaw about trees? You can't just cut down trees."

"What's the address?"

I told him, dreaming of tree police lassoing the savage with the spinning blade.

After several long, saw-filled moments the civil servant said, "They've got a permit."

"How can they have a permit?"

"I guess they don't want the tree in their yard. Some people don't like shade."

"You can't cut down a tree just because you don't like shade. There's supposed to be a bylaw." By this time, huge limbs were crashing to the ground. It felt as though they were my arms being severed.

"They have a permit," the genius repeated.

"What does that mean?"

"It means an inspector okayed the demolition of the tree."

"Why? How could he do that?"

"It was considered hazardous."

"Hazardous? Why?"

"You'd have to talk to the inspector."

"Is he there?"

"You can leave a message."

I realized it was useless. It was over for the tree. Already huge patches of sky existed where her splendour had been. An ugly mesh fence was exposed, and the back of two vinyl-sided houses.

Minutes later, in the shower, I found a lump in my remaining breast. I jerked my hand away as though it had been burned. But my fingers found the lump again, prodded it, while water streamed over me. I couldn't stop fondling it, couldn't believe it was there, still can't believe it's there.

As I left, my tree was being truncated with no sign of disease in her dripping wounds. I ducked into my car quickly, to escape the sound of the shredder. Did humans *ever* have humility in the face of nature? Or were we always this arrogant?

They're probably planning to put in a pool. I must advise them that chlorine is being linked to bladder cancer. So far only in our drinking water, but I suspect that immersing yourself in it isn't such a great idea. Maybe I won't tell them, let them gulp the stuff, let it seep into their pores.

The football player is speaking to me as though I am scum. He has tiny pupils and shiny skin. I'm missing my tree and dreading going home where she will no longer be. Where I will be exposed to ultraviolet rays and people who live in vinyl houses. fixated on my lump, I tell myself it isn't a lump, just a swelling, it'll go away. The gawkers murmur. The jury stares. I must look strange. Without taking my eyes from Blondie's tiny pupils, I try to remember what I'm wearing. It's all right, isn't it? Sedate. Cream and brown. Maybe I forgot to install my breast, would like to check for it, can't, then they'd think I'm really weird. I mustn't look weird. I try to compose my face, sit straight. My lovely tree's gone, my friend. The football player won't stop yammering at me. I can't understand what he's talking about. Speak English, I want to say. He has rubbery lips and yaks and yaks, then stops, and I'm supposed to fill in the blanks. But I can't because I don't know what he's talking about. And I'm terrified I'll say something that will incriminate my son. Sonny Bono coughs, the car salesman adjusts his balls, the cheerleaders recross their legs, the old lady pops a mint. The gawkers, wanting action, fidget and snort while waiting for me to remember my lines. Sweat drips down my left side and I'm afraid my left eye is leaking.

The football player is asking me about my parents. He's asking like he knows something. I try to make it sound as though my parents were perfectly normal, even though they were eaten by a bear. Natasha whispers in Jerry's ear. He nods, continuing to stare at me with loathing. When did he start to despise me? How could I not know he despised me? "Never chase a bus or a man," my father used to tell me. I chased Jerry. He seemed so strong, so sure, so everything I wasn't. Why are we drawn to those who make us weak?

The judge asks me if I'm all right. I nod. The football player leans in closer. His cologne drifts up my nasal passages, fogging my brain. It's so hot in here, why is it so hot in here? Where's Sam? I can't see him, the football player's in the way. I try to look around his big shoulders to see my son. He's there, looking anxious. Am I his last hope? Did he think Mummy could rescue him from this nightmare? I'm failing him again. My baby, who was programmed to seek food and comfort from me. I remember the smell of him, the touch of him as he suckled a breast that is no longer there. My body remembers the feel of his body, so small, so perfect. They want to take him from me. "Sam!" I say, but he doesn't answer. "Sam!" I repeat. I want him to reach out to me, as he reached up from his crib when he wanted to be held. But he doesn't. He looks away. He is ashamed of me. I hate myself. I want to bang my head against the wood around me. I'm trapped in wood, like in the shed dream, surrounded by rats.

I regain consciousness, smelling leather. The couch beneath me feels hard. A woman in uniform frowns down at me. Jerry stands by the door. "That was quite a performance," he tells me. "What were you trying to prove?" I close my eyes to make him disappear. Last week I watched a TV documentary, "Anger in the Family." There seems to be a lot of it. According to the program, we all run around hiding it by presenting "pseudo-selves." I wonder which pseudo-self to present to Jerry. Air whistles through his flared nostrils—a dragon who can't blow fire.

"You wanted me to look distraught," I remind him.

"You didn't look distraught, you looked insane."

"Maybe I am."

The uniformed woman leans over me. "Will you be alright now?"

"Yeah." I want her to go away.

"We'll be fine," Jerry tells her. "Thank you." She leaves. He sits on the couch just beyond my feet. I consider shoving him off it.

"Is it still going on?" I ask.

"The judge is calling it a day."

"He looks so bored."

"I think he's dreaming of retirement." A very loud wall clock ticks above Jerry's head. Grey leafy wallpaper surrounds us.

"I think Sam is being stalked," I say.

"What?"

"The Grundys' daughter. She parks outside our house and watches."

"Call the police."

"Yeah, right, like they'll do anything. Maybe if she tries breaking and entering, they'll show up."

"Does Sam know?"

"If he does, he hasn't mentioned it."

Jerry nods, slumps forward, looking his age. His expensive suit can do nothing for him now. It occurs to me that Jerry and I never presented each other with pseudo-selves. Which may be why we fought. Strangely, I feel a kind of sympatico with him. We're both ancient warriors, survivors of losing battles.

I consider telling him about my new lump because I need to tell somebody. But then he'll feel sorry for me. And be even more repulsed. Nobody wants to get close to cancer. It's as though it's contagious.

"Well," he offers, "maybe the jury will think you're just high-strung, emotional, whatever."

"You didn't want stoic."

"You're right, I didn't want stoic."

We sit, listening to the dock. There's nothing to say.

Bunny's spinal tap revealed nothing. I try to convince Estelle that this is good news.

"Yeah, but now he wants to cut open his throat."

"Why?"

"He says that thyroids control calcium in the blood. So he thinks the high levels might be caused by one of the thyroids."

It seems to me the surgeon could've eliminated this possibility before cutting into Bunny's belly, and before terrorizing Estelle with threats of brain tumours. "I guess they'll have to shave his neck," she says miserably.

I picture the cat with shorn belly, back and now neck and wonder what Bunny makes of all this. He must think he's being tortured, that the humans have gone mad, that there is no hope in sight. I know this feeling.

I leave Estelle to greet a couple of new clients, both male, waiting to be shown houses. Recently, a real estate agent was raped and knifed by a couple of male clients while she was showing them a house. I approach my buyers, trying to assess if *they* are capable of such a crime. They stand to greet me, offering hands. One is Asian, the other looks like an aging Elvis impersonator. When he smiles, he reveals only two teeth. Neither man looks capable of causing bodily harm although, in the press photos, the men who raped the real estate agent looked harmless. Just as my son looks harmless.

They've asked to see houses that need work but can be converted into two units. I show them some "handyman specials." The Elvis impersonator continually cracks jokes I can't understand because, without teeth, he has difficulty enunciating. That I don't get the jokes doesn't seem to bother him because he chuckles anyway. The Asian examines every nook and cranny of each house. It's going to be a long night, I realize, resisting an urge to reach under my bra and feel my lump. It's growing in my mind. Soon I will be all lump. One big malignant mass. I'll call Cheeseburger tomorrow. I will.

I find Sybil on the kitchen floor, unconscious, with a bleeding head. She has a pulse, is still breathing. I call 911 and, to my amazement, an ambulance arrives in minutes. Paramedics make quick work of lifting her onto the stretcher and applaud me for putting ice in a towel on her head. "What do people usually do with head wounds?" I inquire. "Get hysterical," one replies.

I tell them about her heart condition, that she was supposed to get a pacemaker, that she has been attached to a Holter monitor which documented that her heart has abnormal rhythms, frequent pauses. I'm trying to make them understand that she must be prioritized in Emergency.

Why are the wards always so horrible? Why is dull beige compulsory? What is that sickly hospital smell that clings to you for hours? They whisk her away for an electrocardiogram, a CAT scan and blood tests, leaving me to sit and gaze at a TV bolted to the wall. David Letterman is interviewing a baseball player who makes millions and says "dude" frequently. The player has a baby boy who he believes will become a great pitcher because he hurls his Dino Buddies across the room. He shows pictures of his baby wearing his father's baseball cap. The audience oohs and aahs. Letterman's pseudo-self smiles idiotically.

I don't believe Sybil will die because she's too stubborn. She'll want to recover so that she can tell me I was wrong to take her to the hospital. "What a waste of taxpayers' money," she'll tell me. But I am concerned about the blow to her head. "The CAT scan will reveal if there's any subdural bleeding," the doctor told me. "Speak English," I said. Bleeding inside the head, he explained, outside the brain. It puts pressure on the brain, can cause damage. They drill a hole in your skull to drain it. Sybil would not like this.

They're testing her for low blood sugar, diabetes, cardiac enzymes which would indicate if she's had a heart attack. They're doing a chest X-ray, a blood count, a kidney test. Unconscious, she's cooperating with them.

It's not so bad being in the hospital when you're not the one being treated. I feel almost like a regular human, except that my lump is getting sore from all my fingering. They always say that if the lump is sore, it probably isn't cancer. Which is why I think it's just fibrocystic. Maybe I should stop worrying about it, spare myself the aggravation of waiting rooms, patronizing doctors and more tests.

Two portly ladies in black leggings occupy the chairs across from me. They're eating chocolate bars and comparing each other's gawdy jewellery. "Can I try it on?" one asks the other. Rings are exchanged, bracelets. Letterman's interviewing Tom Selleck. I can't believe Tom Selleck is still around. He's publicizing an HBO movie in which he plays an older man who has a love affair with a young girl. How original. Do we really need another movie in which an aging male star simulates sex with a young female starlet?

When Sybil wakens, she's hopping mad. I'm summoned to talk sense to her. In a blue hospital gown, with wire leads attached to her chest and arms and sutures on her head, she reminds me of a monkey caged for research purposes. Against her will, she will be prodded, needled and forced to inject toxic substances.

"I can't believe you let this happen," she says to me.

"I can't believe you fell down and bumped your head."

"Six vials of blood they took from me."

"I wonder if they'll find anything but eighty proof."

"This isn't funny."

I'm so happy she's still Sybil I find myself leaping to her side and kissing her below the suture. "I'm so glad you're back, Auntie." She maintains her grimace. "You look quite fetching in blue."

"Oh stop it. You've got me where you want me."

"Finally."

"They did all these tests before, at the clinic."

"Some of them."

"What a waste of taxpayers' money." She fiddles with the leads on her arms.

"Leave them alone," I caution.

"Pull them off me—I'll take the rap. I'm not staying here."

"No one's asking you to. I think they'll be glad to get rid of you."

"I need a smoke."

"Just sit tight till they come back, please, Auntie, for me?"

She glowers but capitulates. Her skin looks grey. It's obvious to me that her heart is not pumping enough blood. It's obvious to me that she will die if she doesn't get a pacemaker.

"Remember Merna?" she asks.

"The ninety-something-year-old?"

"Her daughter died last week. So Merna died five days later. Refused food and died—didn't want to live without her daughter."

"Makes sense." Somewhere, a baby is crying jagged, desperate wails.

"Her daughter wasn't very nice to her though," Sybil adds. "Institutionalized her." She's starting to fidget, which means she's in serious need of a butt. "Her daughter got divorced and became a lesbian. Broke her mother's heart. Shut her out. I can't believe she didn't die then. She had bleeding ulcers, asthma. I think she even had a stroke, for God's sake."

"What killed the daughter?"

"Cancer."

I nod, not understanding why Sybil's telling me this. Does she think I plan to institutionalize her? Is she warning me that *she* could decide to die, that I'd better back off or else? A technician removes the electrodes.

"Can I go now?" Sybil demands.

"Please, no," he replies. He's Filipino and not very comfortable with English.

"What do you mean, 'please, no'?" Sybil responds.

"Wait for doctor, please."

"Auntie, you can't just do a bunch of tests, then boogie. We have to make sure you're alright."

"What fiddle faddle."

The Filipino disappears behind a curtain. I offer Sybil a butterscotch, hoping this will keep her mind off ciggie butts. The baby has stopped crying. Either a drug has taken effect or it's dead. "Did you see Sam this evening?" I ask.

"Around seven."

"Did he say anything?"

"He never says anything. He ate, watched TV, went to his room."

Sybil was unable to have children. In her twenties, she had severe endometriosis. The doctor's solution was to cut out her reproductive organs. She was young and didn't question him. There was a war on. There were lives to be saved.

Making myself unpopular with the nurses who think we should sit and wait for a few more hours, I track down the

Emergency doctor. He has bed-head and bad breath and sleepy dust in his eyes but otherwise he's relatively pleasant. I explain about the Holter monitor, that we already know that her heart stops beating for as long as six seconds, that the top part of her heart is not producing impulses and that she should have a pacemaker. "She should see her cardiologist as soon as possible," he keeps repeating as I lead him down the hall.

"You don't understand," I say. "You have to scare her. She won't go unless you scare her."

"Blacking out and splitting her head wasn't scary?"

"Is her head okay?"

"Her head's fine. Her heart's another matter. She should see her cardiologist as soon as possible." He rubs his eyes. I stop walking, forcing him to halt. This takes him aback, he's not used to being pushed around. I offer him a butterscotch.

"Listen," I say. "Unless you scare her, she will do nothing."

"That's her choice." He unwraps the candy and puts it in his mouth, then looks around for somewhere to toss the wrapper.

"She doesn't understand what she's choosing." I take the wrapper from him. "You have to scare her. Please."

I push back the curtain and there she is, clothed, cigarette pack in hand, ready to spring. "Oh there you are," she says to the doctor. "I thought you were having a nap."

He begins politely and I think he doesn't have a chance. But not being taken seriously by this old broad starts to irk him because he says, "You're going to drop dead."

This stops her for a second. "When?"

"I'd say you have a fifty percent chance of not making it through the year." The butterscotch is impairing his speech slightly. "Next time you fall, you might get fractures. You break a hip and that's the beginning of the end—you might never get out of the hospital. Your head's okay this time, next time you might not be so lucky."

A nurse hovers, preparing to nab him.

"She wouldn't even feel a pacemaker, right?" I ask.

"You'd forget about it. There's no risk involved. It's not like open-heart surgery." He bends down to tie his shoe, a wonderfully undoctorly gesture. He's wearing ancient desert boots. I'm starting to like this guy. He doesn't straighten fully but stops halfway, eye to eye with Sybil. "You have spontaneous degeneration resulting from aging. It's an easy problem to solve. I wish all the problems I see could be so easy." The nurse fusses. "Gotta go," he mutters.

"Thank you," I say but he's gone.

In the car, Sybil hums. "He was kind of cute, wasn't he?"

"Kind of."

"Could he put it in?"

"You need a heart surgeon to put it in."

"Could we find a cute one?" This is the closest she's come to accepting help. I'm so relieved, my left eye starts leaking again.

"We'll try to find a cute one. I'm not making any promises, Auntie. They're specialists."

"You find a cute one and I'll do it."

"That's not fair."

"Who said life is fair?"

She insists on a nightcap. I agree because I don't want to argue and because I need a drink. Moonlight, no longer blocked by my tree, streams in through the kitchen window. The smell of sawdust hangs in the air.

"We'll plant another one," she says.

"What's the point? It'll take forever to grow."

"Whoever planted that one didn't whinge because the tree would take forever to grow."

"How do you know? They might have whinged while they were planting it."

"So, whinge while you're planting it."

Tucking her in, I'm spooked by the frailness of her. "What keeps you going?"

She squints at me. "What do you mean?"

"Why are you staying alive?" I can only ask this because I'm slightly inebriated.

"I want to see what happens."

"When?"

"Whenever. I want to see how it turns out."

"You'll have to live forever then."

"It won't take that long."

Waiting for my turn at the bank machine this evening I overheard an aging hippie discussing Galileo. He said, "Guess what, guys? The earth revolves around the sun." The woman with the hippie looked very straight. I wondered how they'd met, if she planned to straighten him out. "The universe is a plasma," the aging hippie elaborated. "A living thing. It's been going for ten to twenty billion years. It makes sense that if we keep pouring crap into it, the gravitational force will dissipate and the stars will come crashing into us."

I like the image of stars crashing into us. But it would be too clean, too beautiful. Our extinction will be messy. We'll be submerged in our own garbage, fumigated by our own "progress," destroyed by our own greed. I finish my vodka. "I feel like I know how it's going to turn out."

"That's where you're wrong."

I lift my shirt and stare in the bathroom mirror to look for puckering or dimpling—signs of malignancy. I can't see any. I feel it again. It's very hard. The other lump wasn't this hard. I pull my shirt down again.

If the cancer embodied the hideousness in my makeup, why didn't I feel like a changed person when the butcher cut it out? Was it because I failed to *believe* I was free of it? Just as I'm failing to believe in the innocence of my son? I read somewhere that prayer has helped cancer patients, even if they don't do the praying themselves. Other believers can do it for you. I walk around my bedroom trying to work up a prayer—a sincere, believing prayer. But all I feel is alienated from the familiar objects because they belong to my pre-cancer self. A pseudo-self.

Stopping by the window, I try to see if the only daughter is still out there in her red car. She's quit for the day. Does she eat when she goes home? Sleep? Is there a man in her life? I've noticed no rings on her fingers. I picture her in bed, lying stiffly, plotting the death of my son.

I get into my nightclothes, hoping that the ritual of getting ready for bed will quiet my mind. Of course it doesn't. I can't sleep with this cancer inside me that will not rest until it's drained the life out of me. Would that *I* could be so industrious.

Downstairs, I make myself hot milk and honey and look at the paper. In a British Columbia burb, a cougar attacked a mother and her two children. The mother wrestled with it while the children threw stones and kicked it. The mother ordered the children to run for help. By the time they returned with a neighbour sporting a shotgun, the mother had disappeared. They found her bloodied in some bushes, admitting that she was dying. The man with the shotgun set his dogs after the cougar. Much mauling went on before the man caught up with them and shot the cougar. The article applauds the dead mother's heroism. She's being awarded a medal of honour by a local politician. I must be twisted because my sympathies lie with the dead cougar. How frightened she must've been by the urban development encroaching on her territory. Maybe she was trying to protect her cubs who are now starving in her den. Humans *projected* intent to kill on her when in reality she was just trying to scare them away. Maybe that's what Sam was doing, just trying to to scare them. But then *he* got scared and lost control and now humans are projecting intent to kill on him.

What scared him though? Futurelessness? Lovelessness?

I hear noises in the basement, stop breathing and listen harder, suspecting I'm imagining "the man" again. But the noises persist. Grabbing a broom for a weapon, I creep down the stairs. The light is on in the laundry room. Sam is doing laundry, bleaching his whites. "Sam," I say. He seems not to hear me, just carefully screws the lid on the Javex and places the bottles on the shelf. "Sam . . . ?" Again he doesn't respond and I realize that, even though his eyes are open, he is asleep. My immediate instinct is to run. He could snatch the broom from me and beating me over the head with it. But then I remind myself that he hasn't done this in the past. Before, when I was unafraid of him, I would gently try to coax him back to bed. Now I'm wondering why he's bleaching his whites in the early hours of the morning; did he just kill somebody?

"Sam . . . ? Sweetie?" He starts taking clothes out of the dryer and folding them.

I decide to leave him alone. If they find him not guilty by reason of non-insane automatism, I will have to live with this; my son who becomes a stranger in the night.

I sit on my bed and wait for him to come upstairs. Tense and shaking, I see him small again, in his crib, bashing the frog on his mobile. He didn't hit the duck or the teddy or the rabbit, just the frog. He'd calmly wait for the music box to bring the frog within his reach, then *thwack*.

Suddenly he's on the stairs. Cold sweat soaks the left side of my nightgown. He pauses in the hall. What's he doing? I look around for potential weapons: a hairbrush, a hand mirror? But if I get up to grab them, he'll hear me. It might startle him, frighten him. So I wait. My breast throbs. I wipe sweat from the side of my face. Finally, he steps into his bedroom.

Tomorrow I will buy a bolt for my door.

Ten

Another gruesome crime is being tried down the hall from us. Actually, two gruesome crimes allegedly performed by the same man who happens to be black. The defence is making it into a race issue. The halls are jammed with angry black people who don't budge when I say "excuse me." I have to elbow my way through them to get to my courtroom. I love it that they don't notice me. Even the Wicked Witch of the West pays me no mind as she squeezes between two men twice her size. We are yesterday's news. The alleged black murderer not only knifed two girls repeatedly but tied them to trees and raped them. Sam seems pretty benign compared to this dude. I can't help hoping that this is good timing for us, that our jury will think, Well, at least he didn't rape and murder two girls. At least he was asleep. At least he isn't black. Because, let's face it, it doesn't hurt that my son looks like a nice white boy.

I hope the black kid's lawyer doesn't change his defence to non-insane automatism.

Baldy's final expert looks like Jimmy Durante. I keep expecting him to break into song: "Inka dinka doo, inka dinka dee." He smiles constantly while explaining that my son has electrophysiological abnormalities of the brain rather than anti-social personality disorder. It's hard not to like Jimmy Durante. I even catch the old lady juror smiling. She's probably remembering the variety shows—herself and Walter curled up in front of the TV.

The only daughter looks decomposed today. Initially, she looked churchy. Now she appears to have been sleeping in her clothes, probably in her car outside my house. Periodically, her eyes dart over to the jury and her lips twitch as if she's desperate to speak. Would a conviction give her peace? Would the thought of Sam languishing in a cell offer comfort? It would not make her any less alone.

A nice white boy went gun crazy in a twenty-four-hour grocery store last night. Killed two people, maimed five, then took off. The thugs-in-blue have lost him. I can't help wondering why Sam was bleaching his whites early this morning.

He wouldn't do that. He's not gun crazy. Anyway, where would he get the gun?

On cross-examination the football player doesn't stand a chance with Jimmy Durante. Jimmy actually gets a laugh from the cheerleaders when he talks about crocodile brains.

Yesterday, the Elvis impersonator, while I was showing him a handyman special, figured out that I was the mother of the killer and said, "Don't thweat it, my uncle shot hith wife and kidth and got off on temporary inthanity."

The Asian chimed in, "Guns vewy bad."

"My son didn't have a gun," I explained.

"And my thecond couthin," the Elvis impersonator added, "shot hith wife, then himthelf. It'th no big deal nowadayth. They wath old, wathn't they?"

"Who?"

"The people he terminated?"

"That he allegedly terminated, yes."

"Tho, they had it coming to them. The way I thee it, he did them a favour. Beath thitting around in your own refuth." He leaned against a piece of moulding, which fell from the wall. He immediately tried to fit it back on.

"This house is shit," the Asian observed.

"You get what you pay for," I said. Strangely, I found myself relaxing in the company of these two men. What my son did holds no interest for them. They just want to find a cheap house and crack a few jokes.

I dreamed last night that I was having tea with the Queen—cucumber sandwiches and little cakies. She was very nice but stank of shit. What does this mean?

During his summation the football player "takes us back"

through the murders, draws out the sordid details yet again. Watching the jurors' faces, I'm still denying the indelible truth that these people can put my son away for life. These strangers have more control over my fate than I've ever allowed anybody. The news story about the woman juror who became so infatuated with the defendant she subsequently visited him in prison springs to mind. Eventually, they had nooky while he was on parole. Now, she's on the cover of national magazines looking red-lipped and blousy. "I did it for love," she proclaims. Is this justice?

I haven't noticed any of the cheerleaders eyeing Sam. Too bad.

When I consider all the people in my life who I imagined had power over me, from parents to lovers to employers, I realize that the only power they had was what I gave them. These twelve strangers with sore butts and agendas I can't even begin to fathom, these twelve strangers have actual power over me and my son. I can do nothing but gawk like the excuses-for-humans. And, unlike the only daughter, no words of protest are pushing against my lips. As much as I want him free, I don't want him free. As much as I want him non-insane, I want him insane. I want things to fit. I want to feel that final click of the puzzle.

Who is qualified, really, to decide who's crazy? Everybody looks crazy to me. The patently false interactions I experience with people daily seem insane to me. Why bother? Why feign interest, or niceness, or magnanimity, or self-confidence, or intellect, or ignorance? Does anybody care? We're all just trying to get along here. We all shit and piss and have to find a pair of matching socks in the morning.

Maybe the "insane" are the sane and the rest of us are experiencing non-insane automatism during our patently false interactions. Certainly automatism figures big in the modern age. It doesn't take original thought to turn on your TV, surf the Net, crank your stereo.

I wonder when they'll come up with a study revealing that original thought gives you cancer.

Are there any original thoughts?

Sonny Bono is twiddling his thumbs. I've never actually seen someone twiddle their thumbs in real life, only in movies. It definitely suggests he wants to get on with it. Maybe there's a game on tonight. For the first time, Sam looks frightened, and I can do nothing. I feel the silkiness of his baby head against my cheek, see his baby eyes, so blue, so clear. He sucks on my nipple staring up at me and I see myself reflected in his pupils. I don't want to see myself and shift my position slightly, but something about the light in the room has transformed his eyes into mirrors. Who are you trying to kid? I ask myself in his eyes. You're no mother and he knows it.

This morning, I bribed Sybil into having a bath by promising to take her to her favourite greasy spoon. She hates bathing because she's afraid of slipping in the tub. Consequently, she always has that old-lady smell about her. If I'm awarded the luxury of growing old, will *I* start to smell bad? Is foul body odour as inevitable as death? Maybe the Queen really does stink of shit.

In the restaurant, I knew Sybil was feeling better because she ranted about how Western corruption has ruined Russia. "People block their windows with concrete because they're afraid of getting shot."

She seemed to have forgotten that today was the big day and I didn't remind her. We shared a handy tabloid and comfortably read that Barbra Streisand and Liza Minnelli are on the verge of nervous breakdowns. As in the case of Liz Taylor, their friends are worried about them. Like Raquel, they'd been caught without makeup and looked like normal women. An aging female face without makeup seems to give the media cause to cry nervous breakdown.

Other news included volatility in the stock market, escalation of urban crime and the discovery that the lead content in soft vinyl baby toys causes cancer. Lead in baby toys? What wizard came up with that one?

I asked Sam if he would join us. He shook his head. I asked if he'd buy a tree with me later. He shook his head. I didn't want to appear to be the basket case that I am but to suggest that life goes on.

Not once have we talked about my cancer. I think he thinks I made it up.

Sybil waved a page of newsprint at me. "Check this out," she said.

I read that a man inadvertently ran over his four-year-old son with a bulldozer. He'd told the boy to stay on a pile of sand, but the boy had wandered behind the bulldozer. The father backed up, then looked around for his son. Mortified by this incident, it took me a moment to recognize, on page six, a small drawing of myself, unconscious with my mouth hanging open. "Accused Killer's Mom Can't Take the Heat," the headline proclaimed. I told myself not to read the article. Recountings of my son's trial only upset me. But I couldn't stop looking at the drawing because, if I look like that, Raquel, Liz, Barb and Liza have nothing on me. I look like a woman who experiences nervous breakdowns on a daily basis.

"Doesn't look like you," Sybil offered.

Fortunately, I was able to distract myself with more news about the dead cougar woman. The RCMP thought her corpse should be awarded a medal. A memorial service was held for her. Her cowboy boots and saddle were stacked on bales of hay. Five hundred mourners came to pay their respects.

What about the dead cougar?

An old man sitting in the next booth was telling another old man about an acquaintance of his who won $125,000 in the lottery. "The son of a bitch doesn't know what to do with it. Stays home all day worrying about it."

"I wish *I* had such problems," the other old man grumbled. What problems could he possibly have when he has been blessed with long life. I envy longevity now. I used to dread growing old.

Baldy's summation is not nearly as long or as turgid as the football player's. He goes over the business of Sam being incapable of appreciating the nature and quality of his act or knowing that the act was wrong and ends with "This was not a murder but a tragedy. Sam was failed by his parents and the system that failed to perceive the seriousness of his condition. You can't compound this tragedy with injustice. You must acquit Sam Pentland." I ponder all the courtroom dramas I've seen in which the windup is flashy, edgy, snazzy. For an instant I feel that I'm reviewing this movie; *didactic, dull, lethargic, leaden* are all words I could use. Where's Richard Gere when you need him?

What's Jerry doing? Looks like he's got an itchy butt. Sit still for God's sake. Gingivitis Girl isn't here today. Good move, Jerr. I keep replaying his testimony in my head. He dressed down for the occasion. I guess Baldy'd advised him that Armani suits alienate jurors. Jerr claimed that our son had a very average childhood, very typical, very middle class. The football player was angling for something, probably abuse, neglect. Something that would've produced antisocial personality disorder. But Jerr, Mr. His-shit-doesn't-smell, did not stammer or sweat or pass out, unlike *moi*.

The judge blathers on. I can't listen anymore. Suddenly I want to scream, This isn't fair, this isn't fair! My phantom pain is determined to outdo the pain from my new lump. I got here first, it shouts as it unfurls more burning substances inside me.

There was a For Sale sign on the old-lady-obsessed-with-raking-leaves' house. Guess she's dead. Or they stuck her in a home. Sorry, Mom, we want your money.

"I'll miss her," Sybil remarked, smearing cholesterol on her toast.

"Did you ever talk to her?"

She shook her head. "I watched her rake. The old gal was a constant. Something I could count on."

"Maybe your pacemaker will have the same effect," I offered.

She scowled as she shoved bacon in her mouth.

Beside the hideous drawing of me was a story about a young offender who was killed in prison for "ratting." The guards offered no protection while he was kicked and pissed upon. When he screamed for help, they responded, "Yeah, yeah, yeah." Eventually he was taken to the hospital where he died from "trauma injuries." This offers me no comfort as I look at Sonny Bono and the band.

Sonny Bono's dead, I keep assuring myself.

Having a pee in the greasy spoon's putrefied washroom, I was spied upon by a cherub. His face appeared upside down below the cubicle. "Cameron," his mother chided with her pantyhose around her knees, "don't peek in other people's. You can peek at me."

"What's the fun of peeking at your own mother?" I asked her ankles. She did not respond. No sense of humour. The angel was yanked from view. As usual I wanted my son small again.

Abruptly, it's over. The jury's off to deliberate. Sam and I cower in the car with a murky stillness between us. What can I say, don't worry, sweetie?

"Do you want to buy a tree with me?" I ask.

"What?"

"I need to get a tree."

"What for?"

"For the backyard. They cut down the oak."

"What oak?"

This is where we're different.

You used to stare up at its leaves with wonder from your bassinet.

Say nothing. Best leave it alone.

I trudge through mud at the nursery, ruining my shoes. I'm determined to find a real tree, not a pencil. Price is determined by the width of the trunk. I'm willing to spend doughla on this tree. I can't stop shaking because I fear my beeper will sound and the jury will be back after making fast work of it.

But the trees are so lovely, so soothing, so real. Constant, as Auntie would say. I need a constant tree. The man selling the trees smells of cigarettes and pesticides. "I don't want to have to spray it or anything," I explain. "I want low maintenance, fast growing, flowering." I'm surprised to hear myself say "flowering." Oaks don't flower but offer solace anyway. Maybe I'm moving into a floral phase. Soon I'll be wearing hats like the Queen.

An hour later, I've decided on an Ivory Silk Japanese tree lilac. I get Pesticide Man down slightly on the price because I notice a notch taken out of the bark, presumably by a passing forklift or something. Pesticide Man smokes while writing up the invoice. Around him, garden sculptures offer gentle hands and water tinkles from a fountain. The stench of bug killer burns my nostrils. Will he live cancer-free forever? Probably.

After I've arranged for delivery and planting, I trudge back through the mud to my tree and embrace it. "You will have a home now," I assure her. "You will be free."

"When did you discover the lump?" Cheeseburger asks, fondling it.

"Recently."

"It's quite large. Obviously you haven't been doing self-examinations."

I don't want to admit I slacked off out of fear, and because I figured if there was a lump, it would find me. "I thought it was fibrocystic," I say cheerily. "I mean, it hurts. Malignant isn't supposed to hurt, right?"

He says nothing, just juts out his lower lip as he studies the lump. Clearly it is an unwelcome guest.

I didn't want to come here, didn't expect to be "fitted" in. I expected to talk to voicemail and not have my call returned. But here I sit, once again, with legs dangling from the examining table, hoping that Mr. Mouthspray will tell me there's nothing to worry about. I'm his last patient. The waiting room is empty, ghostly. I miss my sisters-in-pain.

"I'm going to do a needle biopsy," he informs me. Whoops, that's not nothing.

He freezes me locally and uses a hypodermic needle to draw off some fluid. I wait for something to appear in the syringe. It doesn't.

"Hunh," he remarks. "Maybe there'll be some microscopic tissue on the needle that the lab can examine."

I'm thinking, *That's it?* That's all you're going to tell me? He peels off his latex gloves, apparently lost in thought. About what? Me? Vegas showgirls? Lotto 6/49?

"What's your gut feeling on this?" I ask finally.

"What?"

"Lump."

"It's attached to your chest wall. That's unusual for a malignant tumour. Usually, they're loose."

"That's good," I say, hoping he'll say, You're darned right it's good, no worries, babe, etcetera, etcetera.

He scribbles something on his grubby little chart. "The only way to rule out malignancy is with a biopsy."

"More surgery."

"Slow down. Let's take it one step at a time."

"Okey-dokey," I say, reaching for my clothes, wondering why I act twelve around this guy. Because I want him to like me, so he'll treat me like a person instead of a disease.

"You doing anything for the holidays?" he asks.

"What?"

"Thanksgiving."

This kind of make-the-patient-feel-cozy chat is the worst. I would rather he pierce me with needles than do the natter thing.

"No plans," I say. "So I won't get the results till next week?"

"That's right. Don't worry. It's probably nothing." He says this to his tie as he speeds out of the room. I fit my prosthesis into my bra.

It's only life flashing by, I tell myself. Doesn't help.

In the hardware store, I look for bolts. The proprietor has a perfectly round paunch affixed to his stick body and eyebrows which constantly shift. "What kind of bolt would you be looking for?" he asks.

"To put on a door."

"Indoors or out?"

"Indoors."

"Like on a cupboard and that?"

"Actually no, on a bedroom."

The eyebrows merge. "You mean to keep animals out?"

"That's right."

"So's like you're going to be inside and you want to keep the animals out?"

"That's right. Big animals."

The eyebrows lurch up his forehead.

"Nothing complicated," I add. "You know, some kind of sliding doodad."

He scratches behind his ear as he peruses his bolt supply. "How about this?" He shows me a metal sliding bolt.

"Have you got something bigger?"

"You need a thicker door for a bigger bolt."

"I think it's thick."

"Most indoor doors are hollow."

"Oh." I realize that barricading myself in is going to be more arduous than I'd imagined. Better just to get bludgeoned to death. I buy light bulbs because there's no one else in the store and I feel he needs a sale.

Things do not look good for Bunny. Estelle drips tears as she informs me that the fat deposits have come back. I hadn't realized they'd left, but don't admit this, only look concerned for Bunny.

"They're going to try to cut them out," Estelle says. "But they're not sure he'll survive the surgery."

Where are they going to shave him this time? The poor kitty must be bald, chilled in his clinical hell. It's all I can do not to tell the silly woman to let her poor cat expire. But her hands are shaking. She's in agony, has come to the office as I have come to the office—to avoid our real lives.

"I can't believe this is happening," she gasps.

I'm familiar with this feeling and put a hand on her shoulder but immediately feel awkward because she's wearing shoulder pads. I'm consoling a wad of cloth.

"Do they have any idea why they came back?" I inquire.

She shakes her head and blows her nose. What causes kitty cancer? Did Bunny eat refined and processed foods high in fats, additives and sugar? Did he consume more than three alcoholic beverages a week? Pesticide levels are higher in the fat tissue of women with breast cancer. Maybe Bunny ate too much diazinoned grass. Maybe he spent too much time hanging around magnetic fields, maybe he sat on too many chemically treated fences, had too many X-rays. Cancer is associated with the toxic waste of industrial economies. Affluence. It's a disease associated with excess. Maybe Estelle should've been feeding him plain old kitty chow instead of filet mignon.

Maybe I wouldn't have cancer if I'd grown up on a rice paddy.

Maybemaybemaybe.

"He could still make it," I say. "You never know."

She offers me a chocolate-cream cookie. We both nibble on our love-substitutes. "Are you doing anything for Thanksgiving?" I ask. She shakes her head. "Why don't you come over to my place?" As I say this, I realize I must be mad.

"You mean for turkey and stuff?"

"Of course. Sunday."

"Sure. Okay." I can see that she's weighing the possibility of being alone after Bunny's passing against the thought of dining with a murderer.

Driving home, the news tells me that breast cancer rates are 6.5 times higher in countries with nuclear waste sites. Duh.

Driving home, the news tells me that a four-year-old girl was abducted and sexually molested by a twenty-two-year-old man. At least Sam didn't do this, I tell myself. He's not a pervert. He only kills people. Geriatrics, not even four-year-olds.

Stopped in traffic, I see a homeless man staring into a bookstore window. Filthy blankets hang from his shoulders. His trousers are torn at the seat revealing shit-coated buttocks and thighs. His shoeless state, matted hair and beard make him look like a relic from the Middle Ages. Surely no one can live in such abject poverty now in the land of plenty.

What has caught his interest in the bookstore window? *How to Succeed in Business*? *How to Get the Love You Want*? *Martha Stewart's Home for the Holidays*? *Sex Tips for the Twenty-First Century*?

I drive on, leaving him behind. Out of sight, out of mind. I think about my tree—about living to see it flower. I think this is a positive thought.

Eleven

To my amazement, Sam is home and doesn't exit when I enter. He stands around eating a banana. "Guess they're having trouble making up their minds," he says finally.

"They only got a couple of hours in before the end of the day," I point out, trying to sound casual. "Do you want a pizza?"

He brightens at this suggestion and I feel as though I've performed a magic trick. That he is willing to share a pizza with me almost makes me delirious. I order a fancy pizza from a gourmet pizza joint even though I know that gourmet pizza differs from regular only in that it contains whole olives rather than sliced, and one or two pieces of artichoke.

"Where's the old lady?" Sam asks.

"Betty's for a bridge party."

He tosses the banana peel into the garbage. "Her doctor called with the name of a heart surgeon."

"Did he say he was cute?"

"No."

"I told him he had to be cute."

"He didn't say he wasn't." He shows me the slip of paper with the name and number on it.

"Norman Finklestein," I observe. "Doesn't sound too cute."

"Don't you think it's a bit degenerate to keep her alive by sticking a battery in her?"

"She wants to be alive."

He screws up his face as he used to do when he was stumped by a math problem. "What the fuck for?" To think I used to take such care not to swear in front of him.

"She says she wants to know what happens."

"Gee. It's like the world gets more crowded and fucked up."

"I guess she wants to see that."

"Fuck. It's like die already. She's had the good years. It's shit from here on in. The old people have it made, man. They got all the goodies. The least they can do is kick off."

"And relieve the tax burden on the young."

"Right on."

I hate it when he says "right on," makes me think of the sixties, bad trips and venereal disease.

"Well, you might want to mention that to Sybil," I suggest, wondering if the weight of the tax burden was his motive for killing the Grundys.

"Sybil believes," I add, "that people will kill their parents for a nickel. That's why she's against euthanasia. She thinks it would mean open season on troublesome parents. What do you think?"

"Don't play shrink with me, Mum."

He hasn't called me Mum for about a hundred years. It makes me want to hug him but I can't without it being awkward. He's studying a Nike ad in the newspaper. To mask the silence, I pick up the front section and read about emissions of cancer-causing gases from landfill sites. The culprit seems to be PVC or polyvinyl chloride which is a known human carcinogen. Workers who make the stuff suffer from liver damage. But the plastics industry insists that PVC does not decompose. And our Minister of the Environment claims that the emissions are at an "acceptable level." Guess he doesn't live near a landfill site.

"I'm planning a Thanksgiving dinner," I say.

"What the fuck for?"

"Umm . . . diversion."

He stares at me as though I'm mentally incompetent, then looks back at the paper. "That's cool."

"Cool" is a word that must be buried, lost and forgotten so that we can unearth it one day and discover that it means moderately cold.

I break a tooth on one of the olives dotting the gourmet pizza. Fortunately, I feel no pain but my tongue keeps sliding over the wreckage. I show the piece of broken tooth to Sam. "Cool," he says.

No doubt my dentist will want to put a crown on it. My feeling is what's the point of spending eight hundred bucks on your mouth when you could be dying? If I'm not dead in a year, I'll be happy to spend the money. Unfortunately, teeth, when broken, can't wait. They break more and start to hurt. Besides, trying to achieve some kind of compromise with my dentist (who collects cars) would mean explaining that I have cancer. He's British with lethal body odour. He'd lean over me and say, "I'm terribly sorry, bad luck that." While inhaling his armpits and enduring the drill, I would also have to suffer his pity. This would be too much. On the other hand, maybe if I tell him about the big "C," he'll give me a break on the price. Yeah right.

The bummer about breaking the tooth now is that I'm experiencing one of those rare moments when my mind, body and soul feel intact. I'm not loitering in the past or the future. I'm just here and everything seems manageable. Which is bizarre considering the circumstances: biopsy results and a verdict pending.

Sam's on his third slice. I keep expecting him to take his plate and slouch over to the couch and television. He must want to be with me, even though he's studying the want ads. "What are you looking for?" I ask.

"Nothing."

I want to say, Then why are you studying the want ads, but realize this would be intrusive. But, seriously, what can he be looking for? A job, a date, a used car, when he could be in the clink tomorrow? I suppose this kind of delusional behaviour is no different from his mother planning a Thanksgiving dinner. Which explains our need to be together. The doomed want to hang out with the doomed, not the folks with horseshoes up their asses.

"Did you," I begin, "hear about the boy who shot a bunch of people in a grocery store?"

"Missed that one."

"Where'd he get the gun would be my question."

"That's easy."

"It is?"

He snorts and turns a page. My tongue investigates my broken tooth again. "The police can't find him," I add.

"What a surprise."

I look back at the paper. Some new study has concluded that "there is no direct link between high levels of pesticides or PCBs in the body and breast cancer." Who funded this study, DuPont? More interesting is the story about the man who plunged a kitchen knife into his father's chest and watched him die. His father pleaded with him to call an ambulance but instead the son cut the phone line. "I did it for his own good," he told the court. What did the father do to the son to provoke such an attack? Abuse was not raised in the son's defence. He testified that he'd used some drugs, including ecstasy, on the day of the murder and consequently had very little memory of what had happened. His lawyer must've been cheap because the boy was found guilty. It seems to me that, with the right "experts," he could've pleaded temporary insanity resulting from the drugs altering his brain chemistry, making him incapable of appreciating his act.

"This is interesting," I comment.

"What?"

"A boy killed his father." I contemplate the kitchen knives at Sam's fingertips.

"Why?"

"He said he deserved it."

"Maybe he used to beat the shit out of him."

"It doesn't say that."

"Maybe he used to shove his dick up his butt and the kid didn't want to tell anybody."

"So instead of telling anybody, he's happy to go to prison for the rest of his life?" Where more men will shove their dicks up his butt, I'm thinking.

"It's possible."

This is the longest exchange we've had in months and I want to keep him talking. "So do you think being sexually abused justifies killing somebody?"

"If it's your father."

"Why only if it's your father?"

"Or your mother."

The boy, like Sam, was tried in adult court even though he was a young offender. It was probably a mistake to have him testify. It is impossible to look sufficiently penitent to justify brutal murder. I understand why Baldy wouldn't let Sam take the stand.

"Does your tooth hurt?" he asks abruptly, as though we haven't been discussing homicide. I consider claiming that I'm in extreme pain just to see what he'll do—if he'll hold me in his arms while plying me with Advil. But I can't lie to him. "No," I admit.

"You're lucky," he says, and I marvel that someone who has beaten two people to death can be concerned about tooth pain. He must've broken a few teeth while he was bashing their faces. Did he ask them if it hurt? Did he *want* it to hurt?

"Are you scared?" I ask him. Caught off guard he looks me in the eye briefly, then looks away.

"Yeah."

"Whatever happens, we'll deal with it. We can always appeal."

He nods vaguely and pulls a mushroom slice off the pizza. I watch him chew it, wanting him to say more, reveal more, but I can see that he's retreating.

"Do you remember *The Cat in the Hat*?" I ask.

"What about it?"

"Remember how he was always saying 'Have no fear'?"

"No."

"'Now! Now! Have no fear. Have no fear! said the cat.' I loved reading that bit." Sam wipes his hands on his jeans and stands. I've gone too far, he thinks I'm gaga.

"Thanks for the pizza," he says, vacating the kitchen. I hear the TV come on. At least he said thanks. I slap my prosthesis on the table and stare at the remaining olives on the pizza thinking how extraordinary it is that just one of them can cost me eight hundred bucks. Then I open my mail and read a form letter about "a better way to meet someone special." Don't just sit around expecting miracles to happen, the letter urges, meet new, interesting single people and let a special relationship grow. Someone special is waiting for me, the letter advises, but it is up to me to take control of my life. There's that control concept again. Who came up with this idea anyway? Advertising? If we consume these goods and services, we will control our lives. Buy buy buy and ye shall overcome. What crap.

Another piece of mail is handwritten and obviously hand-delivered because it's stampless. The writing is almost unintelligible but after close scrutiny I am able to discern: "I have spoken with the bank and we have come to the conclusion that the only method available to make you PAY WHAT YOU OWE is to foreclose on your house. Be advised that my colleagues and I will be taking possession of said house and all your belongings in the near future if you fail to PAY WHAT YOU OWE."

The signature is illegible. I assume it belongs to one of Sam's pallies who are no longer pallies now that he's murdered people. "Sam," I call, then call again. Receiving no response, I follow him into the living room and hold the letter in front of his face. "Do you know this person?" I inquire.

"I can't fucking read it."

I read it for him.

"It's a fucking joke," he observes.

"Yes, but whose?"

"I don't fucking know."

I throw the letter out and tell myself to forget about it, but of course don't, once again failing to take control of my mind. Which is why I have cancer.

Elvis phones and tells me that he and the Asian want to buy the junkiest house I've shown them. "It juth needth a coat of paint in a few plathes," he tells me. I'm pleased that they're making an offer but sad that they intend to be slum landlords. We arrange to meet to do the paperwork and I call the listing agent to set up an appointment with the vendor. Sybil returns, tipsy on sherry which she hates but drinks when she's at Betty's because it's the only booze available. "How goes it, Auntie?"

"Liberal swines. Two-faced. Soulless."

"Did you lose at cards?"

She searches the fridge for some meat.

"There's Black Forest ham," I say. "Was Betty feeding you cookies?"

"Brainless woman. Spineless."

"How do you feel about the name Norman Finklestein?"

"Who's Norman Finklestein?"

"Your cute heart surgeon. We can call him Dr. Fink for short."

She scowls while munching slices of ham.

"Why don't you have some bread with that?" I suggest.

"Don't fuss."

"What a grump."

I sit with Sam. Lined up on a TV talk show are women with enormous bowling-ball tits. Some are "exotic dancers," but some are just ordinary gals who wanted big boobs. When asked why they have undergone—in some cases repeated—surgery to enlarge their breasts, they insist that they like the way it looks. "It's an addiction," a distraught husband complains. "She keeps getting them enlarged." He appears frail beside her—the drone beside the queen. He declares that he'll divorce her if she gets them enlarged again. She says he's just jealous because men bump into things when they look at her. She says both men and women want to touch her breasts. "It's embarrassing," the husband counters.

"Maybe for you," she smirks.

I don't know what to make of this freak show. What society applauds such self-inflicted deformities? Are the implants not heavy? Do they not drag on their shoulders and neck? Do they not hinder movement? Do they not leak silicone into their bodies which creates a disease in itself? What does it mean when women will put themselves at risk to attain such an image? I feel insulted, mocked, belittled, insignificant. I do not matter in such a world. "Can we watch something else?" I ask.

"Sure." He surfs. It's all the same old stuff—doctors, lawyers, cops and cleavage.

I escape outside into pouring rain. In just a T-shirt and jeans, I walk into a wall of wet. It's cool as in moderately cold. How refreshing, rejuvenating. Free of prosthesis, I know that within minutes my affliction will be visible to passersby but I don't care anymore. Something has snapped, or released in me. I can't compete anymore. So what? Let me live. I begin to run as if away from something. My bare feet make lovely slapping sounds on the concrete. As puddles form I jump into them. My lump and phantom pain welcome the cool, as does my overheated brain. Dog walkers stare. Another crazy, they're thinking. So what? Let me live.

In the ravine, I shout and hop about. The grass squelches between my toes. A squirrel flees from me but not a raccoon. She sits on a branch watching calmly; just another stupid human trick, she's thinking.

It's when I cut my foot that reality comes crashing down. The blood looks Christmasy against the grass and I ponder where we'll be then, if he'll be with me, if I'll be living. Images of Christmases past flash by—especially the first one, when he had no expectations, only delight at the fire engine and Martians. Only later came the inevitable letdown—never the right present, never jolly enough, never cheery enough. So what? Let me live. And I see him in prison, the four concrete walls, the crapper, the sink. The fucking Bible. And I see him in the loony bin, surrounded by the walking dead. Let's do crafts today, a social worker tells his body bloated by drugs, we'll make Christmas cards for our loved ones, and I just start screaming. It's not a cry of pain or even anger. It's not even a cry for sympathy. It's more like a noisy vomit. I'm trying to purge myself of all that I contain—history, cancer, remnants of love.

Limping, shivering, I approach my house and the red car beside it. "Hello," I say, knocking on the windshield. "What's your fucking problem?" I demand. I want her to gun me down. I want it. Sam used to say this when he was two: "I want it." What do you want now, my baby, tell me what you want?

The only daughter doesn't answer, just stares at me with bottomless eyes. I can't be angry with her. "Sorry," I shout through the glass.

She has seen my disfigurement. My secret is out. Will this change anything? Will she drive away, stop at the drive-thru at Burger King, eat for the first time in two days and say, That poor woman has cancer. As she swallows her fourth onion ring, she'll repeat, That poor woman has cancer.

I'd rather she hate me.

"Where've you been?" Sam asks.

"I just thought I'd go for a walk."

"You're soaked."

"Yes."

"Jesus. Don't go nuts on me, Ma."

"I'll try not."

"Like that's all I need."

"I'm not going nuts."

"Your foot's bleeding."

"I know."

"Jesus."

Disgusted, he leaves me to die from the bleeding foot. I hobble to the bathroom and proceed with disinfecting measures. *Don't go nuts on me, Ma.* I hate it when he calls me Ma. Makes me think of Ma and Pa Kettle. Oh well, at least he didn't call me a cunt-shitting bitch. Sybil's in bed. Good. I have a hot bath keeping my Polysporined foot above water. There's no way, no way I will sleep. Best stay immersed.

What if he comes and kills me in the bath? Not a bad idea.

Makes for a quick cleanup.

Her car's gone. Wretched girl. What's to be done about her? Will she go away if he's cuffed and caged? I know she scrawled the threatening letter. She's out of her mind with grief. Does this justify harassment?

STOP TOUCHING YOUR BREAST! LEAVE YOUR BREAST ALONE!

He said the lump's attached to your chest wall. He said that's unusual for a malignant tumour. He said it's probably nothing.

The problem is it hurts more when I lie on either side. I flip onto my back, switch on the radio, fiddle with the tuner. Miraculously, Glenn Gould is playing *The Goldberg Variations.* I am stilled, listening to his humming. And think of the pain he suffered in his arms from his playing posture. Against all advice he wouldn't correct it because it would've interfered with his playing. What a solitary life he led—preferred night to day, phone calls to physical encounters. Greasy eggs at Fran's to home cooking. Loved his mother, depended on her. She tinkled the ivories while he was in the womb.

The music stops and some dickweed with a German accent starts enumerating Gould's eccentricities. "Zis is all very well," he concedes, "but zer can be no doubt zat ze drug dependency posed problems." Says who, you stupid fuck. His playing never stopped sounding good to me. How dare herr moron condemn the man because he failed to stay well. Just as we condemn those who fail to stay "equal." How dare we when there but for the grace of something go we?

Do we have to get sick to feel compassion?

In the twenty-first century, it is estimated that a woman will die of breast cancer every ten minutes. That's a lot of dead people. They can't all bring it on themselves by having fries and pies and negative thoughts.

"A tragedy, really," herr moron concludes.

"You lost the war," I tell him and turn the thing off. The dog's at it. Muzzle it, pal, don't they feed you? Or is yowling through the night a form of therapy? I had a client who hosted "soundings";

a bunch of women would get together and howl. Maybe the dog is sounding, seeking communion with other dogs.

Can't sleep. Is Sonny Bono sleeping? Can they sleep?

I hear the front door open and close. Great, he's going out to kill more people.

On my bed table sits his baby picture. Pudgy-cheeked, a real butterball, it was all I could do not to bite his tushy. I kiss the picture—that's how desperate I am—and sing softly to him, to myself. "The itsy-bitsy spider climbed up the water spout. Down came the rain and washed the spider out. Out came the sun and dried up all the rain. The itsy-bitsy spider climbed up the spout again." I hold my baby against my heart.

Twelve

My dentist is having his dental chairs reupholstered, consequently he has only one functioning torture chamber. Normally he has three and flits from one patient to the other. But due to the lack of chairs, he can't perform his usual assembly-line dentistry. He must get me out of his chair ASAP so he can inflict pain and financial hardship on his next victim. "How did you break it?" he inquires.

"An olive pit."

"Oh yes," he remarks gravely. "Well, we'll have to put a crown on it."

"I figured." As he pokes around in my mouth, the TV bolted to the wall advises me that a study has revealed a possible link between eating squirrel brains and catching the human variant of mad cow disease. A U.S. neurologist is cautioning people against eating squirrels or similar rodents.

"Planning anything for the holidays?" Dr. Dobin asks.

Why do dentists speak to us when we have mouths full of instruments? I grunt, wondering if he really is ignorant of my son's crime. I stare at his "Painless Dentist" sign and remember my dream last night. Sam was turning into an ape. I tried to love him anyway. As much as it dismayed me that he was developing a snout and growing furry, I was relieved that he was turning into an animal because this meant they'd have to drop the charges. I set about making plans to change the house, make it more ape-friendly.

While Dobin fits a temporary arrangement on my tooth, the TV informs me that a young woman was pushed in front of a subway train by a paranoid schizophrenic. As she lay dying in the tracks, she begged the paramedics to tell her mother that she hadn't committed suicide.

"How horrible," I garble.

"Could be worse," Dobin says, thinking I'm referring to my tooth. "Any other problems?"

I realize he hasn't heard, doesn't hear. I look away from the TV, at the pictures of antique cars on the wall. "No problems," I mutter, knowing that given the opportunity—given the extra chairs—he'd dig around and find some other "problem" he must solve for a few hundred bucks. His Scottish squeeze, who's also the office manager and refers to him as "Doctor" in public, pokes her head in the door. "You're getting a wee bit behind, Doctor," she tells him. I know she's his squeeze because I've seen them together in a bar, she sitting with her arm possessively around him. He's *my* dollar sign, her body language said. As he removes things from my mouth, I find myself envying him. He's got cash, a squeeze, a car collection and a complete lack of awareness of the world at large. And, no doubt, practises good sleep hygiene.

Elvis and the Asian are waiting for me at the office with doughnuts and coffee. "You want the fritter or the cruller?" Elvis asks me.

"Gosh," I say, touched by their offering but being in no mood for hard-boiled fat. "The cruller would be yummy," I say.

"Wath I right or wath I right?" Elvis asks the Asian who I've come to know as Lu. Elvis hands me a coffee. "Cream, no thugar?"

"That's right. Thank you."

He cackles with glee and elbows Lu, who is not amused but obviously eager to get on with business. I hand him the purchasing agreement which he studies carefully. I take a bite of my doughnut and actually feel comforted by its doughy greasiness. As the coffee sinks warmth into me, I feel my shoulders loosening slightly.

I checked my messages when I arrived just in case something was screwy with my pager. No news from Baldy's office. What can Sonny and the gang be doing? Is it kind of like group therapy; are they all expressing their feelings and speaking honestly? If so, it will take days. Or are they having heated arguments in which biases surface, he's too good looking for example. I can imagine this myself, not wanting to let a guy off because he's had it too easy, is too cute, too rich, too spoiled. This is why I find the jury system absurd. It is completely human to resent the other guy for having more than you do. It is completely human to ignore the evidence.

"Okay," the Asian says, signing and handing the pen to Elvis who also scrawls a signature.

"If it'th okay by Lu, it'th okay by me," he assures me.

Their offer is low but the house is scuzzy. I don't expect a fight from the vendor. My pager vibrates. I drop the papers and babble. But it's not Baldy's office, it's Estelle. I suspect she's taking a rain check on Thanksgiving. I phone home to check on Sam but there's no answer, just my own irritating voice on the service. I remind him not to go anywhere because we could get news today. I left a note on the kitchen table stating the same thing and signed it "love, Mum." So where is he?

"Oh you're here," Estelle says. "I didn't realize you were here." She's puffy-eyed and blotchy. "Bunny's dead," she gasps.

"Oh Estelle, I'm so sorry."

"I just had to tell somebody."

"Of course." We stand awkwardly. I offer her the fritter left behind by Elvis. She shakes her head.

"Did he pass away during the surgery?" I ask.

"No. It was after that. For a while there, it looked like he might be alright."

"That makes it harder."

"The vet was very understanding. He let me hold him and stuff, till the end."

"That's good," I say, knowing that the "understanding" vet will bill Estelle even though the cat's dead.

She covers her mouth with her hands. "He died in my lap." She begins to sob and I put my arm around her, relieved that she's not wearing shoulder pads. "I gave him Camembert with Valium," she sputters. "I don't normally let him have Camembert because it gives him diarrhea."

"Did he eat it?" This interests me. Do we want forbidden foods on our deathbed?

"He had a couple of licks, but he was too weak."

"Well, Estelle, you did what you could."

Todd skips by jubilant because he's just sold one of his own listings, meaning he scores both commissions. "Yesss!" we hear him say.

I take Estelle with me to the vendor's house because neither she nor I know what else to do with her. She stays in the car listening to a radio station playing hits from the sixties and seventies. Scary.

The owner of the junky house is your basic undershirt-only kind of fellah. Hair bushes out of his armpits and spreads across his shoulders and chest. He feigns astonishment at the low offer, huffs and puffs on his cigarette while shaking his head incredulously. The listing agent I've worked with before. He's a rational man with a family to support. Together we do some fancy stickwork to make King Kong see the light. He signs back for a couple thousand more.

I'm relieved to see that Estelle has eaten the fritter. Where there's appetite, there's life.

My cell phone rings. It's Baldy's secretary. It's time.

Sam's not home, has left no note, no message on the service. Panic clenches my body. I try to think of who to phone. If I tell Jerry, he'll scream at me for letting the boy out of my sight. I try Jackie-the slut's number for old time's sake. Her drunken mother answers, swears at me and insists that she wouldn't let her daughter within ten miles of "that crazy fuck."

Sybil comes downstairs looking pasty. "What's going on?"

I don't want to tell her because it will stress her heart. "Nothing. Have you seen Sam?"

"I heard him moving around."

"When?"

"This morning."

I search again for his shoes and jacket. These days, he always wears the nylon one. I find it crumpled on the couch which suggests he hasn't skipped town. I look in every corner of the basement, imagining suicide; his body dangling from a belt. The phone rings, Sybil answers and informs me that it's Jerry. "Say I've left," I tell her. Sam's been doing laundry. The Javex sits capless on the windowsill. I find the cap on the floor and reach for the bottle. Out the window, I see that the garden shed's door is ajar. I always lock it. A cold mist settles over me. There are shovels in the garden shed. Tools of death.

He seemed so normal last night.

Am I unable to believe he's evil because he's my child?

I tramp through tall grass that is determined to impede me. I can't even remember the last time I bugged him to get out the mower. I stumble over something, a dog bone, and glance at my watch. What happens when the defendant doesn't show up for the verdict?

But he's in there, unconscious in yesterday's clothes. I hold my face close to his to see if he's breathing. Yes. I shake his shoulder because this is no time for a gentle wake-up. If he springs to life and throttles me, so be it.

"What's going on?" he asks groggily.

"What are you doing here?"

"Where?"

"You're in the shed."

He looks around, clearly surprised to be here.

"You must've walked in your sleep," I explain. "We have to move. The jury's back."

"I don't want to go."

"You have to." I grab his arm and begin to pull.

"I'm not going. Who gives a fuck if I'm there or not?"

"Are you crazy? You have to be there."

"They can come and get me."

"Do you want me to call your father so he can bodily drag you in there?"

"Whatever."

"Sam . . ." I hold his face in my hands, forcing him to look at me. "Sweetie, you can't quit on this. It's not going to go away. You have to see it through." I remember when he didn't want to go to school, how I would bribe him with TV shows. I try to think of a suitable bribe. A Caramilk bar? A new pair of Nikes? A gun?

He pulls away from me and heads for the house. I find myself praying even though there is no God. Please make him get ready, please make him hurry up, please make him not evil.

In the car, the silence is like sludge. I think of quicksand in movies. Soon I will be completely submerged. Would this be so bad, dying together in a car crash? Although probably only he would die. I'd be left a veggie in a wheelchair with breast cancer.

Abruptly he turns on the radio. It's still tuned to Estelle's golden oldies—"Killing Me Softly." Fortunately, Sam switches to some rock racket.

Because we're late, we cannot escape the gawkers. I grip his hand as I did crossing streets when he was a child. He doesn't resist but walks with his head bowed as the excuses-for-humans gape. We have a bit of a crowd back today, guess the rapist/murderer's trial is over, or maybe verdicts are must-sees for the court leeches. The Wicked Witch of the West skitters around us, perhaps preparing to hurl saliva. "Shoo," I tell her, looking straight into her demented eyes. "Shoo," I repeat, "or I'll cast a spell on you." This spooks her, she dives behind two pudding-faced women who can't take their eyes off Sam. I want a Gatling gun to mow these lowlifes down. But instead I maintain a dignified stance while shaking within, wobbling actually. It's as though my bones have become tubes of water. To make it into the courtroom seems an impossibility. But suddenly Jerry's there, taking my arm. I can't remember the last time he touched me. "Hold on," he whispers into my ear, "you're doing fine." The gentleness of his tone makes me tear out of my left eye. I hope he doesn't notice.

When I'm obliged to let go of my son's hand it is as though I'm letting go of life. The water gushes out of me. Jerry grips both my arms and places me on a chair. He sits beside me, propping me up, and I remember why I married him. Then the clerk gabs, so does the judge, until it's Sonny Bono's turn. He stands, taking forever to clear his throat, to get the words out. He doesn't sound like Sonny Bono, his voice is deep, accented, Greek maybe. I'm scared I won't understand what he's saying. Then they're there, the words "Not guilty." They're there, they've been said, they can't be erased. The water rushes back into me, flushing my skull, filling my ears, my mouth, my nostrils.

I surface on the leather couch. Jerry's under the loud wall clock. Sam's on the floor at my feet. I reach over and touch his hair. He doesn't pull away from me.

"Is the fainting connected to the cancer?" Jerry asks.

"Maybe," I say.

"You should tell your doctor about it."

"Yes, Jerry."

We've survived a shipwreck. We're on a deserted island somewhere.

"What do we do now?" Sam asks.

"Buy a turkey," I say. "You want to come for Thanksgiving dinner, Jerr?"

"Ahh . . . I'll have to check with Natasha. I think she has plans."

"Forget it," I say.

"No, I'll ask Natasha."

"Forget it." The renewed bond between us is severed and we're back to George and Martha. Oh well, it's not like I thought we were going to live happily ever after.

"How long have I been out?" I ask.

"A few minutes," Jerry says.

"How do we get out of here without being mobbed?"

"We wait. They'll get bored."

I sit up and stare at the grey leafy wallpaper. "Sam hasn't eaten today."

"I'm not hungry," he says.

"Are you okay?"

He shrugs. Oh my God, not again, we're not going back to shrug-talk.

"You're a lucky man," Jerry pronounces and I realize that there is nothing to say. It's still ugly, incomprehensible. We still have to live with it. But isn't that what it's all about? Gouges are taken out of you, but you go on?

What's the only daughter doing? What's she feeling? Is she booby-trapping our house?

"Maybe we should go away somewhere," I suggest.

"Who?" Jerry asks.

"All of us. Or anyway, Sam and me."

"Where?"

"I don't know. Alaska. Is there somewhere you'd like to go, Sam?"

He shrugs and I almost club him.

"I think you're better off staying put," Jerry advises. "Otherwise, it'll look like you're running scared, or celebrating, which would be worse."

There is an interminable, strangulating silence in which we listen to each other's breathing. Stranded on the deserted island, we are debating who to cannibalize first.

"My suggestion would be that you keep your heads down," Jerry offers finally. "Stay out of trouble."

"What kind of trouble would you be thinking of?" I inquire.

"You know very well."

"No, I don't. Don't have a clue."

"He might not be so lucky next time."

"Who's 'he'? If you mean Sam, he's right here. You can speak to him directly."

"He doesn't talk."

"You talk, don't you, Sam? You were talking last night."

"You guys talk enough," Sam grumbles.

"We only talk because you don't," Jerry says. "Please, speak up, we'd like to hear your thoughts. Your future, for example. Any prospects?"

"Now?" I ask. "You're asking him now? Half an hour ago, he had no future. Now he's supposed to have prospects?"

"Your uncle is willing to take you back at the hospital," Jerry says.

"Doing the nightshift?" I ask.

"If that's what's going."

"Are you mad? And screw up his sleep patterns again? Are you out of your frigging mind?"

"He can't live off you forever."

"Why? Because I'm going to die?"

"Oh for God's sake," Jerry says and I can see Sam dissolving in our acid. I grab his hand. "Let's go. Goodbye, Jerry. Give us a call when you're feeling a little less pent up."

The corridor appears to be clear. We move stealthily to the stairs and escape through a side entrance. Brisk night wind buffets us. Sam does not let go of my hand. I don't know what this means.

But the excuses-for-humans have found my car and have scrawled ugly words on it. Do they carry felt pens specifically for this purpose?

"Don't look. Get in," I say, wondering how they knew it was my car. Then I realize it was probably the Grundys' daughter. "First stop, the car wash."

We sit in a doughnut joint adjacent to the car wash and watch them work on the car. I force Sam to eat an egg salad sandwich and drink coffee. A pretty girl sits in a corner smoking a cigarette and I wonder if Sam has noticed her and if he's thinking he'll never know a pretty girl again because he is a murderer. How much will it chase him, dog him? Some boys wear violent crimes like badges. Maybe the smoking girl would be excited by his ability to kill. But then she would be the wrong kind of girl. I remember our fights over Jackie-the-slut. "Have you heard of VD?" I'd ask, "AIDS? Hepatitis B?"

Who's the right kind of girl?

I don't want to fight him anymore. He's so damaged. I must cradle his soul in my hands. "Want a doughnut?" I ask.

He pushes the cart for me at the supermarket. I can't remember the last time he helped me shop. I'm giddy with a feeling of endless possibility. We are together, solid, a team. Normally drab products appear to glow as do normally drab people. I see love between parents and children, kindness between strangers, passion between lovers. I see the reddest radishes, the greenest peppers, the yellowest bananas. I'm inside a cornucopia of life.

"Anything you want, we'll have," I tell him.

At first he shows little interest, but as we cruise the aisles things appear in the cart: Pop Tarts, Fritos, Orange Crush, Eggos, frozen mini pizzas. It's all I can do not to giggle with delight. It's all I can do not to hop up and down and squeal, "This is my boy and he's not guilty!"

We open the Fritos and the Orange Crush in our glistening car and munch while listening to the sparkling strings of Vivaldi. "One more stop," I say.

"I'm in no hurry," he responds and I sense that he too feels safer in the car, on the move.

Elvis lives in a two-bedroom bungalow. I'm surprised to see a wheelchair-access ramp beside his front steps and even more surprised to have the front door opened by a boy Sam's age in a wheelchair. His body is clearly out of his control. His head lolls to one side, his arms jerk, his stick legs are strapped to the chair. One of his hands curls inward towards his wrist rendering the fingers useless. He uses his other hand to open and close the door. He says hello gruffly, then calls, "Dad!" and I realize he is a carbon copy of Elvis minus the sideburns and greased-up hair.

Elvis appears wearing an apron that says "Kiss the Cook." "What'th up?"

"They want two thousand more," I tell him.

"No thweat."

"This is Sam, my son," I explain.

"Hey, kiddo," Elvis says. "Thith ith my thon, Turner, named after Ike and Tina."

"Hi, Turner," Sam and I mutter almost simultaneously. I suspect that he too is dumbstruck by the boy's disability. With his good hand, Turner spins his motorized chair back to the living room where Lu is forking macaroni and cheese into his mouth.

"You hungry?" Elvis asks us. "You had a big day. Theemth to me you should be thelebrating."

"We just ate, actually," I say.

"A drink then. How 'bout thome Drambuie." He's already pulling glasses and a bottle from the sideboard. I hand the purchasing agreement to Lu who peruses it. I look around for signs of a wife. The decor is distinctly male including a nudey girl calender and posters of motorbikes. Fingered issues of *Sports Illustrated* and girly mags crowd the coffee table. Turner grabs a *Chess Master* magazine from the couch, then wheels to his bedroom where I can see a computer. "He'th playing tholitaire," Elvis explains, handing a glass to Sam who says "no thank you." Like Jerry, he doesn't drink because it means losing control. He only loses control in his sleep.

Lu signs the documents and hands them to Elvis who asks, "Everything hunky-dory?"

Lu nods while putting on his coat. "Got work to do," he mutters. "Next week we do inspection."

"Of course," I say.

He hurries out leaving an awkward pause in which Elvis smiles toothlessly and holds up his glass. "Cheerth," he offers.

"Cheers," I respond.

"Take a pew," he urges.

It's only just dawned on me, because I'm slow about these things, that Elvis has a crush on me. I'm not sure if it's the Drambuie or embarrassment that's heating my face. While we discuss weather, real estate, the price of gas, I'm aware that he considers me to be a two-breasted woman with a future that might possibly contain him if he plies me with enough crullers and Drambuie. I'm touched by this and know without a doubt that if I revealed to him my malady, he would not be fazed. Nothing scares him. He has raised a severely disabled son. He catches me watching Turner. "Thee Pee," he whispers. "Umbilical cord wath wrapped around hith neck. He'th had all kindth of operationth. Nothing workth."

"I'm so sorry."

"Hey, we've all got our problemth."

"Where's his mother?"

"She left. Couldn't thtop crying about it, tho we figured it wath eathier on the boy not having her around."

How extraordinary, to leave your afflicted son.

"Does she ever visit?" Sam asks.

"She'th kind of high-thtrung. It jutht wearth him down."

Elvis is probably my age, maybe a bit older. What is he imagining for his son after he is gone? Who will take care of him? Or does he just not think about it? I would be unable to free myself of the vision of my son in an institution. Or worse, lying helpless in his own shit in the house I'd left for him. Would these visions help me to provide him with a reasonable quality of life while I was living? No. Because I'd be terrorized by them. Like his wife, I would be unable to stop crying about it.

I must learn from Elvis.

He starts to pour more Drambuie. I hold my hand over my glass because I'm driving and because I don't want him to imagine that I'm a two-breasted woman with a future which might contain him. As much as I admire Elvis, I do not want to touch him. I've always been a Beatles girl.

We drive in silence; no Fritos, no pop, no radio. "What're you thinking about?" I ask.

"Turner."

"What about him?"

"He's brave."

"Yeah."

Our house is just home: no stalker, no booby trap. Sybil's lights are out. We say good night but do not embrace. We brush our teeth in our separate bathrooms and bed down on our separate planets. I think of Turner being a little boy unable to do little boy things. I think of his mother seeing this and crying. And running from it. And I realize that this is no different from me denying that there was, is, a problem with Sam. I have run from his unhappiness.

Jerry phones. We have a brief dagger-throwing session in which I raise the maybe-Sam-should-be-seeing-a-psychiatrist question.

"You think he'd listen to a shrink after what he's been through?" Jerry asks. "He'd probably kill him."

"Don't make jokes like that. Ever."

"Listen, what he needs is to get off his ass and do something with his life."

"Take control."

"You got it."

"Goodnight, Jerry." He's still gabbing as I hang up. I try to think. *Does therapy actually help anyone?* The people I know who go to therapy have no real problems and lots of free time. They invent problems so they can go to therapy and use up some of that free time. Somebody once told me it's just like having a coffee with a friend. Excuse me, do your *friends* get paid two hundred an hour to listen to you whine? In that case, count me in, pal, I'm yours, let's grab a java.

No. I must simply be there for my son, as I have never been before.

I creep into the hall, see that his lights are out and listen outside his door. Gently, I push it open and tiptoe to his bed. Moonlight no longer bound by the tree illuminates his face. I bend down to kiss his forehead. My angel. Who killed people.

Hey, we all have our problems.

Thirteen

I wake early because today my tree is landing. Running around outside in my bathrobe, I dither about where to put it. The back door swings open. "Get in here," Sybil orders, "you'll catch your death." This is another thing she believes in: chills. Chills are everpresent, waiting to be caught.

"I'm not cold," I assure her.

"Have some eggs."

We look at the paper. One in four Canadians dies of cancer. Gosh, I wonder if this has anything to do with our environment, not to mention our toxic veggies and hormone-saturated meat and dairy products. And then, not because I'm looking but because it's prominently placed, I see an ad for a cosmetic surgery and laser clinic. A tanned young woman, naked from the waist up, smiles ecstatically while cupping her breasts in her hands. "Look after yourself," the ad advises, then lists the clinic's services: breast enhancement, liposuction, hair removal, face and forehead lift, eyelid surgery, nose reshaping, tummy tuck, skin resurfacing, and permanent fat implantation for fuller lips, facial contouring and stronger chin. "That's what I need," I inform Sybil, "permanent fat implantation for fuller lips, facial contouring and stronger chin."

"That girl's naked," Sybil observes.

"Isn't it great? Porno in our national rag. Have you seen Sam?"

"Sleeping."

I used to be glad when he slept late. Now I want him to experience normal sleeping patterns. I turn on the radio, slam cabinets and coffee cups around in an effort to rouse him.

"Your sister's coming," Sybil says.

"Why?"

"Beats me."

"Is Porky Pig coming too?"

"Doesn't he always?"

"When?"

"She said after their errands."

I rarely see Rachel, even less since the murders. Trying to appear normal around her exhausts me. Rachel, because she grew up in a deranged household, has spent her life practising what she perceives to be normalcy. This includes marrying Porky Pig and selling Amway products. The only abnormal thing she does is consult a psychic. Last year "Mrs. Adams" told her that she would be travelling in the "near future." Rachel went nowhere. Mrs. Adams also told her that she would get sick but that it wouldn't be serious. I suggested that this might portend a head cold.

As much as she drives me crazy, I care deeply for my sister. When we were kids, she was often in my care because our mother was busy collecting empty vinegar bottles, hoarding newspapers and sticking pins through insects. Picking Rachel up from school was my responsibility. But one day, I got busy flirting with Guy who was popular and didn't normally notice me. I arrived late at the playground where Rachel was being pinned to the tarmac by boys her age who were tearing her blouse open. "Let's see your titties," they chanted. I kicked their asses but the damage was done. To this day, Rachel denies that this happened. To this day, Rachel insists that my mother did not make her ears bleed with a fly swatter. I don't know that this is bad. Rachel's able to block out the unhappy memories while I sit around gnawing on them. *I'm* the one with cancer.

"Check this out," Sybil says, pointing to the headline "Robbers Kill Mom." Sure enough, some poor teller was shot to death by ski-masked thieves. She'd worked at the bank for nineteen years. I think of her getting up to go to work every morning, not wanting to go but going anyway. Packing her kids off to school as they whine "do I have to?" and "I hate baloney" and "he hit me first." I see her in winter, huddled at the bus stop, glancing repeatedly down the street, hoping for a bus. I see her squeezed into the crowded subway car, staring into coats, thinking, What am I going to feed the kids tonight? Must stop at the IGA, pick up some of those pork chops on special, oh and milk and some kind of vegetable, what will they eat? Forget broccoli, maybe green beans, although they're expensive this time of year. At the bank, customers scowl and gripe—service isn't what it used to be, more fees, less service, what the bank's doing with the record profits is what they want to know. Mom absorbs their abuse, standing for eight hours in dress shoes because runners aren't permitted, thinking, If I have to do this for the rest of my life, I will die.

Then she does. A trigger-happy idiot steals her life, the one that was killing her.

"That's very sad," I comment to Sybil.

"Sad nothing. The point is, it could be over in a second so stop whinging about it."

"I'm not whinging. I'm planting a tree."

A client phones, imagining that I'm going to jump up and show her more houses. "Not today," I say. "I'm planting a tree."

"You're what?"

I'm having difficulty hearing her which means she's calling from her cordless phone. "My wrists are terrible today," she informs me. "I can't open any lids, turn any taps." I hear water running, indicating that she's in her Jacuzzi. "And my shiatsu machine bruised me." I put up with this client because she's listed her expensive house with me and because she intends to buy a less expensive house for her daughter, as well as a luxury condo for herself.

"Well, not today, Muriel," I tell her.

"Oh, I so wanted to look at houses," she says. "What about later on?" She's South African of the imperialistic order, complains about black crime in Johannesburg as though it bears no relation to white oppression. "I'll pick you up," she adds. "Really, we must settle on one soon, otherwise Devon will go potty."

Devon, her daughter, is expecting. I ponder the commissions

and my legal bills. "Pick me up at three," I tell her. "That'll give me time to set up some showings."

"Wonderful. I'll so look forward to it. I haven't been feeling myself. I ate a Fudgesicle yesterday, whilst I was waiting for my tax lawyer, and now I'm feeling it."

"I'm so sorry. Got to go, Muriel."

Rachel and Porky have arrived, actually his name is Bob, he just looks and sounds like Porky Pig. "Good news about Sam," they say.

"Yes."

"How is he?"

"Asleep."

This worries them. And I too am getting a bit weirded out about his resistance to daylight.

"Anyway, it's such a relief," Rachel offers, "isn't it?"

"Of course."

"Sorry we haven't called or anything. Bob's been so busy."

"A lot of cleaning going on, Bob?" I inquire.

Bob starts to stammer, but Rachel rescues him. "Amway isn't just cleaning products."

"It's a way of life," I suggest.

"Ab . . . ab . . . absolutely," Bob agrees.

"Anyway," Rachel continues, "we just thought we'd drop by to congratulate everybody."

"Congratulate" seems an odd choice of word, but I smile benignly. I'm trying to look normal—although I'm braless in my bathrobe. Poor Bob is trying hard to keep his eyes at head level, which is tricky because he's short. Rachel too avoids the missing piece.

"How's Jerry?" she asks.

"Great." I see Sybil pulling out her crosswords. She does this around people who get on her nerves. The doorbell rings, signalling the arrival of my tree. I scamper outside to greet the two Portuguese tree planters. They nod but offer no words, only grunts and gestures, inquiring where I want to put it. I show them and ask if they think this is a good spot. They grunt and nod and start digging. I marvel that the cigarettes don't fall from their lips.

Rachel comes out and hovers. "You look well," she comments. Tell that to my new lump, I'm thinking but don't say because she's been hurt enough. And because she always reminds me of a colt. Anything can make her bolt.

"Are you planting it for any particular reason?" she asks.

"My neighbours cut down the oak that was here."

"In your yard?"

"No. In their yard. I used to enjoy it."

"Oh."

I wish she would stop trying to talk to me because she thinks she should. Why do we persist in doing things because we think we should?

The Portuguese guys are getting mighty sweaty. I offer them juice, but they grunt and shake their heads. I don't think *they're* bothered by my missing breast.

"I saw Mrs. Adams last week," Rachel offers tentatively.

"And . . . ?"

"She said there's something wrong with my liver, but that I shouldn't see a doctor because he would want to medicate me and that isn't necessary."

"What is necessary?"

"She says I should drink eight glasses of water a day. She says it's stress induced. I have to breathe more deeply into my diaphragm. She says so many of our diseases are caused by stress."

It is unspoken, but what she's telling me is that I must drink eight glasses of water a day and breathe deeply into my diaphragm. From the beginning, she has believed I caused my illness. She has to believe this; they're her genes.

I try to think of an excuse to get away from her, even though I care deeply for her. "I should get some duds on," I say.

"We should be going anyway."

"Okay, well, it was lovely to see you."

We perform a clumsy hug in which she avoids contact with my missing breast.

"We've been invited out for Thanksgiving," she confesses, "otherwise we'd have you all over."

"Of course. Don't worry about it."

I remember her sitting in the shopping cart, pleading to get down. "No no no," Mother says. Rachel starts to cry. "Do you want me to smack your bottom?" Mother demands. Rachel wails. Something's wrong, I know something's wrong. "Shut your face or I'll smack your bottom!" Then I observe that Rachel's chubby inner thigh is turning bright pink because it's being pinched between the plastic seat cover and the metal cart. "It's her leg," I protest, but my mother's off down an aisle, and I'm too small to lift my baby sister from her trap. I too start to cry. "Where's your mommy?" a woman in a turban asks. "Her leg's caught," I explain. "Oh my goodness," the stranger says, lifting Rachel free. "Don't touch my child!" my mother shouts, swooping down on the turbaned woman. "How dare you touch my child. You're lucky I don't call the police." She snatches the weeping Rachel and whisks her to the meat counter. I smile feebly at the woman and push the cart after my mother. No point explaining. No point.

Rachel remembers none of this. Rachel does not have cancer. I kiss her goodbye.

I hesitate outside Sam's door but decide not to invade his privacy. I shower, dress and look out the window at my Portuguese pals who are lowering my tree into her hole. How relieved she will be when they unbind the burlap confining her roots.

Passing his door a second time, I can stand it no longer and gently push it open. "Sam . . . ? Sweetie . . . are you awake?" Please don't call me a cunt-shitting bitch.

His bed's empty.

I sit on it feeling dull and stupid, like when the date doesn't show up. How could you imagine, you ask yourself, that he would show up? You're dull and stupid, why would he show up? You look down at the clothes you so carefully selected, inhale the perfume you so carefully applied and feel like a fool. You wipe the lipstick from your lips and swear that you will never let yourself be fooled again. You are, of course, many times.

Why shouldn't he leave without telling me? He always leaves without telling me.

Did you think he'd ask you to make him pancakes?

Sybil appears in the doorway. "What's going on?"

"He's gone."

"So?"

"I just wish he'd told me."

"We all 'just wish' a lot of things. He'll be back. Come see your tree."

"What if he's killing people in his sleep?"

"He's not killing people in his sleep."

The tree planters stand back admiring their work. "Thank you," I tell them. They grunt and nod and head for their truck. I hug my Ivory Silk. "You're so beautiful," I tell her as I look up into her branches that reach out and upwards, as though she's offering them to birds. Her leaves are turning, some have already fallen. "You sleep now," I tell her, "and when you wake up, we'll have a glorious spring."

Sybil leaves me to do her soup-kitchen duty. Sitting alone on the back steps, wrapped in sweaters, drinking tea, admiring my tree, I listen for sounds indicating that Sam has returned. I plan to be casual when I see him, mustn't make him feel that I don't trust him. I trust *him*, it's his brain I'm worried about.

I can't spend the rest of my life fretting every time he goes out.

Make more tea. A study found that women who drink tea are less likely to get breast cancer. Who funded this one, Lipton? My problem with research is that because it's funded by business it must show results that are good for business. Good for business means "make people buy it for the rest of their consuming lives." Drug companies only fund research that involves blind, controlled studies using placebos and whatever drug they're pushing. This eliminates any research that doesn't involve something that you swallow or is pumped into you. Drug companies want sick people to be treated, not cured. They want to kill you slowly with costly medications.

One sparrow, then another, lands on my tree. Eureka.

The phone rings and I leap for it, hoping it's Sam, but it's Ross. "Great news about Sam," he says. "Now you can start putting your life together again."

I think of Humpty Dumpty—all the king's horses and all the king's men not being able to put him together again.

"How are you holding up?" Ross inquires.

My mind swings back to my microscopic tissues being examined in the lab. Don't go there, I caution my mind while my hand reaches for my lump.

"I'm very happy," I say.

"Good. You deserve it." This idea that some are more deserving of happiness than others baffles me. Don't we all deserve some happiness? Doesn't evildoing result from unhappiness? The evildoer has suffered, therefore he wants somebody else to suffer?

Is that what happened to my son? No. He was asleep.

"I thought you might like to go line dancing," Ross asks. "And maybe afterwards, we could grab a bite."

Why? To ease your conscience? It doesn't matter. I don't care that you don't care. Give yourself a break. Delete my number from your life.

I remember, before Jerry, there were "sensitive" guys who'd linger around my apartment, calling themselves feminists. It didn't take long for me to figure out that these "feminists" were draining and self-absorbed and used "feminism" as a passport to free fucks. Ross is reminding me of such a drain. Although, I can't imagine he wants the nooky.

"Listen, Ross, I've got to boogie."

Next up is housecleaning for the big Thanksgiving dinner. I wrestle with the vacuum cleaner. It wraps its tentacles around me. As I drop to my knees to pull the plug I hear a click, maybe the door. I hold my breath, listening. Nothing. I bend down to disentangle my legs, hear my spinal joints creak.

This tension, this feeling of being a spring about to be sprung, reminds me of another time, when Jerry started screwing the first one, the neighbour who borrowed the pots and pans. I'd wait for him, fantasizing about ripping out his entrails. Often, I'd eat an entire bag of potato chips while salivating over the prospect of carnage. But this is different. I'm stretched to the point of breaking, but my heart is down around my ankles, being kicked around, a bruised and swollen mass—like the Grundys' heads. Where is their daughter now? I want to tell her I'm uselessly, grievously sorry.

I wanted a girl, after Sam, should've punched holes in Jerry's condoms. I didn't feel I was worthy. The abortion clung to me. I'm still not free of it. I know it was a girl.

"Whilst I was at Maxim's in Paris," Muriel tells me as we speed in her Alfa Romeo, "I was the belle of the ball. I've always looked younger than I am. I was at a government office yesterday and all the woman could do was tell me how beautiful I am."

Muriel is old. What was once beauty reminds me of the dried petals people put in dishes in their bathrooms. She's a potpourri of vanities.

"I looked so stunning," she assures me, "that I was put at the head table. My ex-husband was furious."

She dyes her hair jet black, wears so much ivory foundation you fear it might crack and large floppy hats in all weather. She brags about making "too much money" in the stock market while complaining that she has to pay "too many lawyers." She owns several rental properties but has difficulty retaining tenants. Probably because she tells them at length about being the belle of the ball whilst at Maxim's in Paris.

"I can't remember what I was wearing," she adds. "Silk, of course, scarlet or the emerald. In any case, heads were turning, I can assure you."

"Here's house number one," I tell her.

She doesn't like house number one. Back in the sports car, she informs me that she's allergic to everything and that she watched *The Way We Were* at four this morning because she couldn't sleep due to the allergic reaction she had to the Fudgesicle she ate in her tax lawyer's office. "It's a splendid movie," she says. "Robert Redford was such a darling. He's aged rather well. I saw him in *The Bridges of Madison County* and he was divine."

"That was Clint Eastwood."

"Surely not."

"Yes."

"I'm sure you're wrong. It was Bob Redford."

No point in arguing. "Here's house number two."

Apparently the kitchen is too small. Devon requires a large kitchen. I advise Muriel that, for what she's willing to pay, house number two offers a good-sized kitchen. Muriel grimaces. "Devon won't stand for it. She simply can't function in a small kitchen." I met Devon briefly; pouty and fat, she was an enlarged version of her mother. Experiencing a difficult pregnancy, she's been bedridden for the past two months. Muriel has hired a live-in nurse for her and has already interviewed twenty-three nannies and hired two. Devon, as far as I can make out, has had everything money can buy and is having difficulty comprehending that her mother can't buy her out of a difficult pregnancy.

Muriel's cell rings and she says "Yes, darling" into it many times as she tries to appease her daughter. Devon uses her mother as a cutting board, but at least she phones her, needs her. I envy Muriel for having a child with problems that she can usually solve.

Saving the best for last, I feel confident that house number three is a real possibility. Unfortunately, the vendor is present and keeps offering suggestions to improve the house. "You could open up the attic," she advises. "The neighbours did that and it looks truly awesome."

"Are they selling their house?" Muriel inquires.

"Well, no."

"Then why discuss it."

The doorbell rings and the vendor has to let the gasman in to read the meter. I make a break for the kitchen which I know to be generous. "Good quality tile," I point out.

"What a ghastly colour."

"It's white."

"It is not."

"What colour do you think it is?"

"Almond or something dreadful."

"Muriel, this is a good kitchen for the money. We're not going to do better than this."

A little hairy dog appears at our feet and starts yapping. "She'll want a convection oven," Muriel says.

"There's room."

"It needs colour."

"Paint it."

Muriel tries to nudge the dog away with her foot which only makes Muffy yap more. "What a beastly creature," Muriel comments.

"It's okay, Curly," the vendor says, picking it up.

"Would you mind if we take another look upstairs?" I ask her.

"Not at all. We were going to insulate the sunroom but never got around to it. My neighbours did theirs and filled it with plants and things. It's truly awesome."

"My daughter's allergic to plants," Muriel tells her, then, as we climb the stairs, "What *is* that woman wearing? Canadians simply *refuse* to dress properly. I was at my real estate lawyer's the other day and he remarked on how refreshing it is to see someone with style."

Is she, can she, really be this deluded? We look again at the upstairs bathroom and I see us both in the mirror. Me looking haggard and Muriel looking absurd. I know that the Muriels of this world see only what they want to see, but when the physical evidence is in your face, how can you ignore it?

My son killed two people and the jury ignored it.

In a dream last night, he had a bald spot on top of his head. He couldn't see it and I didn't tell him about it. I despaired because I couldn't protect him from premature baldness.

"Devon loathes taps that you have to turn."

"Those can be changed," I point out. "She wanted a walkout deck off the master bedroom. This house has it. She wanted a fireplace and a sunroom and hardwood floors. This house has all those things, as well as a new roof and windows. This is it, Muriel."

My experience with Muriels is that you have to beat them up a bit or they eat you alive.

"Yes, well, it's certainly worth considering," she admits.

The vendor agrees to let me take photos to show the ailing Devon. I use a wide-angle lens to make the kitchen look huge.

Before she allows me out of her car, Muriel tells me that her dentist wrote "very beautiful woman" on her dental record, and that she has to take an osteoporosis medication standing up because it upsets her stomach, and that she's in a bind because her housekeeper gave birth in a van yesterday, leaving Muriel housekeeperless. I'm thinking, You had a fully pregnant woman scrubbing your floors? Is it possible to think only of yourself all of the time? Does money blind you?

In an attempt to give her some perspective on being housekeeperless versus dead, I mention the news item regarding radioactive chemical dust left behind by Desert Storm. It's caused a six-fold increase in cancer in Iraq and is blowing back into Kuwait and Saudi Arabia. Children are dying of leukemia, I explain, because few hospitals on the oil patch have the medicines to treat them. Muriel says, "Yes, well, it's a mess, the desert, isn't it?"

"The stuff remains radioactive for forty-five hundred million years."

"Really, well, you can't say they didn't bring it on themselves. I rented to a Muslim once. Never again."

She burns oil daily and buys stock in oil companies but the devastation has nothing to do with her. You could lay the bodies at her feet and she would step over them. No doubt Muriel's devotion to self-preservation will keep her "looking stunning" for years to come.

I really understand why they cut off Marie Antoinette's head.

Sam's still not home, and I'm going ballistic. Must do something, keep busy; preparations for tomorrow. I lift the turkey out of the freezer and eyeball it. Raw bird has never appealed to me. It's a "Grade A Utility," which I took to mean it would be missing innards which is fine by me as I hate touching them (although Sybil loves chicken livers). But as I free it of its plastic casing, I see that the turkey is missing its right wing. How appropriate as I'm missing my right breast. I feel sympatico with the wingless bird and promise to dress it nicely.

"Sybil . . . ?" I call, wanting company but receiving no answer. She's probably browbeating one of her liberal friends. I turn on the TV and surf through doctors and lawyers and cops and cleavage and arrive at a documentary about kangaroos. Startled by cattle, a group of the lovely hopping creatures scampers further afield, leaving behind baby Jacko. The narrator explains that, according to kangaroo rules, a lost baby is supposed to wait for his mum to return for him. But Jacko becomes agitated, frightened by the cattle and the tall grass rattled by wind. He wanders off, which, the narrator advises, makes him easy prey for dingoes (wild dogs). Meanwhile, his mum has retraced her steps and arrives exactly where she left him. She calls for him with desperate barking cries. The camera takes us back to Jacko who can't hear her and continues to wander. Mummy searches for him through dusk, calling plaintively, and I'm thinking, Can't the frigging camera crew show her where he is? But I'm sensing that this is one of those authentic nature shows that don't interfere with natural selection. As night falls and the dingoes start to howl, Jacko cowers, terrified and weak from dehydration. He needs his mother's milk, but she's given up her search as she can no longer see. I want to scream, Get her a flashlight for God's sake, what's the matter with you people? But no, the camera crew desert the helpless baby while the narrator advises us that it is unlikely that Jacko will live till morning. I'm beside myself, sweating down my left side. I want to jump into the TV and grab Jacko, feed him some warm milk and honey. The station breaks to commercials filled with cars, burgers and cleavage. The problem is I can't tell myself that it's only TV because it's a nature show. This *actually happened.* Next day, the crew find Jacko bleeding from a torn ear and limping badly. He's been mauled by dingoes, the narrator explains, and is losing a lot of blood. Get a frigging bandage, what's wrong with you people? He hobbles onward until, too weak from from his wounds and dehydration, he collapses. Mum continues her search all day and eventually finds him, but he's too stressed and confused to nurse. When she urges him to follow her into the safety of the woods, he makes a brave effort, then falters. She comes back for him, gently nudging him on. Believing in Mummy, he makes it to the woods but again dusk is falling and the dingoes are circling. Still Jacko's too dazed to nurse. He lies motionless with the life draining out of him. I can't watch. I turn it off. On the one hand, we're robbing wildlife of their natural habitat, on the other, we're filming them dying.

The front door opens. I jump up and scurry to the hall. Sam looks at me as though I'm deranged. "What is it?" he asks.

"Oh," I say, trying to sound casual, "I didn't know if it was you."

"Who else would it be?"

"Sybil's still out."

He heads for the kitchen. The fridge opens and closes. "There's hummus and pita bread," I call through the wall. He doesn't answer and I feel myself falling down a chasm, relentless gravity sucking me down, down. I don't want it to be like it was before, won't let it be like it was before. It's cold, I'm cold, I look for a sweater in the hall closet, stealing glances at the kitchen. His back's to me as he sits eating at the table. I push my arms into one of Jerry's forgotten sweaters and sidle into the kitchen. Be casual. "I was just watching this show on kangaroos," I offer.

"Oh yeah."

"It was weird. The filmmakers let this baby kangaroo die."

"Maybe they thought that would attract viewers."

"Maybe. I couldn't watch. I turned it off."

"So you don't know that it died," he points out.

"Well, I'm pretty sure. I mean, he was wasted."

"Was he breathing?"

"I guess."

He takes another bite of his sandwich. "So maybe they rescued him at the last minute."

"Doubt it."

"You should've watched to make sure he was dead."

Why? Is that what you did? Before the cleanup? Or were they still breathing? I can't get it out of my head. I can't. "What did you do today?" I ask.

"Nothing much."

"You were gone a long time."

"Fuck off, Mother."

And that's it. I have no strength for it. Just like Jacko's mum, I can do nothing. I go to my room and take Tylenol, knowing it won't even touch my pain, remembering him at two and a half, pulling the plug in the bathtub and freaking out as he sees a piece of lint going down the drain. "It's okay, sweetie, it's only a piece of lint."

"Where's lint going?"

"Down the drain, baby, into some pipes."

More screams as he imagines himself going down the drain into some pipes. I pick him up and wrap him in a towel. "It's okay, sweetie. Mummy's got you. I'm not going to let you go."

I hear him turn on the fucking TV. On my back in my jungle bed I stare up at cobwebs that I've been planning to remove for months, maybe years. All those good intentions rendered void.

I'm not going to let you go.

Fourteen

I am awhirr trying to sort out this Thanksgiving dinner. I forgot about the pie requirement and had to send Sam to the corner store to procure one. Of course, they didn't have any kind of pie and he refuses to drive to the supermarket because he ran over a cat once. Sybil says she can make a pie, but I have my doubts. "What are you going to put in it?" I ask, envisioning kidneys and livers.

"You can put anything in a pie," she assures me as she starts digging around in the fridge.

"Have you ever *made* a pastry?" I ask.

"How difficult can it be?"

"Very."

"It's flour and water."

We look in cookbooks, I who have never followed a recipe in

my life and Sybil who suffers from heart failure.

It's not like I've never produced a Thanksgiving dinner, but usually I'm less distracted. I keep eyeing my amputee turkey who remains morbidly pale. "It's going to be raw inside, I know it."

"Don't fuss," Sybil tells me.

The Grundys' daughter is outside again. In her car. If Sam's noticed, he hasn't mentioned it. Yesterday I pitied her; today she creeps me out.

And Jerry's coming, called at the last minute, said Gingivitis Girl has the flu, could *he* come. What am I supposed to say, he's my son's father. Maybe it'll be like *The Waltons*. Maybe we'll all hold hands and say grace.

Clouds of flour billow around Sybil as she flaps about a bowl. Apples and pears that have been growing mould spores sit in a pile in front of her. "Do you want me to peel them?" I ask.

She shakes her head. "Get the boy to buy ice cream. Pie needs ice cream."

I find him studying a chess manual. "I didn't know you were interested in chess."

"What do you want?"

"We need ice cream for the pie."

"Christ." I give him money and he goes. I look around his room knowing that if I touch anything, he'll accuse me of snooping. But his closet door is open. I peek inside at the shirts arranged by colour. Why is he so orderly about laundry? I can barely bring myself to hang things up, and forget folding, way better to just stuff things in drawers. Maybe he has a future selling men's apparel. All day long he could sort and fold.

I don't know what I'm expecting to find in here, a body?

"Do you have cinnamon?" Sybil calls.

After much searching, I hand it to her. She has flour in her hair, down her front and on her yellow tiger slippers. The "pastry" looks like papier mâché.

"Where's the roller?" she asks.

"You can't roll that."

"Why not?"

"It's too wet. It'll stick to the roller."

"What a fuss-budget."

"You're supposed to knead it or something."

"You don't knead pastry."

"Fine. Alright." I hand her the roller. Sam returns and slaps a carton of ice cream on the table.

"They only had chocolate," he says.

"You're kidding?"

"How continental," Sybil comments, then waves the roller at me. "Buzz off."

In the basement, I visit what used to be Jerry's wine cellar. Actually, it's just wine racks with a few remaining bottles. I know nothing about wine and select two of the dustiest, assuming they're the oldest. Already they're arguing upstairs. I'll hide down here, wait it out. Perched on the stool facing Jerry's workbench, I realize that it's equipped with many sharp implements. I collect them in a pile—chisels, screwdrivers, X-Acto knives, saws, awls. Then the blunt implements beckon: hammers, mallets, files. All must go. I stash them in a laundry basket and throw towels over them. I'll hide them under my bed later.

I hear Sam stomping up the stairs and his door slamming.

Silence except for the sound of Sybil shuffling about.

All my life, I've been in the middle of fights.

In a dream last night, people were waiting for me and I didn't know why. I was afraid they were going to berate me. When they didn't, I became hopeful that they were going to be nice, but then realized that they were waiting for a bus.

The pie looks torpedoed. I stand speechless, trying to think of how to make a quick trip to the supermarket without offending Sybil.

"Did you know," she says, "that Brazil nickel miners worship Satan?"

"'No."

"They worship Satan because they live underground and he rules underground."

"Sounds like a good plan."

"Incredible, the adaptability of human faith." She searches her cardigan pockets for a cigarette.

"Why do we have to believe in Satan or God?" I ask. "I mean, why can't we just get on with it since we're all going to be compost in five minutes?"

She switches on the stove fan and lights up. "Because we need someone to curse and then beg for forgiveness."

"And kill for."

"Exactement."

I look back at the pie. "Auntie, dearest, will you be offended if I buy a pie?"

"What's wrong with this pie?"

I look at the swollen heap. Words escape me.

"It'll be delicious with ice cream," she assures me as she slides it onto the rack beneath the cadaverous turkey. "Go have a rest," she adds. "You're going to need it."

Conversation is strained at the dinner table. We've all expressed sorrow over the death of Bunny. We've discussed the real estate and stock markets and how Toronto isn't what it used to be. We've discussed the *Farmer's Almanac* prediction of a harsh winter, and chiropractors. Estelle swears by hers, but Jerry tells the story of a man at his racket club who developed back pain, went to see a chiropractor and afterwards could hardly move his legs. The chiropractor told him to "ice," which he did on arriving home. Three hours later, he was dead.

"There's always those kinds of stories," Estelle counters. "My chiropractor has a really good reputation."

"More turkey, anyone?" I ask. It is surprisingly tasty, although

Jerry had to crack a few one-armed-bandit jokes. His jokes have never been funny. At the beginning, I used to laugh at them to cover up the fact that nobody else was. He's definitely on his best behaviour. He wants his son to like him. As if the damage could be that easily mended. Sam says little but has eaten lots of mashed sweet potato and Brussels sprouts which gives me hope. He won't touch the bird because it had a face. Only once has Sybil gone into the kitchen for a smoke, and the pie actually smells good, although the top crust slid onto the oven floor.

But the Grundys' daughter is still out there in her car and this bothers me. That we are celebrating while her parents rot.

"Where are you going?" Jerry asks me.

"I'll be back in a sec."

I try the passenger door but it's locked so I tap on the window. She stares at me, twiddling her hair. On the seat beside her I notice a scrapbook. "Won't you come in?" I ask through the glass. "Please? We're having dinner, you must be hungry."

Abruptly she gets out of the car. I wait for her to lash out at me, but instead she whispers, "I can't tell you anything."

"Anything about what?" I ask. She speaks with a British accent. This surprises me as her parents were Canadian.

"People are always asking me," she explains, "but I can't talk about it."

"You don't have to," I say, assuming she's referring to the murders. "Just, please, come and join us. I'm so sorry about everything. I can't imagine what you're going through."

She walks around the car and faces me. She smells of urine. "Promise," she says.

"I promise."

She opens the passenger door and pulls out an umbrella. It's not raining. "Everyone's entitled to their privacy," she adds.

"Of course." I lead her up the walk, noting my "family" watching us from the living-room window. As we enter, they gawp. "This is Lyla Grundy," I tell them. "She's going to have dinner with us. Would you like some turkey, Lyla?" How could anybody name their child Lyla? This in itself would be a cross to bear. I pull out a chair for her.

"I've told them," she explains as she sits, "that I am sworn to secrecy."

"Who's 'them'?" Sybil asks.

"You know."

"No, I don't."

I hand Lyla a plate. "White or dark?" I inquire.

"White, please. I have to watch my figure." She's rail thin.

"Potatoes?" I ask. "Sprouts?"

"Thank you." She carefully adjusts a napkin over her lap. I glance at Sam who looks as though he's seen a ghost.

"They're just people," Lyla adds.

"Who are?" Sybil asks.

"You know."

"No I don't."

I can feel a storm brewing in Jerry. Why are you doing this? he wants to shout at me. And I don't have a good answer for him. Maybe being swarmed by mutant cells has made me want to get to the nub of things.

Lyla eats daintily, cutting her food into little bits, then popping them in her mouth at regular intervals. "I've always said," she tells us, "that fame is a two-edged sword. They're always complaining about their public personas stealing from their private ones. And I've seen it. It's not easy. Everybody wants a piece of you. But there you are."

Sybil pulls her chair closer to Lyla and peers at her. "Dear," she begins, "we don't have a fucking clue who you're talking about."

Lyla appears puzzled. She puts down her utensils and pats her mouth with her napkin. "The Royals," she explains. "The Queen's a witch, contrary to popular belief. She bathes in apple cider vinegar and stinks to high heaven. But that's beside the point. She's cruel. It's no wonder Charles is so screwed up. I told him, forget about her, forget about being king, just live your life. He was crying. A real heartbreaker, I tell you. It hasn't been easy for him. But there you are." She resumes eating. Sybil exchanges a "she's loopy" look with me. I nod but try to appear calm. Because, if we drove her to this, there is a debt to pay.

Jerry's beckoning me into the kitchen. I follow only because I don't want him making a scene in the dining room.

"What do you think you're doing?" he demands.

"Offering human kindness?"

"What do you think this is going to do to Sam?"

"I don't know. Make him feel some compassion? Anyway, you don't have to be any part of it, Jerr. Leave now. You should be getting home anyway, Natasha might need a hot water bottle or something." I pull the hapless pie out of the oven and take it to the dining room while Jerry's jaw continues to flap. After a moment, I hear the front door slam.

"Dodi," Lyla explains, "was really nice to her. Frankly, I think he found her G-spot. I mean, Charles is your basic missionary-position-only sort of bloke. I don't know what goes on between him and Camilla. I think mostly they ride horses. But there you are. It's the boys I worry about, being motherless."

This from a girl who's motherless *and* fatherless. Estelle fidgets. "I should be going," she says.

"Won't you stay for pie?" I inquire.

"No, thank you. It was a delicious dinner, though."

"I'm glad." I see her out. When I get back, Sybil's asking if Prince Philip fools around.

"He's a bit old for that sort of thing," Lyla says.

"Did he ever?"

"I really can't reveal that information."

"No, of course not," Sybil agrees, "you're sworn to secrecy."

Sam appears not to have moved for twenty minutes. I sit beside him, put a tentative hand on his knee. "Are you okay?" I ask. His foot begins to tap.

"The thing you have to understand about Charles," Lyla elaborates, "is that he never had a childhood. I mean, imagine being this little boy and you have to act so serious all the time."

"No fun," Sybil says.

"I tell him, get out there and *savour* life. You know, he's so into organic gardening and so on and so forth. And those bloody historical buildings."

"Serious stuff," Sybil comments.

"Bloody boring. It's like, live a little." Her British accent is fading and she has resumed twiddling her hair.

She did not look insane at the beginning of the trial. She did not. What have we done?

"Dodi spelled fun, I tell you," she says. "He was a real party animal."

"Some people don't enjoy parties," I offer.

"That's true," Sybil agrees. "Maybe Charles isn't a party person."

"Frankly," Lyla says, "I think Camilla's a mother figure because his own was such a witch. I'd be surprised if they get it on at all." She swallows another Brussels sprout. I try to serve the "pie," but it crumbles.

"Spoon it out," Sybil advises, then goes into the kitchen for a smoke, leaving me alone with the murderer and the victims' daughter who appears to be suffering from post-traumatic stress disorder.

"This is meant to be a pie," I explain. "But think of it as a crumble. Sam, sweetie, can you clear some plates and bring me a serving spoon?" I don't want to leave him alone with her. Magically, he obeys me. I guess he doesn't want to be alone with her either.

Fortunately, Sybil returns toting the ice cream. "What exactly," she asks, "is your relationship with the Royals?"

"She made me swear not to say."

"Who, Elizabeth?"

"She banished me."

"That's not very nice," Sybil comments.

"She's a witch, I tell you."

"I've never liked the look of her," Sybil concedes.

"She killed Diana, it's no secret, but there you are."

"Really?" Sybil dollops a massive amount of ice cream on her pie.

"She hated her because she was everything she wasn't."

"How," I query, "did she kill her?"

"The driver. Her people got him drunk, then drugged him."

"Doesn't surprise me," Sybil says. "That old bat's had it in for the girl right from the beginning."

"Does Charles know this?" I ask.

"He's in denial. I tell him, face it and get on with your life. But he's such a good sport. I wish people would stop making fun of his ears, it's *so* unfair. But there you are." Her twiddling is becoming manic and I notice that the hair is sparse on the sides of her head, indicating that she doesn't just twiddle but yanks strands out.

"Have some pie," Sybil urges but Lyla is beginning a meltdown. Anxiety twists her face. Maybe she's just remembered who we are. She stands, gripping her napkin. Realizing this, she drops it as though it's in flames.

I approach her gently. "Do you want to go home?"

"I believe that we all suffer for our sins," she pronounces.

"I do too." At close range, she seems so tiny; a little bird trapped in the house. I open the front door and she flies off. I'm worried that she's too crazed to drive, but once free of us, she seems to regain some composure and pulls a speedy but perfect U-turn, probably heading down the street to her parents' house. I imagine her unlocking their door, stepping over the stains where they lay, brushing her teeth in the sink that drained their blood.

"Why did you do that?" Sam asks me. Standing in the shadows, he could be Jerry.

"I'm not sure. I think I'm hoping to make amends."

"For something *I* did."

"I did it too, in a way."

Sybil butts in. "Don't get into a snit about it, boy. Be glad you're not crackers yourself."

"Why don't you dry up and die?" he demands.

"Because I'm not leaving you alone with your mother."

"Don't fight," I plead. "Guys, let's not fight."

My pager sounds and I see that Elvis has called. Saved by the bell, I use the hall phone so I can stand between Sam and Sybil. Like two weary old dogs, they circle briefly, then go their separate ways.

"I juth wanted to confirm the time for the inthpection tomorrow," he says.

"Two-o'clock."

"We'll be there."

He pauses and I know he's hoping to prolong the conversation with the woman he imagines has both breasts and a future.

"I wath wondering," he begins, "why you never call me by my firth name."

His real name is Arnold. I prefer Elvis. "I'd be happy to call you by your first name, Arnold."

"Arnie."

"Arnie."

"Thank your boy for me. Turner had a really good time."

"What?"

"Tham took Turner to the bookthtore. He'th alwayth nagging me to take him, but I juth don't have the time."

"Sam took Turner to the bookstore?"

"He didn't tell you?"

"No."

"Oh. Anyway, thank him for me."

"Certainly."

"Tho till tomorrow then?"

"Till tomorrow."

I sit at the hall table listening to Sybil load the dishwasher, and notice that Lyla has left her umbrella behind.

"Can I come in?" I ask.

"What do you want?"

"To apologize." I gently push his door open. He's on his bed looking at his chess manual with socks half off his feet. I always had to pull up his socks. "I don't know what I was thinking," I add.

He glances at me briefly. "You wanted me to know that I killed her parents." He resumes studying the manual. "I know I killed her parents."

"But you don't remember doing it."

"Am I going to be on trial forever with you?"

"No," I say too hastily. He makes a sound like air escaping from a punctured tube.

"Anyway," I mumble, "the important thing is that you didn't know you were doing it."

"That's the important thing." He rests one ankle on one knee and absently waves his foot around. The sock flaps.

"It was nice of you to take Turner to the bookstore," I say. "His dad just called and asked me to thank you."

"He's welcome."

I stare dumbly at him, trying to decide if I should proceed with bad movie dialogue like, why won't you let me know you? and why won't you let me in? and how can I make you believe I love you?

"He doesn't know I did it," he says abruptly to the chess manual.

"What makes you think that?"

He shrugs.

"He might know," I point out, "but doesn't feel it's relevant to your friendship."

"We're not *friends*," he says fiercely. "Don't get all excited about us being *friends*. Me helping the crippled guy and all that shit."

"I'm not. I just . . ."

"You just what?"

"Not everybody has to know you did it. I mean, you can't spend the rest of your life feeling people can't be your friends unless they know you did it."

He yanks off his sock and throws it on the floor. "Are you going to invite her to live with us, like you did with Sybil?"

"Lyla? Of course not."

"You fuck things up and you put a band-aid on it."

"I don't mean to fuck things up. Everybody fucks things up."

"Yeah but most people drop it, you crawl around licking it up." The disdain in his voice severs my vocal cords. I stand mute, having no idea, no idea how to cope with this bile he spits at me. He turns a page of his manual, dismissing me, waiting for me to leave. "What's 'it'?" I manage to ask. "What do you mean by 'it'?"

He pulls off the other sock and tosses it.

"Why," I persist, "tell me why it's wrong to try to help this person who's in obvious need? Her parents are dead. She has no siblings and I didn't notice any helpful relatives hanging around."

"Because it's none of your business."

"It is my business. You killed her parents. I'm your mother."

I hear Sybil behind me and think of her heart. "Enough of this," she says.

"We were just talking," I protest.

"You were shouting."

He streaks between us and down the stairs. Where's he going without socks? I grab them and throw them after him, thinking only that I don't want him to get cold but then realizing that the gesture appears violent. I listen for the front door. Instead, I hear him charge into the basement.

"He's not going to change," Sybil tells me. "You make yourself sick trying to make him into Charlie Brown. Forget it."

"I can't forget it," I snap. "*You* don't have a child. *You* can't possibly understand." Why am I wounding her, too? The two people I love I chase to opposite ends of the house. She closes her door in my face.

Happy Thanksgiving.

I wake surprised to find that I fell asleep. Cancer has this way of knocking your lights out when you least expect it. I hear movement downstairs. Getting off the bed, I see that the laundry basket full of tools has been placed at my feet. Great, he thinks I don't trust him. How can I explain that I trust *him*, just not his cortical function? I flop back, feeling my bones turning watery again. Why bother? Why bother to do, to try, anything? Why not just let the tumours have their feed?

Because I'm all he's got.

Most people "drop it," he said. Is that what he's done? Dropped the murders? Like Rachel has dropped the assault and her abusive mother? What else is he supposed to do? Obsess over it? Practise self-flagellation? Write "I will never kill again" ten thousand times on the blackboard? Fast for fourteen days? Stand in the corner? Swear eternal devotion to the only daughter? Join a prayer group? No. He's dropped it. The bodies are free-falling into oblivion. And he's taking a severely disabled stranger to a bookstore.

I lean heavily on the banister as I begin my descent.

He said I "crawl around licking it up." Is this so bad? Shouldn't we take a look at our own shit once in a while? How else are we supposed to spot the blood?

He's sitting at the kitchen table. "I didn't get a chance to apologize," I say to his back. Receiving no response, I try to appear "cool" as I pour myself some juice. "It was too impulsive. I shouldn't have just brought her in like that. It wasn't good for anybody." Turning to him, I see that he's eating Cheerios, his favourite toddler food. Only he's eating them dry. The milk is on the floor, not in the bowl. I look carefully at his eyes. They have that glassy, starey look. He's asleep. "Sam . . . ?" Many Cheerios fall to the floor as he brings the spoon to his mouth.

I've never seen him sleep-eat before.

This means he pulled the bowl from the cupboard, the spoon from the drawer, the milk from the fridge in a state of unconsciousness.

For the first time I believe it's possible, *feel* it's possible, that he didn't know what he was doing. This belief spills frothy bubbles over me. I sit beside him so that our shoulders are touching, and begin to giggle as I watch the Cheerios tumble to the floor.

Fifteen

Of course it's not a laughing matter. He has walked in his sleep twice in the past week. He is not practising good sleep hygiene. There's no question that his stress levels must be reduced. How? Do I leave him alone again? Become an absentee mother again? I ponder this while Elvis and the undervest-only vendor compare notes on their colonoscopies. "You got to do it," Elvis advises. "A guy I know got a tumour, had to have hith colon out and a year later they went after hith rectum. He'th had to do the chemo, the radiation, the whole bit. Bloated up like an orange."

"How'd they take out the rectum?" Undervest Man inquires. "I mean, like, isn't that part of your body?"

"Gueth they juth cut it off."

Undervest Man screws up his face and says, "Ouch." We follow the house inspector and Lu to the second floor. "So he's got to use a bag or whatever?" Undervest Man queries.

"Gueth tho."

"Fuck me."

"What'd *your* colon look like?" Elvis asks. "Did you watch it on the monitor?"

Undervest Man scratches his Molson tumour. "Kinda red with white spots on it."

"No kiddin'? What'd they thay about that?"

"They said I got pouches."

"Poucheth? You're shittin' me."

"No. I'm supposed to eat fibre. It's nothing serious, right. It's not like I got cancer."

No doubt the vendor is hanging around during the inspection discussing his gastrointestinal tract in the hopes of distracting us from the failings of his house. The house inspector has already scrawled two pages of recommendations, and Lu's looking worried. He brought a retracting measuring tape which he keeps snapping.

"What'd yours look like?" Undervest Man asks Elvis.

"Pink mothtly. He removed a polyp. Thaid it wouldn't hurt."

"Did though, right?"

"A bit.

"Lying bastards."

Elvis chuckles. "They got to lie, otherwithe you wouldn't let them in there."

"I've heard," I venture, "that they suffer from cervical spine disorders from leaning over all the time to see in the scope."

They both look at me blankly. "Neck pain," I clarify. "From bending over."

"No kiddin'?" Elvis asks. "Glad to hear it."

My tooth is hurting. Dobin prepared it for a crown this morning while admiring his new upholstery. As each chair was delivered, he'd stop jackhammering the remnants of my tooth and disappear from my cubicle to congratulate Angelo the upholsterer on his good workmanship. "It's a rarity these days," I heard him say while I lay drowning in saliva, "a real pleasure,

Angelo, to see good craftsmanship in these hurried times." Hurry up and finish my tooth, I wanted to scream but couldn't with all the apparatus gagging me. His body-snatcher assistant stared vacantly at the TV news showing a "toxic house" that sits on fifty barrels of toxic waste. The owner only discovered this when he was landscaping his yard years after he'd bought the house and raised two children in it. A spokesman for the Ministry of the Environment claimed it would cost $500,000 to remove the barrels of lead and zinc and decontaminate the soil. "It's not part of our mandate to decontaminate the land," he said. "We'd go after the previous owner if he weren't dead. The problem is there's no way of determining the source of the industrial waste." Here's an idea, how about industry? Meanwhile, the current owner has removed his family from the house, has stopped making mortgage and tax payments, and is waiting to see what neurological damage has been done to his children.

The house inspector who's called "Spidey" because he hops around like Spiderman points to the ceiling. "It's bowed."

"It's what?" Undervest Man asks.

"A lot of roofs been laid on it. Next time, they all got to be stripped, otherwise your ceiling's going to cave in."

"No shit," Elvis remarks. Lu, apparently beside himself, keeps shaking his head and fondling the sweaty measuring tape.

"I was up there last spring," Undervest Man challenges. "Looked fine to me."

"What were you doing up there?" Spidey asks. "Patching a leak?"

"Now look here . . ."

"Mr. Polyschuk," I interject, "we're simply doing an inspection. It's one man's opinion."

"There's nothin' wrong with this roof."

Spidey shrugs and hops downstairs. I can't even begin to imagine what he's going to find ailing in the basement. It's unfortunate that he was the only inspector available. Someone less thorough would've been more appropriate. Elvis pulls me aside. "Ith thith houth like a dump or thomething?"

"It's cheap, Arnie. Cheap houses tend to be dumpy."

"Lu don't look too happy."

"No, well, you have the option to withdraw the offer."

My pager reveals that Cheeseburger's office has called. This is not good. They don't call when it's good.

I hear Undervest Man getting uppity in the basement. I clamber down to run interference. Spidey has located watermarks on some ancient wallboard.

"There's been no floods since I been here," Undervest Man insists.

Spidey shrugs and moves on to the furnace, which looks about five hundred years old. "I've never seen one of these before," he comments.

"Works great," Undervest Man asserts.

It resembles an octopus. Ducts spread from it like tendrils.

I sense Elvis behind me. "Do you mind if I call you by your firth name?"

"Not at all," I say, feeling my tooth pain spreading over my face, consuming my head. I do not need more pain. Is it possible that Dobin's attention to his newly turquoised chairs detracted from his care of my tooth? If so, I want him dead, or maimed anyway. Dentists have the second highest suicide rate among professionals. I dream of Dobin reaching into his medicine cabinet for barbiturates. "Have another," I tell him. "The pink ones are especially tasty. And don't forget the blues. They're really cool."

Lu and Undervest Man are arguing about the lead pipes. "You say copper in listing," Lu points out.

"In the wall, they're copper," Undervest Man maintains. "You just can't see 'em."

"Why would you replace the inaccessible pipes," Spidey asks, "and leave the exposed in lead?"

"It wasn't me. It was the previous owner."

"Then how do you know they're copper under there?"

"He told me."

"Right," Spidey says, then looks at me. "I'm done."

"Good. Let's go, gentlemen."

"You're a liar," Lu tells Undervest Man.

Elvis grips Lu's elbow. "Eathy, boy."

"Are you calling me a liar?" Undervest Man responds.

"That's what I said."

"Enough!" I say loudly. "We'll contact your agent." As we walk out the front door, Undervest Man shouts, "Why don't you fuckin' Chinks stay in your own country?"

Elvis puts his arm around Lu. "Come on, buddy."

"You people don't belong here," Undervest Man sums up. "Fucking boat people. Fucking breeding like rabbits."

I have a feeling this deal is going to fall through.

Cheeseburger's secretary puts me on hold for fifteen minutes, then insists that she can't give me the test results over the phone, I must come in and see the doctor. "Why can't *he* tell me over the phone?" I ask.

"He wants to see you."

"Yes, but I don't want to see him. I'm very busy right now."

"It will only take a few minutes."

"It never takes a few minutes. I always have to wait for at least half an hour."

"You're not our only patient. Dr. Geisberger is also very busy." Her tone is so cold, so completely without feeling. In person, she even looks like a corpse.

"He can bill me for the phone call," I say.

"Mrs. Pentland, we're very busy—would you like an appointment or not?" She knows I have no choice but to capitulate in the face of their ritual. Patient must obey, cower in front of the great doctor while he delivers the bad news using helpful words like "I'm sorry."

"Whenever," I say.

"Can you come in tomorrow?"

It's definitely looking dicey when Cheeseburger fits you in within the next twenty-four hours.

"Fine," I mumble.

"Eleven thirty." Click, she's gone. Does sharing a waiting room with the sick and dying eight hours a day, five days a week, free you of feeling? Does the transience of it all make you think it's not worth caring? Not worth the effort? Just so much diseased flesh. There's more where that came from. Here today, gone tomorrow.

"Fuck her," I mutter feeling completely, utterly out of control of my illness.

Todd limps into the office. "I can't believe it," he tells anyone who's listening. "I'm in such pain, *excruciating* pain."

"What happened?" I ask as I seem to be the only one in attendance.

"I hurt my ankle in my Salsa class." He collapses on a chair. "I can't even walk. If it's sprained, I will die. I've got an open house this afternoon and we've got tickets to Swan Lake, *orchestra* seats."

"Well," I say, "it's not like you have to dance the swan."

"I can't put weight on it. That's the whole point. I can't walk. And the shits won't give me a refund. This always happens to me." He lifts up his leg and studies his foot. "Does that look swollen to you?"

"Not particularly. Take some Advil, ice it, rest and you'll be fine."

"Can you do my open house?"

"Where is it?"

"Forest Hill. Big bucks."

I wanted to go home, relax, talk to my innocent son. But legal bills are pressing. "Sure," I say.

"She's a world-class bitch, I warn you. Just tell her you love the house and ask for the name of her decorator. Act surprised when she says she did it herself."

"Gotcha."

It's a California-style monster home, almond stucco, terracotta roof. The Filipino housekeeper lets me in and asks if I'm Mrs. Todd. "No," I explain, "he couldn't make it. I'm doing the open house for him." She offers me coffee, which I refuse, then leaves me to admire Mrs. Tanenbaum's decorating. I am inside a seashell, ensnared in pink and puce and silvery white.

"Where's Todd?" Mrs. T demands.

"He strained his ankle. He intended to call you."

"Oh I never listen to my messages. They always want something from me." She has blondied hair that has been back-combed and stands high off her head. Her skin, baked in Florida yearly, appears leathery beneath bright pink blush. "I'm not happy with Todd," she announces. "All talk, no action."

"He really is injured."

"I'm sure. Do you have a card?"

"Of course." I hand her one. "Who did your decorating?" I ask.

"Myself."

"Really? It's charming."

"I'm sick of it. If Todd can't get what I want for this house, I'm going to redecorate. I want to go western with it. I like those desert colours." She pushes open some sliding doors to an indoor pool. "It's heated." She points to an exercise bike. "I bought that for my husband, do you think he ever uses it?"

While following this woman through her maze of bad taste, I have no choice but to listen to her condemn her husband, her neighbours, her neighbours' dog, her daughter-in-law, her caterer, her manicurist, her travel agent. Her frown is so constant that the corners of her mouth hang off her face. If negativity fosters cancer, Mrs. T should be riddled with it.

"I tell my husband," she says, "'Don't come home if you're going to complain.' He thinks I have it easy looking after all this. I tell him, 'Easy is a condo.'"

I think about her race, how they have been forced from their homes, separated from their loved ones, robbed of their dignity, their worldly goods, starved, tortured, gassed, and I think, How can I be irritated by this woman who has oppression, persecution and annihilation in her blood?

"I've never met an honest real estate agent," she tells me. "I always say, if you can't do something useful, sell real estate. My son did it while he was waiting to be called to the bar. He told me what tricks you people get up to."

She still irritates me.

The master bedroom contains a king-sized bed, an enormous television and pseudo–Art Nouveau furniture. The seashell palette continues here although shades of pale green have been added, perhaps to create a calming effect.

"I also like that Provençal look," she says abruptly. "Although everybody's doing it." She looks at my card again. "Pentland. Are you related to that killer?"

"I'm his mother."

She is wordless, briefly. It's as though I've cast a spell. In the quiet before the storm, I feel the world revolving.

"Get out," she orders finally. "I want you out."

"May I ask why?"

"Why do you think?"

"He was found innocent."

"Bullshit, he's innocent. Shrinks will say anything if you pay them enough. Get out or I'll call the police." She's making sweeping gestures with her arms as though shooing out a dog. I want out, but at the same time feel I should stand my ground, defend my son. "He walks in his sleep," I explain. She starts towards me as though about to give me a shove, I step back, catching my heel in her repulsive plush carpet. Steadying myself against the door jamb, I feel her prod my shoulder. "Out," she orders and I realize that within seconds we could be brawling. I'm the weaker and would lose.

"I hope," I tell her as I try to maintain some dignity hightailing it down the stairs, "that when tragedy strikes, you will be met with equal compassion."

"Tell that to the dead people."

The front door clangs behind me and I'm left to admire her Audi. I consider keying it but am too chickenshit. Doubtless she's watching me and would press charges. Instead I loiter, hoping to make her nervous. An agent with clients pulls into the circular drive. "It is without a doubt," I tell them loudly, "the *ugliest* house I have ever seen."

But in my car my bravura fades and I see only what's ahead for Sam. He will not be able to live it down. He could perform three thousand hours of community service, donate his wages to charity, raise money for childhood diabetes. He could act repentant, but it would be futile. Only celebrities are forgiven, and only as long as they remain celebrities.

He's not home. *Quelle surprise.* Sybil's in the kitchen with Oscar, one of her soup-kitchen cohorts. She invites him over because he loves her stews.

"Oscar was mugged," she informs me.

"How horrible," I respond.

"Didn't get much." He turns to me and I see he has a swollen eye.

"Who did it?"

"Teenagers. Boys. They've got no shame these days."

"Did they ever?"

"There was a time when stealing was considered a sin."

"Now they're proud of it," Sybil adds.

Oscar nods. He's a war hero, Dutch, ran through a minefield to warn of oncoming Jerries. What the muggers didn't know is that he keeps his cash strapped to his artificial leg. I think of him Sam's age, recovering in the field hospital, realizing he is missing a leg.

Now he's being mugged by "shameless" teenagers the age he was then. What can he think of my son?

What does it matter?

"Look at this," Sybil says, handing me a piece of newspaper displaying a photograph of two young Indian women whose faces are hideously scarred from sulphuric acid. "Men throw it on them when they refuse their advances," Sybil explains. "They use to throw kerosene on them and light up, but acid works better if you're going for permanent disfiguration."

"How do they get away with it?"

"The women are afraid of them. The police don't press charges, probably because they want the option of throwing acid on women who resist *their* advances."

"Disgusting," Oscar intones.

Sybil inhales deeply on her ciggie butt. "A twelve-year-old girl got it in the face because she happened to be sleeping with her sister who was the target. The little girl heard something outside the window, sat up and—splat—her life is over."

Apparently, the two women in the photograph were beautiful. Now blind with cratered skin, missing noses and chins, they have no choice but to become beggars.

"Sybil," I ask, "does it help you to read this stuff?"

"It doesn't help to be ignorant."

Oscar nods sagely. "People didn't want to know about the camps."

"'Didn't want to know' is wilful ignorance," I point out. "That's a little different from seeking out horror stories in the paper."

"Better to turn a blind eye," Sybil mocks.

"That's not what I'm saying, but we're powerless in the face of their suffering. So why put ourselves through it?"

"Because they deserve acknowledgement of their pain."

"So what are you going to do, e-mail them? Tell them how

sorry you are that they have to spend the rest of their lives begging?"

"No. I'm going to talk about it, make waves, so that maybe one will roll over to Bangledesh one day and shame those lily-livered scumbags."

"Hear, hear," Oscar agrees, spearing more kidney and chewing on it.

I guess this is what keeps her going, the belief that she can make a difference. The rest of us feel like just so much flotsam and jetsam.

My pager sounds, it's Muriel. I call her from my bedroom. Her daughter's in the hospital because they induced labour due to her high blood pressure.

"I'm quite distraught about it," Muriel admits. I hear water sloshing, indicating she's back in her Jacuzzi. "Anyway, she adores the house."

What is Muriel doing in the tub when her daughter's in labour with high blood pressure?

"Is there any other interest in it?" she asks.

"I'll check with the listing agent."

"If there is, I expect we'd better make an offer." What if your daughter dies? I'm thinking.

"It's been a dreadful day," she says. "I'm exhausted. And of course, I ate some peanuts at the hospital and am coming out in spots."

"Is her husband with her?" I ask.

"Who? Oh, him. Completely useless. I don't know why she married him."

"But is he with her?"

"Oh, I expect so. They did all those silly breathing classes together."

I think of shouting, screaming, Your child is in need! But then I realize that Devon probably doesn't want her mother around, informing the doctors about her allergies and how she was the belle of the ball whilst at Maxim's in Paris.

Sybil knocks, then enters. She still hasn't brushed the flour off her yellow tiger slippers.

"Are you and Oscar like an item?" I inquire.

"You kidding? He's too old for me." She sits beside me on the bed.

"Soon all the people who lived that war will be dead," I say. "It's weird, it's like they're our conscience."

"Soon we'll be free of them and can get down to serious hedonism." She pats my knee. "I wanted to tell you that the boy was nice to me today."

"Really?"

"I fell down and he helped me up."

"You blacked out?"

"Maybe for a minute."

"You know we're seeing Fink this week?"

"I know. Anyway, he was gentle and made me tea. I wanted you to know."

"Thanks for telling me."

She kisses my cheek. "Try to sleep, baby."

I stand at the window, watching my tree shimmer in the street light, and look for Lyla, but there's no sign of her car. I miss her.

It is entirely possible, I tell myself, that Cheeseburger wants to see you in person to give you the good news. Nothing nourishes a surgeon's ego like a grateful patient.

I turn on the radio and listen to an ad for hair colour. A breathy woman insists that she uses it because she "deserves it." And I'm thinking, Why do you deserve it, you silly cow, what have you done? Fed any starving children lately? How did we become a society of the deserving? I exist, therefore I deserve. What do the girls with burned faces deserve?

I turn off the radio and feel my lump. It feels smaller, it does. I take deep breaths into my diaphragm, and listen to the dog bark.

I wish Sam would be gentle and make *me* tea.

Sixteen

I stand outside Lyla's parents' bungalow, holding her umbrella. Her car is not in the drive, but I ring the bell anyway. The front steps are overflowing with mail.

Does she no longer read it? Sam climbed these steps, opened this door. Did *he* ring the bell? I turn the handle and am relieved to find it locked. My tooth pain has increased. I phoned Dobin's and spoke with his Scottish squeeze. "Sometimes it takes a wee bit of time to settle," she told me.

"Okay," I replied, "but is it normal for it to feel like someone's ramming a chisel into your face?"

There was a little belch of silence before she said, "Why don't I have a word with the doctor about it and get back to you?" She pronounced "you" as "ewe." Of course she didn't get back to me. The doctor's a busy man, just like Cheeseburger who I'm seeing in an hour. I'm so nervous about it my pulse keeps jerking my body around.

I walk to the back of the bungy and see piles of garbage. Lyla seems to have forgotten about garbage day. Big critters have chewed away at the bags, allowing entry of smaller critters. I hold my nose, climb the back steps and peer into the kitchen. It's piled with remnants of various takeout foods, especially Mr. Pong's. I've never ordered from him myself but have seen his delivery cars with sandwich-board menus strapped to their roofs for years. The day I was diagnosed with cancer, I was stopped in traffic beside one and busied my mind by reading about Tai Dop Voy and Moo Goo Guy Pan, understanding I would die and that Mr. Pong's sandwich boards would roam the streets forever. This reminder of my mortality left me feeling no more significant than an egg roll, and strangely calm. I'm still here, though, and so is he, in the mad girl's house. I can't imagine her placing an order. Does she tell the operator about what Dodi did? Seriously, who can she talk to in a day? I've seen no trace of friends or co-workers. What did she do before her parents were killed?

I notice many fortune cookie messages taped to the fridge. Black magic marker shoots off some of the messages and dives into others. The kitchen table is covered with press clippings. I spot the hideous drawing of myself, a photo of Prince Charles in polo gear, and one of the "witch" Queen herself that has been assaulted by felt pen. Why wouldn't Lyla have desecrated my likeness with magic marker? Why have I been spared her wrath?

I look at my watch and realize I must dash so I can sit around and wait in Cheeseburger's office. Speeding downtown, I check my messages. Muriel's daughter is hemorrhaging, but the baby seems fine so Muriel wants to "start the preliminaries" on the house deal. This is good news because Elvis and Lu have backed out of the junk house. I turn on the radio and hear that tomato-based foods *may* cut cancer-risk. The "studies" showed that tomato in many forms including raw, ketchup, spaghetti sauce, tomato paste and salsa offered benefits. Who came up with this one, Heinz? Regardless, I vow to eat more tomatoes, although they're supposed to be bad for arthritis, aren't they? Hard to keep track of the goodies and the baddies. Best not to eat anything.

I've definitely spent too much time in doctors' waiting rooms. When will it be discovered that plastic palms emit cancer-causing gases? Cheeseburger's obviously behind because women fearing death sentences surround me. No one speaks, we listen to EZ rock on his radio and thumb through *Time*, *Maclean's*, *People*. Actually, I'm the only person catching up on my reading. Most of them shift in their seats, sigh, look beseechingly at his corpse of a secretary who does not even glance up as we enter. I would like to leap the barrier dividing her from us and fart in her face. But I've never been able to fart at will. Instead, I pick up a fingered newspaper and read that our Environment Ministry is ignoring public complaints on several environmental threats due to budget cuts. Complaints to be "met with no further response" include illegal dumping of sewage from pleasure boats, pesticide infractions, foul-tasting drinking water, littering, poorly functioning commercial-recycling programs, all filling of wetlands or property, and all discharges to storm sewers. So Joe Schmo can continue to pour paint thinner into our water supply, dump his garbage on our property, and poison our children with pesticides. There's progress for you.

And then, in this very same paper, I read about a woman whose children developed blisters every summer when they played in a municipal park. "It sort of looked like poison ivy," she says. But fortunately, she wasn't your average couch potato citizen. She *investigated* and found out that the park was built on a dump site that was leaking contaminants including ammonia and heavy metals.

Is this how it's going to end? Our garbage will rise up and defeat our immune systems? Is this what we deserve?

Anne Murray's on the radio singing about dreaming and falling in love. This is too much. I try to distract myself with *People.* On the cover is the "sexiest man alive." I don't recognize him. You know you're in trouble when you don't even *recognize* the sexiest man alive. I'm about to read about Madonna's latest transformation when the corpse summons me, I presume because I'm being "fit in." The women with actual appointments glower at me. On entering I smell mouthspray, which indicates that he's just had a squirt. He's at his desk on the phone and signals for me to sit. The corpse places my bulging file in front of him. After a moment, I discern that he's speaking with his accountant. "So you need me to write another cheque," he says several times. "That's no problem, I'll just write another cheque." He's sounding too eager, too willing, there's got to be some tax evasion there somewhere.

I stare at his family photos. Lots of teeth and tan. Is it real?

Are the Cheeseburgers really one happy family? I remember the Velveteen Rabbit wanting to be "Real" and the Skin Horse explaining that you had to be loved to become Real. The Velveteen Rabbit could not imagine this happening. But to his amazement, the boy did grow to love him and make him Real. When the boy came down with scarlet fever, he wanted his bunny by his side. Once the illness passed, the Velveteen Rabbit was snuck away from the boy and thrown on a pile to be burned because it was thought he carried the virus. But the Nursery Magic Fairy rescued the rabbit, kissed him, making him really Real, and set him down among the other rabbits. "That means Mr. McGregor will put him in a pie," Sam informed me.

"Maybe not, sweetie, only if he catches him." And anyway, why think about that? Why not believe that the rabbit will dance forever in the moonlight?

Cheeseburger hangs up, looks at me, opens my chart, picks up a pen, looks at me again. "It's not good," he tells me.

I have one of those moments in which I levitate and hover above, watching him watch my body which is still in the chair. The sun beams in the window and glints off his computer screen. He says something about worrisome cell changes. Sounds familiar.

"However, the results from the biopsy were inconclusive," he adds.

SO YOU WANT TO CUT ME OPEN AGAIN, RIGHT?

"There were hardly any cells on the needle I used to aspirate the lump."

I always wanted to be the Nursery Magic Fairy. It seemed like a nice line of work if you could get it.

"So we're talking about more surgery," my body says.

"Right. We'll do a frozen section of the lump. If it's malignant, we can remove the tumour and some of the surrounding tissue but leave the breast intact. We'll do a separate incision for node sampling."

"Then what?"

"Adjuvant therapy, *if* it's malignant. Don't get ahead of yourself. Wait for the lab results, then we'll talk. When did you last see your oncologist?"

"Ages ago. I thought I was better." I hate the oncologist even more than the surgeon. At least Cheeseburger puts himself on the line, doesn't just send you off for poisoning and burning. The oncologist never leaves his desk, just sits there, growing fungus.

"You're not cured," Cheeseburger reminds me, "until you've lived free of it for twenty-five years."

"I know all that. I wanted to *think* I was better."

"That's understandable."

"I was trying to be positive."

"There's positive, then there's denial."

"If you remove the tumour, and the surrounding tissue, and toss in a few lymph nodes, the breast isn't going to be left intact."

He scribbles on my chart, closes it. "There'll be some swelling, the nipple may drop a little. You may have to get a smaller prosthesis to match it."

"Just cut it off," my body says.

"What?"

"I don't want it anymore. It's over. Cut it off." I crash back into my body.

He looks uncomfortable, even peeved. Here am I, he's thinking, offering to preserve her womanhood, and she's talking about butchery.

What womanhood? What's left? I want life.

"Why don't you think about it for a while?" he says. "We'll book the surgery and you can let me know what you want to do." He's rising from his chair, my file in hand, my time is up. Nowhere to turn, nowhere to go, my frightened self cowers inside my body.

"Don't worry too much," he advises. "Worrying doesn't help and it may harm."

Thank you so very bloody much. I'm going to go out and

celebrate, swallow four gallons of Chunky Monkey ice cream. Not worry, are you *insane*? He must be insane, to do this kind of work. This kind of gruelling, grinding, merciless work. I suspect he never wanted to be the Nursery Magic Fairy.

Todd approaches on crutches. "You're going to have to find a way to deal with being his mother," he advises me. "Otherwise it could ruin your career."

"Thanks for the tip."

"Tanenbaum's told *everybody*. The whole of Forest Hill is going to be on the lookout for you."

"Nice to be famous finally," I say and head for a vacant room in which to make my calls. I set up some showings for Elvis and Lu, prepare a purchasing agreement for Muriel and advise the listing agent that we're going to be presenting an offer. She warns me that it could be a multiple-bid situation. I'm not surprised as it's a good house. Muriel was hoping to lowball, but I leave a message with her suggesting that this might not be prudent. I call Dobin's office again and Scotty tells me to come "straight-way," which I do so I can sit around in his waiting room thumbing through *Time*, *Maclean's*, *People* and a fingered newspaper. I'm pleased to read that the baby who was mauled by dogs has recovered. "The dogs just wanted to help," his mother said. "He was crying and they picked him up like they do their puppies." She'd found the baby in a pool of blood with cuts and bruises all over his head. Do mommy doggies cut and bruise their puppies? How *dumb* can people be?

And more government money's being pumped into prostate cancer research. Our Minister of Health, whose dad died of it, claims that greater attention must be paid to the disease. Before *his* balls have to be cut off, he means.

Then Scotty's ushering me into a cubicle. I recline on the turquoise chair and listen to Dobin chat with a neighbouring patient about his trip to Cuba. "Very nice," he insists, "lovely resort, nothing particularly Cuban about it."

You mean you didn't see poor people living in huts while you sipped your pina coladas?

But when he arrives at my side I try to appear friendly because I want him to fix my pain. He prods around a bit, then gets his assistant to X-ray me. More radiation. Dobin studies the slide and announces that I will have to have a root canal. "What?" I say. "Why?"

"The root looks like it might be a bit swollen."

"'Might,' as in, you're not sure?"

He proceeds to freeze the tooth locally to determine if the pain is coming from the tooth. Even with the anaesthetic, I still feel the chisel. "Could be a sinus problem," he muses. "It's up to you, you can have a root canal or just wait and see what happens."

"What might happen?"

"An abscess. Or it might settle down. Sometimes the nerves get a bit jumpy."

"Is a root canal another thousand bucks?" I ask. He nods indifferently, what's a thousand bucks between dentists. I want to shove metal instruments into his mouth. "I had no pain before you worked on the tooth," I point out.

"Sometimes, if it's a deep filling, the work on the tooth can cause it to crack."

"But it wasn't a deep filling." I know because I looked at the X-ray.

"Not particularly." He looks agitated, eager to move on to the next patient, the next dollar sign. "It's up to you," he repeats.

"I'll wait."

I cruise by Lyla's and see her car in the drive. I park on the street, grab the umbrella and climb her front steps, all the while sensing that I'm being watched from within. She takes ten minutes to answer the bell. When she opens the door, the smell of decay hits me. "Yes?" she asks.

"You left your umbrella behind."

"Where?"

"At my house. You were over the other night."

"Was I? Well, there you are. Come in, come in."

"Actually, I should probably get home."

"What nonsense." Her English accent has been reinstated. "I always say, why bother knocking if you don't want a cuppa." She drops the umbrella into a stand already crowded with umbrellas. "Help yourself," she says waving at the dining table which I realize is the source of the smell. It's laden with cold cuts, cheese slices, devilled eggs, dips, veggies, cupcakes, a trifle, all untouched and days old. Birthday decorations abound, colourful banners, hats, balloons, whistles.

"Were you expecting someone?" I ask.

"Yes, well they came, didn't they, but then they had to go. Horrid lot."

"Who?"

"Sometimes I wonder why I bother? But there you are. Sit, sit, sit." I do and watch her perform a kind of dance. She struts, then pivots and glances over her shoulder at me, only she doesn't seem to be looking at me. I check behind me and see a mirror.

"I've always looked ravishing in periwinkle," she says. "I prefer violet, but there you are."

"Are you dressing up for any particular reason?"

"Questions, questions," she says, striding towards me like a runway model and stopping inches from my feet. She pivots and looks over her shoulder at herself. She's wearing a chiffon dress that probably belonged to her mother because it's distinctly fifties. The silver pumps, too, probably were her mother's because they're obviously too small. Many strings of artificial pearls hang from her neck. Her fingernails are painted fuchsia.

"I've had so many offers on the house," she tells me.

"I didn't know you were selling."

"Well I wasn't, but then all these offers came in and other . . . opportunities." She snatches a large envelope from the mantel and waves it around. "I'm about to be awarded a *large* sum of money." She pulls out an eight-by-ten headshot of Ed McMahon, Johnny Carson's sidekick, the stiff who said "Heeeere's Johnny!" and went "ha, ha, ha" at Johnny's jokes. Lyla kisses the photograph. "Isn't he handsome? And *so* generous." Since off the air, Ed McMahon has had many part-time jobs, including lending his image to publishers' clearing houses.

"Have you actually won any money?" I ask.

"Ed says I'm *guaranteed* to win. If not the grand prize, the Cadillac. Which I intend to sell for a sizable sum."

"Lyla, I think if you read the small print, you'll find that you have to send *them* money, or at least subscribe to their magazines."

"Oh phooey," she says. "Ed's a man of his word. And do you know what else? I have a plan." She fans her hand in front of her mouth as though she's just eaten something hot. "But you mustn't tell anyone."

"Of course not."

"Swear."

"I swear." I notice photos on the mantel: her parents, Lyla with her parents, Lyla in a graduation gown, Lyla as a baby, a toddler, a child, an awkward teen.

"Microchips," she whispers. "It's *tremendously* exciting."

She may be raving, but she's more energized than anyone I've ever met.

"Laminated toenails. *Brilliant.* It's a money-maker. Think of the uses. All those missing children, soldiers, earthquake victims, convicts. And you know what else?"

I shake my head.

"I'm going to sell them *online.*" She holds up her index finger. "But it's *my* idea. I'll go public eventually, that's where the money is. Would you like a sausage roll?"

"No thanks."

"Are you a veggie? I've got veggie wraps here."

"No, I'm not hungry, really."

She wags the finger at me. "It's *top* secret."

"Of course."

"If the witch finds out, she'll want a piece of it. Greedy guts."

"I won't tell anyone. I just think you should be careful about investing money you don't have yet. Wait till you get the cheque."

"Oh phooey." She sits and swings one leg over the other. "I can't decide where to live. Maybe Monaco. Ed favours Saint-Tropez and I'm inclined to agree, except for all those Frenchies." She sticks her finger into the curdling trifle and licks it.

"Lyla, don't you think we should clean up a bit, since they came and left already?"

"Don't worry, the girl will do that."

I know there's no girl. "Please, I'd like to help," I persist and begin clearing the table. Fortunately, she's become absorbed in Ed's photo again. I rummage around looking for a garbage bag, finally find one in a drawer stuffed with plastic grocery bags. I begin removing Mr. Pong's refuse from the kitchen table and surrounding surfaces. It is underneath several chow mein boxes that I discover the empty pill bottle. I quickly slip it into my pocket.

"Have you had any communication with the Royals?" I inquire.

"Oh them. What a lot of babies. She's all upset because her teeth are brown."

"Who is?"

"It's drinking all that tea. I said, 'Spend some of your riches on getting them whitened.' She's too cheap." She brings in a vegetable platter. "You're sure you won't take any of this home?"

"No thanks."

"Seems such a waste. I'd eat it only I'm watching my figure." She stops still and looks at the hideous drawing of me. "That's you, isn't it?"

"Yes."

"Remarkable likeness." She taps her finger against her lips, apparently pondering something, then abruptly turns and studies her fortune cookie messages. "This is my favourite," she says pointing to one of them. I lean forward to read the tiny print: *You have at your command the wisdom of the ages.* A magic-marker arrow points from this message to *Sing and rejoice, fortune is smiling on you.* From here the black line goes to *You are a person of culture,* and from here to *Avert misunderstanding by calm, poise and balance.*

She created this party and no one came. I picture her in a frenzy of preparation, anticipating what? Imagining what? Ophelia thought she could float.

"I'd like you to leave now," Lyla says.

"Okay."

"I'll let you know."

"Okay." I don't ask about what. I grab my purse and escape through the front door. If nothing else, I've reduced the chances of her dying from botulism. I don't want her death on my son's conscience; her delirium is bad enough.

My tooth pain is making me want to tear my head off. How can it be that I have cancer *and* tooth pain. Is this fair? When you have a biggie, you figure you've been dealt your final blow. No more smallies, thank you, my dance card is full. I can't have dental work if I go through chemo because of the risk of infection. Chemo is a "non-selective therapy," destroys everything in its path, good cells and bad, leaving you defenceless.

I'm so tired of thinking about sickness and death. I never used to think about it, it was over there some place, happened to other people. Oh good, Jerry's car's in my drive. If I had the strength, I'd turn around and burn rubber to Thunder Bay. But I'm too weary. I want my bed. I want my son.

"Don't get ahead of yourself," Cheeseburger said. He said the results were inconclusive.

"Fancy meeting you here," I say to my former he-man who's wearing an orange jacket that Gingivitis Girl must've chosen for him because I've never seen him in a bright colour. It makes his face fade, his eyes shrink.

"Sybil let me in," he informs me.

"Did I have a choice?" she asks. She's frying up some gizzards. Maybe the smell will drive him out.

"Where's Sam?" I ask her.

"No one seems to know," Jerry responds.

"Where's no one?" I say. "Let's ask him."

Jerry opens his mouth, closes it again and shakes his head in that I-can't-believe-how-ridiculous-you-are manner.

"Well," I say, "I'm pretty knackered. I'm going to pack it in. Say hi to Sam for me if you see him."

"Don't you think you should *know* where he is?" Jerry asks.

"He's eighteen, almost."

"Oh for God's sake."

"Lay off her," Sybil warns, and I find myself hoping she'll crown him with the frying pan.

"I think he should spend some time with me," Jerry announces.

"What?" I say. "Are you nuts?"

"You obviously need help with him."

"She does not," Sybil says.

He turns to her and holds up his hand. "Could you . . . would you please stay out of this?"

"No."

"It's alright, Auntie."

"If I have to take you to court," he warns me, "I will."

"He's no longer a minor," I point out. "He can think for himself."

"Unless he's asleep."

I look straight into those shrunken eyes. "Is that supposed to be funny?"

"Lord, no, you're the only one allowed to be funny."

I sit because I can no longer stand. "Jerry, you don't even like him, and he knows it. It's over. Fuck Natasha and have another one. See if you can do it better next time."

He leans over me breathing fish breath. "You are sick. You may die."

"We're all dying."

"Some sooner than others. Don't you think he should start making new alliances now?"

"He is."

"What do you mean, 'he is'?"

"Where do you think he is now? Socializing with his enemies?"

"Do you *know* any of his friends?"

"Of course," I lie.

"Well, let's phone them up, get him home, let him decide what he wants to do."

From somewhere deep in my resource centre I find strength to send out don't-fuck-with-me radar. My eyes narrow, and my voice becomes Darth Vadery. "Listen, Gerald, if you want to speak with him, you do it on your own time and not in my house. You pick up a phone and call him and make arrangements. You do not come here uninvited. And I warn you, if you fuck with his head, if you make him think you want him, then change your mind because your twat doesn't want him around, or because you're tired of picking up his socks, I'll kill you. Us cancer victims are facing life sentences anyway, committing murder might be a nice change of pace."

"She's not kidding," Sybil advises him.

He resumes shaking his head. "It's obvious to me that you're losing your mind. I don't know if it's menopause or cancer or what it is, but it's obvious that this is the worst possible place for him. He needs to make a fresh start. Get away from all this."

Something about his repetition of the word "obvious" slows me down. I speak it soundlessly, feel my mouth open for the "ob" and close for the "vious." "That may be so," I concede. "Let him decide. I'm going to bed."

I lie wasted like a gutted whale. Jerry's probably right. What good is watching me go through more surgery going to do him? Or living in the house that sheltered his discordant childhood? I must let my baby go, gently down the stream, merrily, merrily, merrily. He used to love that one, couldn't pronounce the r's of course, "mewily, mewily, mewily, mewily, life is but a dweam."

The Grundys' faces drift before me, smiling, ill-fitting dentures protruding slightly giving them a goofy look. They stand arm in arm, and kneeling before them is their bashful twenty-something daughter, her hair falling over her face, a twisted smile on her lips. They must have had her late. Maybe they tried for years, prayed to their God that He would bless them with a child and when He did, they were forever in His debt, worshipped Him on TV when they no longer had the stamina to visit Him in church. Worshipped Him on TV so that they would be available for slaughter.

When did their baby go mad? Did they know? I feel in my pocket for the pill bottle, pull it out and study it. Lithium. So she's been treated. I check the month, the year. It predates the murders. She was there before, Sam, we poured salt into the wound but we did not make it. This offers me some comfort, some.

Seventeen

The phone wakes me. It's Elvis and I wonder why he's phoning me in the middle of the night, then I look at the clock and see that only an hour has passed.

"You want to come to McDonald'th with uth?" he asks. "Tham'th over here. They're doin' thtuff on the computer."

"Umm . . ."

"You ate already? Come for a coffee or a McFlurry or thomething."

"Does Sam know you're calling me?"

"How do you think I got your home number?"

"Oh. Right. Well, can I talk to him?"

He calls "Tham" once, then twice while I try to shake myself free of my dream. I was on a flying trapeze with my son small between my legs. "Hold on," I kept warning him. He tried desperately to grip my thighs, but his little hands kept slipping. I knew that if I reached down to grab him, we both would fall.

I hear the receiver being passed and Sam's voice. "Hi."

"Hi," I respond. "Arnie's asked me to go to MickeyDee's with you and I just wanted to know if you're comfortable with that?"

"Sure. Whatever."

If I let you go, we both will fall. "I don't have to come."

"Come, just hurry up, we're starved."

"Okay."

He hangs up. I'm so excited to be going for burgers with my boy. I'm so excited. Of course my prosthesis is playing hide-and-seek and my mascara is crumbling and I've got bed-head. But I'm going for burgers with my boy.

"Tho what kind of name ith Greer anyway?" Arnie asks me as he frees his Big Mac from its wrappings.

"She was a movie star, in the forties."

"Your mom wanted you to be a movie thtar?"

"I don't know what she wanted." She wanted a son, I would say if Sam weren't present.

"Maybe *she* wanted to be a movie thtar," Arnie suggests.

"That's possible." There have been no warm greetings, but Sam did open the door for me, and got us napkins and little containers of ketchup. Turner manages to feed himself with his good hand, but occasionally Arnie catches falling food with practised ease. At regular intervals, he wipes his son's chin with a napkin.

"That'th thome thtory about the old lady got hit by a bike."

"Yeah," I agree.

"Imagine that, eh? Cruithin' along and wham, a two-wheeler thendth you to your maker."

"Not what you'd expect."

Before, in another life, the one without end, I would have been embarrassed to be seen in public with a man who looks like an aging Elvis impersonator. Now it feels absolutely appropriate. I look at the stiffs around us, stuffing hydrogenated fat into their mouths, frowning into their Diet Cokes, and I feel gloriously unencumbered. But Lyla should be here, in her fifties chiffon, telling us about what Charles did to Di. Then we would be complete.

The boys depart for the game centre. I watch as they become absorbed by the violence on the monitor.

"Do they talk much?" I ask Arnie. "Who?"

"Turner and Sam."

"Don't think tho. Don't need to." Arnie's wearing glasses, I guess usually he wears contacts. The lenses are thick and transform his eyes into spheres.

I bite my burger, feel that secret sauce dribbling down my chin. "Does Turner know what Sam did?"

Arnie shrugs. "I didn't tell him."

"Don't you think he should know?"

"What differenth would it make? The boy wath athleep. It'th not like he'th a killer."

"No."

"Don't thweat it."

"I suppose there's a possibility that he does know," I muse. "That he saw it on the news."

"It'th pothible." He finishes his fries and wipes his hands on a napkin. "Tho, theen any good movieth lately?"

"Ah, no. I don't go to movies."

"Why not?"

"I don't know. I just never think of it."

Arnie nods. "They're not ath good as they uthed to be."

"What is?"

"What'th that?"

"What is as good as it used to be?"

He sucks on his straw. "You know, I wath thinking about how you theem thad all the time."

"I'm not sad all the time." This is where he tells me how he's going to show me a good time.

"I'm thad too," he admits. "There'th a lot of thingth goin' on that don't theem too good to me."

"Like what?"

"Children being abandoned, abuthed, thtarved. That thtuff really geth to me."

"Me too."

Sam asks me for money for ice cream which I give him with pleasure. I watch him stand in line, gazing up at the menu. He's so tall, so lovely, so innocent.

I consider telling Arnie about the cancer, thereby relieving me of my womanly duties. But then he wouldn't invite me out for burgers with my son. Besides, being considered normal is kind of fun. I find myself trying to show him my "good side," the side with the real breast. Which gets me to thinking about breasts again. Todd told me that one of his clients had a breast reduction. They cut off her nipples, sucked fat out and sewed the nipples back on again. But one of them didn't take, shrivelled and dropped off.

"Do you play cardth?" Arnie asks me.

"No." I realize it's beginning to look like I'm a stick-in-the-mud. I try to think of what I like doing. Gardening. "I enjoy gardening."

"No shit? You got to come over and give me thome tipth. I've been meaning to plant thomething in back of the houthe. You know, flowerth and whatnot."

Two hugely fat women absorb the chairs beside us. Between them they must be consuming every cancer-causing food ingredient available. After a brief inspection, I am left with no doubt that their breasts are real.

"I'm big on shrubs and trees," I tell Arnie. "Privacy."

"Thoundth good."

The fat lady with the Marilyn Monroe do talks on her cell. "We're pissed at you, Corky," she chides. "Me and Liz have just about had it wit' you. It's not like we don't got nothing better to do."

"If you plan it right," I advise Arnie, "you can have a shrub in flower most of the summer."

"No shit? And you don't have to weed 'em."

Beside the fat ladies, a little boy jabs another little boy with a straw and chirps, "Do you watch wrestling? You got to watch wrestling. We watch it every Saturday."

"Ass face," the bloated Marilyn says into her phone before shoving it in her purse.

"Asshole," the other fat lady agrees.

Sam has returned to the game centre with the sundaes where a square-headed bully has pushed Turner aside and monopolized the controls. Sam speaks quietly at first but then I hear "cocksucker." Squarehead stands and starts pushing my slight son who can't push back because of the ice cream. Instead he tries to circumvent Squarehead to deliver the sundae to Turner whose head has begun to wag from side to side. Squarehead lands a punch on Sam's shoulder, launching the sundaes into space. Sam spins around and tries to reciprocate the punch. But Squarehead's clearly no stranger to skirmishes and ducks out of the way. Meanwhile, Arnie has jumped up to pull Turner out of the line of fire. Squarehead wallops my son again in the solar plexus. "Stop it!" I hear myself scream as I run towards them.

"That's the murderer!" the bloated Marilyn shrieks. "That's the psycho who killed those seniors!"

Sam tries to kick Squarehead, but my grip on his arm throws him off balance. He tumbles into me and we crash to the floor, into the ice cream. A circle of ugliness forms around us, squinty eyes and snarling mouths. Arnie forces his way through. "That'th enough now, he wath found innothent in a court of law."

"Bullshit," declares a pumped-up short boy.

Arnie helps me to my feet, Sam jumps up ready to fight, but I grip his arm again. "It's not worth it," I say into his ear. "Think of Turner. We have to get Turner home." This works, he scowls at the crowd, but allows me to lead him away, like a prisoner.

"Drambuie?" Arnies asks.

"Please."

We've sponged the ice cream from our clothes.

In the car, all Turner said was, "Is it true?" Sam didn't get a chance to answer because Arnie repeated, "He wath found innothent in a court of law." We drove on in fetid silence.

Now the boys are watching some inane futuristic movie in which women with cleavage scamper around in metallic body-suits while men with shaved heads stand at control panels looking grim. I don't know what we're still doing here. It's as though we're afraid to be alone together, especially home alone together. I thought Sam might leave without me, walk the city as he has been known to do. But he lounges on an easy chair, Nikes off, ankle crossed over knee, foot jiggling, sock flapping.

"Thometimeth you jutht got to look the other way," Arnie says. I nod in solemn agreement although I don't know if he means look the other way from the bullies or look the other way from the killer. I remember this horrible, horrible period when Sam was being tormented by boys at his elementary school. I only knew about it because the principal called and told me that Sam refused to go out at recess and would I please speak with him about it. After much questioning, Sam admitted that one boy shoved him.

"Just one?" I asked.

"It's usually him."

"Why do they shove you?"

"I don't know." He looked at his knuckles. "I'm not supposed to hit back, right?"

I didn't know what to say to this. Experience had taught me that you do hit back, really hard, so they don't ever hit you again. But was this something I wanted to teach my son?

"There's this one guy," he added, "who's smaller than me. I could probably beat him up."

"Why would you want to?"

"To show the others."

"They'll just pick on you for beating up someone smaller than you are. I'd just try to ignore them."

I told the principal to let him stay in at recess. My actions taught my son that it's okay to be afraid and do nothing. Now he wants to fight.

Arnie gestures grandly for me to sit on the couch under his bay window. Once sitting, I lose sight of the boys on the other side of the dining-room set. I hear only the TV emitting outer-space noises. Arnie sits beside me on the couch, a little too close. His body odour, a cross between mildew and putrefied socks, permeates my nostrils.

"Did you hear about the black kid?" he asks.

"What black kid?"

"The one that raped and killed the two girlth. He'th goin' down."

"Doesn't surprise me."

"Don't think *he* wath thleepin."

"No." I remember his face though, one day as we crossed paths among the gawkers. He looked bewildered. Prison will not be kind to him. If he ever gets out, he will rape and murder many more girls.

"Tho, Greer, what do you do for fun?"

"Not a lot."

"You ever play bingo?"

"No."

"Oh, you got to try it. They got Thuperthtar Bingo goin' now that'th provinthe wide. Like the bingo callerth on TV, right, tho everybody acroth the provinthe ith doin' it. The jackpot'th like twenty-five thouthand."

"Wow."

"Or the Bonanza—you win that—you could thcore fifteen hundred."

I drink more Drambuie. "Have you ever won a jackpot?"

"I got a full card one time. Couldn't believe it. Won three hundred buckth."

"Must've been nice."

"I'm tellin' ya, there'th nothing like shoutin' 'Bingo!' The thing ith, you gotta thtay awake, right? Thnooze, you lothe. I took Lu one time and he wath gettin' all worked about hith bingo dabber. It wathn't working perfect, right, like the rubber part wath coming off or thomething. Or maybe it wath the thponge. Anyway, he picked a thparkle colour, which ith a bad idea, I alwayth thay go for the red or the blue, you know, tholid. Anyway, he had two lineth going and he *mithed* the bingo."

"Bummer."

"He could've won a hundred and thixty buckth."

The thing about alcohol is that it impairs me. Before it used to relax me, but now I actually feel clobbered by it.

Arnie shifts slightly closer to me on the couch. This must come to an end.

"Arnie," I say. "I have breast cancer."

"What'th that?"

"I have breast cancer."

"Are you shittin' me?"

"No."

He shifts slightly further from me on the couch. "I'm thorry."

"Me too." Although the Drambuie is paralyzing my frontal lobes, it is softening my tooth pain. I drink more.

"Tho, have you been operated on and whatnot?"

"That is correct. I'm missing one breast and about to lose another."

"I'm tho thorry."

"Hey, it's only flesh."

I don't look at him because I know what his face is doing. The muscles are dashing about trying to form an appropriate expression. His mouth is probably gaping slightly, maybe an eye has started to twitch. A spaceship crashes on the TV, explosions follow, and women's screams.

I stand. "Time to go. Sam, you coming? Sam?"

He stands but appears dopey, as though he's been sleeping. "Pull your socks up, honey," I tell him.

"You don't have to go," Arnie says.

"It's been a long day. We're both tired. Thanks for the drinkies."

Sam pulls up his socks but stares strangely at his shoes, as though he has no idea what to do with them. I kneel beside him and slide them onto his feet. The gesture sends me back, back. You were so little once, so vulnerable, and yet you scared me.

"Is he okay?" Turner asks me.

"Of course," I say, but am not sure. Sam's got that dilated-pupil look about him. "Come on, sweetie."

I fit him into the car, lock his door and drive to the lakeshore. We can't go home because that would mean separating and I'm not leaving him alone in this semi-conscious state.

I stare where the lake should be. There is no horizon, only blackness. And the sounds of cars whizzing past. And Sam's soft breathing as he sleeps. I carefully pick up his hand and kiss it.

We've disappointed our new friends. Him by killing, me by dying.

"Mum . . . Mum, wake up, what are we doing here?"

A stretch limo has pulled up not far from us. Men get in and out, adjusting their flies, and I can only hope that the prostitute within is getting well paid. "I just thought we could use some fresh air," I tell Sam.

"It's fucking freezing."

"Okay, well, we'll go home. Is that what you want to do?"

"I don't know."

"Are you hungry?" I was dreaming something weird, about a crippled baby, I was trying to adopt a crippled baby.

"I don't really feel like going out in public."

There is nothing worse than a liqueur hangover. I rub my temples. The baby had hands where his shoulders should have been, and feet attached to his hips.

"Can we pick something up?" Sam asks.

"Of course."

They wouldn't let me adopt the baby because I had cancer. "I'm not dying," I kept telling this old bag with hair on her face. "Who else is going to look after him?" I demanded. "Who else?"

Even when we're safe in our kitchen with our Kentucky Fried Chicken, my son's eyes will not meet mine. How can I free him of shame, if that's what this is? And shouldn't he be ashamed? Isn't that what I wanted? But why now? When it's over? Did he need the enemy of the judicial system to remain obstinate in his remorselessness? And now that the opposition has crumbled, so has he?

What an interesting way to treat criminality—take the retribution away. Of course that only works if there's a conscience.

Does this mean my son has a conscience?

He looks at his hands as Jerry did when I told him I knew he was screwing what's-her-face. He holds his palms outward as if he's searching for answers encoded in his palms.

"Your dad was here," I tell him.

"What did he want?"

"To see you."

"Did you tell him to go fuck himself?"

"No. I told him he should call you and make arrangements."

"Not this century."

"I think he's serious." Please don't go live with him, I want to say, please don't go live with him.

"All he's serious about is fucking his bitch wife."

"Anyway, I thought I should warn you. That he might be calling."

"I'm warned." He collects chicken bones, stuffs them in the bag, the bag into the garbage, washes his hands. "How are you?" he asks abruptly. "You don't look too good."

He never asks me how I am. I gulp, swallow. "I'm fine," I say.

"I don't think so."

"I just . . . it's nothing. I have to have a bit more surgery, exploratory."

"When?"

"Soon. I don't have a time yet. Sometimes they get cancellations."

"So they're in a hurry?"

"I don't know, not really. I think the surgeon likes to keep busy. He's got to pay for his kids' education."

"The same jerk as last time?"

I nod meekly.

"You hate him."

"How can you not hate someone who disfigures you?"

He opens the fridge, stares into it for the longest time, as though he's waiting for someone to come out of it, maybe the Nursery Magic Fairy. She'll kiss his mother and make her Real. "You wouldn't hate him if he saved your life."

"This is true."

"Is he going to cut off the other one?"

"Umm, I don't know. It depends on what he sees. Him and the oncologist, they . . . confer while they've got you on the table."

"When you're unconscious."

"That's right."

He pulls a can of ginger ale from the fridge, snaps it open. We listen to it fizz.

"Sam, I just had a thought. It may be crazy but I . . . anyway, what if you changed your last name? You could use my name, Dawes. It's a nice name, I always liked it. I would've changed it back, but it got too complicated." I'm babbling on because he's not responding. "Sam Dawes," I blather, "sounds like a detective, Sam Dawes, Private Eye. Or maybe a spy, Special Agent Dawes."

"Don't make a joke of it."

"I'm sorry."

He leans his forehead against the wall. "I really hate my life." He says this with wonder, not anger or despair.

"You mustn't, sweetie, you're at the very beginning of it. You have no idea how things will change. They do. We think oh my god, it will be like this forever but it isn't, it just isn't. The good and the bad, they fade like the photographs. Years later, you hardly recognize them."

He sits, drops his head into his hands. The foot begins to tap. "I don't know what I'm supposed to do with myself."

"Nothing. You do nothing. You heal. You sleep. If you want, I can set you up with professional help."

"Forget it."

"Okay." I'm jittery, because of the intimacy, I'm not used to it. He's never acknowledged my cancer before. Do you want me to keep the breast? I want to ask but don't because I know this would be unfair. But does it *mean* anything to you, this gland that gave you life? Because if it does, I will not let them take it away. If it does, it is not just so much diseased flesh.

Sybil shuffles in and for once she is not welcome. "I wondered what happened to you two," she says. Sam's retreat is instant. Safe in his shell, he can resume that surly air.

"Are you hungry?" Sybil asks. "Do you want some stew?"

And he's gone, up the stairs to sleep with his demons.

"Everything alright?" she inquires.

"Not really, but there's not a fuck of a lot I can do about it."

"That violinist died today. The Brit or whatever he was. Eighty-two. He was a vegetarian, used to do yoga, stand on his head." She pours herself a glass of milk, adds Ovaltine, stirs it around, and I ponder how many hundreds, maybe thousands, of times she's done this, mixed her pre-bed cocktail. Is Ovaltine what keeps her going?

"What's it like to outlive everyone?" I ask.

"Lonely."

"Kind of like the last person to leave the party."

She nods. "You're left looking at the garbage."

"That sounds a little bit negative, Auntie."

"You don't have a monopoly on it."

I kiss her on a cheek as frail as parchment paper and climb up to my jungle bed. Tomorrow I will buy cream sheets. I will.

Eighteen

Dr. Norman Finklestein is small and spry, reminds me of a jockey. As he explains the Holter monitor documentation, he holds his hands forward as though he's urging on his horse. Giddy-up, giddy-up, I keep expecting him to say.

"There's these big pauses," he elaborates, "when the blood's not getting to your noodle, so you black out. The thing is, if the pauses get any bigger, and they will because you've got spontaneous degeneration"—he urges the horse into a gallop—"if the pauses get too big"—whoa, he pulls back on the reins—"you may die."

"Sounds pretty serious," I offer.

He leans over his horse and looks down at Sybil. "I don't get the feeling you're ready to die."

"Not really."

"Well, then"—he leaps from the saddle and sits on the edge of his desk, facing her—"seems to me a pacemaker might just do the trick."

"How big is it?" Sybil asks.

"Little, about the size of a hockey puck."

"Won't it stick out?"

"We spread the muscle and skin, make a bed for it, cover it up. Piece of cake. You won't even know it's there. End of grey-outs, blackouts. You'll be a new woman."

I can see that the idea of becoming a new woman in the hands of Norm is growing on Sybil. His energy, his enthusiasm for his trade and his unconditional admiration for someone who has lived for eighty-seven years is making her girlish. She even blushes when he says, "I would never tell someone your age how to live." So no scolding about smoking or drinking or fat, just plain old respect for the aged; a rarity these days. As he twinkles and says things like "in a jiffy" and "no prob," I sense that Sybil is becoming smitten with him and this fills me with the same satisfaction I felt when Sam loved his first grade teacher.

"I'm not staying in the hospital," she says pertly.

"May have to, Sybil, we'll have to see. Chances are we'll send you home."

"How long is the procedure?" I ask, assuming the role of the concerned parent.

"Half-hour to an hour. There's no risk, no general, just happy drugs and some local freezing."

"What about infection?" I inquire.

"Low incidence," he says. "It's a two- to three-inch incision left of the clavicle. We find a vein, thread the wire through to the atrium, the right ventricle . . ."

"Speak English," I say.

"The pumping chamber. We hook up the pump."

"I don't like the idea of wires in my body," Sybil admits.

"It's covered in plastic," he says as though this makes it okay. "Sybil, you are a formidable woman, and I don't want to tell you what to do, but I'm going to anyway. Get this done, you won't regret it."

She stares at him without blinking for what feels like ten minutes. "Okay," she says finally. "If *you* do it. No one else touches me. If you get sick, or your wife has a baby or something, you call me."

"I will."

"Promise."

"I promise."

I wish *my* surgeon rode horses.

How serendipitous that The Bay is having a white sale. Unfortunately, everybody seems to be here; our entire pulsing, multicultural society is riffling through row upon row of tables stacked with bath and bedding supplies. Scouting for cream sheets, I drag Sybil behind me. I don't want beige, brown-beige, yellow-beige, coffee, I want cream. "What's wrong with blue?" Sybil asks. "Here's a nice navy, or royal's nice."

"I want cream."

"What a fuss-budget."

She, of the new lease on life, cannot understand, or accept, that it is possible—and I'm not being negative but there is a possibility—that I may die in these sheets. Therefore, it is essential that they are *cream.*

She grabs another packet. "Geometrics are nice, stripes and

zig-zags. Or what about floral?"

"I hate floral." I don't want to die in a bed of roses, or an ocean blue, or a cosmic hell.

Then I spot them, on an island, with no crowd around them.

Because even marked down they cost eighty-nine ninety-nine. "You're not paying that," Sybil tells me.

"Oh yes, I am."

"That's highway robbery."

"They're all cotton, Auntie."

"Means they'll wrinkle."

"I don't care, they feel nice."

"What nonsense."

We recuperate in the cafeteria already occupied by middle-aged and old ladies. "There's probably a pacemaker or two around here," I comment. Not to mention a few fake breasts.

I returned the laundry basket full of tools to the basement this morning, laid them carefully and obviously on the workbench. I had to leave early because Todd had found Iranians who wanted to buy Muriel's house. I've had trouble selling it because it's too ostentatious, what with marble everywhere and spiral staircases. But this suits the Iranians. How apt that Muriel should sell her home to the Muslims she so abhors. When I told her the nationality of the buyers she said, "At least we know the cheque won't bounce." They're paying close to asking price, which means a sizeable commission, which is why I've bought two sets of ninety-dollar sheets.

And Muriel wants a fast close on Devon's house because she wants to get decorators in there. I suggested that maybe Devon would like to make some of the interior design decisions herself. "Absolutely not," Muriel said. "Devon has frightful taste."

"But she has to live there," I pointed out.

"Yes, but it's *my* investment. I'm not having the house devalued by her gaudy choices. If I let her have her way, it will be flowers and pine, flowers and pine. And lace curtains. Dreadful."

"Flowers and pine sells," I advised her. She ignored me and insisted that she must lose five pounds and that the pottery tour she took last year in England was a great disappointment because it rained all the time.

Anyway, this is all good financial news. Next I have to find a condo ostentatious enough for Muriel. Something grotesque, right downtown; shouldn't be difficult.

"Here's a feel-good story for you," Sybil says, handing me a section of the paper showing a photo of a black man in a baseball cap. "Chased a purse snatcher," Sybil explains. "Some scumbag grabbed an old lady's purse and took off with it." She points to the black man. "He caught him. Could've looked the other way, but he went after the little squirt. Gave the purse back to the old lady. That's nice." She forks a piece of napoleon slice into her mouth.

"The world is not lost," I offer.

"Not today anyway."

"I'd like to buy you something. Can I buy you something?"

"No."

"Please, Auntie? What about a new sweater or slippers?"

"Save your money for the boy," she says.

"Did you see him this morning?"

"Stayed in his room." She looks back at the photo of the black man. "The old lady offered him a hundred-dollar reward, but he refused it. 'It could've been my own granny,' he said." She nods. "That's nice."

Estelle has become wan. She drifts about the office with Bunny's ashes in a locket around her neck. Not all of his ashes, the remainder she keeps by her bed in a cookie tin shaped like a cat who resembles Bunny. While I'm waiting for Todd to return with the signed purchasing agreement and deposit, I tell Estelle the uplifting story about the black man who rescued the old lady.

"There's crime everywhere these days," is her only comment.

While showing Arnie and Lu houses this afternoon I distinctly noticed a change in Arnie's treatment of me. He held doors open, offered chairs, glasses of water. "I'm fine," I kept assuring him.

It's so sad that we can't tell people we're sick because then they'll treat us as though we're sick.

But I think Lu's cooling on the house idea. He's starting to see that cheap means trouble. I don't expect to hear from them for a while, if ever.

"I don't have *one* listing," Estelle grumbles.

"You got to get out there and hustle."

"My life just feels, my life just feels . . . over." She fondles the locket.

"It isn't, Estelle, trust me."

"How would *you* know? I mean, I hate how people act like you're being immature when you grieve for your animals. We should be allowed to *grieve.*"

"Of course."

"There's nobody home anymore. I hate it. Echoes, all I hear is echoes. Sometimes I think it's him. I wake up and think he's on the bed, that he's going to snuggle and stuff."

She's starting to cry again. I look around for a Kleenex, snatch one, feel in my pocket for a butterscotch. "Here," I say, offering both.

"Everybody says, 'Just get a kitten, you'll fall in love all over again.' How can they say that? That is *so* insensitive. Like he could be replaced."

"People say stupid things."

"I hate people. I really do."

We listen to her unwrap the butterscotch. Now might be a good time to suggest she find another line of work, something less people-oriented. But then I know about grief, how nothing eases it but time, and sometimes not even that. I put my hand on her shoulder pad as Todd charges in gleaming with the purchasing agreement. "A major score," he informs us. "Major." He offers me a high-five which I take. His palm feels sweaty; he's obviously been working his ass off. "Mrs. Halib was getting a little weird about the wrought iron," he advises me. "But I said, 'Look, it's cosmetic. You can change the house, you can't change the location.' Then she says, and it's totally strange, right, because she's all covered up, like you can't see her face because she's wearing a burka, right, so she starts whining about the marble, like it might hurt her feet or something—she's got joint problems from having twelve kids or whatever—so I said, 'Look, that can be changed, in the meantime you don't have to buff or polish, we're talking low maintenance here, and let's face it, nothing looks as impressive as marble.' Anyway, Mr. Halib loves the pillars, so there you go." He hands me the agreement which I peruse.

"I'm going to paint my condo in Ralph Lauren colours to celebrate," he announces. "Have you seen them? They're to die for."

"Why don't we take Estelle for a drink?" I suggest. He looks stunned briefly, then attempts to smile enthusiastically.

"You don't have to," Estelle murmurs.

"Of course we do," Todd says.

We go to our local bar, which claims to be Irish but is run by Sikhs. An "Irish" band is playing winsome Irish tunes about bonnie lasses and clover. The singer has a huge gut and pants falling off his butt, but he's rosy-cheeked and apparently merry and I find myself tapping my foot.

"One of my clients," Todd begins, "who shall be nameless, has taken off for the Philippines to screw his cyber-sex mistress. It's so depressing, it's totally screwed up the deal. His wife's a mess."

"Does his cyber-sex mistress know he's married?" I ask.

"Doubt it, she's probably hoping he'll marry her and bring her back here."

"What's cyber-sex?" Estelle asks.

"You wire up an internet camera to the Web," Todd explains, "and speakers, and pull out your willy and go crazy. He's filmed his genitals, she's showed him hers, it's disgusting. Happens all the time though. Anyway, I told his wife he'd be back, if she wants him, because there's no way that Filipino lassie is going to put up with a fifty-year-old with no assets. The house is in his wife's name, thank God. I told her, sell it, teach him a lesson, you don't want to be here when he gets back anyway. But she says she doesn't want to grow old by herself, can you believe it? It's pathetic." He sips his lime and lager. "I was so close to selling that house. It's got a four-car garage, central air, vac, two walkout decks and *three* working fireplaces."

"Bummer," I offer as I hum along with "Irish Eyes Are Smiling."

Estelle's getting tipsy. She keeps adjusting her hair which doesn't require adjusting. The merry Irish singer winks at her and she giggles. We must pour more spirits into her, give her some respite from her melancholy. I signal another round to the waitress and get up to use the loo. After peeing and studying graffiti about the size of Denzel's penis, I phone home. Sybil answers. I ask if Sam's home.

"He's in the basement."

"What's he doing?"

"How should I know?"

"Right. Okay, well, I'm having a drink with Todd and company."

"Good, enjoy yourself, we'll be here."

I check my messages. Jerry has called for Sam. The sound of his voice increases my tooth pain. I see my face distort in the mirror. He's not going to let go; something admirable but also scary about Jerry is his tenacity.

There's another message from the listing agent of Devon's house; she's dropping the papers off at my office in the morning. Excellent. And then a strange, stammering message which I realize is Turner phoning for Sam. "Just wanted to see if you wanted to go to the bookstore." Good, that'll get him out of the basement.

Back at the table Todd's describing an associate's gruesome, humiliating death from AIDS. "He got these slimy, wet, oozy skin lesions all over his body, and herpes on his anus, and candidiasis that totally clogged his throat so he couldn't swallow, and these creepy crawly parasites, and massive diarrhea, blindness, dementia. The whole deal. He was just one big pus receptacle by the end of it."

Not clear why we're talking about this when we're trying to cheer up Estelle. "How did he die in the end?" she asks, wide-eyed.

"Pneumonia. His lungs couldn't clear. He drowned in his own pus."

Estelle shakes her head in astonishment.

"So," Todd adds, "anybody running around saying we've got AIDS under control is full of it."

Estelle adjusts her hair again. "I don't think Bunny felt much pain."

"I'm sure he didn't," I say, then get Todd talking about what he's good at, real estate.

"Earl Verman got the listing on that bungy your son did his thing in," he informs me.

"What?"

"The bungalow, where the murders happened. Verman got the listing."

"But it's not for sale."

"It is now. He's only asking two-eighty-nine, which is a crime. It's worth at least three-fifty. I guess he wants to move it before people figure out whose house it is."

Earl Verman is the white-shoed, Caribbean-cruise-anticipating agent who sold the house of the woman with Lou Gehrig's disease to the perfect couple. He acquires listings by reading obituaries and sniffing out surviving relatives. He is vermin, and he will sell Lyla's house within a week.

"Are you showing it to anyone?" I ask Todd.

"No, but I might have somebody for your house, if you're still interested. They're friends of the Halibs, just got here, so they don't know your history. You know, the whole time I was working out that deal I was thinking this woman's had her clitoris cut off. This woman's had to spread her legs for this guy at least twelve times and it must've hurt. I mean, what about lubrication? It's pathetic. I don't know how any doctor could do that to girls, I don't care what his religion is."

"They cut off girls' clitorises?" Estelle asks. I put cash on the table and tell them I'll see them in the morning.

As soon as I get into the car I page Earl Verman. Thinking I'm interested in one of his listings, he gets back to me within minutes. I wait for him to express surprise at my interest in a house in which my son committed murder but Earl, always looking for the deal, only yabbers on about the two-car garage, "newer" windows, roof and furnace. "All in all it's a good house," he tells me. "Although the murders are a bit of a neg. Congratulations on your son getting off, by the way."

I consider explaining that he didn't "get off" but was found innocent, but decide that this will only start a philosophical discussion with Verman and this I do not need.

"Have you shown the house to anyone?" I inquire.

"Not exactly. Problem is it's a bit tricky to show. The young lady won't give me the key."

"So how are you showing it?"

"Haven't yet. Had a couple of drive-bys. Feedback's good."

"It seems underpriced." I hear him inhale on a cigarette.

"The vendor's eager to sell." He exhales.

"Is she bridging a deal?"

"Not exactly. But, as you know, it was her parents' house. You know how it is, memories and so on."

"Yeah. It just seems odd that she won't give you a key if she's eager to sell." I pretend to know nothing about Lyla's mental health.

"Well, she's a bit flighty. Lives alone, doesn't want strangers in the house, that sort of thing."

"I see. Well, if I want to show the house, what do I do?"

"Give me a shout, we'll work something out."

"Alright."

"Super. Good talkin' to ya."

I must stop Lyla from eloping with Ed to Saint-Tropez. If she sells her house, she will be left with nothing. I pull into her drive so she'll recognize my car. I ring the bell only once and the door swings open. She's been on a buying spree, is decked out in a new dress with tags still attached, new shoes, straw hat, light jacket (still tagged) worn over the dress and a silk scarf tied loosely around her neck. She pivots and turns for me. "It's a bit summery," I observe.

"Yes, well it's summer over there, isn't it?"

"Where are you going?" Boxes and suitcases have been packed and unpacked. Clearly she thinks she's going somewhere.

"Would you like a cuppa?"

"No thanks."

"He needs a friend right now. I feel I owe it to him."

"Ed?"

"No, silly, Charles, of course. I think something's up with Camilla. He was dancing with a native girl in Trinidad and I don't think old horse-face liked it. I mean, she's so bloody ancient, he's bound to stray at some point. Anyway, he's devastated, of course. I told him she'll come round, who else will have her? He disagrees, but there you are. Did you know the first thing she said to him was 'My great-grandmother was your great-grandfather's mistress, what do you think of that?' What a floozie, honestly."

One of her scrapbooks is open to a newspaper clipping about the July '81 wedding of Charles and Diana. In the photo Diana, seated, smiles shyly with eyes cast down while Charles stands with his hands on her shoulders, also smiling with eyes cast down.

"The Coldstream Guards played 'Now Your Philandering Days Are Over,'" Lyla informs me. "It's so sad. He said, 'I'm amazed that she's been brave enough to take me on,' and she said, 'It cannot go wrong if he's there with me.' Which was true, wasn't it? He wasn't there, was he?"

"No. Listen, Lyla, I was surprised to see the For Sale sign on your lawn."

She spins around. "Whatever for?"

"Well, I didn't realize you wanted to sell."

"Earl's very positive about the whole thing."

"I'm sure he is. It's just . . . I think it's worth more than what he's suggested, and I think this is all a bit sudden. I mean, you might regret selling your home."

"How would *you* know?" There is desperation in her righteousness. She drops a photograph of her parents into a box, then takes it out again and sets it back on the mantel.

"All I know is that sudden moves can be dangerous, that grieving takes time and it's best not to make hasty decisions."

She struts towards me and leans in so close that I can smell her rancid breath. It is the breath of someone who no longer eats, whose body is beginning to feed on itself. "I would say," she hisses, "that it is none of your beeswax."

"I'm only concerned. Do you have a relative who can advise you, offer help?"

Like a bat she is on me, fuchsia nails clawing my face. I see only red and think I'm going blind as she tries to dig her fingers into my eyes. But then her face appears above me, the mouth gaping, saliva flying as she screams, "Leave me alone, bitch, leave me alone, leave me alone!" I try to get up but she's kneeling on me, her bony knees boring into my thighs. She begins to tear at my hair and I fall into the kind of trance I used to escape to when my mother flew at me. I would feel nothing, would not resist. This is what I've been waiting for: Lyla's wrath, her scorching hatred. I will wait until it is over.

And, as in a tornado, I'm only vulnerable while in its centre. In minutes she backs off, tears only at her own hair, her own face. This is a child in more pain than I have ever known. This is a child losing pieces of her mind as I am losing pieces of my body. I'm not sure which is worse.

I stand, remove a card from my purse, write my home number on the back and place it on the table. "If you need help, for anything, please call."

She has resumed twiddling her hair and seems to have forgotten about me. She flips through her scrapbooks, her only friends.

"Goodbye, Lyla."

Sam's out of his room the one time I want him in it. "What happened to your face?" he asks.

"I was attacked."

"By who?" He spreads peanut butter on a slice of bread.

"I don't know. Some crazy."

"There's blood on your shirt."

"Is there? I'll soak it." I should ask him to take care of it, he knows how to remove blood stains.

"Why did they attack you?"

"I have no idea. Paranoia."

"Man or woman?"

"Woman."

"Did she get your money?"

"No. It wasn't that kind of attack."

He looks at me and I'm thinking he knows.

"Your doctor's office called," he says. "They've had a cancellation. Want to know if you can do it next week."

"Really? Goody-goody gumdrops." I watch him smear jam on the peanut butter.

"I guess sooner's better than later, right?" he asks. "For that kind of thing?"

"I guess."

Only now is my face beginning to hurt. I see in the bathroom mirror that the tracks left by her nails are beginning to swell. I wash carefully, get out my Polysporin. He startles me at the door. "You're going to do it, right?" he asks.

I consider emotionally blackmailing him, saying, Only if you want me to, tell me that you love me and I'll go under the knife, swear you'll never leave me.

"I'm going to do it," is all I say.

He nods, is about to return to his room. "Turner called for you," I say to stop him. "It was on the service. He wanted you to take him to the bookstore. Do you have their number?"

"Don't need it."

"So you're not going to call?"

"He's only phoning because his dad told him to."

"How do you know that?"

"His dad wants to fuck you, if you haven't noticed."

"He doesn't anymore. I told him about the cancer."

His eyes meet mine in one of those crystalline moments when I know I'm getting through.

"Why did you tell him?" he asks.

"So he wouldn't want to fuck me. Since I don't want to fuck him."

He considers this, leaning against the door jamb. "Makes sense," he concedes.

"Anyway," I persist, "my point is Turner phoned of his own volition."

"Point taken."

"Don't desert him, Sam."

His eyes are on me again, with that dressing-down stare his father has, a stare that makes me feel like a cadaver on an examining table about to be disembowelled. "It was her, wasn't it," he demands, "who scratched your face?"

I try to look as though I don't understand, I raise my eyebrows slightly.

"The Grundy girl," he says without waiting for an answer. I listen to his door close.

You fuck things up and then you put a band-aid on it.

I take off my blouse, drop it into a basin of cold water, take off my bra with the prosthesis still tucked into it and look at my remaining breast in the harsh fluorescent lighting. "How are ya?" I ask it. "Seen any good movies lately?"

The whole thing is so ugly, my body, it's beyond words. I cup number two in my hand, immediately feel the lump, drop the breast like a hot coal. A decision, I have to make another decision. Why don't you just strike me dead? Please? Why this extended torture? I never hit anyone, I ate my spinach, I haven't sold dying people's houses for fifty cents.

Useless thinking, waste of time. I touch the breast again, more gently this time. The nipple may drop a little, Cheeseburger said. What does this mean exactly? Will I confuse it with my belly button?

The nipple hardens against the cool air. Jerry used to suck on it, had this trick he'd do with his tongue, kind of a dance around the nipple. I wonder if he does this with Gingivitis Girl. Probably.

Sam used to be so greedy, would suck and suck, fall asleep, wake up, cry out for more. Then I deposited him in daycare, pumped milk into sterile bottles for him. My breasts would swell wanting him, and leak through my blouse while I smiled winsomely at commercial clients. I developed a blocked duct which burned. I needed him to suck more to unblock it. What kind of message was this? You can't have my breast during the day but suck till you drop at night?

Sometimes, like right now, my mother appears in my face. It's not a pretty sight, more like catching a glimpse of the devil. Can she see me now, her disfigured daughter? I caught her putting lipstick on her nipples once. Standing in front of the mirror in her shrine of a bedroom she was not embarrassed, only annoyed at being disturbed. "What do you want?"

"Can I borrow a sweater?" She was always very generous with her clothes, let us wear any of her finery.

"Of course, honey," she said, suddenly friendly. Without covering up she opened drawers for me. "Which one?"

"Well, I was thinking the purple."

"Of course, honey." She found it, handed it to me. I tried not to look at her ample breasts.

Maybe she was just some kind of wonderfully liberated woman, at ease with her sexuality. At a time when feminists were encouraging women to hold mirrors in front of their genitals to do self-examinations, my mother was comfy masturbating at the piano.

I so badly wanted to love her. It's unfair that while young we believe that things have a correct time and place, that there is order. Only later do we discover that the disorder is actually order. That within that apparently chaotic framework there is a structure all its own that must be respected, just as we must respect the grain in a piece of wood before building with it.

I must let all this go. Let it go. What a concept, like it will go anywhere when we release our grip. Mostly it just sits there, this big lumpy mass. Out of our grasp it remains a stumbling block. I want to push it down the hill, watch it roll into the river. Would it sink? A drowned body sinks to the bottom, led by the head which is its densest component. It stays down there, headfirst, until the decomposition begins. By the time the body surfaces, it is well on its way to being compost.

What's Lyla doing now? I wish I could hold her, restrain her. Soon there will be no hair on the sides of her head. What can she be seeing in that house of death? There's a satellite dish on the roof, maybe she's watching an Australian cooking show. "Throw another steak on the bahbie, mate. Good on ya. No worries."

One of my fears which I keep shoving to the back of the closet is that the cancer will metastasize in my brain and I will become demented. Losing memory and rational thought wouldn't be so bad if it happened all at once; you got boinked on the head and that was it. But losing it in fragments over a period of months, maybe even years, is not an appealing prospect. Already I have "senior moments" when I do things like put the cheque for Hydro in with the phone bill. I tell myself that everybody over forty does this, that it doesn't mean that my malignant tumour has eroded through the wall of a blood vessel or lymph channel, dropped a few cells into the passing stream of blood which have then headed skyward to implant in my brain.

Metastasis. *Meta* is a Greek preposition meaning "beyond" or "away from" and *stasis* means "position" or "placing." Don't we all want to move beyond or away from our position or place? Dissatisfaction is part of the human condition. Complacency is for the brain-dead.

For this reason, I have a kind of respect for cancer. It's asocial, nonconforming, rebellious. It escapes the constraints that rule non-malignant cells, those regulated, programmed automatons. Fuck you, it says, I'm doing my own thing. It fights its way into vital structures that support the system, prevents their functioning, chokes their vitality. Thrives in the face of adversity.

We admire this in people.

Sybil knocks and enters. "What's going on?"

"Nothing."

"What happened to your face?"

"The crazy girl attacked me."

"What were you doing there?"

"I don't know. Trying to help."

"Leave well enough alone." She hands me a *Time* magazine. "I wanted to show you this. Says you can eat fat, says any kind of fat doesn't harm the breast. They did a new study."

Who did? Hostess Frito Lay?

I pretend to read the article for her benefit, my auntie who believes that if I eat greasy meat, I will thrive. It's so lovely to have someone who cares. Lyla has no one, except her paper kings and queens. Which may be why I'm drawn to her, or maybe I'm imagining she's the daughter I terminated. Years later, I still gaze at little pink dresses and grieve.

I had a miracle in my belly and I destroyed it. How dare I ask for mercy?

"I'm going to do the heart thing next week," Sybil says. "Norman's there Tuesday."

"You guys are on a first-name basis already?"

"Will you come with me?"

"Of course." I only hope my surgery is after her surgery.

"The boy's building something downstairs. Did you see it?"

"No. In the basement?"

"Looks like a coffin. Or a boat."

"How bizarre."

"Anyway, it's keeping him busy."

"That's good. I guess."

"I think he's going to be alright," Sybil pronounces.

"Why?"

"It's a feeling I have."

I nod, not asking for further evidence, knowing there is none.

I lie back on my jungle bed, realizing I have no strength to change the sheets. "Was my mother crazy?

"She was different."

"Yeah, but so are you and you don't go around being nasty to people."

"Doesn't mean she was crazy. Lots of people are nasty."

"You didn't like her."

"She wasn't my type."

Sybil has said this before. It's as much as she'll reveal. It's as though she's vowed never to say a bad word about her beautiful younger sister. There is a loyalty there that I recognize because I feel it for Rachel.

"I'm going for a smoke," she says.

"Okay."

I consider going down to look at the coffin/boat but I can't. What if he's lying in it? My son, the vampire. Too much today already, I must rest, start again tomorrow.

Nineteen

Dr. Hooey shoves his fingers in my mouth and fondles my gum. "Any pain?" he asks.

"There's always pain, that's why I'm here."

"But does it hurt more when I press on it?"

"Not really." He's alarmingly fit, wears running shoes that look like space boots.

He sticks a wad of cotton in my mouth. "Bite down." I do. "More pain?" he repeats. I shake my head. I suspect he eats only veggies and tofu and runs for miles and miles. He pokes a hose in my mouth and blows cold air on the tooth. "Ouch," I respond. Next he rubs an ice cube over my gums. "Tell me when it hurts."

"It all hurts."

"What hurts most?"

Dobin, who will not speak with me directly but communicates through his Scottish squeeze, has referred me to this endodontist who has pictures of sailboats hanging where Dobin has cars.

"It's hard to tell," I admit.

He slides away from me on his stool, drops the ice cube in the sink and rubs his hands. "I'm going to freeze the tooth."

Oh goody, more needles.

"If it stops the pain," he explains, "the problem is in the tooth."

"Where else would it be?"

He leans over me and swabs my gum with a numbing agent. Lyla's scratches don't hurt anymore and everyone seems to believe my story about a pruning encounter with an aggressive rose bush.

"Open wide," he says, needle in hand.

And I checked out the coffin/boat this morning. It just looks like a box, quite large, to put things in, not a body necessarily, odds and ends.

The sting of the needle subsides.

"Alright," Hooey says, "I'm going to leave you for a few minutes, give it a chance to work."

I've already waited forty-five minutes to see marathon man. If I have to read another *Time* magazine, I may begin breaking things, vases that contain plastic palms for example. What gives doctors the right to keep us waiting? Is this something they learn in medical school, make them wait, keep them humble? I'm supposed to be meeting Rachel for lunch, am already late. She sounded subdued on the phone, something's up with Porky Pig. If he's hurt her, I'll kick his ass. My pager sounds. It's Earl Verman. I call him.

"Just thought you might want to know," he begins, "there's been a bit of a snafu with the Grundy bungy. I . . . umm . . . was trying to take a couple of buyers through, phoned Miss Grundy, she seemed fine. But when I got there she wouldn't let us in. Now these people had driven by a couple of times so I have to admit I was a littlle persistent, showed her the signed listing agreement and so on. In any event, she let us in, we had a quick look-see but . . . umm . . . in the meantime she'd called the police, said we were planting a bomb."

Good for her, I'm thinking.

"Unfortunately, when they showed up she went berserk. They had to call for reinforcements."

Lyla? Tiny Lyla? Two big cops couldn't handle her?

"A SWAT team arrived. Maybe that's routine when there's a bomb threat, I don't know. Looked a bit scary, I have to admit. They have those masks on, you know, helmets and knee pads and so on. It took six of them to carry her out. She was screaming 'Burn in hell' the whole time—she's quite a fireball."

"Where did they take her?"

"Wouldn't say. That's confidential." He inhales on a cigarette. "Anyhoo, I noticed your card on the table and thought maybe you'd been in there."

"Briefly." That's why he's calling. He thinks I'm trying to steal his listing.

"For any particular reason?" He exhales.

"A social call."

"Is that right? Well, like I said, if you have anybody interested, just give me a shout."

"Of course."

"I have another bungy listed, very similar. Not quite as shipshape, but that's reflected in the price. It's an estate sale, the heirs want a fast close, you know how it is, they don't want to keep paying taxes and so forth. Anyhoo, I just thought I'd mention it."

"I'll keep that in mind."

"Super. Good talking to ya."

Where is she now? In a padded room? Buckled to a bed with leather restraints? Shot up with antipsychotics that will fuzz her brain and give her the shakes?

Hooey jogs in. "How's it goin'?"

"I still feel pain."

"Really? Well, I can't promise a root canal is going to help."

"If it's not the tooth, what is it?"

He grimaces, clasps his hands. "Facial pain."

"What?"

"Neuralgia. It happens."

"But why?"

He shrugs, determined not to implicate Dobin.

"I did not have 'facial' pain before Conway Dobin worked on the tooth."

He shrugs again. "I can do a root canal, if you want, but it might make it worse."

"I don't want a root canal. I want the pain to go away."

"Well, I can give you some painkillers." He starts scribbling on a prescription pad. "And you might want to see a neurologist who specializes in this sort of thing. I can give you a name."

I don't want to see another doctor. "What can he do?"

"There's medications that can help."

More medications. "Like what?"

"Antidepressants, anticonvulsants."

"What do antidepressants and anticonvulsants have to do with facial pain?"

He taps his temple. "The pain centres are in your head. You've heard of phantom pain? Same thing. I really don't know that much about it." He snaps off the prescription and hands it to me. "Go see Dr. Shankes. He'll fix you up." And he's off and running. A hundred dollars later.

"Bob's become a Scientologist," Rachel informs me. She hasn't touched her quiche. I refrain from forking it into her. She seems to be shrinking. The dress she's wearing, she used to fill. "It's been going on for a while," she admits. "He's been taking courses. They're so expensive, all our savings, even some RRSPs he's spent on them."

"With your permission?"

"I want him to be happy." She fiddles nervously with one of her gold loop earrings. "He says he wants to be 'clear.' That's what happens after you've been 'audited' over and over—you become clear. They hook you up to an E-meter. I think it's supposed to be able to tell if you're getting emotional. You're not supposed to get emotional. The auditor keeps saying words that bring back bad memories. He says them over and over until they don't upset you anymore." She stares at the dregs in her coffee cup. "It's not much to look at, the E-meter, just these two cans attached to a string or something. Reminds me of when we used to play phone, remember that, with orange juice cans?"

I nod but withhold comment knowing that no matter what I say, it will be interpreted as big sister's intolerance for little sister's foibles.

"Anyway," she adds, "it's expensive."

I sip wine, fondle the stem of my glass. A man is washing the window, making lovely rivulets with his squeegee. He spins it in his hand and wipes them dry with the rubber edge. "Rachel, Scientologists are scum."

"Well, I knew you'd say that, that's why I haven't told you about it."

"So why are you telling me now?"

She looks down at the linen napkin on her lap. "Because I need money."

"How much?"

"Ten thousand dollars. It's just credit cards, you know, they just . . . pile up. I'll pay it back."

I sigh, look around the restaurant that's been drained of the lunch crowd. The sweaty waiter, with no business left but mine, starts scurrying towards me. I indicate that I'd like the cheque.

"What does Mrs. Adams say about all this?" I ask.

"She says I'm facing a fork in the road, that I must find my centre before making a decision."

"That's helpful." I sign for the cheque and hand it to the waiter who says, "Enjoy your day now."

"The deal is," I tell Rachel, "I'll give you the ten thousand if you cut up the credit cards, or just the ones he uses."

She nods meekly, my little broken sister. I reach for her hand and grip it. "Scientology isn't going to go away," I advise her.

"No, I know that. At first I thought maybe it would be good

for him, he's always trying to improve himself, there's nothing wrong with that. So I thought maybe *I'd* try it, you know, see for myself. So I went down to the 'Org,' that's what they call it, and did a personality test. You know, you answer questions and they show you on graphs what you need to work on."

"And recommend courses."

"That's right. According to the graphs I'm . . . I need a lot of work." I can see she's trying not to cry, the little girl with the bleeding ears. "It doesn't hurt," she said.

"But you didn't want to take the courses?" I inquire.

"Well, no. The man interviewing me seemed like he needed a lot of work. He was very edgy, and had bloodshot eyes. Bob told me *he* was clear. So I thought, if that's clear, I don't want any part of it. Anyway, you don't stay clear. After a while you have to be audited all over again."

"It's a money pit," I suggest. "What's happened to Amway?"

"Oh, Bob's just . . . he's lost interest. I'm doing what I can but I've never been that good a salesperson. I'm better on the business end."

My pager sounds. It's Todd. He showed my house to the Halibs' buddies this morning. I wonder what they thought about the coffin/boat.

"I know it's none of my business," I tell Rachel, "but if you want to leave him, you're welcome to stay with me."

"Oh I would never do that, leave the house? They're not getting my home."

"That's the spirit. Please eat something."

Ten thousand dollars, I must be mad.

"They want your house," Todd tells me. I hear something in the background, skin being slapped. He's calling me during his massage. He has this big Latvian who beats him with switches and throws ice on him.

"What do you mean, they want it?" I ask.

I'm in the hospital having my presurgical workup. I've peed in a bottle, bled into test tubes, had yet another chest X-ray and an ECG. Nuclear waste is flowing through my body because Cheeseburger ordered another bone scan. I have to wait at least an hour more before I lie down like Frankenstein and let them zap me with more radiation.

"They *love* your house," Todd explains.

"Are they going to dicker on the price?"

"Doubt it." Slap, slap. "Of course I can't say for sure until we present an offer."

Somebody in a bathrobe with a bandaged head bumps into me. "Excuse me," I hear him mumble. "That's alright," I mutter back. Apparently lost, he looks up and down the corridor.

"If I do this, Todd, I don't want to be wanked."

"I understand."

No, you don't, I want to say. The bandaged man is lumbering back towards me. I quickly step aside.

"I'll think about it," I tell Todd.

"Don't think too long, I'm telling you they're *very* interested. If you're serious about selling, I wouldn't wait."

"I'm sure you wouldn't." Already the commission is making him foam at the mouth.

I call home to talk to Sam, but of course he isn't there or isn't picking up. He had lunch with his father today. I can imagine the bribes: Come live with me and I'll buy you all the Tommy Hilfiger clothes you want. Why is he after him now? Does he really believe he can make him better?

Sitting on a plastic chair, I flick through, yes, another *Time* magazine and read about the physiological benefits of "forgiveness." Tormented by anger you can heal yourself in a "forgiveness laboratory" where you'll be hooked up to electrodes that will monitor your heart rate, blood pressure, sweat and muscle tension. At the sound of a beep, you'll be instructed to vent your fury by imagining doing horrible things to the person you hate. At the sound of the next beep, you'll be instructed to switch to "empathizing" with the offender. After another beep, you'll be told to imagine ways to "wish the person well." Physiological differences will be noted between your forgiving and unforgiving states. Studies have shown that stress is significantly greater when we consider revenge rather than forgiveness.

I try this with Jerry as my subject. First of all, I burn all his expensive clothes and make him walk to the office naked. Next, while he's still naked, I make him go to the bank and give me ten thousand dollars. Then I force him to eat one of Sybil's stews, especially the kidneys. The beeper sounds and I try to empathize with him, poor fuck has to live with Gingivitis Girl, has a son who hates him, has to rape and pillage small businesses to make a living, has to comb his hair in that special way to cover his bald spot. The beeper sounds and I proceed to "wish him well." Here there's a glitch. I try again. Hmmmm. Okay, leave me my son and I will forgive. Does conditional forgiveness reduce stress?

The article tells the story of a man determined to forgive the boys who were playing around with automatic weapons and happened to shoot his wife and eight of her grade-school students. She died in his arms, leaving him alone with his two-year-old son. "Hate and anger are sins," he whispers. "I need to totally forgive." She had gun wounds in her leg and chest and died a slow, agonizing death. He goes to church every Sunday and prays that he will be able to forgive.

This is just a suggestion, but how about focusing some of that energy needed to forgive on petitioning for gun control?

I find a phone book and look up the admitting number of the Queen Street Mental Health Centre. An icy voice informs me that professional ethics and law dictate that psychiatric patients remain confidential. Which makes sense. People will be more willing to admit themselves if they know their identity will be protected. However, it does mean that I've lost Lyla. But then so has Verman. For now, at least, she's protected from herself.

Sybil adds more animal innards to her stew. "A couple moved into the old-lady-obsessed-with-raking-leaves' house."

"What'd they look like?" I put my prosthesis on the table.

"Ex-hippies. They invited us over for a brew once they get settled in."

"There's something to live for."

"Did you read about the boy who killed his father with an axe and then hacked off his arms?"

"Must've missed that one."

"He was mentally ill."

I eat more potato chips since they don't cause cancer. "I wonder how he got that way."

She chops away at carrots. "That would be something, hacking off a pair of arms. He didn't run or anything. Just sat there till the police arrived."

The father must have held the boy in those arms.

"Have you seen Sam?" I ask.

"He went out for lunch with the pig."

"I know that. Did he come back?"

"Not that I noticed."

What did the father do with those arms that made the son feel they must be severed?

"My point is," Sybil declares, "you should stay away from that mentally ill girl."

"She's been taken away. She's in a psych ward."

"Just as well."

I pull a chair out, rest my feet on it. "I know you're hoping I'll forget, but it's your birthday on the weekend."

"So?"

"I thought maybe the three of us could go for a drive in the country, have lunch in Elora, enjoy the autumn colours."

"You think he's going to want to go?"

"All I can do is ask."

In my bath, I do my exercises, walk the wall with my right hand, and notice mould sprouting in the grout. Hopefully the Halibs' buddies didn't notice it, not to mention the cracking tile around the toilet. If we sell, I would be free of this: the house that requires maintenance that I resent giving because my ex resents helping me pay for it. I contemplate the yard sale: Come and get it, Jerry, or the staring man's going to buy it for five bucks. Actually, I don't think there's much left that he wants, Gingivitis Girl did a recce when they were first married, requested some antiques that we'd bought twenty years ago. I didn't get half what they were worth.

There I go withholding forgiveness again.

Safe in my bathrobe, I bundle up the jungle sheets and stuff them in a pillow-case. I take great care making my bed with the creamy cotton. Out of habit, I glance out the window to see if Lyla's there. The dog's barking, phew, for a second there I thought I might experience silence.

I lie back, determined to luxuriate, and peruse the paper only to learn that U.S. shipments of hazardous industrial waste to Ontario have quadrupled in the last five years, up to 288,000 tonnes. U.S. rules forbid them to dump the stuff south of the border so they're heaping it on us because we have lax environmental laws. And our government is thrilled because they're paying us fifty cents. Meanwhile, our own hazardous waste production has doubled, making the U.S. donations look meagre. Made-in-Ontario hazardous waste amounted to 2.1 million tonnes. "Hazardous" means sludge containing cyanide, toxic heavy metals, corrosive and flammable liquids, solvents, pesticides, fuels, oil and batteries. Our Minister of the Environment said, "As long as it's being dealt with in a proper manner, the quantities, I guess, are a secondary concern." It's so comforting to know he's only guessing about it.

Add to this that Health Canada estimates that air pollution causes 5,000 premature deaths annually in Canada, along with additional misery for asthma sufferers (predominantly children) and others with respiratory ailments, we're talking one great country.

Why, why, why are we so willing to destroy flora, fauna, air, ocean? Do we imagine we can survive without them?

Time for some Sleepy Time tea.

I'm startled by Sam eating Libby's beans out of a can. With only the stove light on, his face is in darkness.

I switch on the overhead, causing him to squint. "I thought you were out," I say.

"I wasn't." His hair looks slept on and he's sockless but at least he's answering me, which suggests that he's awake.

"Were you sleeping?" I ask. In the daytime? This is not good sleep hygiene.

"We're out of ginger ale," is his response.

"Make a note on the list." He doesn't. I reach for it, scribble "ginger." "What else do we need?" I ask in an attempt at conversation. "Are we out of mini-pizzas?"

"Don't know." He starts to toss the can in the garbage. I grab it from him. "That's recyclable," I explain. My action causes the lid to cut his hand.

"Jesus," he gasps, noting the blood.

"I'm sorry, sweetie, run it under the tap."

He does as I scramble upstairs to look for gauze. I hurt him, can't believe I hurt him. Fortunately, the Polysporin is where I left it, but coming downstairs I have this walloping pain in my breast and have to sit for a minute. "Sam . . . ?"

"What?"

"Can you come here for a sec? I want to bandage you up. Bring the scissors."

I hear him pull them from the drawer. "Is it still bleeding?" I ask.

"Not much." He sees me on the stair. "What's the matter?"

"I just got a cramp or something. Show me your hand." The cut is small, on the palm. I squeeze the tube over it, sneak a look at his lifeline while I'm at it. The crease becomes jumbled towards the base of his palm. Doesn't everybody's? I tape the gauze in place but don't let go of his hand. "I have to ask you something."

He doesn't say "What?" so I continue. "Someone wants to buy our house."

"Who?"

"Some Iranians."

He withdraws his hand and studies the bandage. "Are you going to sell?"

"How would you feel about that?"

"Where would we go?"

I'm so pleased he says "we." "I don't know. We could find something smaller, maybe a condo."

He sits on the stair below me. I stare at the back of his head, aching to put my arms around him.

"If we buy a condo," I expound, "it might have facilities, you know, a gym and a pool, sauna, maybe some tennis courts."

"I don't play tennis."

"I know you don't. It was just a thought."

"I want to stay here." He says this with the conviction he had at two and a half when he didn't want to go out. "I want to 'tay in the house."

"Okay," I say.

"Dad wants to sell, right?"

"I haven't spoken to him about it yet."

"He'll want to buy his bitch-wife jewels."

"How was your lunch?"

"He's an asshole." He looks at both his palms in that Jerry

manner. Outside a siren sounds, grows distant; a drama in somebody else's life. "Why did you marry him?"

I fit the surgical tape back in the box. "It seemed like a good idea at the time."

"Why?"

"I thought he made me stronger. I thought strength was something you could get from other people."

"He's weak, though."

"Yeah, well, it took me a while to figure that out. Actually, now it's his weakness that keeps me from hating him."

"You still hate him."

"You think?"

"Oh yeah."

"How regressive."

He stands. "We need peanut butter. Smoothy, not that health-food crap."

"Okay."

He turns on the TV. I could be reckless, go in there and ask him about the coffin/boat. But what if he's building it in his sleep and my drawing attention to it stresses him out because he wasn't conscious that he was building a coffin/boat? Or what if it *is* a coffin intended for me or a senior citizen? What am I supposed to do about it? Phone the police? Forget it. I'll keep an eye on it, maybe move it into a dark corner, see if he forgets about. Kids always start projects, then lose interest. He's still a kid. People forget that. He's still a kid.

"How close to list price?" Jerry asks. He picked up on the first ring. Maybe conversation's getting a bit strained with Gingivitis Girl.

"Probably close." I'm one of those naive types who keeps promises. And I did promise to let Jerry know of any "serious" interest in the house.

"Okay, so let's do it."

"The thing is"—I pull my sheets up to my neck—"Sam doesn't want to sell."

"Sam is a confused young man—he doesn't know what he wants."

"Well, I think selling his home might confuse him more."

"It might also shake some sense into him."

Definitely don't want Jerry seeing the coffin/boat. "The other thing is"—and I really don't know how to say this without making him throw up or something—"I've got another lump."

"Oh, love . . ."

He hasn't called me "love" in a hundred years.

"Is it malignant?" he asks.

I feel tears collecting in my left eye. "Geisberger is operating next week, he isn't sure."

"Oh, love . . ."

The dam breaks and I look around for Kleenexes, can't find any, use a corner of my cream sheets.

"Greer . . . ?"

I try to answer but choke on the words.

"Do you want me to come over?" he asks.

I remember this, that he would be there for me when I least expected it. And for an instant I do want him here, want to bury my face in his Armani suit, but within seconds I realize that this would feel false, forced. "I'll be okay," I say. "But please understand I can't sell the house right now."

"I understand."

He really isn't all bad. We bring out the badness in each other, suck out each other's poison, thereby poisoning ourselves.

He clears his throat and I wonder if a tear is trapped in there. "Will you let me know what happens?" he asks.

I'm not used to him asking, only demanding. "Do I have to? I mean, I hate talking about it."

"I'm the father of your son."

"Right. Okay."

"Promise?"

"Promise."

I hang up and unwrap a butterscotch, place it on my tongue, away from my teeth which I've already brushed, and contemplate my neuralgia. If the pain centres are in my head, what's real and what isn't? Obviously it doesn't matter. Pain is pain. "Pain centres" suggests busy places filled with jangled nerves venting about how they became stressed. If only they could forgive.

I ponder the word centre, how Rachel will stress herself out trying to find hers. And I think of us earthlings believing for centuries that we were the centre of the universe only to discover that the cosmos contains tens of billions of galaxies hurtling about, expanding, swirling, ballooning. The further away they are, the faster they're racing away. Just like life. The further it is from us, the faster it's racing away. Yet we grab at it, as if that tiny darkening speck were still within reach. In the face of tens of billions of galaxies, we continue to behave as though we are the centre of the universe.

And I think of Lyla's mind hurtling, expanding, swirling, ballooning. In the old days we locked them up. Now we provide medical restraints. But still the mentally ill walk alone. I can think of no other disability so reviled. I will not abandon this girl.

I can't sleep. In the basement, I stare at the coffin/boat. It's quite ingenious actually, built from odd pieces of lumber left behind by Jerry. I try nudging it with my foot but it's heavy, solid. Bending down like a sprinter readying for a race, I grip one side of it and push, using my weight as leverage. It takes me ten minutes to move it to the darkest corner.

Twenty

I've trapped my loved ones in my car with me. It's a blazing, brilliant, azure-skyed autumn day. The kind of day you stand in knowing there will never be another like it because within hours the leaves will begin to lose their fire. In days, they will shrivel and fall, leaving behind the dull grey of ash.

"Does anybody need to pee?" I ask them. "Do you want to stop at Tim Hortons?"

"I'd like a coconut doughnut," Sybil announces.

"Then you shall have one."

We pull into the parking lot and I release my prisoners. On the whole, they're behaving rather well. They didn't fight at breakfast, and Sam actually wished her a happy birthday.

It relieves me that he orders two double chocolates rather than a whole wheat roll. I settle for a carrot muffin hoping that the beta carotene will miraculously heal me. We sit by a window and stare at golden fields. Pop music blares; Bette Midler singing about you being the wind beneath my wings. Coffee's good. Sybil adds about four pounds of sugar to hers.

"Are we having fun yet?" I ask. Sitting across from me, they both nod politely, humouring the old gal, and I have this feeling that really, really all is going to be well, peachy, hunky-dory. "Maybe we should move to the country," I suggest.

"Boresville," Sybil says. Sam wipes chocolate icing off his lip.

"Do *you* think it would be boring?" I ask him.

He shrugs, then says, "You have to drive everywhere."

"That's a point." This would be awkward for him as he doesn't drive because he ran over a cat once. I've told him everybody runs over an animal at some point in their driving lives, but he's remained resolute in his resistance to taking the wheel.

I dropped off a cheque for ten thousand dollars at Rachel's yesterday with the intention of kicking Porky Pig's ass but he was at the Org. Rachel wouldn't stop cleaning even though the place looked spotless. I suspect her obsession with cleanliness results from having lived with our mother's slovenliness. Besides, it's a world she can control, with Amway products. She thanked me so profusely for the money it became embarrassing. We had tea together, accompanied by the leaf blower next door. There was too much to say and no way to say it, because words can't bridge the gap between us. We don't even know each other anymore, and I'm not sure we want to. I miss the orange juice cans, but don't have the energy to tiptoe around the choices she's made. I can't relate to her marriage, her business, her need to consult Mrs. Adams. I miss the little girl with the bleeding ears, but adult Rachel keeps her well hidden.

"The bimbo on that beach show," Sybil tells us, "she's getting her implants taken out. Says she wants to go back to her natural look."

"Her tits were humongous," Sam offers.

"Won't the skin flop?" Sybil asks.

"Probably," I say. "I don't know how floppy tits are going to work in a bikini."

"She'll get them tightened up," Sam advises us.

This is what I've dreamed of, good company, stimulating conversation.

"Anyway," Sybil adds, "I thought it made a nice change, a sexpot getting her titties made smaller."

"It is a nice change," I agree.

In Elora, we explore twee touristy shops. I force Sybil to let me buy her a hand-knitted cardigan with a Canada goose on it. "You want to look good for Norm," I tell her and she blushes. Sam lets me buy him a pot of raspberry jam to put on his smoothy peanut butter. But really there isn't much to do in Elora. We have sandwiches in the Mill Restaurant by the gorge and listen to water rushing. Sybil drinks one vodka and then another and I worry that soon she'll be preaching Marxism. The cute waitress has been admiring Sam and he knows it. He's been smoothing back his hair and slouching "cool." I try not to giggle about this as Sybil and I discuss important topics like what we must do to keep the neighbour's cat from spraying on our porch.

But something changes over the apple crumble. The cute waitress stiffens and no longer offers us coffee refills. Eyes behind aviator glasses fix on us from the kitchen and I realize that the cook has recognized my son. I consider running back there, offering him cash if he would please just act normal. But already it's too late. My preening son folds his feathers, leans his elbows on the table and covers his face. With her back to all this, Sybil rants about our hatchet-job government's treatment of the homeless. "They won't even let them sleep in the parks. If the cops find one on a bench, they hit his feet with billy clubs and write out a ticket. All so we don't have to see their suffering. Drive them out of Toronto, keep the city clean, doesn't matter if they freeze to death as long as we don't see it."

I don't need to ask for the bill because the waitress slaps it on the table, then hurries away as though afraid we might chase her. Should I acknowledge what has occurred or pretend I haven't noticed? What would help my son? "Let's go," I say, "we want to get back in daylight." I leave a large tip hoping that maybe, maybe, she'll feel some guilt, maybe, maybe she'll forgive.

In the car, silence reigns. Sybil dozes off and Sam, sitting in the back, stares out at passing fields. I can feel his foot tapping behind me. When Sybil begins to snore, I turn on the radio and learn that U.S. apples, peaches, grapes, green beans, pears, spinach and winter squash contain a hundred times higher levels of toxic pesticide levels than other foods. A single daily serving of these fruits and veggies delivers "unsafe levels of toxic pesticide residues to young children." All the foods tested were within legal limits, although these limits are at odds with what the U.S. government deems safe for children. So why doesn't the government change the legal limit? Hmmm. Could conglomerates have anything to do with it?

We find Rachel sitting in the kitchen, drinking Sybil's vodka. We've always given each other keys so the fact that she's in the house isn't surprising. But the redness and swelling on her face is. "What happened?" I ask.

"Nothing. I just thought I'd sleep here tonight, if that's okay."

"Did Bob hit you?"

"Of course not."

"Then what happened to your face?"

She fumbles, pretends to be looking for something in her purse. "A door. I bumped into a door."

"I'm going over there."

"Please don't."

"Alright, I'll call the police."

"Nothing happened," she insists. "Just leave it, can't you leave it?"

"No. This is unacceptable."

"It was the credit cards," she moans. "I should've told him what I was doing."

"Why? Did he come up with ten thousand dollars?"

She flails her arms and I realize she's drunk. "I wouldn't've come if I knew you were going to be like this."

"Has he hit you before?"

"Of course not." She can't even look at me, the little girl with the bleeding ears.

"That's it. I'm going over."

She's hysterical now. "Don't! Please don't!"

"I won't do anything. I'm just going to talk to him."

"I'm coming with you," Sam says.

"What? Why?"

"So he can't hurt you."

"He's not going to hurt me, he's a chickenshit."

"Greer!" my little sister pleads.

"Now, now," Sybil says. "She's only going to talk to him. Have another drink, dear, put some ice on that bruise. We'll just sit tight till they get back."

In the car, I'm steamed. I can't abide hitting. I've suspected that the little worm had tantrums and hurled ugly words at my abuse-receptive sister, but I thought he was too cowardly to use physical force. But then isn't it always the cowards who attack the weak?

Does this mean Sam's a coward? No, he was asleep.

"I want you to wait in the car," I tell him, remembering that he's capable of murder.

"No way."

"Sam, he's a wimp. It's better we sort this out between us."

"Yeah, like if he takes a swipe at you, you're going to be able to defend yourself. You can't even swat a fly."

He has a point. But I feel invincible, endorphins must be surging because I feel that old battle lust. All my anger at the world who mistreats my son has found a focus. I'm going to blow this little shit out of the water. At this moment, he represents everything I despise: wilful ignorance, greed, selfishness, deceit, arrogance, brutality.

He's sprawled on the couch slug-like, beer cans in a pile beside him, watching Mel Gibson shoot a bad guy's face off through a pillow. I press the power button.

"If you ever hit my sister again," I say, "I will kill you."

"Well ahh, now let's ahh get this straight, I aah did, did, didn't hit anybody."

"Oh yes, you did, you little worm." It's hard to beat up on someone who stutters.

"Aahh . . . all I'm ahh saying is, she she shouldn't . . ."

"I gave her money to pay off your debts. It is *my* money, for *her*. If you run up more bills on becoming enlightened, I will have no choice but to sic my son on you. He's killed people, you know."

"T . . . t . . . tell me about it."

"I don't think I need to." I avoid eye contact with Sam because I don't know how he feels about being used as a weapon, but he's the only one I've got. "Now where can you go?" I ask Porky.

"Wha . . . what?"

"You can't stay here. You must have friends, at the Org perhaps? Just till the legalities get settled."

"Le . . . legalities?"

"Abuse is a criminal offence."

"Nn . . . now look here . . ."

"I am and it would seem to me that the only honourable thing for you to do is to provide a safe haven for your wife. She'll stay with me tonight, but she's not giving up her home. Whether or not she presses charges is her affair." Something's going on with my body, a power failure. I lean my hand against the wall for support.

"Le . . . let me talk to Rachel."

"Not tonight."

"Nn . . . now look here . . ."

"Oh stop saying that. Finish your brewskies and get some sleep. We'll be back tomorrow and will expect to find you gone. Leave a number where you can be reached. Come on, Sam."

My head's doing strange things, lights coming and going and the relentless chisel driving at my tooth.

Sam opens the car door for me. "Are you alright?"

"I just have to sit for a bit."

We do, in suburbia, the land of no sidewalks where people spray toxic chemicals on their lawns. Maybe we were designed to self-destruct, maybe it's all part of a master plan. My waiting-room reading has informed me that, in 1950, New York was the only city with a population over ten million. By 2015, there will be twenty-seven such cities, twenty-three of them in the developing world. Even now, a quarter of urban dwellers in developing countries don't have safe water supplies and half of them lack sewage facilities. So here's a question: How's an expanding population going to be accommodated when we've already hit our global carrying capacity? Could be tricky. Can't be too pleasant dying of thirst immersed in shit.

"It's weird out here," Sam observes.

"Yes," I agree. "Lots of wife beating going on, I figure."

"You probably get persecuted if you don't mow your lawn."

"Or allow dandelions to grow between your interlocking bricks."

I rummage in my purse for butterscotches, hand him one. The crinkling of the cellophane soothes me, and the sound of us sucking. A doughy man in argyle everything waddles by and I'm certain that he was once a woman. What happened that made her feel she had to become a man? Was she wounded in love and determined never to love again but to move to the suburbs and wear argyle everything?

"I think men who hit women should be publicly spanked," I say.

"Won't stop them hitting."

"Sure it would, having their tushies hanging out in public, their peepees shrivelled up?"

"It's not like they choose to hit. It just happens."

"Kind of like ejaculation."

"Oh, Mum."

What glorious words: "Oh, Mum." I feel better already.

My little sister lies on my bed emitting little animal snores. I pull up a chair and watch her. With the tension gone from her face, she is beautiful again, apart from the bruise. She has Sam's golden hair, which I gently stroke. Why do the vulnerable get pummelled and then pummelled again, making them more vulnerable? Their wounds never heal as they limp into the next cruel embrace. Why Porky Pig? My God, she had all kinds of guys calling her, one of them must've been decent. Porky Pig was in the army, looked bigger in his uniform. His courtship of my sister reminded me of the soldiers "freeing" Europe in '45—basically raping young girls emerging from the rubble who were frightened, in desperate need of comfort and cigarettes.

I note a bit of drool leaking from her mouth.

When our parents' feuds extended into the night, we'd sleep together, my knees tucked behind hers, my arm around her waist. If I do that now, she'll think I'm perverted.

I can't sleep anyway and decide it's time to bury Jerry's golf trophy since he doesn't want it. I've left it on the mantel because I thought it held meaning for Sam but, as he thinks his father's an asshole, I feel it's time to take action. I switch on the outdoor light and find a spade in the shed. It's fun digging; I imagine the trophy being unearthed years from now, after the apocalypse, by aliens who'll put it in their museum of human art.

"What are you doing?" Sam asks, making me jump about ten feet.

"Burying your dad's golf trophy."

"Why?"

"Because I'm sick of it. Do you want it?"

"No way."

"Well, it'll be here if you change your mind." I drop it in the hole. He takes the spade from me and fills in the dirt.

"Couldn't you sleep?" I ask. "Do you want me to make you some hot milk?"

"Okay."

Good, I have a purpose. I bustle back to the kitchen and pour milk into a saucepan, dig around in the cupboard for honey—"a little something," as Pooh would say. Sam loved those stories. Especially Eeyore's birthday; poor old Eeyore didn't think anybody would remember and was beside himself when Piglet presented him with the burst balloon and Pooh gave him the empty honey pot. Dear old Eeyore sitting there, putting the burst balloon into the pot, then taking it out again, happy as a clam. Making so much of so little when most of us make so little of so much.

"Should we put a cross over it?" Sam asks.

"Only if we can tie a skeleton to it."

He sits and throws his feet up on a chair. "I don't think that guy's firing on all cylinders," he comments.

"Who? Bob? He's found religion."

"Marriage sucks, man."

"Not always. You just haven't been exposed to good ones."

"Gran and Grandad loved each other."

He never talks about them; I try to appear unfazed. "An obsessive kind of love."

"What other kind is there?"

"The kind in which you are friends above all else." I pour the milk into mugs and hand him one.

"You've never had that."

"No. I was too busy looking for fireworks." I place the saucepan in the sink, run water into it. "I talked to your dad. We're not selling."

"Cool."

I put the honey back in the cupboard. "Did you like that waitress in Elora?"

"She's trash."

I nod, not knowing what else to do. His fingers twitch around his mug as though it's electrically charged. Waiting for him to talk because I'm tired of filling in the blanks, I sit and lean my head against the wall.

"No girl's ever going to go out with me," he says.

"Sure they will."

"Not if I tell them what I did."

"Sweetie, you have to start thinking of it as a horrible, tragic accident. You did not voluntarily kill these people."

"I still killed them."

"People driving cars kill people. Do you think it stops them dating?"

He shrugs, sips his milk.

"You are," I continue, "a kind, intelligent, sensitive, attractive person with a sleep disorder that you're dealing with and will probably grow out of. Any girl who rejects you on the basis of an unconscious act isn't someone you want to be around anyway. That tart in the restaurant wouldn't even give you a chance. She's going to marry Joe the truck driver, live in a trailer and pop fourteen babies. Forget it, you're not going to find the girl of your dreams in Elora."

He slouches further into his chair, becoming Eeyore; nobody cares about me, nobody'll ever love me. I'm reminded of a "total mind and body self-improvement course" I was forced to attend. The key doofus had us chanting "inspirational" mantras such as "The universe loves ME!" I feel like shouting "The universe loves YOU!" to my lost son, but he'd think I'm making fun of him, which I'm not. I do believe he's been graced with a second chance. "I love you so," I tell him because I don't know what else to say. That word, the vessel of all those feelings beyond words, sinks through the floor into the coffin/boat. I shouldn't have said it, it's begging him to reply "I love you too," and he's not ready for that, may never be. And why should he? It's the mother's job to love unconditionally.

"You want to watch *Letterman*?" he asks.

"No. I'm pretty wiped."

"You're okay, though?"

"I'm okay." And he's gone. So be it. I'm back in my place. I got a little too soppy there, a little too demonstrative. God knows what would happen if I tried to hug him.

I curl up beside my baby sister, being careful not to disturb her. Wind rattles my window and I imagine shingles lifting off my ancient roof that I'm not selling to the Iranians. Guess I'll have to get it repaired.

Twenty-one

The thought of Sybil's fragile skin being cut open has me fidgeting and pacing about the hospital. Norm won't let us down, I keep assuring myself, it's a simple procedure, no probs, piece of cake. To distract myself, I call agents and set up appointments to see hideous condos suited to Muriel. The chisel's at my tooth again, probably because Dobin fitted the cap this morning. "What a beautiful crown preparation," he told himself, or me or his body-snatcher assistant. I can't imagine what Scotty has to do to keep the doctor's ego inflated. Does she wear crotchless Little Red Riding Hood outfits and say, "Oh, sir, what big teeth you have"?

Out of desperation, I pick up a *Time* and sit beside two old ladies probably waiting to be hooked up to pacemakers. One of them has the kind of cough you don't want to be near. "I caught it from a friend," she explains apologetically to the other. "She wanted me to do something for her."

"You should've stayed home," her blue-haired companion responds.

"Well, she pressured me a bit, you know how it is."

"You've got to resist that."

"Being pushed."

"That's right," Blue Hair concedes. "I've pushed at it my whole life and now I've quit. Now I let my children do the pushing."

Pushed at what exactly? I want to ask.

"I'm in a seniors' tower now," she says. "Gave my car to my granddaughter. She needs it more than I do."

"Don't you miss your home?" the consumptive old lady inquires.

"The garden mostly."

"And your friends?"

Blue Hair doesn't respond to this and I cop a quick glance at her. Her chin is thrust forward in a proud I-don't-need-anybody kind of way. "They can come visit me if they want," she pronounces, and I'm sure they won't, because the tower's too far away, too high up. "It's got a nice view of the city," she adds, as though this makes it okay that she's going to live out her days entombed in concrete, far from the familiar. Who "pushed" her to sell her home in the first place?

Uh-oh. *Time* informs me that heartburn can lead to cancer, that we must avoid fatty foods. Bummer. I was really enjoying mainlining potato chips again.

"I pay the insurance," I hear Blue Hair explain. "Anybody can drive it so long as I pay it." And I'm thinking they got you to sell your house, surrender your car *and* pay the insurance? Aren't children wonderful?

I get this feeling, and it may be completely transitory as most good feelings are, but I get this feeling Sam wants me around, and not just because of the money. Like I said, it's probably transitory.

A buxom nurse retrieves me. "Your aunt's asking for you," she says.

Great, that means she's alive.

Trapped behind bed rails, Sybil looks wounded. "Let's go," she grumbles.

"I think they want you to rest for a bit. Has Norm talked to you?"

She shakes her head. "I need a smoke. Where's my purse?"

"At home."

"Get me a cigarette, I'll take the rap."

"Forget it, Auntie."

She keeps fiddling with the bandage over the incision. "Leave it alone," I tell her. "A picked wound doesn't heal."

"I want some bread and butter."

Old people lie stranded around us. General Norm gallops into the battlefield, jumps off his horse and leans over Sybil. "How you doin'?"

"It feels funny."

"How so?"

"Foreign."

"Sybil," he says, "you've overcome all kinds of things in your life, don't tell me a little jump starter's going to faze you?"

"I guess not," she mumbles and actually smiles at him. I wonder if this is the kind of guy she would have married, given the chance. It makes sense. She would've killed anybody who took her seriously.

"You're looking good," he adds. "You've got colour. Soon you'll be hopping and skipping." He turns to me, suddenly serious. "It went well, no complications, but keep her hands off it if you can."

"I'll try."

"Gotta go, Sybil. Come and see me soon, alright? We gotta keep tabs on you." Astride his horse, he offers a salute and is gone.

"My podiatrist," Muriel tells Spidey the house inspector, "says I have the most well preserved metatarsi he's ever seen."

The inspection of Devon's house is taking way too long because Muriel has felt it necessary to convince Spidey that she was the belle of the ball whilst at Maxim's in Paris and looks much younger than her years. Spidey, being a man of few words, simply nods vaguely and continues to make endless notes on his clipboard. Unfortunately, he has spotted leaks in the skylights and some buckling in the hardwood around the sliding doors to the third-floor deck. Fortunately, Muriel seems to be absorbing none of this during her hot pursuit of Spidey's undying admiration.

"Of course I *must* lose five pounds," she admits. "It gets more difficult as you get older. But it's a stunning dress. Silk, of course. I told the salesgirl I was too old for it and she said, 'Absolutely not, you have elegance.' Which is true, of course. The length was a concern—short is *au courant* but I didn't really feel it would be suitable. 'Just above the knee,' I told her. 'But you've got the legs,' she said."

Spidey steps outside and starts clambering around the deck. I fear that within minutes he'll spot wood rot.

"He's not very gallant, is he?" Muriel asks me.

"He's a house inspector."

"That's no excuse for rudeness." She adjusts her floppy hat in a mirror. "I must dash. I'm seeing my cranial therapist in twenty minutes."

"Give my regards to Devon."

"Oh, she's not speaking to me. We had a blazing row. She's having postnatal depression, so she says."

"I'm sorry."

"Yes, well, I think it's an excuse to do absolutely nothing." She pulls out her compact and powders her nose. "Do tell those Iranians to quit spying on my house."

"Have they been around?"

"And all their friends. Bloody Muslims. In frightfully expensive cars, of course."

"I'll mention it to Todd." Although Todd's pissed with me for not selling the Halibs' buddies my house. "It's unprofessional," he told me. I apologized for waffling on the issue, but he's remained huffy. This may have less to do with me and more to do with the loss of his parakeet. Todd left it in the care of a neighbour because he thought the fumes from the Ralph Lauren paint would be bad for the bird. But the neighbour let Liberace out of the cage and he escaped through a window.

"Don't birds have homing skills or something?" I asked.

Todd sighed heavily. "If something happens to Liberace, I will die."

"It's quite a big bird, isn't it?" Estelle queried. "It's not like a budgie. A cat can't get it."

He turned on her. "How can you say that? He's a *domesticated* animal, he doesn't know how to survive in the wild."

"It's not exactly the wild," I pointed out. "Pigeons survive. Tiny sparrows." I was trying to offer hope. "I bet if you cruise around your neighbour's place, you'll find Liberace nibbling on bread crumbs or something."

"He only eats whole grains." He collapsed into a chair and absently flicked through some real estate listings. "My life, it's just, like why bother, you know? I'm just trying to live a life here, mind my own business—first I sprain my ankle, then I lose my bird."

"Put up notices," I suggested. "Offer a reward. Is he green?"

Todd threw the listings on a desk. "With a yellow breast."

"Does he talk?"

"He shrieks when he's stressed."

"That's good. That'll get attention."

"We . . . we've been through so much together. Maybe he thought . . . maybe he thought I was abandoning him." Todd's voice cracked. I handed him a butterscotch which he refused because he's on a sugar-buster diet.

"He's not here," I tell Rachel who prowls around her house as though fearful of being attacked. Thankfully the little porker has gone AWOL. I half thought he might display some courage, hold his ground, and that I would have to call the police and generally cause a scene. He has left a note for Rachel which I'm sure is loaded with emotional blackmail. I hand it to her anyway. She opens and reads it, gasps, clutches her throat, slides down the wall to the floor and sobs. I want to snatch the note from her, burn it, because I know he's playing games with her. But instead I sit on the floor beside her and put an arm around her shoulders, which she immediately pushes off. I move over, giving her space, wondering why I continue to meddle in people's lives. Maybe a life with an evil dwarf suits her. Isn't there supposed to be ecstasy in pain? Don't we kill the thing we love? Maybe Porky loves her in a way I can't understand, having had such limited experience of the thing.

"Do you want me to go?" I ask.

"Yes."

This definitive response gouges me. I move slowly, awkwardly, hoping for a word like stay. When it doesn't come, I close the door quietly behind me, and tell myself I will not call her.

It's while I'm loading groceries into the car that I spot the flash of green. Beside a dumpster, behind the supermarket, eating white bread, is Liberace. I stop breathing for a second, take out my cell and page Todd, then stand very still, keeping an eye on the bird. When a minivan bursting with children pulls in beside me, I gesture "sshhh" and point. Soon a crowd has gathered and I know that momentarily Liberace will have had his fill and be disturbed by the attention. Therefore, it is crucial that I formulate a plan. I try to remember the contents of my grocery bags. What would be tempting for a parrot who usually eats whole grains? Mini-pizzas? Peanut butter? Aha, pecan pie. I open my car door, slide the pie out of its box and move stealthily towards the bird. He stares at me out of one eye as he beaks his Wonderbread. "I'm a friend of Todd's," I explain. "And I have some nut pie I thought you might enjoy." He stops beaking briefly, then resumes eating. Within yards of him, I freeze and continue chatting. Behind me I hear the mother of the many children repeatedly saying, "Shut the fuck up!"

"Liberace," I continue, "Todd was having your place painted, which is why he took you to the neighbour's. He's very sorry if he upset you." I creep a little closer. He's not very big, maybe a foot long including the tail feathers. "He was trying to protect you from toxic fumes. Carcinogens. He loves you very much." I place the pie a few feet in front of him. He cocks his head, eyeing it. "It's going to be a harsh winter, according to the Farmer's Almanac. I don't think you'll want to be outside." I slowly slide the scarf off my neck. "Besides, your place is going to be newly painted in Ralph Lauren colours." Liberace takes a couple of steps towards the pie. "I've felt neglected myself from time to time, but often I find it's because the alleged neglecter got busy with other things. They didn't *intend* to neglect me." He takes a peck at the pie, beaks a nut, savours it, goes for another. When his head's down, I throw the scarf over him and try to get a grip, but he shrieks and flaps. A struggle ensues and I worry that I'm going to break his wings. Or die from parrot bites. "It's going to be alright," I shout over the screeching as I bundle him to my car. His claws scratch, his beak jabs. But I toss him in and slam the door. The shrieks penetrate glass and metal and I feel the crowd turning hostile because of my cruelty to parrots. "Get the pie," I tell the mother whose bottom jiggles as she hurries to retrieve Liberace's treat. I take it from her and, with one swift movement, open the door, put the pie on the seat and slam the door.

"You're not going to drive with him in there, are you?" Jiggly Bottom asks me.

"No. I'm going to wait for his owner to come for him."

"He's pooping in there," she observes.

"Well, he's stressed," I point out.

"Hope he don't overdose on that pie. Caramels killed our gerbils."

"Well," I respond, "I think he's just eating the nuts."

"Better hope so otherwise you could have one dead bird on your hands."

She has been of assistance but I wish she would leave. Her children press their snotty noses against my car windows and squawk.

"I think he needs some peace and quiet," I say.

"With all that shrieking he's doing he can't hear nothin'," Jiggly Bottom replies.

This is the kind of thick thinking that clogs the world's arteries.

"He's shrieking," I explain, "because your children are frightening him. Please go ahead and do your shopping. We'll be fine here."

The dullard stands there. "Yeah, okay," she says finally. "Come on, kids, let's go get weenies." Fifteen minutes later, she's herded them into the store, but Todd has not returned my call—I fear because he's mad at me. My car interior is covered in shit and Liberace looks overfed and waning. I start to worry about oxygen; how to roll a window down without letting him escape. Nothing for it but to get in there with him. I swing open the door and dive into the driver's seat. This starts a fresh outburst of shrieks. I wait for him to attack me, peck my head, my face, but the poor sod's exhausted. He blinks at me, gripping the upholstery. I phone our receptionist who believes that Todd's at the Irish bar run by Sikhs. I drive slowly, carefully, but there is no question in my mind that I will be stopped by the police and charged for driving with an unrestrained bird.

I find Todd exchanging dying-pet stories with Estelle and, to my horror, Earl Verman who's spitting on a napkin and wiping dirt off his white loafers.

When I give him the news, Todd presses his hands together as though in prayer. "How can I ever thank you?" he asks.

"Stop being mad at me for not selling my house."

"Done."

I hand him my keys. "He's all yours. Is your car nearby?"

He nods and scampers off, in spite of his "sprained" ankle. Earl pulls out a chair for me. "Take a load off your feet." I do because I'm depleted from bird hunting.

"Can I buy you a drink?" he inquires.

"Sure. A draft."

He signals the waitress. "I was just telling Estelle here about the Grundy bungy being vandalized."

"What . . . ?"

"Last night. Somebody broke in. Took the stereo, TV and so on. Seems they knew she was out."

"Are the police investigating?"

"As much as they can. Don't seem to be too interested, what with her being in the loony bin and so on. Not exactly an influential citizen, if you know what I mean."

I try to imagine Lyla "recovered," doped, walking into her violated home. This will plunge her back into darkness.

"The snag is," Earl continues, "there's no lights on in the house. You wouldn't happen to have a key, would you?"

This is why he's skulking around our office. He thinks I have access to his listing.

"You said you were paying her a social call," he explains. "I thought maybe you'd have a key, or know somebody who does."

"Nope," I say.

Estelle lights up another cigarette. "Just be thankful she doesn't have animals."

Earl crosses one leg over the other and jerks his foot around. "Anyhoo, my buyers are interested in making an offer, if you happen to talk to her."

"Earl," I venture, "maybe you should chill out on that house for a bit. Wait and see how she feels when she recovers."

"*If* she recovers. My sister-in-law's a social worker. She's seen a thing or two, I can tell you. Girls slashing themselves, bleeding to death and so on."

"Lyla's in a hospital," I remind him.

"It's revolving doors these days," he says. "She'll be out in a week. Deinstitutionalization. My sister-in-law says the only place left for the crazies is the jails. And you got to do more than shout 'Bomb!' to get invited there." He drains his glass. "Anyhoo, give me a buzz if you hear anything."

Todd hurries in and hands me my keys. "Liberace is *very* angry with me. He nipped me, he's never nipped me." He shows us the bite mark on his wrist.

"You should stay home for the next few days," Estelle advises. "Whenever Bunny came back from the hospital, he was angry with me and I had to stay home with him. He'd hide under chairs and stuff like that. Sometimes he'd stop eating. I'd have to cook him something really special, like veal parmigiana or something."

Todd scrutinizes the bite. "I can't stay home. I have open houses."

Estelle gives him a searing look. "If you love Liberace like you say you do, you'll make sacrifices."

Earl stands and hitches up his pants. "I'd be happy to help out with your open houses, Todd."

Todd grimaces, but I love the idea of Earl sliming Mrs. Tanenbaum. Maybe he'll offer her some decorating tips.

Estelle puts a hand on Todd's shoulder. "Do it, Todd. You won't regret it. Liberace *needs* you."

"Alright," Todd concedes, barely glancing at Earl. "I'll call you tonight with the details."

"Super," Earl says. "Give me a shout anytime." He slinks out without "buying" my beer.

I'm thrilled to see Sybil awake and drinking tea. "Feeling better, Auntie?"

"Much."

"You've got rosy cheeks."

"The boy brought me tea."

"You're kidding?"

"He's going to be alright."

"Where is he?"

"Around." Her hand moves to her bandage.

"Norm told you to leave that alone," I warn her.

"I'm just feeling it."

"You're fiddling with it. There's delicate wiring in there. Leave it alone."

I search the house for him, end up in the basement where I find the coffin/boat missing. I gasp, sit on the steps and breathe deeply into my diaphragm. It is entirely possible that he took it to pieces again, or moved it with help from someone, although I can't imagine who since he has no friends. There has to be a simple explanation. Best to forge ahead, do some laundry, fry some pork chops for Sybil. Hours pass. I read the paper—bad idea: war, savagery, man-made famines, ruthless dictatorships, child porn rings, teenage prostitution, political scandal. Stop reading. On goes the television. Flicky-flicky past doctors, lawyers, cops and cleavage. Off it goes again. I lie back on the couch and listen to the noises of the house; a groan here a creak there. Tomorrow this breast may be gone.

Hey, it's only flesh.

I told Cheeseburger I want to keep it if possible. Because I believe it will make me less grotesque to my son.

Did I rescue Liberace today, or was he happy off limits? He bit Todd, what can this mean? I have a horrible feeling I robbed that bird of his longed-for freedom.

I dropped the car off to be cleaned. Coming home on the subway, I saw only misery in faces and wanted to jump up and say, Guess what folks? You're not going to the hospital tomorrow to have your breast cut off, rejoice!

But I knew there'd be no point. True, marrow-deep appreciation only comes with loss.

A raving lunatic wearing two coats kept scurrying from seat to seat, cursing people who weren't there. We all looked the other way.

Liberace in a cage, Lyla in a cage. Earl Verman at large.

Maybe the mad girl is waiting for Prince Charles to rescue her, since he was expecting her in Trinidad.

Stop thinking Sam's in trouble. Have faith. Sybil says he's going to be all right.

Jerry didn't want him in the bed with us. This was a law I abided for some reason I cannot now understand. He'd tug on my blankets, "Mummy, I want to get in da bed wit' you." He stopped asking after a while. Don't we all. It's called socialization.

I'm with Jerry in a house I don't recognize. He keeps touching me in what could be interpreted as a sexual manner. I find this hard to believe and try to ignore it. I'm pulling up floorboards for no discernible purpose. Underneath, I find maggots.

"Mum . . . !"

He's hurting me.

"Mum, wake up!"

"I'm awake, stop pinching me."

"You scared me."

"I'm sorry." He's in his jacket with a smell of autumn leaves about him.

"Why are you always falling asleep?" he asks.

"Am I? I don't mean to." I sit up and try to look lively. "Are you hungry? Do you want me to make you grilled cheese or something?"

"I ate already."

Of course, I want to ask where. He heads for the kitchen, glugs his usual gallon of ginger ale. Slowly, trepidatiously, I follow and try to appear busy at the sink.

"Your doctor's office called," he offers, "to remind you about the surgery."

"Like I could forget."

"Are you going to stay there overnight?"

"No, it's just day surgery," I say, trying to make it sound like it's just a bit of fun, a quick visit.

"Do you want me to come and see you?" he asks. "After?"

He's never come to see me. "That would be nice. Although I'll probably be pretty out of it."

"How are you going to get home?"

"A cab."

He considers this. "Where's the car?"

"Being cleaned." Is he asking because he's thinking of picking me up, overcoming his dead-cat-in-the-road phobia? It would be so nice to have someone waiting on the other side. But then I remember that his licence is expired. "I'll be fine," I say.

He opens a bag of Tostitos and crunches one after another. Resuming my busy work, I feel hot and sweaty under my prosthesis and would love to whip it out, but this might disgust him. "Sam . . ." I begin. "There was something in the basement, made of wood . . ." I wait for him to say "yeah" or "so" but another Tostito vanishes into his mouth. "It was a box of some kind," I continue, "to put things in, I think. Anyway, it's gone."

"Did you want it?"

"No. I just wondered where it went."

"Why?"

"Well, it was rather large and I . . . I've been having difficulty visualizing its departure."

"Arnie helped me move it."

"Arnie?"

"He's really hurt you don't call him anymore."

"What? He said that?"

He nods, gulps more ginger ale.

"I don't call him because he doesn't call me. I'm his real estate agent."

"I guess it's none of my business."

"There is no business. There's nothing. He's a fine person and all that. Anyway, we're getting off the topic here. What was the boat for?"

"Boat?"

"The coffin thing."

He stares at me and I realize my blunder. "I mean the . . ." I stammer, "the wood thing."

"You thought it was a *coffin*?" he says as though I've just accused him of murder, which in a way I have.

"I didn't know what it was, it was just there."

"Why didn't you ask me?"

"Because"—how can I say, Because I feared you might be building it in your sleep, or that you might have intended it for me or a senior citizen—"I didn't want to intrude," I murmur finally.

I feel him drifting away from me. All that ground we've covered in the last few days, slipping.

He shakes his head. "I can't believe you thought it was a coffin."

"Well, what was it?"

"A bookcase."

"A bookcase?" We stare at each other. I see in his eyes the disappointment we feel when someone we thought we understood proves incomprehensible. Or worse, untrustworthy.

"It was for Turner," he says with disdain. "He needs somewhere to keep his encyclopedias and crap."

"Well, that's . . . that's wonderful. I'm so glad you're—"

"Not building coffins," he interrupts. "Get a grip, Mother." He stuffs the Tostitos in the cupboard, the ginger ale in the fridge and takes refuge in the living room with his pal the TV. God, have I blown it. I start blubbering again. This will really make him sick. I run the tap to block out the noise but the sobs keep erupting. I try to plug my mouth with Kleenex as I hurry upstairs to my room. *Stay in your room.* When I'd get mad at him, the kind of mad that knows no bounds, I would make him stay in his room. Not for long, just long enough for me to recover. He would scream, implore. God, I blew it. Try to trust, can't you trust? What's the matter with you?

I fall face down on my bed as I remember falling after the abortion. I didn't want to be inside my body, my head. I wanted to claw my flesh, rip out my entrails. I wanted to die.

I can't die. He thought I was dead. That's what scared him. This is what he lives with now—the constant fear that I'll kick off. Behind the shrugs, the foul mouth, is a frightened little boy who hasn't heard too many cancer stories with happy endings. We should talk about this. How, now that I've betrayed him? Do I beg, plead? He'll stamp his boot in my face. He's gone now. I scared him away.

A bookcase. For Turner. How many times in a life can we say "If only I'd known"? We don't know. That's the whole point, stop thinking you know. Let it transpire and deal with the consequences. You don't hear the bomb when it's directly overhead.

"What's going on?" Sybil asks. This I do not need.

"Nothing."

"Charlie Brown upset you?"

"I upset myself. Please leave me alone."

"It's stuffy in here." She opens the window, amplifying the fucking dog's barks.

"I'm very tired," I say, still buried in my pillow.

"Why are you crying?"

"I don't want to talk about it."

"Okay." I feel her sit at the foot of my bed. I refuse to face her. If she weren't old and dear, I'd boot her off.

"How are you?" I ask.

"Good."

"Good. I'll see you in the morning."

She stands, I feel her hand on my shoulder and her kiss on the back of my head. "Good night, baby."

"Good night, Auntie."

"I'm going to come see you after your surgery."

I wasn't even sure she remembered. "You don't have to. I'll be home in a few hours."

"I want to." I hear her pad to the door, then stop. "You are the most precious thing in the world to me," she says. "I know I don't show it."

"Thank you."

"Thanks has nothing to do with it. You made me get better, now you do the same."

"I'll try."

"We'll get through this."

"Okay."

And I'm drifting on a raft somewhere. At my parents' cottage, we'd lie on air mattresses and let the water take its course, send us down river, into boats, docks, we were fearless, immortal. A luxury enjoyed by the young which my son does not possess.

The night before last, we watched a TV show together about attractive teenagers in designer casuals who go to exclusive high schools, have great sex during commercial breaks, and experience angst over bad hair days. They drive nice cars and live in nice houses, are never without phones, and have supportive, attractive friends who help them get through their bad hair days. Is this what Sam is afraid he'll never have? Is the pouty blonde who gets six invites to the prom the girl of his dreams? Is he robbed of expectations because he knows he can't expect this? Wasn't this always so? Haven't there always been movies starring unattainable starlets? But this is different, because it pretends to be real. And juxtaposed to Nike commercials and Mel Gibson shooting faces off, it does seem real or, anyway, realer. And certainly more entertaining than life as Sam knows it.

Before Spidey showed up, Muriel was complaining to me that her self-tanning lotion had turned her skin orange and blotchy.

Self-tanning lotion? Are we nothing but actors, *pretending* to be tanned, to live nice lives in nice cars and houses while really, really we're all just scared that our tans don't look real and our cars and houses aren't nice enough? Who set these standards? The God of Consumption? There must be one. Nothing but a god could exert this kind of mind control.

If another person tells me that there are "good things" on TV, I may have to club them. The point is there are many more BAD THINGS on TV that rob us of imagination and will, that blur what is real and what isn't. How can I feel for the earthquake victims when the anchorwoman announces that the death toll has climbed to thirty thousand, then smiles warmly and tells me what's new in entertainment? Why should I care? Nobody else does. Besides, the footage is a joke, Steve Spielberg could do it way better.

My son is staring into a world in which there is no delineation between actual wounds and simulated ones, in which actors, body builders and champion wrestlers become heads of state. In which materialism is the norm, in which ruthlessness is perceived as strength, and compassion weakness.

My son believes he has no future and yet he built a bookcase for a disabled boy. He takes no satisfaction from this. He sees nothing gained. Helping Turner does not bring him any closer to the nice life presented to him daily with digital clarity. His own life is murky, unresolvable, without commercial breaks and final episodes.

We were so close for a second there, so close. I could almost smell his skin, could almost feel his muscles relaxing into mine. The little boy who watered his pansies with great care has once again turned to stone.

Twenty-two

The nurses don't even pretend to be nice or concerned. They have the overworked, underpaid expressions of pieceworkers in the garment industry. After endless waiting in a hospital gown, with my butt exposed to the breeze, one of them wordlessly hooks me up to an IV; I'm just another sleeve to her. Almost immediately, I become woozy and disconnected from what's being done to my body, which is a good thing. They wheel me into the world of stainless steel and masked bandits. Defenceless in the face of their weapons, I watch as the bandits begin to shake, rattle and roll. The anaesthetist injects his poison and I am relieved to be leaving the party.

I'm diving off concrete into the ocean because I can't afford the sandy beach. The sandy beach belongs to the expensive hotel and I'm living in a shack, on the concrete. The undertow sucks me down, down. I struggle to surface, reach up, but can only feel the coarse underbelly of the concrete. The ocean slams me against it. Salt water burns the scrapes on my arms and face. Don't panic, I tell myself, let the current pull you away, it *will* pull you away, and you'll be able to swim into the clear.

I wake hearing my voice, which doesn't sound like my voice, responding to one of the pieceworkers who's taking my vital signs. "How do you feel?"

"Nauseated."

She gives me a shot of Gravol. I'm back on the air mattress, drifting.

The voices first, then thirst. And a smell I recognize—Sybil who hasn't bathed for days. "How are you, baby?"

"Okay."

"Jerry brought us, me and Sam. You look fine, sweetie."

"Aren't I going home?" I ask.

"Of course you are," booms my former he-man. "They just want to observe you for a bit. Geisberger wants to see you."

"I don't want to see him."

"He has to let you know how it went."

And then he's there, my son, hovering above me, my angel, my love. "It's over," he tells me and I think maybe, maybe he's forgiven me.

"That's good, isn't it?" I say.

"Yeah."

I'm trying to determine, without touching it, if my breast is still there.

Jerry holds out flowers for me, which is so silly, so absurd that I feel myself on the verge of a chuckle. But my throat hurts from the doohickey they shove down it to open your airway. "Water, please . . . ?"

"You're only allowed ice chips," Sybil warns.

"Whatever." She shuffles behind the curtains.

"How did you know I was doing this today?" I ask Jerry.

"I have my ways."

A constipated silence descends upon us. I'm one of those animals who prefers to lick my wounds in private. I'm not thrilled to be the centre of attention on this day. Sam leans against the wall as though he's feeling for a trap door that will swing open, allowing him a speedy escape. I attempt to sit up but of course pain stabs me. Another pieceworker zips in and advises me about the drainage tube and the "collecting chamber." "Pin it to your nightie, your blouse, whatever's convenient," she instructs. "Empty it every twenty-four hours, but don't forget to measure the fluid."

"I know all this," I tell her. "I've done this before."

"Oh," she says without surprise. "That's fine then."

Fine?

I'm in a house with many rooms overlooking an alpine valley. Water runs in rivulets down the slopes towards me and I know that soon I will be flooded. The sun glints off the streams and I think what an extraordinarily beautiful day this is. As the water approaches me and the house with many rooms, I find a shovel and calmly begin to build a dam to redirect the water.

I wake again to hear Cheeseburger giving bad news to the woman in the next bed. Hidden behind a curtain I hear only her wails. I suspect that I'm next and feel myself trembling, which could be due to the anaesthetic or my terror, or both. My nearest and dearest must be having a coffee break because they're nowhere in sight, thankfully. Cheeseburger approaches with that preoccupied look of his, and stands over me breathing mouthspray which makes me want to hurl. "I did a lumpectomy and a quick section," he informs me. "Some of the cells appear to be changing. I removed a fair amount of tissue. With any luck, that's all we'll have to do."

"But we won't know until we get the lab results," I say before he does. The woman in the next bed moans.

"That's right," he agrees. "Make an appointment to see me next week." Before exiting, he does this creepy smile, the smile you see frozen on politicians' faces. "Get some rest," he says.

So I still have my breast. How novel. And he didn't tell me to get my affairs in order.

A pieceworker brings me tea and sandwiches and advises me that after I eat something, I can go home. I try to be a good girl but the bread's stale and the cheese so processed it sticks to the roof my mouth. I look around for a wastebasket but can't see one. I toss the sandwich behind the bed just as my entourage returns.

"How are you, baby? We were just getting caffeinated."

"I figured."

"The nurse said you can go after you eat something," Jerry says. I present my empty plate.

"Good. Let's get out of here."

"Do you want to talk about it?" Jerry asks me.

I hand him the won ton soup container. "Not really." I actually feel quite good now that the nausea has subsided and I'm tumour-free, back in my creamy bed. I've accomplished something, survived the knife again. "They can't say anything for certain until they get the lab results," I add.

"Which is when?"

"Next week."

He looks into the container. "You don't want your won tons?"

"You have them." I know he adores the doughy doodads and watch as he gobbles them, suddenly boyish. I don't know why he's hanging around. The three of them seem to be taking turns watching me, as though they're afraid I might jump out the window or something. I'm actually glad they're here. Last time I hid from view, stayed in bed trying to "rest" and got edema. This time I'm keeping my arm propped up at all times when stationary and planning to continue with my life, in spite of the codeine which is spacing me somewhat. I hope to take less of it tomorrow because it bungs me up. Always prepared, I'm armed with laxatives and stool softeners.

Gingivitis Girl phones in a flap. I watch Jerry's face contort as he listens to her. At one point he winces.

"What was that about?" I ask after he's hung up.

"She crinkled the car."

"How'd she do that?"

"Parking."

I try to smother a snort.

"I knew you'd find that amusing," he says, chewing another won ton.

"Wasn't she supposed to be taking driving lessons?"

"She does."

"With one of those macho driving instructor dudes?"

"I don't know if he's macho. He certainly isn't cheap."

Maybe this is why Jerry's hanging around. Gingivitis Girl's

been having a bit of a flirt with her driving instructor, maybe even a toss in the back seat.

"Was he with her when she crinkled the car?" I inquire.

"No, she ahh . . . she drives to Starbucks. She doesn't like making her own coffee. She likes those venti lattes."

"Who doesn't?'

"Don't be a wiseass."

How, I want to shout, HOW could you marry this viper? Boinking them is one thing, but marrying? Goodbye bank account.

"I should never have left you," Jerry says.

"What . . . ?"

"I should never have left."

"Yes, you should have," I reply, thinking it's interesting that he's forgotten I kicked him out.

He sits with his elbows on his knees and his forehead in his hands, revealing his bald spot—his vulnerability. He's blaming himself for my cancer. How hilarious. As if he could be that effective. "You're not blaming yourself for my cancer, are you?" I ask.

"You got sick during the divorce. It was ugly. Unnecessarily so."

"Divorce is always ugly." I don't know if it's the drugs or what, but the evening sun dancing through my window has me feeling—and this is mondo weird considering the circumstances—but I feel uplifted. "Oh come on, Jerr, take your head out of your butt. Nobody knows why anybody has cancer. Blame it on aspartame, that's a good one, too many diet Cokes."

"Stress is a factor," he persists.

"If you don't feel stress, you're dead. I think stress is underrated. Imagine a world full of West Coasters. Scary." I sip some cranberry juice. "I'll tell you what," I offer, "if you want to blame yourself for something, take some responsibility for what's happened to your son."

"What am I supposed to do about it? He hates my guts."

"He desperately, and I mean *desperately*, wants your approval."

"For what? Murdering people?"

"For trying to go on, in spite of the world and you condemning him. He built a bookcase for a disabled boy. And he takes him to bookstores and McDonald's and stuff."

"What disabled boy?"

"One of my client's sons."

"Are you dating one of your clients?"

He's jealous. What a riot. "We're not serious," I say for fun. "Anyway, the point is, he's doing good, he's trying. Maybe, if we don't beat him up, he'll go back to school."

"I doubt that."

"See, that's what I'm talking about. He smells it on you. Doubt."

Jerry stands, walks over to the window and stares out, heaving a Chekhovian sigh. "That tree wasn't there before."

"No."

He fondles his five-o'clock shadow. "He was telling me about the honeybees, he's quite upset about them, and I can't help thinking there's something abnormal about becoming obsessed with honeybees."

"He hasn't talked to me about honeybees."

"Really. Well"—he slides his hands into his pockets and jiggles change—"apparently there's a mite that kills them. Came from Asia on a ship or something. It's destroying the North American honeybee. That and pesticides."

"That's horrible."

"Yes, I suppose it is, but on the other hand, that's evolution. I don't think it's worth losing sleep over."

"What do you think *is* worth losing sleep over, Jerr?" I feel a fight coming on and I'm not up for it. I take another Tylenol No. 3.

But he disarms me with a tender look I haven't seen in years. "Your health."

God, I hate it when people worry about me because it doesn't help.

"My health is fine," I say.

"You have to start taking better care of yourself."

Bring on the violins, as Sybil would say. "I need to fix the roof," I tell him. "Are you willing to cough up fifty percent?"

His tenderness dissolves into concern for fiscal restraint. "Is it leaking?"

"It's twenty years old. The shingles are crumbling. It's stressing me out. It would help my health if we got it repaired."

"Fine. Just don't hire one of your Polish hacks. Use a reputable company."

"It'll cost more." He hesitates, contemplating the number of venti lattes that could be bought for the price of a roof. If I didn't have cancer, he would never repair the house he wants to sell. Every cloud has a silver lining.

"Just send me the bill," he says.

"Half the bill."

"I'll pay for it, Greer, for God's sake."

"I'm not dead yet. Pay for stuff when I'm dead."

"You're not going to die. How do you think he feels when you talk like that?"

"I don't talk like that to him."

He stares down at his five-hundred-dollar shoes. "Will you do chemo this time?"

"I don't know."

He looks at me. "You have to do chemo this time."

"Why does everybody who doesn't have cancer think chemo's a cure-all? It's chemical warfare. The casualties are horrific. That's how it got invented in the first place, soldiers being poisoned by mustard gas."

"Has it not occurred to you that if you'd done it the last time, this wouldn't be happening?"

"No, Jerry, no. Don't start pretending you understand this disease. Nobody understands this disease. My nodes were clear."

He sits on the edge of my bed, our bed, and covers his face with his hands exactly as our son does.

"Is this supposed to be making me feel better?" I ask. "Because it isn't. I'd like you to go now."

He stands wearily, the long-suffering husband. "I wish you'd listen to reason."

"Cancer isn't reasonable. I'm very tired, Jerry. Thanks for picking me up and thanks for helping with the roof. I want to get it done before the snow flies."

"Of course."

"Bye for now."

"Yes."

I listen to his tread on the stair, a sound that used to make my heart skip beats, and think how strange it is, how *strange,* that one person can contain so much of my life. All those years, digested by his body, spewed out his anus. He knows me better than anyone, but he doesn't know me at all.

Whatever was keeping me afloat ruptures and I come tumbling down. I check the fluid in my collecting chamber pinned to my nightie as the pieceworker directed. Shaped like a grenade, it's clear plastic so I can observe what's leaking out of me. A bit of blood, but mostly it's the clear, yellowish stuff. Nothing to fret about. My arm's numb from the constant elevation. I move it gingerly. My shoulder feels like I had a run-in with a Mac truck and my armpit's on fire. I get up to pee but avoid the mirror. Returning to my bed I hear Auntie plodding up the stairs. Quickly I switch off the light and pretend to be asleep.

The home-care nurse is way too perky. She's got perky hair, perky tits, perky buttocks, her name is Patti with an i and she says "that's excellent" frequently.

"I had a bowel movement," I told her when she asked.

"That's excellent."

Her perkiness overwhelms me. I have that feeling you get when you show up dateless to the prom thinking *some* boy will dance with you, that not all the boys have perky dates and then you realize that of course they do. Girls you didn't know were perky have been transformed into runners-up for the Miss America beauty pageant. You stand there in your unpink dress that belonged to your mother one hundred years ago that sort of looked all right after she took it in but now looks atrocious, and you just feel . . . overwhelmed.

"Have you been drinking lots of fluids?" Perky Patti asks.

"Yes."

"That's excellent."

I can see her in the bathing suit for the best-personality quiz. "What hobbies do you enjoy?" a crewcutted judge asks.

Patti shifts her position to make her perky butt more visible. "Helping the poor. Especially the little children. They're excellent."

My only hope is that Patti will be taken off duty due to personal matters, her fiancé having a tummy ache, for example, and my wound will be dressed by an embittered old nurse who pines for the good old days before health care cuts.

"If you increase your fibre," Patti cautions, "you must drink more fluids."

"I understand."

"Otherwise you could block your bowel."

"Right."

"And don't forget to measure the fluid in your collecting chamber and mark it on your chart."

"I won't forget."

She gauzes and tapes me. The diamond on her engagement ring is enormous. Guess she's marrying money.

"Call your doctor if you get more than 70 to 80 ml or 30 cc's."

"Yes."

"The incisions look excellent right now, though."

"Good."

"Is there anything you'd like me to do? Would you like me to brush your hair?"

"No thanks. It's pretty short. Low maintenance."

"Okay then." She packs up her supplies. "Well, keep up the good work, you're doing great."

"Thank you."

My framed poster of Van Gogh's *Iris* has caught her eye. "Is that by Monet?" she inquires.

"Van Gogh."

"Oh he's excellent."

"Yep. Anyway, I've got to pee."

"Good for you."

I wave. "I'll see you tomorrow."

"Definitely."

"Mary Sunshine says you're doing fine," Sybil tells me, handing me a cup of tea.

"I wanted to get up and do stuff, but I just feel too shitty."

"What'd you expect?"

"It was only a lumpectomy."

"'Only.' Give yourself a break." She hands me the newspaper. "They're giving that pedophile two years. He molested sixteen kids. They have to live with it for life and he's only going to be out of service for two years."

"Sick."

"One of the boys he did it to jumped off an overpass after he heard the sentencing."

"Dead?"

She nods. "Couldn't live with it. Telling the world what had happened to him, then seeing the guy get off so easy."

"Sickening."

She straightens my duvet. "That escaped bank robber, if they catch him, they'll lock him up for good and *he* never hurt anybody."

"There's no justice, Auntie, you know that."

She puts my used juice glasses on a tray. "I'm worried about the boy."

"Sam?"

"He's sitting around not doing anything, not even watching TV. I think he's worried about you."

"Why doesn't he come up and see me?"

"I think he's scared."

"That makes two of us."

Liberace's in the room with me, flapping about, banging into walls, the window. "It's okay," I keep assuring him. "I'll let you out." But he's in a panic, shrieking and diving until he smashes into the *Iris* which shatters. Glass shards scatter and Liberace thuds to the floor. He barely moves and I see that he's been stabbed by a piece of glass. He squawks feebly, trying to flap a broken wing. As I pull out the shard, purplish blood spurts out of him. "I'm so sorry," I tell him. I know that he's going to die here, at my feet, and that the only decent thing to do would be to put him out of his misery. The pillow method would work. I grab one and clutch it, bracing myself. His eyes implore me to do something. He thinks I can save him. Maybe I should just cradle him in my arms, just cradle him in my arms.

The phone wakes me. Why doesn't somebody answer it? "Hello . . ." I say. No response. "Hello . . ." I repeat. "What are you selling?"

"It's me," a flat voice says and I know it's Lyla.

"How are you?" I ask. "I'm glad you called."

"You said I should if there was anything you could do." Her English accent is missing, as is her mania. She speaks slowly, deliberately; tranked.

"What can I do for you?" I ask.

"Could you bring me some oranges, seedless? The food's not very good here."

"Are they not letting you out?"

"Oh yes. But I don't want to go out. Once you go out, it's hard to get back in. It's hard to get in here."

She makes it sound as if it's an exclusive resort.

"You *want* to be there?" I ask.

"You have to get doctors to believe you and they don't want to see you. They put you on waiting lists. It's okay here. I've been here before. I don't like group very much. The men stink and smoke cigarettes. But I'd really like some oranges. The food isn't very good here."

"You're at Queen Street?"

"They want me to leave, but I've got these parasites and they're so . . . they're so disgusting, they're . . . I can't . . . if I go home, they'll get on the carpet. They'll *breed.* Can you make sure the oranges aren't from Africa? Poisonous frogs jump out of African oranges. I want California oranges. Seedless."

"Of course." The line goes dead. I stare at the *Iris* which hasn't shattered.

At least she committed herself. At least she's not a forensic patient in a locked ward.

I measure my fluid, mark it on the chart, pour it down the drain, glance in the mirror and see an ancient woman there. I consider lifting up my nightie and having a peek. Nah. I take a laxative. The phone rings. It's Muriel. "I'm in such a state," she tells me. "I took my osteoporosis medication per instructions and my throat feels dreadful. I'm virtually choking to death. These bloody doctors prescribe this, that and the other thing with no warning of the dreadful side effects. It's criminal, they're so busy worrying about billing they wouldn't notice if you dropped dead." I hear water lapping, she's in her tub. "Are we on for tomorrow?" she asks.

The prospect of showing hideous condos to Muriel is not a

pleasurable one. On the other hand, I need the money and I hate lying around. "If you drive," I say, aware that operating vehicles on codeine isn't prudent, "my car's in the shop."

"Certainly. I'll pick you up at one. Cheers."

My door creaks open and Sam appears.

"Hi, sweetie," I say, trying to figure out if he's asleep.

"Who keeps phoning?" he asks.

"Clients."

"Don't they know you're sick?"

"I haven't told anybody." Relieved that he's conscious, I pat my bed, hoping he'll come and sit beside me. Of course, he doesn't. He walks over to the window as his father did before him.

"I want to kill that dog," he says.

"Me too. But don't."

"You think I would?"

Here we go again. Me suspecting him capable of brutal acts. "No . . . it's just . . . *I'd* like to kill it. I fantasize about plugging it with bullets."

"Kill the owners for keeping it penned up like that."

"I agree." Don't fall asleep with this on your mind, I'm thinking. "Was Dad alright today?"

He shrugs. "His car's so fucking clean. I want to wipe my ass on it."

"I know the feeling."

"Do you think he's going to stay married?"

"Probably not. And she'll sue him for all he's got."

He sits at my dressing table and absently picks up a brush, puts it back down, picks up a comb. I can see his face in the mirror. There is a desolation there I haven't seen before.

"Did you have some Chinese food?" I ask.

"It was mostly meat. Sybil ordered it. My fortune said I'm going to get a new television."

"You're kidding?"

He shakes his head.

"I've never had one that specific."

"Are you going to die?" he asks my comb.

Air is sucked out of me. "At some point."

"You know what I mean."

"I don't think so."

"You 'don't think' based on what? What did the doctor say?"

"He can't say much until they get the lab results."

"Which is when?" he asks, echoing his father.

"Next week."

He puts the comb down. "There's no pictures of Gran and Grandad in this house. I've looked everywhere."

"Have you? Well I . . . we should ask Rachel, she might have some."

"Did she hate them, too?"

"I don't think so. I didn't really hate them, Sam, I just . . . I had nothing in common with them."

"So why don't we have any pictures?"

I can't tell him I burned them. "We weren't a picture-taking family. You know, they were more into cars and the cottage and stuff."

I burned them because seeing them brought back the hurt. And because I was angry with them for dying and deserting my son who, for no reason that I can fathom, loved them dearly.

He stands and rubs his hands on his jeans as though touching my implements has soiled him. "You want anything?" he asks.

I want you to be happy, to understand that you're loved, *feel* loved, but these words would ring cheap in a world in which your mother may die and your father's adhered to a whore.

"I'm fine," I say.

"Good night then."

"Sleep tight, love."

He's grasping at gravestones. Because they're solid, grounded and cannot betray him.

Twenty-three

Perky Patti's mopping me with saline solution while telling me how her fiancé took too long to propose to her. She's wearing a tight sweater. As she leans towards me, I have to restrain an impulse to tweak her nipples. "First of all," she explains, "he gives me two boxes, one's green and one's gold, and he says, 'Choose one and I'll return the other.' And I'm like, are you serious? I mean, you don't offer two gifts, then take one back. But he's like a kidder, right, he loves jokes, so I'm thinking, okay, this is just his way. So I'm looking at these two boxes and trying to figure out which one's got a ring in it, right, because I know he's giving me a ring, I mean, he *better* be giving me a ring. So I unwrap the smaller box and inside it there's this other box wrapped in gold paper. So I undo that one and there's another box, and the whole time Steve's sitting there grinning. And my family's all around because it's Christmas and everybody's expecting him to give me a ring, it's all anybody's been talking about. So I get to a Birks box and I'm thinking *finally*, and everybody's like apoplectic and I open it"—she pauses for effect—"and it's earrings." She waits for me to absorb the impact of this. I try to look moved. "So that's it," she concludes. "They're nice earrings and everything but I was so upset, I was scared I was going to start crying right there. So anyway, the next day he gives me the green package, which I know has to be the ring. And my little brother's there and he's announcing it to everybody, 'It's the ring, it's the ring!' So I open it up and guess what?"

"It's not a not a ring?"

"It's a watch. Rolex, really beautiful and everything."

"But not a ring."

"You know what he said after I opened it?" I shake my head.

"He said, 'You should've seen your face.' It was a joke to him."

"That's not very nice," I offer.

"He's just a kidder. He's always doing stuff like that. One time, he tied a plastic bag to our poodle so he wouldn't have to stoop and scoop."

"Not very comfortable for the poodle."

She spreads her fingers, displaying her oversized diamond. "Anyway, isn't it gorgeous?"

"Very striking."

"I just love it. Some days, all I want to do is sit around and look at it."

I've never figured out the jewel thing—how possessing them provides a reason for living. Jerry once gave me a natural sapphire and diamond ring which produced a callus where it rubbed above my knuckle. I lost it gardening. Jerry accused me of not "valuing" it, which was true. It will be unearthed one day by the aliens, along with the golf trophy.

Patti begins taping me up again. "The incisions look excellent, and your fluid levels are perfect, so I'd say you're doing really well."

"Thank you. When's the wedding?"

"Oh, I haven't been able to get him to commit to a date yet. He keeps saying, 'What's the hurry?' I tell him I don't want to be one of those women having babies in their late thirties. My girlfriend's sister had one when she was forty and he had club feet and turned out schizophrenic. She says she knew something was wrong when she caught him talking to the milk." She starts to pack her bag. "Is there anything else I can do for you?"

"No, that's fine, thanks."

"Okay then. Keep up the good work. You're doing great."

"Thank you."

I listen to her skip downstairs and ponder, is she really that vacuous or is it some kind of front, some kind of protective mechanism?

Maybe she's frustrated because she wanted to become a neurosurgeon but ended up a home-care nurse. Maybe Steve's a neurosurgeon and she puts up with his crap because she feels he's her superior, and being the subordinate to the Jokester fulfils her needs as a nurturer. Or maybe he's "excellent" in bed. Maybe none of the above and she's really that vacuous.

"It's so pedestrian," Muriel says of the third luxury condo I show her.

"It's got a great view," I point out. "And the patio's big enough for a garden. Put a few large terracotta planters out there and you could even grow some shrubs."

"I can't bear terra cotta. Makes me think of sweaty Italians." She scrutinizes the condo's information sheet. The fact that she's not making a beeline for the door is a good sign. I'm definitely waning and seek restoration on the couch.

Muriel taps her index finger against her lips. "I suppose the walk-in closet could be converted into a room for Darwin."

Darwin is Devon's baby.

"Devon insists I take him on the nanny's night out so she and that dimwit can go dining and dancing. I'm sure he'll break everything in sight."

I want the sale, but I'm a little worried about Darwin. "There's no ventilation in the walk-in closet."

"No, perhaps not," she admits. "I suppose I could always leave the door open. What ghastly fixtures."

"Those can be changed. It's a great location. You're near the opera, the symphony, the ballet."

"Oh, I saw what's-his-name's rendition of *Swan Lake.* Absolutely dreadful. Why are Canadians so determined to convert ballet into clog dancing? I'm not going to subscribe next year." She catches sight of herself in a mirror and adjusts her hat.

"Muriel, take a closer look at the kitchen. The counters are granite and the taps are levered. Good value for the money." I don't have the energy to walk her through the place again. On the coffee table is a fitness magazine with a girl barely covered in a towel. "Look Great Naked" the headline reads. Beside this is a magazine with Cheryl Tiegs in a bikini and I'm thinking, Isn't Cheryl Tiegs old yet? "Still Making a Splash Twenty-Five Years Later!" the headline reads and I'm thinking, Is this how we measure worth as a female in mid-life? Your brain may be atrophying, but if you still Look Great Naked, you may still grace the cover of magazines? You've come a long way, baby.

"Do you hear anything?" Muriel asks me.

"What?"

"I hear a hum." We both listen.

"I don't hear anything."

She shivers. "I can't bear hums."

Between condos, stopped at a light, we observed an old man in rags carrying seven tins of cat food stacked between his hands. My first thought was that the cat food was his breakfast, lunch and dinner for the next week, and being stoned on codeine, I admitted this to Muriel who immediately said, "Don't be ridiculous, he probably has a house full of cats. One of my tenants took in strays. Absolutely disgusting. I had to have her evicted."

Sometimes, when I listen to Muriel, I envy her conviction. My bottom line is usually "okay, maybe I'm wrong." Muriel's doubtlessness must be the artillery that keeps her forging ahead.

"I had a house that hummed," she tells me. "Beside a fire station. Drove me balmy. I threatened to sue the fire department. That stopped the hum, I can tell you."

"I really can't hear anything."

"In any event, I must dash. One of my tenants is trying to sell *my* vanity and medicine cabinet, the bugger. He's a Jehovah's Witness. You can't trust them. I said, 'Those are *permanent fixtures.*' He claims he put them in. I phoned my lawyer, of course, and he said what I knew he'd say: Tell him you'll sue him for the cost of the fixtures and installation."

The prospect of a quarrel with the Jehovah's Witness has Muriel glowing and adjusting her hat again. Oh, to thrive on confrontation. I don't think a cell would dare mutate inside Muriel, she'd sue it.

She drops me off outside the Queen Street Mental Health Centre. I tell her I'm visiting an old friend's disturbed teen. "Oh, they're all disturbed these days," is her only comment. During our time together, she has not once mentioned my son.

It looks like a mental hospital. I'd hoped it would look like a regular hospital with portraits of doctors on the walls. Or at least the Queen. And maybe a gift shop filled with Disney stuffies. But the place is bare. Maybe it was decided barren was best because otherwise the patients might start talking to the pictures, or to Mickey Mouse, or think the pictures and Mickey were talking to them. I try to get the attention of a stolid Jamaican woman at a reception desk behind what looks like bulletproof glass. I'm forced to talk loudly through a little speaker-hole. Making myself understood proves difficult, understanding her response even more so. Her irritability grows as does my incomprehension. Around me, mental patients meander; some trapped in their own worlds, others watching me warily as if waiting for me to do something though they don't know what but are scared I'll do it anyway.

I find Lyla in the lounge dressed in the same tagged dress she wore at our last encounter. Presumably they couldn't get it off her to wash it. She's watching a soap opera. Beside her on the couch sits a woman with hair that has seen too many bleachings, neatly pinned into a French twist. The woman holds a cigarette between her index and middle fingers in what I suspect she considers to be a sophisticated manner—wrist held high, hand flexed back, pinkie slightly extended—because when she was young, smoking was considered sophisticated. "Good day," she says to me.

"Hello," I respond, then offer my oranges to Lyla who doesn't seem surprised to see me.

"Thank you," she says, taking them.

"They're from California," I assure her.

"Thank you," she repeats, looking back at the TV.

"I told her," the French-twist woman says, "it could be a hairline fracture. My hairdresser fell on her rump and got a hairline fracture. So I said, 'Take that child to the hospital. She shouldn't be crying like that after a week.' I said, 'That's no bruise, that's a *hairline fracture.*' I said, 'Get that child X-rayed.'"

Behind us a man wearing sunglasses paces while making whistling sounds like dropping bombs.

The French-twist woman flicks ash into an ashtray. "She went to one of those walk-in clinics, you know, I *hate* those places. The doctor said, 'She can move it, it's not broken.' For a week she was crying. I said, 'Take that child to the hospital and get it X-rayed, it's a *hairline fracture.*'"

I'm trying to figure out if this is an extension of a dialogue the woman was having with Lyla or if it's a monologue I just happen to be witnessing. Either way, Lyla isn't participating but continues to stare at the big-haired men and women on the screen. The French-twist woman stubs out her cigarette and lights another. A wild-eyed man sprawls on a chair across from us and slides his hands into his sweatpants.

"How are you, Lyla?" I ask.

"This is Erna," she says, pointing to the French-twist woman. "We're in group together."

"How do you do?" I ask.

"I've been better," Erna replies. "Her grandpa'll buy her anything. I said, 'I don't want *ants* in this house.' She wanted traps, the kind that don't kill ants. I said, 'What's the point of an ant trap that don't kill ants?' 'They can't come out,' she tells me. 'Please, Grandma?' So *he* buys it for her. I said, 'No ants are coming into this house.' Her father was the same, collected worms, spiders. 'Don't kill it!' he'd say. Anything creepy-crawly." She shudders and inhales daintily on her cigarette.

The man in the sweatpants starts thrusting his pelvis forward. A staff member looks sternly at him. "You can do that in your room, Mr. Finlayson." The man cowers and obeys, scurrying down the corridor.

I'm assuming that the better-dressed people are staff but this could be a mistake. Coming out of the elevator, a "normal" looking man offered me guidance and showed me from room to room until a staff person reprimanded him for impersonating staff again. The more obvious crazies smoke and drink coffee constantly to wet their mouths, made dry by medication.

As I watch the soap opera, I try to deduce its appeal to Lyla. It seems to be about reunited high-school sweethearts. The man's wife died of cancer (no explanation of what kind), so he's alone in a lonely world pining for Melissa who is well endowed and married to a bodybuilder who wants to have a baby with her. "But it just doesn't feel right," she confides to her high-school sweetheart who must be intended to look "sensitive" because he's wearing glasses. The sensitive guy (Joseph) wants Melissa to break free of the bodybuilder and run away with him, but she can't bear the thought of hurting Luke (the bodybuilder). Melissa and Joseph look longingly into each other's eyes. He caresses her face with his hand and the network breaks to commercial.

"They'll be in the sack next," Erna informs us.

"He shouldn't be doing that to her," Lyla protests.

"She's doing it to herself," Erna argues.

"She loves him."

"So get a divorce, what's the big deal?" Erna speaks forcefully, like she's telling it like it is, or anyway, like she thinks it is. I wonder if this is her "mental illness"—an inability to accept that it isn't the way she thinks it is. Kind of the Don Quixote thing.

"She doesn't want to hurt Luke," Lyla counters meekly.

Erna looks at me and nods towards Lyla, indicating "she's a flake."

"Lyla," I begin, "I was wondering if you'd like me to check on your house, water the plants, make sure no food's going rotten, that sort of thing."

Her drug-induced tremors are becoming more pronounced and I'm worried that I'm freaking her out. "If you want," she says.

She'll be more freaked if she returns to a vandalized home.

"I'll need a key," I point out. She stares at a bra commercial displaying all kinds of breasts requiring all kinds of support. The bodies don't even have heads.

"Lyla, I'll need a key."

"Under the toad," she murmurs.

"You mean 'toad' as in lawn ornament?"

"I had one of those," Erna informs us. "Water spouted out of its mouth. Real cute. That girl busted it. I said, 'Leave that toad alone, it's not a toy.' Cost me thirty bucks."

The soap's back on and, sure enough, Melissa and Joseph are in the sack.

"What'd I tell ya?" Erna says. "They won't go all the way though, she'll feel too guilty."

They cut to a construction site where Luke the bodybuilder is blissfully ignorant and sporting a hard hat over his big hair.

A bloated man sits in the chair that was vacated by the masturbator. He breathes noisily and smells of sour milk. The ash on his cigarette is an inch long, nicotine has stained his fingers. "Why are you defending Victor?" he demands explosively of no one in particular. "Why are you defending him? I know for a *fact,* I know for a fact, Victor's a bad boy. Why are you defending him? He's not your friend, he's not. *I'm* your friend, I am. Why are you defending him?"

That Lyla wants to be here in this place of loose connections dumbfounds me. Can it feel safer than the world outside? Where boys kill your parents? Probably. I place a magazine I bought for her about the Royals on the coffee table. "Call me if you need anything," I tell her.

She looks at me briefly. "Can you tell Mum and Dad I'm alright? They get embarrassed when I'm here." I think my heart stops.

"Parents are *bad* news," Erna interjects. "Forget parents. I told my parents, 'If you can't take the heat, get out of the kitchen.' I said, 'You fucked me up more than all my husbands put together.' I said, 'Drop dead,' that's what I said."

Lyla's riveted to the screen again and not waiting for my reply. I wander off, like a mental patient. As I step into the elevator I hear, "Why are you defending Victor? I know for a fact, I know for a *fact,* Victor's a bad boy."

"You don't look good," Sybil tells me. She's blending me a banana milkshake with yoghurt, orange juice and yeast. She seems to think this will be good for me. At least it's not cow brains. "You're overdoing it," she adds.

"I just had some stuff I had to get done."

"You always have stuff you have to get done."

"Is Sam around?"

"He was. Don't know if he is." She hands me the concoction. "Drink this. It's got B vitamins."

It tastes yeasty, but I force it down. "Does he seem okay?"

"He's not talking much."

"Does he ever?"

"He hasn't called me old witch recently."

"That's an improvement."

"That bank robber shot himself," she says. "First thing he did when he jumped the wall was go see his mum."

"He shot himself in front of his mum?"

"No, no, at his girlfriend's. Told everybody to leave before he did it. Blew his head off as the cops were breaking down the door."

"That's very sad."

"As long as we let the pedophiles go free, I'm happy." She lights up a cigarette.

"He was a robber, Auntie. He threatened people with guns."

"Who doesn't want to rob a bank? Record profits year after year, they *should* be robbed."

I drink my shake and pretend to be engrossed in the paper, read that the feds aren't protecting us from the risks of toxic chemicals and pesticides. "We are paying the price in terms of our health, and our legacy to future generations," said the Commissioner of the Environment and Sustainable Development. Among major industrialized countries, only Canada and the Slovak Republic do not track pesticide sales. "We are concerned about the absence of a comprehensive strategy to manage the environmental risks posed by pesticides," the Commissioner said, "and about the inadequate tracking of releases of toxic substances and pesticides into the environment." Our Prime Minister was tracked off the golf course and commented, "He (the Commissioner) is making recommendations and every department will make sure it has been studied and corrections will be made." Wow, there's action for you.

"The boy was talking about monarch butterflies," Sybil tells me. "They're doing something to the corn, genetic engineering, and it's killing the butterflies."

"Why's he so concerned about bugs all of a sudden?"

"They're pollinators. It's not like the wind can do it for all plants. So we're looking at a world with no apples, almonds, blueberries, cherries, plums, pears, currants . . ."

"Pretty tasteless."

"Everybody thinks a human can do it in a lab somewhere. Dream on." She hands me a number on a scrap of paper. "Somebody called Arnie phoned for you."

"What did he say?"

"Nothing. Asked you to phone." Why's he calling? Am I a charity case?

"There's a spring in your step, Auntie. I think the pacemaker's doing you good. Either that or you're infatuated with Norm."

"You wish."

"What, is he too old for you?"

"Why don't you go rest and leave me in peace?"

"I wath wondering if you'd like to come to the mutheum with uth. Turner'th got thith thchool project."

"I'll ask Sam."

"Turner already did."

"Oh."

"I thought maybe we could go tomorrow afternoon."

I've been racking my brains trying to figure out who could help me restore Lyla's house, someone physically strong, with a truck, who's discreet and has no part in my life. "Arnie, I have to get a used TV and stereo for a friend and I was wondering if you could help me out with your truck?"

"Abtholutely."

"Maybe before the museum?"

"Sure. How you feeling?"

"Fine," I say. "I'm fine."

"I wanted to tell you that a friend of mine got canther and beat it."

"Good."

"Lymphoma. That one'th thupposed to kill ya. He drinkth about a gallon of carrot juith daily. Turned him orange, but he thwearth by it."

Do I tell him that there's a type of lymphoma that goes into remission all by itself? Nah. Let him dream. "Interesting," I say. "I'll keep that in mind. See you tomorrow."

"You bet."

It doesn't surprise me that Porky Pig answers the phone. I consider hurling threats at him but what would be the point? I got him out, she let him back in. Screaming at the captor when the captive, once freed, returns to her cell is futile. "Is Rachel there?"

"Ju . . . just a moment." A moment turns into ten and I'm left perusing *The Economist* which informs me that the reason so many hormones are reaching us through beef is that most farmers can't be bothered implanting them behind the ear, which is a fiddly process, so instead they shoot them into the neck muscles. More blood circulates through muscle than skin so the animals' hormone levels soar. Consequently 500 grams of meat can contain more hormones than a young boy produces in a day. The hormone estradiol-17-beta has been linked to endometrial and breast cancer. Hmmm. All so we can have leaner burgers.

"Hi," Rachel says.

I must not reveal that I am sickened that she is back in Porky's pen. If I berate her, condemn her, I will lose her. "Sam was asking me for photos of Mum and Dad and I couldn't find any. Do you have some?"

"Sure."

"Could I borrow them?"

She hesitates. "How do I know you won't destroy them?"

I never told her about my mini-bonfire. "Why would I destroy them?"

"What does he want to do with them?"

"Look at them. I promise we'll take great care of them." Her loyalty to her abusers astounds me.

"Okay. There's also a video. Of their fortieth anniversary. You were there."

"I'd forgotten about that." A scary time, Porky Pig cruising with his camera, stammering jokes that weren't funny. My mother dressed to the nines acting "charming," my father cursing a busted cork in a bottle. "If we could look at that, it would be great," I say. "Should I come and get it?"

"No, don't come here, I'll drop it off."

"That would be excellent," I say as perkily as Patti.

While brushing my teeth, I spot Sam in the backyard, lit by moonlight. He sits with his back to me in one of the

Adirondack chairs. I experience one of those déjà vu moments except the already-seen is my father. He'd just quarrelled with my mother who was locked in the bedroom (she'd wedge a chair under the doorknob). I'd needed money for a school trip and Dad was the best person to ask. But as I got closer to the chair I saw that he wasn't moving, which was unusual for my father; he always had a foot tapping or a finger twitching, not unlike Sam. It occurred to me that he might be dead. I'd just read a Nancy Drew novel in which a dead body was discovered in a chair. I froze on the grass, wondering if I would be charged as a murder suspect. I looked harder at him and saw that his eyes were open, but his face didn't look like his face. It looked how I imagined a dead person's face would look—flat once the blood had drained out of it. But since he wasn't dead, there had to be something else wrong with him. I deduced that he must've been very upset by the fight with my mother. It was possible, I concluded, that he was feeling sorrow and this was scary. I wanted him to go back to fixing cars, watching sports and telling us to "keep it down."
"Dad . . . ?" I ventured. Then "Dad . . . ?" again.

"What is it?"

"I need money for a school trip."

"How much?"

"Five dollars. It includes lunch."

His face remained toneless as he pulled a five out of his wallet.

"I guess Mum isn't making us supper?" I inquired.

"Guess not." Structure returned to his face and he prepared Kraft dinner as he always did in her absence. Rachel and I loved Kraft dinner but conversation was strained. "How was school?" he asked.

"Alright," we both replied.

"Very good," he said with his mind on the woman upstairs.

I push the back door open noisily because I don't want Sam to have a toneless face. I don't want him feeling sorrow.

"What's up?" I ask.

"Nothing. Shouldn't you be in bed?"

"Eventually." I sit on the other Adirondack chair. We're side by side, as though in a cockpit waiting for liftoff. "I talked to Rachel, she's going to drop some photos of Gran and Grandad off, and a video of their fortieth anniversary. Do you remember that?" He nods. "You were in grade one," I add. "Such a smarty pants, spouting your vowels and counting to a hundred. Remember that, A, E, I, O, U and sometimes Y? You said it over and over again." I'm carrying on a monologue again. Me and Erna. "Dad and Sybil told me about what's happening to the bees and the butterflies. That's horrible." He doesn't respond, only stares at the moon. "It's really amazing," I continue, "how mankind is bent on destroying itself." Wow, there's an original thought for you. He must think I'm such a deadbeat. "Is it alright if I go to the museum with you and Turner and Arnie tomorrow?"

"Whatever."

In the Merc with Muriel, we'd passed a rotund woman with a bulldog face wearing a T-shirt that said "Whatever": the ultimate noncommittal word. A word that makes me want to shout, "Shit or get off the pot!" But I can't shout at my son, he'll run away.

"Did you hate daycare?" I ask, trying to jolt him into communicating.

"No. Why?"

"It's just sometimes you cried when I dropped you off. Sometimes you cried when I picked you up."

"All kids cry."

"Yeah. I just wish you'd told me if you hated it."

"I didn't hate it." His foot begins to tap. "I hated napping when everybody else did. I never slept."

"What did you do?"

"Just lay there. They told me to keep still."

I find this out sixteen years later? My little boy was sleepless even then, held in invisible restraints? Sitting beside him, not facing him, I find the courage to probe. "What did you think about?"

"Can't remember. There were kids I hated, who were always taking stuff from me. Stuff they didn't want until I had it. It got so I'd grab any piece of shit just to see if these morons would take it from me."

"And did they?"

"Of course. It's all about sharing, right? The teachers were always telling us to 'share.' Didn't matter who got there first."

Interesting that kiddies raised in daycares dedicated to instilling the desire to share grow into teenagers who shoot each other in schoolyards.

"Yeah, I guess I hated it," he admits finally. "You're stuck in a room with these monkeys and there's nothing you can do about it."

"I wish you'd told me."

"What would you have done? Moved me to another daycare. Big deal."

"Would you have preferred to have stayed home with me?"

"Are you looking for forgiveness or something? I forgive you. Forget about it."

"I can't."

"Well, that's *your* problem." He stands. "It's fucking freezing. I'm going in."

"Okay."

I look up at the moon, its eyes and gaping mouth, and think of the robber stuck in a room with all these monkeys and not being able to do anything about it, except scale a ten-metre wall. He could have been my son. Could be my son if the verdict is appealed. The robber looked up at this moon as he ran for freedom. It guided him through trees, between buildings. It watched as he ran so fast the air scorched his lungs, ran so fast his legs burned. Until he collapsed at Mummy's feet. She knelt beside him and stroked his sweat-soaked hair, knowing that he had no future, no escape, just this second for her to say she loved him, forgave him, would always be there for him. But she didn't, because she was choked, terrified, imagining the bloodhounds, the men with sticks and handcuffs. Guns. The men who would make him suffer for proving them fools. And then he was gone again. Running away from her. She listened to his footsteps receding and with them went her soul.

I wonder who they'll get to play it in the movie. A Brad Pitt clone, or that *Titanic* kid whose name I can't pronounce. They'll get a bosomy nubile thing to play the love interest. And we'll all go to it and feel sad for the *Titanic* kid and the nubile thing and completely forget that a man really, really, really put a gun in his mouth and blew his head off because our judicial system insured that he would not be released until he was an old man. The same system that releases pedophiles after two years, enabling them to destroy more children. The same system that sentenced a woman who suffocated her four-month-old baby with a pillow to one year in prison. One year for murdering a helpless baby. She did not plead insanity, or postnatal depression, or automatism. She offered no explanation and showed no remorse.

The same system that allowed my son to walk.

"Mum . . . ?" he calls, and it is as though he has thrown me a life preserver.

"Yes?" I reply.

"You coming in?"

"Yes."

Twenty-four

"How's Liberace?" I ask Todd who's doing his ankle exercises.

"He's not speaking to me, won't even look at me."

"He's still angry with you," Estelle advises.

"Like I don't know that," Todd says.

"Offer him treats," I suggest. "You know, something sweet, pecan pie or something." I haven't told him about the pie binge because I feared he might accuse me of poisoning his bird with refined sugar.

"He doesn't like sweets," Todd declares.

"How do you know?"

"He only eats whole grains."

I'm quite certain that what Liberace needs is a sugar fix. "Pigeons like sweets, doughnuts, that sort of thing."

"He's not a *pigeon*," Todd says with disgust.

It's so curious that the more we think we know someone (or some animal), the more we limit their options. You'd think it would be the other way around. "You could always try a butter tart with walnuts or something," I persist. "He likes nuts."

I'm feeling goofily optimistic because a house I've listed for over a year has hooked a buyer. It's an attractive semi in a good location but attached to a Dog Patch house occupied by hairy, sixty-something twins who use the front yard as a dump site. During open houses I've scrambled to greet potential buyers in attempts to divert their gaze from the dump to the wonderful perennial garden. But this proves difficult in winter. Heavy snows have blanketed the toxic waste for short periods, but inevitably more car parts, paint cans and old tires have soiled the white. My vendors accepted the offer in a stupor. After the buyer's agent left, I sat in their kitchen assuring them that yes, the offer was real, that yes, they should start looking for another house. They expressed some concern for the buyer, which I thought was sweet, but I explained that she was a twenty-four-year-old neo-hippie waitress who planned to start a commune. Her magnate father was paying cash for the house, freeing her of financial obligation. She would be smoking doobies, having love-ins and listening to Cat Stevens. I did not expect that she would notice the garbage.

I'm currently completing the paperwork on this deal and considering which roofers to contact for an estimate on my own premises. And—this is really radical—I'm thinking about renovating the basement, getting rid of the doom and gloom, making a pad for Sam: a safe, quiet, private place.

"Greer doesn't know about my new cat," Estelle enthuses. "His name's Girly, but I'm calling him Harvey after the rabbit. Harvey sounds like Girly, don't you think?"

"It does not," Todd says.

"Harvey after the rabbit in that movie," Estelle clarifies as though this compensates for the lack of rhyme.

"I know which rabbit," Todd says. "You can't just go and change his name because you happen to feel like it. Girly's his name. You call him Harvey and he's going to think you're nuts."

"Not if I make it sound like Girly. Girlee, Harvee."

"Both two syllables," I point out.

"That's pathetic," Todd says, limping from the room.

"This is great news, Estelle," I offer. "I'm really happy for you." She sits on a desk and swings her legs. I've never seen her swing her legs before. "They wouldn't just *give* him to me. Her stepson's niece was also interested, so I had to prove myself. He's four years old, you know, he's not like a kitten, he has habits and stuff. Anyway, his owner's ninety-seven and broke her hip so her daughter's putting her in a home and they needed somewhere for Girly, I mean Harvey. And they just didn't think the stepson's niece was responsible enough. So she invited me to tea, the daughter, to meet me, her name's Inga, and she had all these little cakies laid out and stuff like that and I was so nervous. I said, 'What do you need to know about me?' and she said, 'I learned everything I needed to know the minute you walked in.' Isn't that marvellous?"

"Great. Where was Girly, I mean Harvey?"

"In a cage. Inga didn't want to stress him too much. She let him out at the end and put him on my lap. I stroked him and he purred. Isn't that wonderful? I suppose I should've gone to the Humane Society and taken a cat nobody wanted, but I just couldn't face seeing all those poor kitties. You just know they're going to be destroyed. It's so hard, it breaks your heart." And I'm thinking, Isn't it better to rescue one poor kitty than none at all? Is witnessing some suffering so terrible if you're performing some good? Is it better that we just not look because it's so hard and breaks our hearts? This approach would explain our growing indifference to genocide, man-made famines, wars, child abuse. The homeless dying in the streets.

Everybody's out. Good, I don't have to act healthy. I put on a wash, thinking about how snazzy the basement's going to look doodied up, and notice a pile of Sam's laundry. This is unusual, he always folds his laundry. Oh well, it's not like he doesn't have other things on his mind. I fold it, carefully, lovingly, and take it upstairs, knocking on his door just to make sure he isn't there. His bed's unmade, this too is strange for the neat freak. I start to make it for him, discover a porno magazine between the sheets. This is normal, isn't it, boys giving themselves hand jobs while gripping girly mags? I'm curious though, haven't looked at one of these for years, since I found one in Jerry's closet. I remember feeling betrayed, becoming red hot, taking the presence of the magazines personally because I knew I could never live up to their air-brushed, implanted standards. Jerry's excuse was that "it released tension" and had "nothing to do with us." This was the same excuse he used when he started shtupping the neighbour.

I start to flip through the glossy flesh and realize that the women's breasts and faces have been cut out. Every one, every digitally perfected model, is faceless and breastless. He must've used an X-Acto knife, the tool with which he once carved his face.

I don't think this is normal.

What's even weirder is that he's left their glistening ever-ready vaginas intact. Why, so that they'll be available for penetration? All I want is your huge dick inside me, baby, and I'm one satisfied girl. Don't think, don't feel, just cut me up and buy another one.

Some teenaged boy slashed a woman's face before raping her. And shoved a hot curling iron inside her. He's still out there, the cops can't find him.

I feel sick, dislocated.

Where's the knife? I open drawers, search shelves. There is no knife. Shove the magazine between the sheets, he mustn't know. I take the laundry back downstairs, mess it up, leave it as it was.

Who's he hating? Women? Just these women? Does he think that by severing their breasts he can save his mother's? Will he forever hate women who are whole? Seek vengeance on their cancer-free bodies, cut them to pieces in his sleep?

I search the basement for the knife, the kitchen drawers, cabinets. No knife. My breast is burning, my arm is swelling; must lie down on the couch.

Pornography, the mind-altering substance that allows little and big boys to think that real women, the imperfect ones, should also be ever-ready, in awe of their erect members, grateful to be fucked. And when we're not, when we tell presidents and boxing champions that we don't want their penises inside our vaginas, anuses and mouths, they get righteous, indignant, call us frigid, and sometimes they beat us up or kill us.

My son's not like that.

They're just magazines. Think of something else. Do something. You're supposed to call roofers. Pick up the phone and dial. They speak gruffly, not pleased to be dealing with a woman. I imagine bowling-ball tits and spread buttocks on girly calendars inches from their faces. The most "reputable" company has a slippery sales rep who offers to drop by first thing in the morning to "take a boo at it." Turn on the TV. It tells me a fifteen-year-old boy poured turpentine on his shoes and set them on fire to see what it would look like. As he ignited, he tried to bat the flames down with his baseball cap. Meanwhile, his sixteen-year-old "friend" sloshed the remaining turpentine over the burning boy, causing his torturous death. The sixteen-year-old's defence is that they were "fooling around." What could possibly have gone through his mind as he watched and smelled his friend burn? Did *anything* go through his mind, or was he watching special effects? Cool.

How did this desensitization come to pass? The face of youth is hard-edged now, arrogant, with the innocence gone. It's cool to be cruel, to sneer like the lean and mean on the Calvin Klein ad.

I suppose we have no one but ourselves to blame for this change since we've powered the machinery that has cultivated their minds. *We've* supported the conglomerates who've produced the "entertainment" our children ingest. And the video games that tap their sensorimotor brain centres, providing entire environments of testosterone-stimulating virtual violence. *We* wired ourselves to the Net because we didn't want to miss anything in this information age. Therefore, we shouldn't be surprised that they view life as one big show, and that the important thing is to be on it, preferably in a starring role.

And we can't just look away because it's so hard and breaks our hearts.

I insert Rachel's video, needing to see Sam small again, innocent. She must've been so relieved to find me out of the house. I think about weeding, how I've always enjoyed freeing the earth of the invasive, allowing the more delicate to thrive. If I pulled Porky up by the roots, Rachel would never forgive me.

It starts with a shot of the ham, pink and greasy, my mother fluttering above it while responding coquettishly to Porky's admiring comments. Rachel's doing dishes and waving Porky away whenever he veers the camera in her direction. I pop up in the corner of the frame, vodka in hand, looking like a mental patient. I sport the hairstyle of the time, short on top, wavy on the bottom, blonde highlights (like Cheryl Tiegs), Ray-Bans balanced on my head. To think that I thought I appeared sophisticated. "Hi, Mum and Dad, seen any good movies lately?" My breasts look wonderful, firm, Real under a T-shirt that reads, "Don't worry, it will never work out."

Sam buzzes into the frame, pushes his face into the camera to explain that the red stuff inside the olives is pimento paste. Off-camera, my father curses the busted cork and asks what time it is. I tell him eight and Sam declares that it's not eight, it's seven-fifty-seven. Inebriated, I try to smile warmly at my smartassed son, then make some inaudible comment about the ham, to which Sam replies, "We didn't have *ham* for lunch, we had *baloney*. Don't you know the difference between *ham* and *baloney*?" And I remember this phase, when whatever I said stood to be corrected. "Don't speak to your mother like that," I hear my father say.

"Sometimes she's so out of it," Sam grumbles as my mother complains that I didn't bring the right kind of mustard.

"This has tarragon in it," she says. "I asked for Dijon."

"You didn't specify," I protest, "you just said mustard." Were the camera not on she would have reminded me of all the other times I'd failed her.

"Mum's always forgetting stuff," Sam contributes. "She can't even drive me to Karl's house, she's always getting lost."

"I don't always get lost." I can see that I'm irritated that my child, even my child, can find fault with me.

"Greer's never had a sense of direction," my father says.

In every shot, I'm standing, holding a glass, forever holding a glass, as though it could shield me from the steady fire of criticisms. Jerry must've had one of his "late meetings" because he's nowhere in sight. The pewter candle holders I spent two hours deliberating over receive little attention. Why did I care? Why couldn't I have moved beyond that? Metastasized. What did I think I was doing? That pose, the dull-witted smile, what did it cost me? Were the cells plotting their mutiny even then? Why didn't I grab my little boy and run? Because I feared he would turn against me, his out-of-it mother. Would he, though? How many actions do we not take out of fear? Fear of what? Rejection? You're going to get that anyway. At some point your mother pushes you off the breast, that's life, you recover. Maybe without the interference of my parents and my husband, Sam and me would have been forced to communicate. You can kill me and feast on my flesh, but then what? Better we hunt and forage together. You chase the animals off the cliff, I'll hold the net. We can make a life this way, form a trust this way.

He pushes a sausage roll in front of the camera. "There's pig's guts inside here," he explains. "And every piece of the pig—brains, feet, bum . . ." He presses his face into the lens and whispers, "Dick."

The doorbell rings. It's Arnie. I feel to make sure I'm wearing my prosthesis, and check my face in the hall mirror to ascertain that there's nothing paranormal about it.

He smiles toothlessly. "You ready?"

I focus my attention on the task at hand.

Cash Converters provides excellent parking and the kind of friendly service that gives me the heebie-jeebies. "How can I help you today?" the young men smile, and I know they're on commission and that I'm a fish in their pond that must be caught. I say, "I'm just looking," but they hover anyway, pressing power buttons for me as though I can't do this myself. "Is there anything else I can help you with?"

"I'm just looking," I repeat, inhaling their cologne that could kill flies.

I can't remember anything about Lyla's TV and stereo. I'm just hoping that if I buy used appliances and cover them with doilies, she won't notice. Kind of like the mother replacing the dead turtle, praying that the child won't notice the different markings.

"Here'th a Thony," Arnie tells me.

One of the smiling fishermen leans between us and presses the power button. "This one's worth twice what we're asking," he informs us.

"Then why aren't you charging twice what you're asking?" I inquire.

"I don't do the pricing," he whispers in a playful, hushed tone. Maybe he has a child at home in need of food, who's suspended in his Jolly Jumper right this second pleading for Cheerios. For this reason, I accept the fisherman's lure. He shows me stereos, fiddles with dials, talks about "good sound." They all sound the same in this room already blasted by a sound system tuned to a rock station captained by a rabid DJ.

"This one's a beaut," the fisherman says, patting a Sanyo. "Nobody does it like the Japs."

I consider advising him that Sanyo's a Canadian company, but what would be the point? "I'll take it," I tell him, thinking only of his starving child.

I find the key under the toad. As we enter the house, the stench nearly makes me vomit. Arnie rushes around opening windows. I've explained the entire story to him, every detail, and he has not balked. Nor has he said, Wow, what a good plan, you're doing the right thing. He is simply there for me. I'm not used to unconditional support and keep sniffing around for ulterior motives. I vow to buy him several bottles of Drambuie.

I phone home. Sybil answers, says she hasn't seen Sam, that I shouldn't get my knickers in a knot every time he goes for a piss.

The cleanup required is huge because not only is Mr. Pong's refuse strewn about but raccoons have been visiting via the broken window and have shit all over Mrs. Grundy's peach carpet. We toil, a camaraderie forming. I find myself relying on my right arm as my left is useless. The knock on the door startles me. "It'th probably thomebody thelling thomething," Arnie says.

"Just ignore it."

But the knocking evolves into pounding and window tapping. Arnie looks at me and I nod. He opens the door and there stands Earl Verman. "Hey, Greer, how goes it?"

"Busy."

"Is that right? Well, I happened to be driving by and noticed your car, thought I'd say hello."

"Arnie, this is Earl Verman, he's the real estate agent listing the house."

Verman offers his hand. "How you doin'?"

Arnie hangs on to his mop and pail. "You want to lend a hand here?"

"Wish I could, would make selling the house a whole lot easier, but I can't stay. Greer, how'd you get in?"

"Through the window."

He laughs at my joke but I only stare at him.

"The coonth got here firtht," Arnie offers.

Earl jangles his car keys and looks around. "You doing this for any particular reason?"

"When your listing expires," I explain, "I'm planning to take it over. I've already got a buyer lined up." I say this dead straight. He looks at me, waiting for me to crack an I'm-just-kidding smile.

"You know that's against the rules," he admonishes.

"Oh Earl, get a grip. The girl is sick, she needs her home. Leave her alone."

"An agreement's an agreement."

I feel as though I've run up against an NRA guy. Guns don't kill people, people kill people. Excuse me, are you *nuts*? Earl assumes a Charlton Heston stance. "I could report you to the board."

"Please leave now," I say quietly. "You're out of line."

"I was never in line. Get out, please."

"Have you heard from the girl?"

"No."

There's nothing for it but to charge at him with my scrubbie. I wave it in his face. "Bye, Earl."

"Now don't get excited."

The scrubbie makes contact with his pasty cheek. He backs off as I pat his nose.

"This is completely unprofessional," he protests as he trips over Mrs. Grundy's swan planter. I slam the door, lock it and peer through the curtains. He hitches up his pants, gets into his American boat of a car and cruises away.

"Wouldn't want to meet you in a dark alley," Arnie remarks.

"He's a bottom feeder," I say.

"No kiddin'?"

Inside the museum, entombed in concrete, I feel safe. Nothing bad can happen here. And Sam's acting normal, there are no blood stains on his clothes, although he'd have washed them off by now, wouldn't he? The boys leave us to look at insects and I clue in to the fact that Turner must be the source of Sam's bug obsession. Arnie and I amble through the European section while he shares important cancer information with me. "I talked to Wethley yethterday. I call him every now and then to make sure he'th okay, and he thaid you should be eating grape-theed extractth."

"Really?"

"And thomething from peacheth. From the pit. I gueth they grind it up or thomething."

The Victorian display shows corsets and nighties and little

pointy shoes. To think we were ever that tiny. A dress on a stand has a waist that can't be more than sixteen inches.

"Are the grape seeds and peach pits helping Wesley?" I ask.

"He thinkth tho."

"I thought carrot juice was helping him."

"He doeth that too, and thome Chinethe breathing. And lotth of garlic."

The ladies with the tiny waists didn't know they had cancer until the tumours pushed against their skin. Surgeons cut their breasts off anyway. Anaesthesia hadn't been invented, not even ether. Patients had to be held down on the table. Imagine the screams.

Are we better off though, pursuing brutal, dehumanizing, often futile treatments?

Best not to think about it. I head back through the Industrial Revolution, back to the Renaissance. Here we were left to die. Bled of course, many happy leeches gaining life as we were losing it.

"Thing ith," Arnie adds, "he doethn't go out anymore."

"Why not?"

"Thcared of getting thome infection that'll thcrew up hith immune thythtem."

"He must go out to get grape seeds and peach pits."

"He orderth them in. And geth organic vegetableth delivered."

"What does he do all day?"

"He uthed to thurf the Net for canther cureth. But then he figured the magnetic field from hith computer wath bad for him. He doethn't like uthing electrithity at all."

"What's he do for light?"

"Candleth. Goeth to bed early."

This is no life. But can you blame him? An article yesterday linked magnetic fields with childhood leukemia. A study found that children exposed to magnetic fields were two to four times more likely to develop leukemia. Breast cancer cells, from women taking tamoxifen, exposed to magnetic fields continued to mutate in spite of the hormone block. Meaning magnetic fields (we're not talking just power lines, but your regular household wiring) affect hormones. "He'th pretty pothitive about it though, old Weth. Figureth ath long ath he keepth doing what he'th doing, he'll be alright."

A life sentence. I try to imagine staring at my own walls day in and day out, popping peach pits and grape seeds, grinding carrots, chewing garlic. Doing Chinese breathing. I admire Wesley for his will. Will I do not have.

"Good for him," I say.

"I juth wanted to tell you a thuctheth thtory."

"I appreciate it."

On the way to Lyla's, we stopped at a dollar store to pick up cleaning utensils. As I was determining which environmentally unfriendly product to buy, an old lady in a floral head scarf, wearing a shabby raincoat and masses of face powder, smiled at me. "My, aren't things cheap here?" she mused, leaning heavily on her grocery cart filled with grubby plastic bags.

"Yes," I agreed.

She picked up a framed portrait of Jesus. "I can't believe how cheap they are," she re-emphasized.

"Everything for a buck," I said, looking around for rubber gloves.

"A clock for a dollar," she remarked with awe. "Probably won't last long, but still. You'd get some use out of it. Good for kids. Kids love playing with clocks." And I contemplated how many children she'd watched playing with clocks, how many children she'd outlived, and how miraculous it was that she could be enthused about a dollar store when she must remember a time when a dollar was a day's wage. When she must remember wars, and rationing, and polio. And I felt this incredible affection for her, and wondered what she'd think of the term "pesticide showers" to describe rainwater contaminated by toxic pesticides.

Sybil informed me this morning that Swiss scientists have found samples containing 400 nanograms per litre of the widely used pesticide 2-4-dinitrophenol, which is quadruple the limit set by the EU for *any* pesticide.

"So are they going to put up Don't Drink the Water signs for the cows?" I asked.

"It's not funny," Sybil said.

"I didn't say it was."

And I had a feeling the clock lady, on hearing that the water that feeds our lakes and streams is being poisoned, would simply buy her dollar clock, even though experience had taught her that it wouldn't last long. And I admired this, even though I knew the clock would shortly become landfill, even though I despair over our "disposable" society. Because her action would require a recognition that you can't have everything, but that you can still get some use out of it. I kind of feel this way about my life.

"Let'th go check out the dinothaurth," Arnie says.

Sam didn't want me to cook him dinner. I told him about Rachel's video and asked if he'd like me to watch it with him. "No," he replied. I sat in the bath worrying that seeing the dead in action would upset him. I've left my bedroom door open, hoping he'll come and talk to me about it, and give me an opportunity to ask what he did today, if he mutilated any girls. He's moving around in his room, I hear drawers opening and closing. "Sam . . . ?" I call, then call again.

"What?"

"Could you come here for a sec?"

He stands in my doorway. "What do you want?"

"Oh . . . umm . . . I was just wondering if you happen to know if we have an X-Acto knife?"

"An X-Acto knife."

"Yes."

"What do you want with an X-Acto knife?"

"I want to cut out a recipe." Hopeless at lying, I pretend to be straightening my cream sheets.

"Since when do you cut out recipes?"

"Since . . . well . . . it's just it's a really good recipe."

"For what?"

I've drawn a blank. What do I cook? "Brownies."

"You need a recipe for *brownies*?"

"Sam, just tell me, do you know where the X-Acto knife is?"

He stares at me with glacier eyes. "Use scissors. And stay out of my room." His door slams.

At least I know where he is.

I wake hoping it's morning but there's no hint of dawn in the sky. I was dreaming that I was on a roof and couldn't get down because the roof went on and on. My digital clock, while producing a magnetic field, reveals that it's 3 a.m. There's no way I'll get back to sleep with visions of mutilated playmates in my head. And I've got jumpy legs, a sore back, armpit and tooth pain. I take more drugs. Patti didn't say "excellent" once today and I worried that I'd affronted her in some way. Or that I wasn't healing properly. But then she admitted that she and Steve had had a fight, "big time," she emphasized. He works too hard, she complained, won't even let her plan a Christmas vacation, and if they don't commit to a trip now it's going to be *humongously* expensive. She wanted to go on a walking/wine tasting tour in Italy, but Steve hates Europe because of the plumbing. He said if he's going anywhere, it's got to have good water pressure and a beach nearby. "Which is totally boring," Patti complained. "I like adventure."

"Why don't you go on the tour by yourself?" I suggested.

She looked at me as though I'd just suggested she cut off her arm.

"If it's a tour," I elaborated, "you won't be alone."

"The whole point is that we have some time alone *together*."

What if he doesn't want "some time alone together"?

"He never takes time off," she added and I could hear her chanting this refrain for years to come, after the rings, the babies, *you never take time off.* I no longer envied Patti's life that would be spent tailgating the Jokester. I even stopped envying her breasts because I felt that they would never be caressed, only handled. Even her children would take their cues from their disinterested, disrespectful dad. I wanted to grab Patti and shake her and say, You can do better than that. But she wouldn't have believed me. If a forty-something woman missing one breast and a chunk of another had shaken the babe with the Cheryl Tiegs do and Ray-Bans, would she have believed her?

I'm hearing something outside, thumping or something. The only good thing about having insomnia is that the dog's asleep and I can open the window. Leaning out, I try to see in the darkness. It sounds like shovelling. So what now, he's digging graves? I check his bed, he's not in it. I scramble downstairs and search the broom closet for my flashlight, throw on Jerry's sweater and step out front, because it sounds like it's coming from the tree-killing neighbours.

Barefooted, I move stealthily towards the sound and lurk beside some forsythias. I peer through the bushes at his shadowy figure. "Sam . . . ?" I ask quietly, understanding that if he's asleep it will be impossible to wake him. It doesn't look like he's burying a body because he's digging randomly, making potholes all over the cropped, pesticided grass. I pad closer and peer at his blank and starey face. How terrifying to be murdered by a face stripped of expression. You'd prefer to be killed by a face contorted with fury, resentment, hatred. Staring at Sam's face, as consciousness was leaving them, the Grundys must've felt that their death held no meaning for their murderer and was therefore meaningless. Much better to die at the hands of an enemy, much better to die for a cause.

What can he be looking for in the neighbours' yard? The golf trophy? Then I remind myself that he isn't looking for anything, that there is no reason behind his actions.

Shivering, I glance at the upstairs windows, anticipating a light show, but they remain dark. Maybe Ativan has the tree-killers soundly sleeping.

There's really nothing I can do about any of this. I have to "chill," as Sam would say. Otherwise I will go mad. I can only watch over him, make sure he comes to no harm, does no harm. I can do this, will be glad to do this, for the rest of my life.

We woke the dog.

Twenty-five

"What are you doing sleeping down here?" Sam asks me.

I look around and see that it's morning. "I didn't sleep down here."

"You were asleep in the chair."

"I was? Hunh. I came down early, felt like a cup of tea. Guess I dozed off."

"Where's the tea?"

I make a show of looking for it. "I guess I fell asleep before I made it." He knows I'm lying. Where did *he* wake up? I only remember coming inside and discovering a slug between my toes which I squashed with a Kleenex while Sam did his zombie thing on the couch. I watched till his eyelids slid over his eyes, then told myself I'd have a quick snooze.

"It's so weird the way you're always falling asleep," he comments.

"I'm not *always* falling asleep." A replay of the Cheryl Tiegs wannabe's protest that she doesn't always get lost.

Sybil of the new ticker bustles around us. "Who wants bacon and eggs?"

Sam stares at her. "I'm a *vegetarian*, remember?"

"Vegetarians eat eggs."

"Eggs are baby chickens." He leans over her. "Baby chickens die so you can OD on cholesterol."

"I'll have some," I intervene. The doorbell rings and it's Sid, the slippery sales rep, coming to take a boo at the roof. I must look like a bag lady, and every part of me aches. Patti will not be pleased to hear I slept in a chair.

Sid and I stare up at the roof. I cop a quick glance at the tree-killers' front lawn. Must be a big year for groundhogs, I'll tell them, those little guys get high on pesticides, it's kind of like glue-sniffing to them.

Sid taps his clipboard with his pen and appears concerned about the condition of the roof. He's wearing a pretend Rolex and a chunky high-school graduation ring. His permanent-press pants fit so tightly across the ass I can see his panty line. I have a disturbing suspicion he's one of those guys who wears bikinis that have ice-cream cones printed on the crotch.

"Needs to be replaced," he observes, "no doubt about that." As he swaggers around the back, I nip inside to make sure no carnage has taken place. "Smells good," I tell Sybil who's standing over a smoking frying pan. "Where's Sam?"

"How should I know? Why are you always asking me where he is? Maybe he's taking a crap."

"Okay, sorry."

"Leave him alone. I've never seen such a fuss. The boy can't breathe."

Muriel phones to tell me that she wants to have another look at the condo with the walk-in closet for Darwin. "It's the stalactites in the lobby I'm not too keen on," she remarks.

"Those are chandeliers."

"So it would seem. Dreadful. Makes me feel like a bat."

"They're planning to remodel the lobby."

"Can you get that in writing?"

Sid's on his way in. "Muriel," I say, "I've got to go, I've got a roofer here."

"Smells faaabulous," Sid says. "Not too many people cookin' up eggs these days. I always say a good day starts with a good breakfast."

"How much for the roof?" I inquire.

"Well," he takes in a big breath, expanding his chest, "there's good news and bad news." He exhales, looking grief-stricken suddenly, as though breaking the news is too much to bear. "There's rot up there. Some of the boards are going to have to be replaced."

"You can see that from the ground?"

"Ma'am, I'm only giving you my professional opinion."

"What's the good news?"

"Your eavestroughs look shipshape."

"I had them replaced last year."

"That would explain it."

Sybil slides greasy eggs onto plates and points to a chair, indicating that I should sit. The shower turns on upstairs which means Sam's behaving normally which makes me feel light, ethereal, Nursery Magic Fairyish. "How much, Sid?"

"Well," he feigns wistful regret about having to gouge me for twenty grand, "I'd say we could do it for seventeen-five."

"Great. Go ahead."

He stares at me as though I'm speaking in tongues.

"Go ahead," I repeat, "I want it done before the snow falls."

"Great. Good. We'll get right on it."

"Good." I sign the estimate and see him out. I can't help worrying that there's a woman out there who pines for Sid, who dreams of quitting her dry-cleaning job so she can have his babies and fold his ice-cream-cone bikinis.

"Read this," Sybil orders, pushing one of her alternative health magazines at me.

"Do I have to now, Auntie? Can't I just drink my coffee?"

"Those drugs women take so they won't get menopause come from pregnant horses' pee."

"I know that." I look down at a photo of a mangy mare in a tiny, dark stall. A rubber "urine-collection bag" has been strapped between her legs and hooked up to the ceiling.

"For six months of the year they have to wear that," Sybil advises me. "It chafes and gives them sores. They never go outside. They can't turn around, can only take a step forward or back. Can't even lie down comfortably." She shakes a pound of salt on her eggs, pinches a slice of bacon between her fingers. "They're kept pregnant for twenty years or until their bodies break down. Their foals sometimes replace them, but usually they're sold to 'kill buyers' who fatten them up for a year, then slaughter them for the meat market."

"This isn't a great breakfast topic, Auntie."

She waves the bacon at me. "Nobody knows this. Millions of women pop those pills and they don't even know where they come from." She stares at me, waiting for a response.

"It's horrible," I mutter. "I don't know what to tell you."

"Tell people, women who take those pills."

"Sure, okay." I look into the yellow eyes of my eggs—baby chickens. Their mommies spend their caged lives under light bulbs so they'll think it's day and never stop laying eggs. Do they ever question why they don't have babies? Do the horses ever wonder why their babies vanish?

"Farmers restrict their drinking water," Sybil continues, "which gives them kidney and liver damage, but the farmers don't give a rodent's rectum because thirsty mares produce concentrated pee with more hormones in it. When the bastards give them a few drops, the mares hurt themselves struggling to drink it because they're so thirsty. The stinkers don't even treat their injuries. Just let 'em get sick and die."

Speechless, I can only shake my head and stare at the dismal photograph and consider that, once again, man has proved himself barbarous in the name of business.

She peers at me. "Do you take those pills?"

"No, Auntie."

"What's wrong with menopause? What's all the fuss about menopause?"

"Some people suffer from it."

"It's not a disease. It's life."

"The drugs do reduce the risk of heart disease and osteoporosis." I can't believe I'm towing the line for drug companies. "But there are alternatives. Yams, they're getting estrogen from yams, and progesterone to balance the estrogen." I wonder what pesticides they spray on the yams.

Sybil munches on a particularly fatty piece of bacon. "You think our ancestors fussed about menopause? They were too busy working. Get out and work instead of sitting around on your fat ass—that'll strengthen your bones." She finishes her eggs and drops her plate into the dishwasher. "Capitalism," she comments disdainfully.

I could say, "You don't think communists abuse animals?" but this would only lead to one of our nonsensical arguments in which I inquire if she's ever heard of Joe Stalin and genocide. Despite all evidence to the contrary, she continues to believe communism means happy peasants with health benefits.

Patti wooshes in perkier than I've seen her. "Up and about," she observes. "That's excellent." I plod up the stairs behind her and listen while she explains that Steve bought a house yesterday to surprise her.

I start to disrobe. "You mean he bought a house without you seeing it?"

"I saw it last night. He got an excellent deal. The only problem is the people next door have Rottweilers that chew the bark off trees. The fence is pretty high though. I don't think they can get out. Anyway, it's got green shutters which I really like, green's like so calming."

You're going to have children in a house beside Rottweilers?

She digs around in her bag. "It's not like the kind of house you walk into and say, 'Wow what a great house,' but it's got potential."

"You'll make it great," I say, wanting to be supportive because, let's face it, the girl has been kind to me.

"Exactly. Steve's already got plans for the third floor—it's, like, pretty gross right now. The guy who rented the place kept lizards in it. There's all these mice running around because he fed them to his lizards. Anyway, Steve got a really good deal. He's really excited about it. He says it's just a starter home. You know, he'll fix it up, then get something bigger."

"But, Patti," I have to say, "has he not included you in any of his plans?"

"We're engaged."

"I know. But it would seem to me that you'd like to shop for a house together."

She smiles knowingly. "Is this sour grapes because you weren't the agent?"

I give up, really. It's her delusion, her bubble. Whatever gets you through. Extraordinary that in our post-feminist era, girls still yearn for proposals and rings. All that burning and we're back to push-up bras.

"Steve's got excellent taste," she emphasizes. "And he's really sensitive about the marriage issue right now because"—she stops cleaning my wounds—"this mustn't go beyond these walls."

"You don't have to tell me," I assure her.

"His best friend's girlfriend," she whispers, "got pregnant so he would have to marry her."

"Well, presumably she didn't get pregnant all by herself."

"You know what I mean. Anyway, his mother's furious. She says she'll kill him if he marries her. She's Sicilian so I don't know."

She starts taping me up. "So anyway, Steve's a little on edge right now. And who can blame him? I mean that is so totally tacky. I would never do that, I swore I would never do that. I mean what kind of marriage is that?"

How different, I'm thinking, is this from your proposed liaison? One partner takes action without consulting the other? I can see Steve arriving at the lizard house late one night and announcing that he's impregnated a surrogate mother because he doesn't want Patti to get stretch marks, and because he wants her tits to himself. How many soul-suppressing, mind-retardant compromises will we make to live lives we imagine to be normal? Lives that mimic the ads for the SUV, mortgages, life insurance, mutual funds, dairy products, meat, Disney, Viagra, diamonds. Premarin.

Should I tell Patti about the horse abuse? She'll retort that only some farmers mistreat the mares, and that medical research depends on the use of animals because we can't go around injecting people with AIDS. Aren't there enough people *with* AIDS who would be more than willing to experiment with a cure? Starving children in Africa for example?

"This is my last visit," she tells me. "You're doing excellent."

"Great."

"You seeing the doctor Monday?"

"Yes."

"That's excellent. You're doing really well."

"Thank you." She starts to pack up.

"Patti . . . ?"

"Uh-hunh?"

"Would you like the *Iris*?"

"Are you serious?"

"I'd like you to have it. A house-warming present. But you must promise me you'll hang it where you want it. You won't let Steve decide."

"Okay." She looks at the picture. "It's totally awesome."

I try to take it down but can't lift either arm high enough. "I'll do it," she says.

"It's a bit dusty," I apologize.

"No problem. This is excellent, Greer, really. I really appreciate it."

"I hope you enjoy it."

"Big time." She holds it at arm's length to admire it.

"I've got to pee," I say, feeling very sad suddenly because I know, just know, the *Iris* will be closeted in the lizard house if Steve doesn't like it. I've betrayed Vincent who's been my pal for years. It's only a poster, I tell myself, don't be a sentimental wheeze-bag. But I'm also sad for Patti because she has no idea, no idea of her power. I sit on the toilet trying to collect myself while listening to her decamp.

My hope is that the *Iris* will remind her that it *is* possible to move beyond.

I wipe a tear from my eye, which continues to leak despite the missing lymph nodes, toss the Kleenex in the wastebasket, and see that Sam's deposited the desecrated porno mags in my wastebasket. Okay, so he wants me to know he knows. That's fair. *Stay out of his room.* But I can't stand having them near me. I grab The Bay bag that contained the sheets, fit it over my hand, and pick them up in the way that dog owners collect their dogs' shit. Good thing it's garbage day.

"Darwin is absolutely the fussiest baby I've ever met," Muriel complains. "He cries constantly."

"He's a newborn," I point out.

"Devon never cried like that. Had she cried like that, I would have locked her up and thrown away the key."

She was probably too scared to cry.

"I smoked through my pregnancy," she adds. "Everyone did then. It resulted in much calmer babies."

Too brain-damaged to cry.

"And I promise you they weren't the spoiled ninnies they are today. Smaller too." She adjusts her hat in the mirror. "They didn't have to tear you open to get them out. Devon hasn't been able to sit for days. I told her to take up smoking next time."

The property manager has been kind enough to show us the plans for the lobby upgrade. While he stands with arms crossed looking down at them, I marvel at his toupee. It's wavy, not curly, and each wave is immovable, anchored in some way. Most toups have hairs straining to escape, but this is one secure rug.

I keep suggesting that Muriel look at the plans, but she's too busy telling the property manager that she was the belle of the ball whilst at Maxim's in Paris. Which begins a discussion about botulin being injected into faces to preserve the look of youth. Apparently the poison paralyzes the muscles, releasing tension, thereby smoothing the skin. The manager's daughter has been doing it regularly and he asks if Muriel has ever tried it. "Absolutely not," she says. "It sounds absolutely disgusting."

"Works a charm," he says, "and it's a lot cheaper than a lift. She was a little disappointed after the last injections because he paralyzed her upper lip. She couldn't smile or talk for a week or so. And her eye drooped a bit."

"How old's your daughter?" I inquire.

"Facing the big three-O next month and she's not too happy about it."

"She's thirty and she's worrying about lines on her face?" I ask.

He nods. "They all want to look like models these days." Which is weird when you consider that we're an aging population. You'd think our bulk would tip the scale in favour of aging well but aging none the less. Maybe what's happening is we're looking at each other's jowls and thinking, Oh my god, I hope I don't look like that, I *can't* look like that, better go get some botulin injected into my face. And the twenty- and thirty-somethings are saying, There's no way I'm going to look like that, better go get some botulin injected into my face.

"All my life," Muriel confides to the manager, "people have thought me younger than my years."

"When is the lobby reno scheduled to take place?" I inquire.

"January."

"That's eons away," Muriel says. "In the meantime, I'd have to walk through a *cave* to get to my apartment."

I pick up the plans and hand them to the manager. "Thank you for your help." He welcomes the opportunity to exit. Muriel grimaces as the door closes behind him. "What an appalling little man. Absolutely no sophistication. Probably watches hockey. Why are Canadians so *obsessed* with hockey?"

Which brings to mind the Canadian in Texas who, according to my watch, will be injected with lethal chemicals in four minutes unless granted another stay of execution. His whole time on death row he remained loyal to the Montreal Canadiens.

"Anyway, I must dash, Devon's nitwit of a husband took the Range Rover on an off-road course and got it scratched. Ridiculous. It's in the shop, meaning Devon's without a car and I have to do her errands." She pulls out her compact and powders her face. "I know she's hoping to annoy me so much I buy them a second car."

"Muriel . . . ?" She looks at me as though I've interrupted some very profound thinking. "Are you interested in making an offer on this condo?"

"It's the best of a bad lot really, isn't it?"

I look into her dull grey eyes. "Yes. If you want a fast close."

"Very well. I'll call you this evening."

I glance at my watch. The hockey fan's dead.

Erna sits on Lyla's couch watching a soap opera in the exact same posture she assumed in the ward's common area: legs neatly crossed, cigarette held high, French twist immaculate. "Good day," she says to me.

"Hi," I respond. "How are you?"

"I've been better." She inhales on her cigarette and continues: "I said, '*Don't* you tell me that bitch hasn't been snooping around here.' I said, 'That woman's no good.' I said, '*Don't* you go drinking her coffee and eating her muffins.' I said, 'That woman's only interested in one thing and it's not what's between your legs.' I said, 'She wants me dead so she can get in my house, and let me tell you, once she's in it, there's no way you're getting her out of it.'" She jabs the air with her cigarette. "I said, 'After I'm dead, you'll know how good you had it. Once I'm dead, you'll be on your knees cryin' at my grave . . .'"

"Erna . . ." Lyla interjects. "Could you be quiet for a few minutes, please?"

"What?"

"I need to talk to Greer."

Lyla phoned my service, left an almost coherent message. She's looking plumper in striped pyjamas, probably her father's. She beckons me into the kitchen. "Someone's been here," she informs me.

"I was. You asked me to, remember? You told me the key was under the toad."

She considers this while pushing Swanson dinner remains past the flap in the trash can. The hair's growing back on the sides of her head in soft tufts, meaning she's stopped yanking it out. I wait for her to ask me where her parents are.

"A man's been here," she tells me.

"What man?"

"The toilet seat was up."

"Oh. That's my friend, who helped me. He also nailed the plywood over the window."

"Why?"

I could lie and say a baseball broke the glass, but that would not explain the TV and stereo. "Lyla, your house was vandalized while you were away. I've ordered a new window and my friend has promised to install it."

"Who is he?"

"He's just a man. His name's Arnold."

"I don't like men." She opens a kitchen cabinet, stares into it, then closes it again. "Why was I robbed?"

"Why is anybody robbed? Luck of the draw. They saw your lights out." I watch her peel the fortune cookie messages off the fridge. She still has a tremor. "Why is Erna here?" I ask.

"They don't want her there. They want her in a rooming house, but she says all the people there are crazy, and the bathroom stinks of piss. She really likes my bathroom. We went shopping and bought all kinds of soaps . . . shaped like ducks and turtles." She bunches the fortunes into a ball. "And fish." She drops the ball into the garbage. "Her granddaughter's missing. That's why she's so upset."

"'Missing' as in she ran away or got kidnapped?"

"Nobody knows. Yesterday was her ninth birthday. It was a bad day yesterday. Did you know they've done things to the viaduct so people can't jump off it? I think that's so disrespectful."

"Were you planning to jump?"

"Of course not. Erna just wanted to look at it. One of the guys in group was always talking about it."

"How long has her granddaughter been missing?"

"Almost a year."

I think of rape and mutilation and child-porn rings. And how I stare straight ahead when whisking past the missing-children signs at Wal-Mart because it's so hard and breaks my heart. Oh it's always relatives who abduct the kids, people say, divorced fathers wanting revenge, that sort of thing. So we'd like to think. The missing child is old news when they find the bodies later, much later, or not at all.

"Are the police doing anything?" I inquire.

"Erna says they stop looking after three days. She says after that you're just another statistic."

I would be more than insane if I were Erna. I would have attacked many piggies by now, would be a forensic patient in a locked ward.

"Erna's mad at her all the time."

"Her granddaughter?"

Lyla nods. "Our group leader says it's because she's not accepting the loss."

This whole idea of accepting loss drives me nuts, I mean it's gone, that piece of you, you can never accept that. You can learn to function without it, but the feeling of loss, that suction in your gut, remains.

"What about the girl's parents?" I ask.

"Erna hates them. All they want is her money. Now that she doesn't have any, they don't care what happens to her. They're separated anyway."

"And her husband?" I ask.

"Oh he's dead. Our group leader says she has to accept his death before she can heal."

Erna brings her loaded ashtray into the kitchen and dumps it in the trash can. "Nice day if you like rain," she says.

"It's not raining," I assure her.

"It will." She turns to Lyla. "So she's pregnant with Joseph's baby."

"You're kidding?" They both hurry back to the living room and stare at the TV. I follow and see chesty Melissa in tears as she tells her sensitive high-school sweetheart that the only right thing to do is to abort. He grips her by the shoulders and exclaims, "You can't do that. This is a *love* child!"

"What'd I tell ya?" Erna says.

I leave my card on the kitchen table and take out the garbage which is beginning to smell. Maybe Erna is good for Lyla. Watching someone else's suffering tends to mute our own. Maybe this is also true of madness.

As I get into my car, rain begins to fall.

Jerry's hanging around again. I don't get it. It's as if he thinks he's been a bad boy who must be forgiven. Which is pretty hilarious. What's to forgive? I was a consenting adult who made my own hell. He sits before me in a compliant pose, head bowed, hands in lap. Somehow cancer seems to sanctify its victims. It's as though the healthy hope that the sick will put in a good word for them in the afterlife. Tell God I didn't mean it.

"Why are you here, Jerry?"

"You don't call me. I wanted to see how you are."

"Is Natasha out for a drive?"

"Natasha is at home. She sends her regards."

"Is she getting venti lattes delivered now?"

"Please don't be a wiseass."

"My ass is not wise. But I'm very tired. Zonked."

"I just wanted to see you," he says in an urgent, blustery confession-of-a-lover kind of way. Lord. I collapse on a kitchen chair. Where is Sybil when you need her?

"Have a drink," I tell him. "Pour me a small one."

Just like the naughty doggy allowed back in, Jerry jumps up and scampers to the liquor cabinet. I imagine his tail wagging. He trots back with large drinks. "Is this good for you?"

"Nothing is good for me. So what's up? Something's up."

He takes a swig, sets the glass on the table. "Actually, it's my mother."

His mother? I hate his mother, and she hates me. I never go to her snotty fundraisers for worthy causes like her social club. "I think she has Alzheimer's."

"How old is she, a hundred and ten? That's called your garden-variety dementia."

"She's only eighty-nine."

"A spring chicken."

"She goes . . . she's been getting on buses and trains and things. Planes. She takes cabs for two hundred miles. I had to pick her up in Kingston."

"Maybe she wants to explore new horizons."

He shakes his head to indicate that I don't understand. "She has trouble getting around so she hires people to help her. Cab drivers, waitresses. She pays them twenty bucks to carry something for her, help her sit up, sit down, climb stairs. It gets expensive. Last night, she calls and breathes on my service, and I hear this Puerto Rican woman in the background shouting, 'Leave message! Leave message!' Finally my mother says, 'Pearson. Nine thirty.' She doesn't say morning or evening, doesn't say where she is, no flight number, nothing. I show up at Pearson at nine, check for nine-thirty arrivals, of course there aren't any. To date, she hasn't left the country so I hang around Terminal Two for three hours. Sure enough she shows up with some poor schmuck carting her luggage."

"Where'd she been?"

"Calgary."

"Does she know anybody there?"

"Not a soul. She went to Winnipeg last week, came home and took a cab to Stratford. Cost two hundred bucks."

"Maybe she wanted to catch some shows."

"This isn't funny."

I shrug. "I don't understand the problem."

"It's costing a lot of money."

"It's her money." Like all heirs-in-waiting, Jerry thinks of his mother's money as his money. He drinks more and broods.

"Okay, here's what I think," I say. "Do you want to know what I think?"

"Shoot."

"She's lonely."

"I talk to her every week."

"On the phone. That must offer comfort. Jerry, how dense can you be? She's running away to get your attention. Didn't you ever run away? It doesn't mean she has Alzheimer's. Everybody wants their parents to have Alzheimer's so they can stash them in a home and forget about them."

"Natasha thinks we should institutionalize her."

"What a surprise. Forget it. Your mother's fine. Just visit her more often. Buy her some flowers."

"She mentioned you the other day. Said you were the salt of the earth."

"She must really hate Natasha." I lost complete interest in his mother when she lost complete interest in Sam which was immediately after the murders.

The front door swings open and our boy lumbers in. "This is different," he comments on seeing us. He avoids eye contact with Jerry as he pulls ginger ale from the fridge. He looks at me. "Is he moving back in?"

Jerry drums the table with his fingers. "Not exactly."

"Why not?" Sam asks me. "Now that you're dying. He could move in here with his sow, steal some more furniture."

"Sam . . ." I say.

"What's he doing hanging around? It's sick. We don't see him for years and now you're dying, he's like breathing down your neck."

"I'm concerned," Jerry ventures.

"Bullshit."

"I'm not dying," I interject.

"You've got cancer, for fuck's sake," Sam says.

"Do you think it helps her to hear you talk like that?" Jerry asks.

"What the fuck do you know about helping? You fucking tore her apart."

"Okay," I say, "that's enough. I don't need this."

"What are *you* doing for her?" Jerry demands. "I don't see you making her life any easier."

"What am I supposed to do?"

"Get a job, for starters. Contribute to the household."

I start screaming, a kind of Munch thing with a bit of

Pavarotti thrown in—a piercing, continuous sound. It stops them. Requiring oxygen, I take in a breath and hear the pitter-patter of Sybil coming down the stairs. "Everybody clear out," I order. "Now."

And they do. And I find this remarkable. Cancer gives you superpowers because everyone is afraid of you, since you embody cancer and everyone's afraid of cancer.

But Sybil, of course, returns in minutes because nothing stops her for long. "What was that all about?"

"Fights. I'm sick of them. No more fighting."

"Okay. Have you eaten? There's stew."

"I'm not hungry." The hatred between them scratched like sandpaper. I can still feel it against my skin.

"You have to keep your strength up." She pushes a bowl of the stuff at me and I eat a lump or two in an effort to make someone feel good.

I don't want their rough edges scraping my face. I want to be the shoulder that's there, just there. Forever.

Twenty-six

"How's Harvey?" I ask Estelle who's eating one of the mini Mars bars she bought at a Halloween sale.

"Willy," she corrects, "not Harvey. I'm calling him Willy."

"For any particular reason?" Todd inquires.

"Because he looks like Willy."

"I see." Todd's eyes roll skyward. Estelle offers us the bag of Mars bars. "Stay away," Todd protests. "I inhale those and I gain weight."

"So is Willy settling in?" I ask. I've prepared Muriel's offer and am waiting for her to sign. She's late, of course.

"Well, he's got his own towel," Estelle explains, "that Inga brought, and his own bowl and litter box and stuff like that so . . . he's a little timid though, he's hiding a lot."

"Could that have anything to do with the fact," Todd queries, "that you're calling him Harvey or Willy instead of his *name* which is Girly?"

"Willy sounds more like Girly than Harvey," Estelle counters. "I couldn't call him Harvey, he's too shy. Harveys aren't shy."

Todd flips through his daytimer. "Honestly, Estelle, get a life."

Muriel glides in, hat flopping, scarves billowing. "I had a dreadful time getting here, some dreadful march going on, lesbians or something." I hand her the offer which she peruses.

"The Halibs are just so excited about your house," Todd tells her. "Mr. Halib's gone ballistic over the gargoyles."

"Yes, well they were imported from Rome," Muriel explains. "Priceless. I have half a mind to take them with me."

"Won't work in a condo," I point out.

"And I *love* your hat," Todd says, recognizing that a change in topic would be useful. "Is that European? You just can't find hats like that here. Very elegant."

I try again to page the listing agent. Estelle follows me to the desk. "Willy plays hockey," she informs me breathlessly. "We were watching hockey on TV and he started batting the puck with his paw. Isn't that the cutest?"

I can't stop thinking about the roofers who descended on my house this morning and are currently hacking the shingles off it. Their skin has been baked brown by the sun. Is melanoma a word they're familiar with? Are they aware of the carcinogenic properties of tar? My library reading informed me that chimney sweeps developed cancer of the scrotum because they were sent up the flues naked so they could squeeze through all the nooks and crannies. By fourteen they had to have their balls cut off.

By eighteen they were usually dead. Which got me thinking about the current news regarding tar ponds in Sydney, Nova Scotia, that contain 700,000 tons of toxic sludge left behind by the coke ovens. Residents of the steel town are 50 percent more likely to develop cancer than other Nova Scotians. Which got me thinking about Ontario's coal-generated production of electricity doubling since seven nuclear reactors were sidelined which results in 3 million metric tons of hydrocarbons being pumped into our atmosphere yearly. My query is, is this prudent? What about solar heat? What about windmills, waterfalls? What about designing energy-saving buildings instead of glass towers that require constant heating or cooling? What about allowing things to grow which provide shade and oxygen? What about consuming less?

Estelle unwraps another Mars bar. "And I just got so tired of him not sitting with me, you know, on the couch and stuff, so I picked him up and put him beside me and stroked him and he started purring. Isn't that darling?"

"It is."

The vendor of the hideous condo is the only daughter of the owner who recently died of—and this is not cheering—breast cancer. Anticipating an emotional meeting, I plan to present Muriel's low offer as tactfully as possible. But when I arrive the daughter and the listing agent are discussing the pros and cons of mammograms. It turns out the agent recently had a cancer scare due to what her radiologist described as calcifications in her breasts (didn't Bunny the deceased cat have calcifications?). The radiologist recommended an excisional biopsy. "I'm one of those people," the agent tells us, "who goes *whoa* when doctors talk about incisions. I mean, it's a business, right? So who can you trust?" Her fingernails are maraschino, matching her lipstick. "And my cousin's had a bunch of biopsies, every time they do a mammogram they cut a piece off her. So now her breast's scarred and half the size of the other one. It's not like they grow back. So I told this guy I wanted a second opinion. I got three. Only one said I needed the procedure. But I'm like, *one,* one's enough, right? One's enough to keep you up nights."

The vendor has the face of the haunted. She believes that cancer is stalking her, as it did her mother. She can't be more than forty, but grey hairs have already dulled the shine of her hair.

"So I go to the States," the agent continues, "to this specialist who does mammotomes, which locate the calcifications with a digital X-ray."

"Without making an incision?" the haunted asks.

"He cut me but it was, like, teeny. You lie face down on this table with a hole in it for your breast and he inserts this hollow probe that sucks the calcifications out. End of story. Off it goes to the lab. A few days later I get the news they're benign. I'm telling you, if you get sick, go to the States. It's a joke here."

"It's costly," the haunted points out.

"Listen, it's your life you're talking about." The agent is one of the many who refuse to believe that some people just don't have the cash to hop on a plane to the Mayo Clinic.

"My mother was treated here," the haunted says, crossing her arms so tightly I fear she might crack a rib. "She did everything. Whatever they offered, she took without question. She weighed seventy pounds by the end—couldn't eat, move, talk, breathe."

"It doesn't mean *you're* going to get it," I say, startled by my own directness. I want to advise her that my family was cancer-free and yet I'm the proud owner of three-quarters of a breast. But if I confess, the maraschino cherry will spread the word and I will be shunned.

"They wouldn't give her adequate medication for pain," the haunted tells us because she needs to tell someone. "I could see she was in agony, but they wouldn't provide further relief for fear of killing her. As though such a side effect could be anything but merciful." She has the strained, studious look of someone who never stops reading. Who needs books like some of us need drinks. "She's still with me," she tells us. "She appears to me. Cautions me to be strong. I have her photograph on my desk. When she sees me weakening, she knocks it over. Initially, I assumed it was incidental and tried bumping the desk to see if the frame fell over easily. Other pictures collapsed but her photo remained standing, watching me."

The maraschino cherry's purple-eyeshadowed eyes are beginning to bulge.

"And she makes me do things I don't usually do," the haunted adds with an eerie little laugh. "Last night, I made Pilsbury turnovers. She used to make them regularly. I never ate them, certainly not with the icing. But last night, I craved something sweet, which is completely uncharacteristic of me. It was my mother trying to comfort me. She made me squeeze icing onto them. I ate four."

"How does your mother look when she appears to you?" I inquire.

"As she looked before she got sick." She pulls out a Tupperware container and lifts the lid. "Would either of you care for a turnover?"

"No thanks," the cherry says. "I'm on a diet, *comme toujours*."

I take a turnover and hope that the action will make the dead condo owner forgive me for presenting her beloved daughter with such a shitty offer.

I am absolutely wiped and not thrilled to be approached by the male component of the couple who bought the old-lady-obsessed-with-raking-leaves' house. "Greetings, neighbour!" he heralds, then proceeds to quiz me about security systems. When I explain that I don't have one, he appears aghast, as though I'd just said I had no beating heart. Next he wants to know "if there's a good Thai restaurant around here." His wife skips towards us and insists that I join them for a drink. I agree because I rarely turn down drinks, and because I believe in being neighbourly until the neighbours prove to be callous tree-killing louts.

"Did you happen to notice what happened to your neighbour's lawn?" the husband asks me. "Was that vandalism or what?"

"Probably groundhogs," I say. "They crave pesticides. It's kind of like glue-sniffing to them."

His eyebrows rise. "Seriously?" He's in faded-denim everything, with a pair of pink sunglasses suspended from a tropical green cord around his neck.

Inside their house, we drink "Far Niente," a California wine which he informs me is "well balanced with a long finish." We squat on "designer" chairs that hurt my back. "Are you interested in gardening?" I inquire.

"We had a banana tree in L.A.," the wife offers. "Sweetie, can you get us more pretzels?" He obeys. She kicks off her espadrilles and massages her feet. "I'd like to get a banana tree for here, but I guess it would die."

"You wanted a white Christmas," Sweetie reminds her from the kitchen.

She flexes her toes. "I don't see why we couldn't treat a banana tree like a big annual."

Watch it freeze to death. Buy another one next year, and the year after that, transform your yard into a banana-tree killing ground.

Sweetie offers me the pretzels. "They're organic," his wife assures me. I eat one and notice only that it needs more salt. "This house," she informs me, "was our Christmas present to each other. There's so much we want to do to it. I really want a slate floor in the kitchen."

"Not this year, hon," says Sweetie. "We made a deal, remember?"

"I know." Hon sulks playfully, bobbing her head, causing her native people's handcrafted earrings to jiggle.

"Did you like L.A.?" I inquire.

"L.A.'s great," they both reply.

"We had a great house," Hon elaborates, "near Sunset and LaCienega. There were a few shootouts, but you get used to it."

"Just stay inside," Sweetie adds, chuckling.

"We met some great people," Hon says. "Stewart broke his wrist rollerblading which delayed us coming back. Which was great."

"Great," Sweetie echoes.

"We took some great courses, did a lot of training."

"It was great."

"What kind of courses?" I ask.

Hon sucks on a pretzel. "Self-healing, growth-oriented."

"Wholeness," Sweetie clarifies.

Hon nods. "It was great, we connected with some great people. Stew got treated by a physio who was into the whole mind/body experience."

Sweetie nods. "Miguel. He was great."

"Miguel believes that your body has memory and that you have to teach it to forget. Sweetie, what did he used to say to you?"

"Every cell in your body remembers death."

"Wow," I comment.

"He was great," Sweetie repeats.

I'm curious about what happens to people in L.A. that compels them to use the word "great" in every sentence. Is it kind of like if I *say* it's great, it *will* be great? If you *look* great, you'll *feel* great?

"Did you know," Hon tells me, "that you can't cross the border with an open wound?" I shake my head. "Stew, tell her about your near-death experience."

He shrugs. "I just saw light, and there was this great music."

"This was when you fell off your rollerblades?" I ask.

He nods. "It felt great. After I got over the shock of seeing my bone sticking out."

"Miguel says he was accepting death. Which is why his cells needed so much training."

"Wow." My mind, of course, is wandering away from greatness and visualizing the horrific near-death of a two-month-old baby who was left in his crib last night with a pet ferret. The infant was strapped to a car seat and unable to move while being severely mauled by the ferret. His mother was "sleeping" in the bed beside him. The neighbours heard the baby's screams, but decided it was a cat. The mother had previously been charged with "failing to provide the necessities of life" to her many illegitimate children. Did the infant see light and hear great music? If he lives, will every cell in his body remember death? Certainly the scars won't let him forget. Why, why are there so many neglected children in this "civilized society"? Last week, one was found lying on top of his mother who'd overdosed on heroin. He'd been there for three days and was nearly dead from dehydration. *What* is the Children's Aid Society doing these days? Making sure babies stay with their drug-addicted, abusive, alcoholic, neglectful mommies? When there are baby-starved infertile couples scouring the globe for unwanted babies because adoption here is fraught with government brouhaha resulting in long delays and often no bambino?

"This is a great neighbourhood," Hon tells me.

"Don't think there'll be too many drive-by shootings here," Sweetie remarks.

"Or quakes," I offer. Being new in town, they obviously don't know who I am, or who my son is. This is good.

"I was thinking," I tell my aberrant son, "that we could renovate the basement for you. Give you some privacy."

"What for?" He shoves Tostitos into his mouth.

"You don't want privacy?"

"You don't want me upstairs?"

"Are you kidding? Of course I do, I just thought you'd like more space."

"What for?"

"I don't know. Whatever it is you do."

"Jerk off with magazines."

"Right, well, whatever."

"Cut off their fucking teats."

"Sure," I say, gasping inwardly, "if that works for you." I know he's trying to shock me, scare me. Try as I might, I can't convince him that I'm on his side.

He turns his baseball cap around and hides under the brim. "You don't think that's a little weird?"

"We're all a little weird, Sam. Everybody masturbates, or if they don't, they should."

He makes that punctured-inner-tube sound again.

"Seriously," I elaborate, "everybody has sexual fantasies, and some of them aren't too pretty."

He snorts. "Like *you* have sexual fantasies."

"Of course. You want to hear them?"

"Spare me." He rummages around in the fridge, pulls out olives and starts eating them from the jar.

"Did you watch Rachel's video?" I ask.

"Yeah."

"What was that like?"

He unscrews the cap of his ginger ale. "I was some little shithead."

"No you weren't. You were smart. Are smart. Probably too smart."

"What's that supposed to mean?"

I'm not sure. I try to think of something. "Only that you might not want to do what everybody else is doing."

"I don't want to do anything. That's my fucking problem."

"Why is that a problem?"

He heaves a huge how-dumb-can-this-woman-be sigh.

"You will want to do something at some point," I assure him. "Then maybe you'll change your mind and want to do something else. This whole idea that we're supposed to know what we want and how to get it is absurd. Life isn't like that."

"What's it like, Ma?" he asks in a Jerry-derisive tone.

"It's confusing. You think you think something and then you think something else. You think you want something, then you want something else. It's this big chase. After all kinds of things. You score some of them and find out they weren't worth scoring. Sometimes things you weren't chasing just kind of drop in your lap and you can't believe how lucky you are. I mean, it's like that. Confusing."

"Sounds groovy." He drinks more ginger ale.

"I don't understand why you're so hard on yourself."

"I don't understand why you're so fucking forgiving."

Find an answer to this one—because I *love* you, that overused, undervalued word again? Because the umbilical cord is still there in my mind? What wouldn't sound unbelievably hollow? "Do you want me to make a salad?" I ask.

"*Stop* doing things for me, alright, just stop," he says this urgently, as though if I don't stop, the floor will split open and we will perish.

"Okay," I answer, knowing this is not possible.

He abandons me for his television. I sort listlessly through the tulip bulbs I bought, feeling as if every joint in my body is loose. Because without him, without the prospect of doing things for him, I have no stabilizing force. My basement fantasy goes the way of its many floods: lots of gushing and gurgling, then mud.

I bought the bulbs for Arnie's backyard. I wanted to plant them before I see Cheeseburger. While I still believe in the possibility of clear skies.

But now it just feels pointless: treading water, biding time. Useless endeavours. Why bother to make things pretty? Who gives a fuck? I grab the bag of Tostitos and start mainlining hydrogenated fat.

I peed at the garden centre, shared the ladies' room with a woman in a wig. On seeing her, a rock lodged in my throat because I assumed she was a chemo patient. But as I squatted in my cubicle I overheard her chatting with another woman about the abundance of artificial curls on her head. "I can't be bothered curling my own hair," she said with a *Coronation Street* accent. "I'm at my health club at seven and then at work. Wigs are so much easier."

"But your own hair is so nice," her mousey companion offered.

"I like a change. It gets a bit boring, having the same old hair all the time, don't you think? And the truth is, I've got a bit of grey now and I haven't made up my mind about a colour. Some days, I feel like being a blonde but not always, you know what I mean, that's the thing."

"Well, auburn looks lovely on you."

"You think so? Sometimes it's just a bit too tarty for me, you know what I mean?"

While washing my hands, I took a good look at her and her breasts. Definitely real, droopy, as was her face. I considered mentioning she might want to get some botulin injections but decided that no, I'd best haul my jaded ass out of there. I could think only of all the women, *all* the women who feel their hair being pulled out by brushes and combs. Usually you start noticing it three to four weeks after you start chemo, but it can proceed quickly after that. You can be bald in days. Imagine collecting the hairs, fishing them out of the drain, pulling them off your loved ones, clothes, towels, sheets, carpets—stuffing them in the garbage.

"What's the matter with you?" Sybil asks.

"Nothing."

"You look miserable."

"I'm not." She's got her hand on her pacemaker. "You've been twiddling that, haven't you?"

"I'm just feeling it."

"Norman said to leave it alone. If you keep touching it, I'm telling Norm."

She fits her empty glass into the dishwasher—meaning she's had her constitutional and is tipsy—and pushes a *Harper's Magazine* at me. "Read about the chickens."

"Do I have to, Auntie? I know chickens have it rough."

"It's not just the chickens. It's the workers. The deboners stand for hours chopping through chicken gristle and bone with blunt scissors and knives. Sometimes, the blades slip off the slimy carcasses and the workers gouge each other by mistake. They get joint pain and hurt their backs slipping on the muck on the floor. They lose their fingernails because of the bacteria in the carcasses."

Tostitos clog my throat. "Don't they wear gloves?"

"They're supposed to, but lots of them don't want to spend the money since they're only making six-fifty an hour. Cleanup workers go blind because they aren't given eye protection from the ammonia they use to clean the floors."

"This is in America?"

"You think it's any different here?" she demands, getting red around the gills. "It's hard to find Americans desperate enough to do the work so Congress is setting up a *government-run* 'guest worker' program that will employ immigrants for up to two years, or until they burn out, then send them home."

"Blind, in pain, and without fingernails," I comment. "What a great country. Sybil, I know this is hard for you to understand, but this information doesn't make me feel better."

"Who said it was supposed to? Who says we have to *feel* good all the time? Since when did *feelings* rule the day? If people would stop fussing about their feelings and pay attention, these kinds of killing lines wouldn't exist."

"Sure they would. People want their boneless chicken breast. Got to watch those waistlines."

She's hopping mad now. "That's exactly the kind of defeatist thinking I'm talking about. It *has* to stop. People *have* to know."

"I think lots of people do know and don't give a shit. That's the difference between us, Auntie. You believe people are ignorant and that if enlightened, they would care and do something about it. I believe they do know, don't want to know, choose to forget about it and go shopping."

Jerry phones sounding frightened—very unusual for him. "My mother's . . . I'm at my mother's. She had a fall, she's . . . there's shit everywhere and she thinks I'm trying to kidnap her."

"Are you?"

"This is no time for jokes. Can you come over? She'll listen to you."

"Where's Natasha?"

"My mother hates Natasha."

"What about your brother?"

"You know they haven't spoken in years."

"So call an ambulance or something."

"Greer, I want some confidentiality here. Please, I don't ask you for much, please . . . ?"

I'm thinking about the seventeen-five plus tax for the roof job. "Okay."

Hedley Pentland lives in a gargantuan house in Rosedale all by herself. She has a housekeeper who's currently in Greece visiting her hometown. A housekeeper who's been Hedley's uncomplaining slave for years, who has a deaf-and-dumb twenty-eight-year-old daughter she supports and takes to Greece with her. "She come to flower in Greece," the housekeeper told me. "It's cold here. People. She prefer Greece."

My former he-man greets me rubber-gloved, bucket in hand. The place stinks of shit. "It's been quite a mop up," he admits.

"Where is she?"

“Top floor. She won’t come down. Thinks I have kidnapping cronies down here.”

The first thing Hedley says is, “None of this would be happening if Pinkerton were here, call Pinkerton.” Pinkerton was her money manager and has been dead for nineteen years.

“If Pinkerton were here,” I say, “he would be a hundred and seventeen.”

“He may be old,” Hedley tells me, “but he goes to the office every day.”

“Would you like some tea or something, Hedley?”

She pulls her housecoat tighter. “He went to the moon and has the rocks to prove it.”

“Pinkerton?”

She resumes rocking in her chair. “There’s no atmosphere on the moon,” she explains. “You have to wear a mask.”

Maybe Jerry’s right. Maybe it is time for a room that locks from the outside.

“When you want to talk,” she advises me, “you have to take off the mask.” She mimes taking the mask off, then putting it on again. “Call Pinkerton,” she repeats.

Jerry gave me some pills for her, hopefully sedatives. I offer one. “This’ll make you feel better, Hed.”

“I’d rather shoot you dead than take those pills.”

“Okay.” I sit on a zebra-skin pouffe. “Is there anything you’d like to talk about? Are you in pain from the fall?”

“You’d like that, wouldn’t you? No, I’m just fine, thank you very much. Just fine. Call Pinkerton.”

“Pinkerton’s no longer with us.”

“That may be, but he goes to the office every day.”

Jerry appears with something in a bowl. “Here’s some of that tapioca you like so much, Mum. Might settle your stomach. I put some raisins in, just the way you like it.”

“I’d rather shoot you dead than eat that.” He sets it beside her anyway and she gobbles it. She’s always been a sweet freak.

"Did you tell Greer about the crocodiles?" Jerry inquires.

"They were standing on their tails to greet me. They opened their jaws and stuck out their tongues." She demonstrates the crocodiles' greeting with her own jaws and tongue. "Very friendly," she adds.

"I've always felt crocodiles get a bad rap," I offer.

"Very cordial. Standing on their tails. Quite magnificent."

"I'd like to have seen that," I say.

"Beautiful country, a bit swampy, but lovely water lilies. I'd like to buy a house there. No tennis though. I'd miss that."

"Maybe you could take up boating," I suggest.

"Yes, I don't get seasick like your father did. The man couldn't look at water without vomiting. Very inconvenient. Of course, there's always airplanes. I'm quite fond of air travel. Apart from the ear trouble."

She seems to be fading, her head's lolling. I slip a pillow behind her. "Seats are smaller now though," she adds. "Cram you in like sardines. I always travel business class. They give you slippers." And she's out.

"What was in the tapioca?" I ask Jerry.

"Sleeping pill. She was tired anyway, just needed a push. So is that Alzheimer's or what?"

"I don't know what it is. I think you should seek professional help."

"I promised my father I'd never put her in a home."

"So don't. Get help in."

"She won't cooperate."

"She may have to. Are we going to leave her here?"

He lifts her gently, carefully, and carries her to her room. I leave them alone, the mother and son, wander back downstairs and look at old photos on the mantel, mostly of Hedley looking smart in spiffy clothes. But then I notice one of young Jerry that could be Sam. I pick it up to examine it under the light. The eyes are different. Young Jerry already has a predatory look about him.

"Thanks for coming," he says. "Can I offer you something?"

"No, I want to get back."

He pours himself a Scotch. "I realized that you were the only one I could trust. Pretty shocking."

"You're going to have to come out of the closet on this one, Jerr. Talk to her doctor."

"Her doctor suggested the pendant she's wearing so she can page me. The problem is she's paging me constantly. She bumps it by mistake. I come rushing and she's fine, talking about crocodiles."

"What a nice dementia though," I comment. "Greetings from crocodiles, visits to the moon."

"Nice if it's not your mother."

"Jerry, she brought you into this world, wiped your ass, fed you, clothed you, the least you can do is look after her now."

He sighs and sits on a chair covered in animal skin. Hedley's always been big on safari booty. "Can we talk about Sam?" he asks.

"Of course," I reply, wondering if, subliminally, this is why he called me.

He sips his drink, takes a long time to swallow. "Do you think he will ever forgive me?"

"Do you think you deserve to be forgiven?"

He stares at a table lamp made from a hoof, maybe a water buffalo's, and shakes his head. "I don't even know what I did wrong."

"There's your first clue. Maybe if you figure that out, he'll forgive you."

"Has he forgiven you?"

"I don't think you ever forgive your parents. Have you forgiven Hedley?"

"Hedley's always been a coquette. She never consciously hurt anyone. We just got pushed aside if we interfered with her social life."

"Doesn't sound like you've forgiven her." I step off a dead tiger. "Anyway, I think forgiveness is overrated. It's just a word. I just want Sam to like being with me. That's all I want. Sometimes I think that's happening and then I do something stupid, something well intended but wrong, and I lose him again."

"You really don't think he'll kill again?"

"I really don't think he'll kill again."

"Why?"

"I don't know."

He strokes the arm of his chair. It's brown fur, maybe an impala. I picture the graceful creature sprinting about the savannah, getting plugged by bullets.

"It smells of dead animals in here," I remark.

"It's a strange passion of hers, the skins."

"Just think, you'll inherit all this."

"God, you just . . . you never back off, do you? It's always a joke to you."

He has no right, no right to say it's always a joke to me. "You know what isn't a joke to me, Jerr? A father who has his head so far up his own ass he can't even see his son. He's standing there, facing you, *within your reach,* and you tell him to get a job. Are you nuts? He hasn't recovered, I don't know if he'll ever recover. I don't want him to get a job, I want him to heal. I want him to relax into who he is instead of despairing about who he isn't. Forgiveness is your wank, it's got nothing to do with him. Quit whining about it. And don't come around unless you're willing to beg, because that's what I'm doing. I'm letting him walk all over me and when he's finished, when all his fury is spent, I plan to still be here. Broken in places, but still here. I'm going home. Find some help for your mother. I'm sending you the bill for the roof." I leave him on the impala, lips working, about to spit out words.

I know I shouldn't dwell on these things, even read about these things, but they're there in the paper. I try to skip past and read about important things like what the TSE's doing and Fall Fashion Trends. But then my eyes get sucked back to the stories that shake my bones. A three-year-old girl was raped, beaten, sexually abused with a "blunt instrument," whipped with chains and a cat-o'-nine-tails, shackled while her feet were burned—all by her mother and her current beau. The girl was left naked, soaked in blood on their bathroom floor. It took her four hours to die of internal injuries. The mom and the beau's defence? She fell down some stairs. It was in an apartment, for God's sake, couldn't anybody hear her cries? Are we so absorbed by our TVs with stereo sound that we don't hear? Or do we just not want to hear. Oh it's only domestic violence, you know how it is, he's a disciplinarian after all. Kids these days, you never know what they'll get up to. A *three-year-old*?

What about the Grundys' cries? Who heard the Grundys' cries and did nothing?

As much as I want the mom and the beau tortured as they tortured her daughter, I understand that many want such a fate for my son. And I can only retreat into my little psychic shell and say, You don't understand, you don't understand. Like a snail, I must stay here, poke my head out only occasionally. Because once outside and in the world as we know it, I may get myself a gun—(the paper said it's easy these days)—and start shooting. I would begin with the mom and her beau, proceed to the ferret-mauled baby's mother, take out a politician or two, some industrialists and certainly any miscellaneous pedophiles.

"Mum . . . ?"

"Yes?" He's calling me "Mum" again?

"Can I come in?"

"Of course."

He sits on the end of my bed—sits!

"Sybil told me you were with Dad."

"That's right. His mother's going dotty."

"Hasn't she always been a nutbar?"

"More or less."

He takes his baseball cap off, puts it on again. "Is he mad at me?"

"No."

"I don't know what I'm supposed to do about him."

"Why do you feel you have to do anything?"

"Because he's my dad."

"By that standard," I point out, "*he* should do something."

He looks down at his palms à la Jerry. "I changed my name."

"You did?"

He nods without looking at me. "Sam Dawes."

"Oh that's great, sweetie, I'm so pleased, I mean, are you pleased?"

He sort of nods and for one second looks at me and sort of smiles. "Secret Agent Dawes."

I want to hug him, want to hug him, but he's up at the window again. I can't chase him around the room. Sam Dawes.

"What the fuck happened to the neighbours' lawn?" he asks.

"What do you mean?" He can see it in street light?

"They've fucking dug holes all over it." He leans out, a little too far, I'm thinking, don't do this in your sleep.

"Oh that," I say. "I think it's a new way of applying pesticides. You know, so it gets to the roots. Fungus on the roots. Below ground. You need to dig holes."

He ducks back in. "They're fucking psycho about bugs. Someone should spray them with anthrax or something. Let 'em know what if feels like."

"I agree."

He sits at my dressing table, close to my prosthesis. He's never seen it in the buff and I'm afraid it'll spook him. "Did you know the Russians have this arsenal of biological weapons?" he asks. "It's like fucking huge. They've been brewing the stuff even since the cold war ended. They've got the bubonic plague, smallpox, ebola. They can just pack 'em in melon-sized bombs and drop 'em. Five hundred kilograms of the stuff could wipe out Toronto."

"Charming."

"I told Sybil."

"And she said don't believe everything you read."

"You got it." He picks up one of the pages Patti left behind featuring stick figures demonstrating post-op exercises for mastectomy patients. "Why do you like her so much?"

"Who?"

"Sybil." He puts the paper down and starts tapping his foot.

"Because every fibre of her is decent."

"I just wish she'd shut the fuck up about all the crap in the world. I mean like we really need to hear that shit."

"I think we do. I think we do need to hear that shit."

"Why?" His foot stops.

"I'm not sure."

"It's not like we can do anything about it."

"We can acknowledge it, maybe even feel it a bit, maybe even try to think of ways we can improve things in a minor way."

"I just tell her to bite it." He picks up a photo of him at three, watching the seals at the zoo. He said they were "bootiful." "Are you nervous about seeing the doctor?" he asks.

"A little."

He puts the photo down. "Do they make mistakes on those tests?"

"Rarely."

He picks up a *New Yorker* that's sitting on the dresser and flicks through it. "Turner wants to be an etiologist. He can't even crap on his own. It's not like his dad's going to be around forever."

"He'll get help."

He leans back in the chair and stretches his legs. "There's nothing wrong with me and I can't get off my ass to do anything."

"You will."

He rolls the magazine into a tube and looks through it, not at me but at the floor. "I'm sorry I swore at you before."

"I don't think you actually swore at me."

"Whatever."

"It's okay."

He puts the *New Yorker* down and heads for the door. "You should get some sleep," he advises.

"You too."

"See you tomorrow."

"You bet."

He goes downstairs and I'm thinking, It's two in the morning, shouldn't he be in bed? This is not good sleep hygiene. Then I sneak over to the dressing table and pick up the magazine and feel it. Just feel it, because it's still warm from his grip.

Twenty-seven

Cheeseburger's corpse of a secretary is on her phone frantically trying to locate hockey tickets for tonight. Apparently Cheeseburger's nephews are in town and want to catch a game. Seeing the corpse animated unsettles me, particularly over such an insignificant detail. But Cheeseburger wants good seats, not your regular scalper's offerings. The corpse sees positive pathology reports daily and is unmoved, but following her sports fan's orders has her in a flush. Actual colour spreads up her neck and onto her cheeks.

He's on the phone as I enter. "It's too bad," I hear him say. "I'm surprised. Things seemed to be going so well." He sees me and gestures for me to sit. I stare at my file in front of him and know that within it lies my fate. "Thursday night's better for us," he says to the phone. There's a doodad on his desk, one of those woodpeckers on a stick. You slide the bird up the stick and gravity sucks it back down, pecking. I do this a couple of times while wondering why I don't just grab my chart? Why do I have to wait around for the great doctor to sort out his social life? But he's off the phone and looking at me in that Spock way of his: eyes slightly narrowed, a crease between the eyebrows. "What is it, Doctor? Have the aliens invaded the Starship Enterprise?"

"How are you feeling?" he asks.

"Alright."

"That's good, can I see it?"

I lift my shirt, unfasten my bra. He steps around the desk. "Looks good," he comments without touching it. "Still a bit swollen. Eventually, it'll get smaller. As I said, the nipple may drop a little. You might want to get a smaller prosthesis for the other breast. But wait till the swelling's gone down. Need any more painkillers?"

"I think I'm alright. Although I wouldn't mind some sleeping pills."

"Sleeping pills?" He gives me a you're-not-going-to-off-yourself look. As if he'd prescribe enough for that. If suicide's in your plans, you've got to get prescriptions from all your cancer doctors.

"I'm having trouble sleeping. Pain."

"Of course."

"Seconal works best."

"Alright." He scribbles a prescription and hands it to me. "Just call if you need anything else." He sits down again, opens the chart and takes the requisite pause. "The report shows that three nodes tested positive. The good news is there's no metastasis." He waits for me to say something, do something, jump up and down, tear my hair out—*How long have I got, Doc?* I do none of this because my skin is sagging off my bones, my jowls are flopping around my knees.

"I'm surprised," he admits. "Things seemed to be going so well." Didn't he just say this on the phone, that he was "surprised" because "things seemed to be going so well"? How often is he surprised?

"That's fast for a recurrence," I comment.

He shrugs. "Cancer moves at different speeds in different people. Anyway, you should consider adjuvant therapy. Deb's set up an appointment with Dr. Wozniakowski. He can give you more details. See what he recommends. I'm sure he can fix you up with a good treatment plan." Already he fidgets and wants me out. Why? Is he feeling guilt? He did what he could, he tells himself, gave it his best shot, *twice,* what more could he do? The patient failed to heal. On to the next one, preferably a set of hooters that don't surprise him. I stand because I'm sick of looking at this man. It feels good to be on my legs, they're still there, still solid, one step, two step. "Enjoy the game," I say at the door.

"What's that?"

"Enjoy the hockey game."

"Oh. Yes. Thank you."

The appointment took less than five minutes. I sat in his waiting room for sixty-five. Never again. I'm not seeing any more doctors. I don't believe in them, in what they do. I believe they are sheep rushing with the herd. I believe they stay interested as long as your disease remains "treatable" by butchery and big pharma. Once you fail to be cured, they rush to the next feeding ground. There will always be more grass to graze, more cancer to treat.

The Starbucks near his office seems as good a place as any to recuperate. Certainly I can't drive in this condition, with my skin sagging off my bones. I think of the Elephant Man carting all that flesh around, and the weight of it crippling him. I order a venti latte, because I feel I should live what's left of my life to its full, and realize that I am the Elephant Woman. But nobody knows it. I'm hiding behind a falsie and a realtor's smile, but really I'm just this big bag of cells gone wrong.

Three nodes. How did it get to three nodes if he did such a swell job the first time around? I'm blaming him because I need to blame someone. My hatred for him is burning a hole through my throat. I want to spew poison at him, maybe some of that chicken bacteria Sybil was talking about. How about freeing him of fingernails? How about blinding him with ammonia so he can't butcher any more women? Stop. This doesn't help. Stop.

"Thank you," I say to the young Goth who hands me my latte. Does it fulfil you to whiten your face? I want to ask, to purple your lips? Does shoe-polish black hair heighten your spirits? Tell me, I need a pick-me-upper.

Sit, I tell myself. You're in shock, this is normal. You don't have to talk to anyone. Look around you, feel the sun shining through the window, you're not dead yet.

And really I am remarkably composed. No tears, no moans. No one can possibly detect that I am the Elephant Woman. It's so sad how he died, attempting to lie down like a normal human in spite of his deformities. Snap goes the neck. Snap. Two women at a nearby table wearing cloche hats look at me and I realize I've said this out loud. "Snap," I repeat and give them a realtor's smile. They smile back. How nice. The Elephant Woman's fooled them again. The latte's yummy. Maybe Natasha's onto something. Maybe I'll start coming here regularly, hoping for glimpses of Cheeseburger so I can dangle on the edge of his conscience, as unsightly as one of Muriel's gargoyles. Not dead yet, I'll tell him, in pain, losing weight, appetite, breath, but hey, nothing a venti latte can't set right.

"Oh that's so cute," one of the cloche-hat women exclaims regarding a stuffed pink pig.

"Isn't it adorable?" the other says, clutching it. "I was going to get her a sleeper, you know, a nice one, hand knit, but it was thirty-eight bucks and, I mean, they grow so fast."

"They do," the other cloche hat agrees, nodding little flapper nods.

"So I thought, get a stuffy, but different, you know, not a teddy."

"Everybody gives teddies."

"That is so true. And this was seventeen bucks which is a bit much for a toy."

"She *is* your sister."

"That's what I thought. But isn't it cute?"

"It's darling." And I'm thinking that's one ugly pig. That pig is going to scare the shit out of that baby. That pig's going to traumatize that kid for life. It's got bulgy black eyes with snaky eyelashes, and cavernous nostrils, and it's neon pink—no calming pale pink piggy for this bundle of joy. I really feel I should speak up. Do one good deed before I die. Spare the baby the pig. "Excuse me," I say, "but that pig is atrocious, actually quite scary, I think." They stare at me, their eyes dead below the brims of their hats. "I mean," I clarify, "I don't mean to intrude, but I think that pig would give me nightmares."

"Did we ask for your opinion?" the pig giver snarls. I notice that she's pencilled her lips over her natural line to make them look fuller.

"No," I admit. "I just thought I'd mention it."

"Mind your own business," she snaps, stuffing the monstrous pig into a bag.

I do. And leave wondering what got into me, besides cancer. Or maybe this is the new me, the speak-the-truth Elephant Woman. Here she comes, with nothing to lose, so you better watch out. She's going to spew chicken bacteria on you, blind you with ammonia.

I must think straight. Where'd I park? In the parking lot. Good.

That's a start. One step, two step.

I'm trying to find Muriel's survey. It's in the office somewhere, I had it in my hand. Estelle's chasing me, breathing Laura Secord bargain outlet chocolates down my neck. In an effort to lose her, I'm trying to look busy, I *am* busy.

"Last night Willy sat in my lap," she informs me. "I was on the armchair and he was on the table and he stretched his arms over to like, to like feel my legs, sort of testing to make sure it would be okay and stuff. Then he jumped on my lap and started purring. Isn't that wonderful?"

"It is." She has no idea that I am the Elephant Woman. More than that, I'm combustible.

"It's at the point where," she persists, "all I have to do is look at him and he starts purring." She demonstrates his purr, "Ggrrrr. Isn't that the cutest?"

I find the survey, probably where I left it. I'm not thinking straight, I'm . . . this is bad. I have to get . . . I have to pull myself together. I've got to cut off that extra skin. I just want it off, so I can lie down like a normal human.

She pops another chocolate. "This morning, I looked at him and not only did he start purring, but he rolled over onto his back." She demonstrates, tipping her head back and holding up her "paws." "And it was like he was saying, rub my tummy and isn't life grand? Isn't that the sweetest?"

"It is."

Todd parades in. "I just sold Tanenbaum's morgue. Yabadabadoo!"

"Congratulations," Estelle offers.

"Those Halibs," Todd says. "What a connection, I'm telling you. Greer, can you do an open house for me this afternoon? I've got to push this through."

"Sorry. Can't. Get Estelle to do it. Or I'm sure Earl Verman's available." I leave them, heaving my sagging bulk through the glass doors. As they close behind me I hear Todd say, "What's *her* problem?"

In the car I think about what I haven't done, the places I

haven't seen, the love I haven't felt. Highly constructive. Get busy, I tell myself, and drive to Arnie's where I'll plant the bulbs I didn't plant yesterday because Sybil and Oscar (the one-legged war hero) had offered their services as garden slaves. All day long I ordered them about, hoping my son would appear. I didn't see him all day, didn't even hear him. His absence punched yet another hole in my heart. Because I'd thought we were at peace, sort of. Never think you're at peace. If you're at peace, you're dead. There's something to look forward to.

No one answers the bell. Good. I want to be alone with my trowel. Dig, it feels good to dig, in spite of the pain. I no longer expect to be free of pain, therefore pain no longer defeats me. These bulbs will present their splendour in the spring, if the squirrels don't eat them first.

The back door opens and I hear Turner's chair wheeling down the ramp. "What're you doing?" he inquires.

"Planting bulbs for your dad."

"Why?" When he says few words I can understand him, it's when he elaborates I get muddled.

"I just thought it would be pretty," I explain. "He said he wanted to do something with the backyard." I find it hard to look at him, because of the spasms. Or more to the point, I don't know where to look. How does Sam cope with this?

"Nice," he manages to say. I expect him to spin back into the house but he remains, watching me. I associate being watched with being criticized—you're doing it wrong, do it this way, don't do it like that, do it like this. But he makes no sound. He's a friendly presence, like the birds twittering above him. I continue with my work thinking only of how beautiful the tulips will be, even if I'm dead.

Whoops, a negative thought.

"I should wash my hands," I say finally. He scoots up the ramp, props the door open for me with a corner of his chair and watches as I rinse at the kitchen sink. I pull some paper towel from a dispenser, dry my hands, and look around for the garbage. He opens a cabinet door for me, revealing a bag. I stuff the towel into it, wishing that there was some way I could help this boy who is so obviously kind and gifted.

"Come 'ere a sec," he says. I follow him into his room and see the coffin/boat. Filled with books, it looks less like a coffin/boat. "Sam did this," Turner tells me.

"Yes, I know."

"Great?"

"It is great."

Beaming, he slaps it with his good hand to indicate it's sturdiness. There are books everywhere, this boy lives in books.

"Looks like you could use some more shelves though," I point out.

He makes a sound that could be a giggle or a garble. I check his expression and see bliss on the child's face. In his room of books, he is in a safe haven, free of his body. He touches the coffin/boat again, more gently this time, almost a caress, and I feel as if I'm intruding on lovers. This is his world he has allowed me to see, I mustn't outstay my welcome. I reach into my bag and pull out a bottle of Drambuie. "Can you give this to your dad?"

Turner giggle/garbles again and nods, taking the bottle.

He opens the front door for me and I say bye and he says bye and I feel as though I've brushed against someone holy, even though I don't believe in holiness. To have been dealt the blow that he has, and to have surfaced in spite of it. To have moved beyond makes him more than human.

Meanwhile the Elephant Woman sags in her car, not wanting to go home, because if I go home, they'll want to know and I'll have to tell them, and once I tell them it will be real. Now I can still pretend, go shopping like everybody else. What for though? I don't need anything. That's never stopped anybody, there's always something to buy. What about a prezzie for Sam? He's so picky, I haven't been able to buy him clothes for years—what about a book? Yes, a bookstore, a safe haven. I can go to one of those freighter-sized ones and score another venti latte.

Buzzed on caffeine, I stand looking at shelves and more shelves, trying to remember a book I really loved when I was his age, a book that got into my veins and stayed there long after I'd put it down. A girl in black everything nudges me aside to grab a paperback. "I want it to be a multimedia event," she explains to her male companion who's also in black everything. "Dancers with painted headpieces," she clarifies, "that I can project images onto, like Vietnam and stuff."

"Cool," he says. He has an earring in his eyebrow.

"They're like sculptures, right, the dancers. It's like *performance* sculpture, three dimensional, you walk into them, they touch you, you touch them. It's an experience."

"Cool."

I loved Dostoyevsky, but then I'm weird. What about D. H. Lawrence? You can't go wrong with him. What about *Lady Chatterley's Lover*? It's got nooky in it, and it'll show him how twisted the love thing is, unlike what he's being told by television where happy endings abound.

Don't I want him to believe in happy endings? I buy the book anyway.

I must go home, I am losing power. Maybe they'll be out, maybe they'll have forgotten today was the day.

And they are nowhere in sight and this relieves me but also robs me of the opportunity to say things like it's not that serious, no metastasis, with adjuvant therapy it's curable, etcetera, etcetera. Lies, I've been robbed of the opportunity to lie—to them, to myself. Therefore, I have no choice but to face the thing, in my house filled with objects belonging to my pseudo-selves, and all I can think is what everyone thinks in this situation, WHY ME? And I find myself shouting this question even though I know there is no answer. Soon the words merge into a generalized wail erupting from my abdomen, a sound unfamiliar to me. As I'm making the sounds, I'm fascinated by their depth and tone, and decide that they're animal-like. An animal caught in a trap with a severed foot. The animal looks at her bleeding stump and moans, throws herself against the trap causing herself more harm, but what does it matter when she has no way out? She bangs her head against the steel grid so hard it ruptures her skin and blood spurts over her face into her eyes, blinding her. My arms lash out causing my hands and elbows to hit counters and walls, but I don't feel it. I'm swaying on my feet, rocking. And shaking my head repeatedly, denying, denying, denying. I start running but there's nowhere to go. I run in circles, losing breath, getting dizzy. Maybe I can die this way. Maybe I can tornado myself into oblivion. I look at the order of it. My life. All the proper things in their proper places. I take swipes at innocent objects, oven mitts, wooden spoons in ceramic pots. The teapot crashes to the floor. What order? There is no such thing. We create it thinking it means something, thinking it gives us some control. No control here, ducky, just one rambling disaster after another. Fuck order. I'm tired of it. I can't do this anymore.

Abruptly Sam's behind me, throwing his arms around my torso. It is not an embrace but a straitjacket. I appreciate this. I need confinement. Bludgeon me to death now, would you please?

"What's going on?" he asks my ear.

"Cancer's back. Never left."

His grip loosens slightly and I feel my wounded body preparing to fling itself around again. But he holds tight. I feel the strength of him. We have not been this close in years.

"You'll get better," he says. "You'll do chemo this time."

Baby boy, it's not that simple. I know you want it to be that simple.

I'm out of steam. He's supporting me now. Don't let go. You let go and I fall.

"Dad got better."

I don't want to explain the difference. "Yes, he did."

"You've just got to do the full treatment. Blast the fucker."

Does he want me to live? Why does he want me to live? If I die, he'll get money.

He guides me to the couch. I sit like a little old lady who's shit her pants. What am I ashamed of? Grief? Getting sick again?

"Do you want anything?" he asks.

I want to hold you, I want to kiss you, I want everything to be okay.

"Mum?"

"Can you just sit with me for a minute?" I plead.

"Sure." He arranges himself awkwardly beside me, ensuring that there is a space between us through which cold winds can howl.

"I didn't know you were home," I say.

"I wasn't. So are you going to do chemo?" He says this as though it is a panacea.

"Mum . . . ?"

It destroys me when he calls me "Mum."

"Mum, you *have* to do chemo this time."

"We'll see." This is what I told him when he was a little boy demanding grotesque toys he didn't need which I would never buy.

"Promise me you'll do chemo this time."

Should I tell him that it's still not proven that chemo actually cures a greater proportion of breast cancer patients than good supportive care? That it only postpones relapses and death, making life unlivable while you're dying?

Should I tell him there is still no DIRECT EVIDENCE that chemo prolongs survival?

I can't tell him any of this. I look at the floor, the Persian carpet he rolled around on, and in my mind I hear Sybil saying, "Children go blind weaving those rugs," and I feel faint, my elephant hide is smothering me, squeezing the breath out of me. Let me lie down like a normal human, please, just let me lie down.

I regain consciousness on the couch and feel a breeze on my face. Sybil's fanning me with a magazine, probably an alternative one about animal abuse. I feel a wet cloth on my forehead. "Drink some water," she orders. Sam hands me a glass and I drink because I don't want to talk.

"It's so freaky the way you're fainting all the time," he says and I don't argue because I am freaky. I try lifting my arms to see if I'm still the Elephant Woman. Miraculously, they feel sore but like mine.

I look at Sybil. "Did he tell you?"

"Yes. Rest now."

"I don't know what to do," I whimper, feeling my left eye preparing to gush.

Sybil mops my brow again. "You're not going to do anything."

"She *has* to do something," Sam interjects.

"Not right now," Sybil says.

He shakes his head, runs his hands through his hair, shoves them into his pockets, pulls them out again, runs them through his hair, shoves them into his pockets. "She's just going to die, I know her, she's . . ." Suddenly his hands jerk in all directions and he starts running down the hall, away from me. *Don't run away, please don't run away.* I hear the front door open. "You're fucking giving up," he shouts. "I know you. I can't believe you're fucking giving up!" The door slams.

"He's upset," Sybil tells me.

"No really?"

"He'll settle down."

I sit up, my head does a little spin. "I'm going to bed."

"You going to be alright?"

"Yeah." I stand, relieved to feel my legs feeling like my legs, and start for the stairs but she hops around me, the woman with the pumping heart. "Listen," she says, taking my hand. "Whatever you do, I'm there for you. Whatever."

"Thank you, Auntie."

"And he will be too, once he comes around."

"What goes around comes around."

"What?"

I lean on the banister. "It's hard to imagine a time when 'fucking' wasn't used as an adjective or adverb. What did people say before 'fucking'?"

"Can't remember. They cursed God a lot. They still believed in him."

"They don't anymore?"

"Only the really deluded ones."

I start my climb. "I sure as hell am angry at somebody."

"I know, baby."

"Might as well call him God."

"If it makes you feel better, baby."

"Good night."

"I'm here, lovey."

"I know."

I lie awake, waiting for him to come home, remembering the feel of his body holding mine. I lie awake listening to the dog.

Twenty-eight

Erna, as usual, is sitting on the couch smoking, in mid-conversation with invisible people. Beside her, in an orderly line, sit plastic dolls who are missing limbs and, in some cases, heads.

She jabs the air with her cigarette. "I said, 'What she needs is a *psychological assessment.*' I said, 'That girl's got a screw loose needs tightening.' I said, 'What she needs is a *psychological assessment.*'"

"Erna," I interject, "is Lyla around?"

"In her room."

"Is she okay?"

"She's not the sharpest tool in the shed, if you know what I mean." She sucks hard on her ciggie butt and resumes her verbal assault. "I said, 'Any time there's trouble you fold like a cheap suit.' I said, 'Get that girl to a shrink, what she needs is a *psychological assessment.*'"

The place appears to be spotless. Erna must be a whirling dervish of a house cleaner. "Erna, this is my friend Arnie. He's putting in the new window."

"How are ya?" Arnie asks.

"Been better."

"The dolls are interesting," I offer. "Are they yours?"

"They just throw 'em out, after all they've done for them."

Some of the doll amputees have toilet-roll prosthetics decorated with lace and ribbons. In the lap of every doll is a small bar of soap shaped like a turtle, duck, or fish.

"It's going to be tough to replace their heads," I point out.

Smoke streams out of her nostrils. "A lot of people would do a whole lot better without heads."

"People think too much, you mean," I suggest.

"*Don't* you go thinking you know what I mean." She hauls on her cigarette again, snatches the remote and turns on the TV. Arnie sets to work on the window while I search for Lyla under a heap of bedclothes. "Are you okay?" I inquire.

"Yeah," she mumbles, but it's obvious she isn't. She's puffy-faced with shadows under her eyes, and wearing the same pyjamas she had on the other day. I suspect she's stopped getting out of bed.

"Would you prefer it if Erna weren't here?" I ask. Even with the door closed I can hear the madwoman's tirade. This constant barrage of aggression would drive me into bed and under the covers. "Because you can ask her to leave," I add. "She's your guest."

"She cooks for me. And cleans."

"Okay, well, just so you know, if you want her to leave, you can always ask me to find somewhere for her to stay. Do the dolls bother you?"

"They're just dolls."

And I wonder if this is what lithium does: grounds you, frees you of imagination so that maimed dolls are just dolls and not all the lost and brutalized children. Maybe *I* should be taking lithium.

"Have you seen your doctor?" I ask.

"Which one?"

"The one who prescribes your medication."

"They all do that."

"Aren't you supposed to be monitored?"

"Erna says it's a racket. She's stopped taking her meds."

We hear Erna shout, "*Don't* you tell me you shovelled the goddamn snow! How many times did I ask you to shovel the goddamn snow?"

"Is she talking to her husband?" I inquire.

Lyla nods. "She says she broke her hip because he didn't shovel the snow."

"You think I don't got eyes in my head?" Erna continues. "You've been sneakin' around with that woman, eating her muffins and drinking her stinkin' coffee. *Don't* you think I don't know what's going on."

"Have you tried reminding her that her husband is dead?" I ask.

"She has to get mad at somebody," Lyla explains. "Better him than me."

"Why does she have to get mad at somebody?"

"Everybody does."

I think about my own rantings at Cheeseburger, and Jerry, and now "God." Tirades in my head. The only difference between me and Erna is that I keep my mouth zipped behind a realtor's smile.

"He had a heart attack watering their lawn," Lyla explains. "She came home and he was in a lawn chair, still holding the hose. He'd been dead for five hours. It was a swamp, she says."

Arnie pokes his head in. "All done. Lookth ath good ath new."

"Great."

"That real estate fellah'th been thircling the houthe with thome folkth."

"Lyla . . ." I kneel beside the bed, making it difficult for her to avoid my eyes. I put a hand on her arm which she stares at and I immediately take it off. "Do you want to sell your house?"

"I don't know." She's so listless, so not the Lyla I know.

"Would you like me to tell him to go away?"

She pulls the blankets over her head. "He said once you get parasites in the house you can't get rid of them. He said I'd be better off moving to a new house that doesn't have parasites. But they're still on me so . . . I don't want to move yet."

"Lyla, there are no parasites in your house or on your body. He's saying that to make you sell. I'm going to tell him to leave you alone. If he speaks to you again, you call me. Alright?"

She shudders, emitting a small animal noise. The old Lyla wouldn't take this shit. Where is she, Charles' confidante, the transcontinental traveller, the fancy dresser, the high financier? I'm really not convinced she's better off drugged, although obviously she's more manageable, which is what counts in a world that distrusts the eccentric, the idiosyncratic, the individual.

I spot Verman behind some bushes, pointing at the roof which I'm sure he's claiming is "newer." "Earl, could I have a word?"

"Greer, I thought that was your car, how are ya? Beautiful

day, isn't it?" He's being budsy in front of his clients. He scuttles towards me, clearly hoping to prevent me from jeopardizing his sale.

"Where are the parasites in the house?" I ask loudly to ensure that his dowdy buyers hear me. "You told the vendor there are parasites in the house. I was wondering where you saw them."

Verman's doing throat-cutting signals at me. I don't know if he's suggesting I'm cutting his throat or he intends to cut mine.

"I was just kidding around," he says, breathing Clorets on me.

"Really? Because she's feeling them on her skin, fleas or something, from the carpets. Or I suppose parasites can thrive in dank places, like the leaky basement. Or the grout in the shower? That's mighty mouldy."

Already the buyers are backing towards their car.

"What I say to the young lady," Verman hisses, "is not your affair."

"I was just curious. I mean, *parasites*, that's gross, that's worse than cockroaches, or is that what you meant? I guess cockroaches are parasites. Man, are they tough to get rid of. I had them once. They'd crawl into my shower cap, my Mini-Wheats."

He definitely looks ready to bludgeon me to death. What a way to go, no adjuvant therapy decisions, just a painful but fairly rapid death. Although Arnie's bound to try to save me. He's just stashed his ladder in his truck and is speedily approaching. Verman looks around for his clients, sees them retreating and hurries towards them, hitching up his pants. "Have a nice day," I shout, smiling my realtor's smile.

I take Arnie to Starbucks for a venti latte since I'm becoming an addict. And because he won't let me buy him a beer, says he never drinks before six. "That old gal'th one brick short of a load, eh?"

"Her ten-year-old granddaughter's missing. She's been missing for months."

"Are you shittin' me?"

"No."

"Tho like she'th probably dead in a trash can thomewhere."

"Probably. Anyway, that's why Erna's disturbed."

"Or she could be thomebody'th thex thlave. That happened to thome kid. They made a movie about it."

Beside us, two young women are having a heart-to-heart. "I was in *mega* pain," the one wearing a baseball cap backwards over her ponytail says. "I mean, it was like pain pain pain and then suddenly no pain. But I went to the hospital anyway because I was like puking my guts out. So they did this ultrasound and there was this cyst and it was like twisted. And it had kept twisting until it twisted right off. Which is why I'd stopped feeling pain, but then there was this *dead thing* inside me."

"Weird," her friend in tie-dyed everything offers.

"Arnie," I begin, "I was reading this article about a new treatment for CP. It's called hyperbaric oxygenation. Have you heard of it?" He shakes his head. He's wearing his glasses again, giving him an owlish look. "They put the patient into a pressured chamber," I explain, "with a hood over his head through which he breathes pure oxygen. The extra oxygen gets into the blood and to areas which are normally hard to reach. It stimulates dormant cells surrounding damaged brain tissue. It's supposed to increase motor and verbal abilities."

Arnie looks unimpressed, like a man who's been sold a bill of goods one time too many. *Buy this drug, cure your son.*

"How much doeth it cotht?" he asks.

"Well, that's the thing, it's expensive. A hundred dollars per treatment and they can need as many as three hundred sessions."

"Doeth it latht?"

"They don't know yet. And it doesn't work on all kids with CP. And it's only available in B.C."

"Tho we're talking a shitload of dough 'cauthe you got to get there and thtay there. And there'th no guaranteeth."

"That's right."

He stares at me with the washed-out eyes of someone who's been robbed of hope again and again. And I feel bad for having brought it up, but I just thought he should know. I think I would want to know.

"It wasn't cancer," the baseball-capped girl emphasizes. "I mean what he said was it *could* become cancer. He said I had a twenty percent chance. Which means two out of ten, right? I mean, like where am I in that percentile, near the top? He said, 'If I were you, I'd have them out.'"

"You mean both?" the tie-dyed girl asks.

"He said that was the only way to eliminate the risk. And I mean I didn't want to live in fear."

I presume we're talking about her ovaries and my question is, how did the surgeon know what *he* would do if *he* had a twisting cyst since he's never possessed a pair of ovaries? And my mind starts speeding into the danger zone, firing too many questions. Remember bubonic plague? Didn't some doctor wizard come up with the idea that the fleas carrying the bacteria were on the dogs and cats and ordered all the dogs and cats to be slaughtered? And didn't the carcasses lie in the streets providing good eating for the rats who were the *actual* carriers? And didn't the rats who no longer had predators, once the cats were dead, thrive, incubating more fleas who carried more bacteria that killed more people? Sounds a lot like cancer treatment, doesn't it? Annihilate the good along with the bad, see what happens. Whip out her ovaries, see what happens.

"It was mega weird," the girl admits.

"Weird things happen," her friend offers.

I put *Lady Chatterley* on Sam's bed this morning after he'd left to go I don't know where. This was after Sybil had forced one of her alternative mags on me, citing more news of amoral drug companies. Apparently, they sell formula to Third World countries, depriving Third World babies of the immunities they need from their mothers' milk. Unable to fight off the bacteria brewing in the formula because it's mixed with tainted water, they die. Drug companies know this. But dead black babies in distant lands are not a big concern for them—or for the Western world in general. We expect them to die, what with famine and civil war and AIDS. We see pictures of black children dying all the time. It's sad, but what can you do? Buy another drug from your local pharmacist.

"That wath thtome thory about that guy lothing money in the thtock market and gunning down all thothe people."

"Yeah."

"Theemth to me there'th a lot more killing going on."

"It gets your name in the paper. Sometimes a front-page feature."

"It'th how he axed hith wife and kidth I can't figure out."

"He said in his note they were his demise."

The girls are off the topic of cancer and discussing cosmetics tested on animals. "The cruellest is the eye-irritancy test," the tie-dyed girl explains. "They put these toxic chemicals into rabbits' eyes that basically destroys their eyeballs. And in the lethal dose test animals are forced to eat, inhale and suffer skin exposure to all kinds of chemicals until half of them die."

"I only buy Body Shop anyway," the girl without ovaries says.

"I've been thinking," Arnie begins, "that men are really thcrewed up right now. Kind of like they get hurt, their parenth abuthe them and whatnot, and they don't know what to do about it. Tho they get angry."

"And kill people."

He takes off his glasses and rubs his eyes. "It'th thith wuthy buthiness. Guyth are thcared of being wuthieth, and I'm thinking, what'th a wuthy? A guy who crieth? Who like, talkth about hith feelingth?"

"I think that's it. Feelings are for wussies."

"That'th a shame."

"They don't *need* to do these tests," the tie-dyed girl points out. "They do them because they think they'll protect them in case they get sued by a user of their products. Something like fourteen million animals are tortured annually."

"That's heinous," the girl without ovaries remarks.

"Arnie, how do you feel about letting Turner loose in this world?"

"Thcared."

I nod, stare out the window at the concrete wasteland. "How do you cope with that?"

He puts his glasses back on. "Everything I do, I do for him. That'th all I can do. For now, for ath long ath I've got, that'th what I do."

A man in a filthy suit jacket, wearing mismatched shoes and a Frank Sinatra hat, bends down to pick a butt up off the pavement. He holds it to his lips and sucks on it even though it isn't lit. I wait for him to start singing "My Way."

Sybil told me that some of her soup-kitchen homeless suck on toothpaste tubes because it contains a small percentage of alcohol and is easier on their internal organs than cleaning fluids.

"This mass of contradictions we call life," I say apropos of nothing.

Arnie reaches across the table and holds my hand. Nobody touches me these days and I feel myself recoiling because he's Elvis and smells, but then the warmth of his hand moves up my arm and into my body. His skin is rough from manual labour but even this is comforting, a hand that's never graced a keyboard. "You do what you can," he tells me.

I look down at my hand that has been swallowed by his and feel like that child, that little girl who so badly wanted her mother. She's always there, inside you, this battered creature in too small shoes, she's always willing to believe, unlike you who requires botulin injections, who's become so distrustful you can't even trust yourself.

"Greer . . . ?"

"Yes?"

"You're doing what you can."

"I guess."

"You are."

My little sister bends over her interlocking-brick driveway, spraying chemicals on baby weeds. She's so thin her vertebrae make tracks on her sweater. Should I tell her about the forty-eight-year-old breast cancer "survivor" I met in Cheeseburger's office, a former agricultural researcher whose cancer had been in remission for eight years but now is spreading from her solar plexus to her groin, making her look hugely pregnant? "I'm dying," she told me, "because morons have decided that innocuous plants like dandelions have no right to life on this planet."

No, Rachel will not want to hear this. "Hi," I say.

She straightens swiftly, as though about to flee from an attacker.

"Oh, it's you."

"I brought the tape and pictures back. I had copies made for Sam."

"Did he enjoy them?"

"I don't know."

The bricks are damp from the pesticides. I try not to inhale while wondering if she'll invite me inside. We stand, motionless, waiting for the music to begin. Lawn mowers buzz, and of course leaf blowers. She takes the tape and photos from me.

"Are you okay?" I ask.

"I'm fine. You?"

I have to tell her, she should know. "Three nodes tested positive."

She stares at me as though I'm already a corpse, risen from the dead.

"I'm so sorry," she mutters finally.

"Me too. Anyway, I thought you should know."

"Are you going to do chemo?"

"Haven't decided."

"You should do chemo if it's in the nodes."

I don't want to go into my nobody-knows-shit-about-chemo rant. Instead I look at her anal-retentive garden; marigolds and impatiens are hanging on till the frost. Mums—funeral flowers—squat in plastic planters. We are so different, I'm thinking, please let this be true of our DNA.

As no invitation is forthcoming and there's no sign of Porky's ass to kick, I give her a peck on the cheek and depart. Driving away, this ruptured feeling spreads in my abdomen, as though tumours are busting through tissue there. Profuse bleeding after the relationship has been in remission for years.

She doesn't want to see you anymore. You remind her of death. And her parents whom she wants to remember well. Let her go, gently down the stream; she may float if you don't stuff rocks in her pockets.

Determined to wait up for him, I drink coffee, eat butter tarts, watch a movie in which Meryl Streep dies of some unnamed cancer. Her hair falls out but there's no commode by her bed, no emesis basin. After the wheelchair, she becomes bedridden and redrimmed around the eyes. Lacquered with pale makeup that was probably tested on bunnies, she smiles graciously and tells her daughter she loves her, to which her daughter replies, "I love you, Mom." Very nice indeedy. But Meryl's having a hard time, what with not being able to walk or breathe and all, so somehow, in the night, she miraculously exits her bed, boogies on down to the kitchen to swallow a bunch of morphine tablets. Wow, no plastic bag required. Cut to daughter sitting at bedside holding her dead mommy's hand. Meryl looks neat and tidy as usual.

What *I* heard is that when you're that incapacitated, it gets real hard to swallow or keep stuff down if you do manage to swallow. So hard in fact that it becomes impossible to snuff yourself. However, it's only a *movie,* can't have people barfing narcotics in a movie.

"Why are you watching that?" my son who never says he loves me demands.

"Hi, I didn't hear you come in."

"Because you've got the TV on. Why're you watching that?"

"It's a movie."

"It's about dying."

"Kind of. I think it's more about box office."

He shakes his head in disgust as his father does and disappears into the kitchen. Cabinets get banged around, drawers. I meekly follow. "Are you okay?" I inquire.

"Quit asking me that."

"Okay." I start eating the cashews I put in a bowl because I know he loves them. I'm not hungry but require an activity.

"Shouldn't you be in bed?" he demands.

"I'll get there."

"I mean, you're sick and you don't even sleep. That's why you're blacking out all the time. I mean, try to take care of yourself for fuck's sake."

"I do."

"No, you don't. You're fucking worrying about everybody else all the time. It's fucking pathological."

What would Meryl do in this situation?

"Why don't you invite the fucking homeless into the basement?" he says. "That'll keep you busy till you die."

Arnie believes guys who get hurt become angry because they don't want to be wussies. Is that what this is about? Your mother's dying but don't you dare cry about it.

"Sam . . ."

"What?" he snaps.

"I need to know how you'll feel if I don't get treatment."

"Fuckin' great. I'll feel fucking great." He stuffs a pickle in his mouth.

I chew another cashew, suck the salt off it. He turns his back to me and starts smearing peanut butter on his bread. The fridge seems to be experiencing indigestion and keeps belching and groaning. It would be wise to go away, let him cool down. But I've got that Crazy-Glue-on-the-soles-of-my-shoes feeling. "Sam . . . ?"

"What?"

"I just don't believe in the treatment. I haven't seen it work in the long term."

"It must work. You always hear stories about women who beat it."

"Many of those women 'beat it' for a time, then get it back again. Kind of like me with the surgery. I mean, my cancer seems pretty determined."

He turns on me like a man ready to swing. "So fight it, fucking fight it—what's the matter with you?"

Only now do I see the tears, microscopic ones, escaping. He hastily wipes his eyes. "It's *your* life," he says hoarsely. "Do what you want." And he's gone again, my roadrunner, up the stairs and under the covers. *He's* probably bought a bolt for his door.

The fridge and I wait for our stomachs to settle. I think I'm experiencing cashew burn. God. Do what I want. I want to be well.

There *were* tears. I saw them.

Twenty-nine

Henry Kissinger, alias Dr. Wozniakowski, unlike Cheeseburger, likes to talk. While his chin wags I notice his ears wiggle, particularly during a's and i's and o's. Saying "chemo," for example, causes an ear flutter. I'm paying more attention to his ears than his words because I don't want to hear "aggressive tumour" and "progressed further" and "high risk of recurrence." I think of Dumbo the Elephant, it was Dumbo, wasn't it, who flew around, flapping his ears? I imagine Henry in flight, his gut ballooning, his legs dangling. It occurs to me that I've never seen him standing. Maybe he can't. Maybe he's physically challenged. Maybe there's a wheelchair stashed under his desk which would explain why he never moves. Maybe he's as ashamed of his wheelchair as I am of my prosthesis.

"It's a lot to absorb," he advises me.

"Yes," I agree, having absorbed nothing except that my chance of survival, according to Henry, *with* adjuvant therapy, is 66 percent over five years. Which sounds a little better than a fifty-fifty chance, which doesn't sound great when you consider a large part of those five years (if I don't die) will be spent consuming drugs, including tamoxifen which I may have to take indefinitely. Drugs which will dramatically reduce my quality of life. In fact, make me sick.

I woke at dawn and dared to skim a cancer book that I actually bought (it was half price) because I wanted to make an "informed" decision. I was reminded yet again of the side effects of said drugs beyond your basic hair loss, weight gain, and ovarian death. Special things like candidiasis (overgrowth of yeast causing swallowing difficulties and vaginal infections), diarrhea or no bowel action, metallic taste in mouth, buzzing in ears, loss of high-tone hearing, bloated abdomen, darkening of skin folds (sometimes mouth), heart problems resulting in breathlessness (worse when lying down), impairment of bone marrow resulting in the loss of white blood cells resulting in an inability to fight infections (particularly of the skin, mouth, lungs, urinary or reproductive tracts), anemia, bruising and bleeding (of gums, nose, digestive tract) resulting from the destruction of red blood cells, fatigue and weakness, chills, double or blurred vision, headaches, drooping eyelids, dizziness, numbness and weakness in fingers and toes (neurological effects which can persist for years after treatment stops), acne, redness and itching, dry skin, brittle nails, wheezing, endometrial cancer.

Yes, but you may live longer.

"Do you follow me?" Henry inquires.

"Not really," I admit.

"Oh," he says, twitching his ears. "What I'm recommending is the Bonadonna cycle."

Bonanwhat? Bonanza? Is that like bingo? Arnie says if I win the Bonanza, I could score fifteen hundred. Maybe this is an omen. Take a chance, win the Bonanza.

"This would include," Henry clarifies, "large doses of adriamycin three weeks out of the month followed by six months of a combination of Cytoxan, methotrexate and 5-Fu."

He can't seriously think I understand any of this. It just sounds like a lot; one month plus six equals seven months. Seven months of chemical warfare.

"How many cycles?" I ask.

"We do one then re-evaluate."

Lady Chatterley was on the couch this morning, slightly fingered. No sign of Sam. I didn't look for him, didn't want to fight. But his tears remain in my mind, rare jewels. I can't go back and tell him I quit. I'll lose him, he'll be gone before I am. I'll live out my days in the empty box of a house thinking only what if . . . what if . . . ?

"Let's do it," I say.

Henry humphs. "My advice would be that you take some

time to think about it."

"I've done that. I want to start as soon as possible. Is there a waiting list?"

"Not necessarily."

"Swell. Can we start tomorrow?"

"Tomorrow?" Big ear action on "tomorrow."

"Yes," I persist.

He shuffles papers on his desk and continues humphing. "I suppose it's possible."

"Good. I don't want to schtoomp over this. I just want to do it."

"I understand. We'll . . . we'll see what can be arranged. My secretary will call you."

"That's excellent. Thank you so much." I stand and offer him my hand waiting to see if he'll stand and reveal fully functioning legs. But he doesn't. And his handshake is limp.

Maybe he's a double amputee.

"You understand we have to monitor you carefully," he cautions. "There's no room for error with chemotherapy."

You mean 'cause the stuff is POISON? A couple of cc's extra and I'm one dead survivor?

"I understand," I say, smiling my realtor's smile, because I want him to get me in there, in the line of fire. I want to prove to my son that I'm not a coward.

"We must take it day by day." He scribbles a prescription for an anti-nausea medication. "And Mrs. Pentland, you might find it advantageous to purchase a wig now, while you still have the strength."

"Righteo," I say.

"I kept imagining it was bigger," Muriel remarks of her condo bedroom. She's measured and remeasured about fourteen times. "This is disastrous," she says. "I don't think it will fit."

"Why do you need a wardrobe when there's a walk-in closet?"

"That's for Darwin."

"Right, I forgot. Well, there's still one closet."

"Minuscule little thing. Absolutely useless."

"So spread into the hall. It's not like you have to share closet space with anyone."

"I can't bear having to rush about hunting for clothing."

"Sell the wardrobe, buy a smaller one."

"This wardrobe's been in my family for years." Oh, you mean black slaves have dusted and polished it? Minutes ago she was ranting about the fishermen out east being bloody lazy and ungrateful about the compromise being offered by the government which has forbidden them to fish. "They're refusing the jobs," Muriel insisted, "simply because they'd have to commute for an hour."

"I don't think it is that simple," I countered. "I think we're asking them to give up a way of life, a kind of freedom, by forcing them into fish-processing plants. Working in an assembly line is a little different from sailing the open seas."

"They shouldn't have fished so bloody much in the first place."

"Corporate trawlers robbed the sea of fish, not independent fishermen."

At this point she noticed a run in her nylons and was "absolutely furious" and ready to sue the manufacturer. And the medication she's taking for her arthritis is giving her hives which are "positively hideous" and making it "unthinkable" for her to wear a backless gown to the gala as planned.

"My ex-husband will be there," she said. "It's *absolutely* essential that I look stunning."

I take the tape from her and measure the opposite wall. "It'll fit here," I advise her.

"Yes, but then where do I fit my vanity and chest of drawers? I'd have to put them side by side, which I loathe. Makes me feel like I'm living in a galley."

And all I can think is, You stupid woman, you have *life,* throw things away, give to charity, free yourself of clutter. Embrace nothingness. You've been given the chance to begin again.

"At first I didn't want to let him outside and stuff," Estelle explains, "because it said in the paper another cat was found chopped up and I just couldn't . . . I mean . . . but he so badly wanted to go out so I attached a little leash to him, and taped a paperweight to it so he couldn't wander off. Well, he was just *so* depressed, he kept looking at me with those big eyes and I thought I can't do this. I mean, this is cruel. So I took off the leash and he just kind of stayed there with me, sniffed around and stuff, and chewed some grass, and I thought everything was going great, but I guess he got startled or something because all of a sudden he bolted like lightning up the tree and I thought, that's it, he won't be able to get down, he won't know how, and my heart was in my throat and I was thinking who can I call, fire departments don't answer cat calls anymore. So guess what happened?"

I take one of the mini Oh Henry! bars she offers. "What?"

"He climbed down, just like that. Isn't that wonderful?"

"It is."

"But then," she adds, "he runs under the fence, and I thought, Oh my god, how am I going to catch him? But I stayed calm and went into the neighbour's yard, which I never do, they're Korean and very hostile, and there he was, looking at me. Isn't that the cutest? He was playing games with me. So I go to pick him up and he darts under the fence again. I go back in my yard and he's sitting there looking at me with those big eyes." She mimics Willy's big-eyed stare. "And it was like he was saying, 'Look what I did? Aren't I clever?' He's such a darling."

I'm having trouble focusing but am determined to find a house for the stupefied couple who sold their home beside the Dog Patch house. They're nice people and I really, really want to set them up in a good house. They've been looking on their own because I've been indisposed, but so far they seem only discouraged. They're afraid—and I can completely understand this—of investing in another house that proves to be a toxic dump. I'm looking for something detached with a huge lot (meaning large borders around it), in a good neighbourhood, fairly central but not a gazillion dollars. In other words, I'm attempting the impossible.

I phoned the doctor listed on Lyla's lithium bottle. Of course, he wouldn't speak to me until I'd insisted, repeatedly, that it was an emergency. "Are you a relative?" he asked, sounding annoyed.

"A friend."

"Obviously I can't discuss her case with you." He had very sibilant s's.

"No, I know that. I just wanted you to know that she's living at her parents' house, and that she doesn't seem well."

"Is she taking her medication?"

"I believe so."

"In what way doesn't she ssseem well to you?"

"Just listless. She sleeps all the time."

"This is normal. In her condition. Is she sssuicidal?"

"I don't think so."

"Mrs. . . . ? What was your name?"

"Pentland."

"Mrs. Pentland, if she wishes, she can contact me. Without her taking the initiative, there is nothing I can do."

"You can't even call her?"

"Do you imagine that we call all our patients when we don't hear from them?"

"No . . . I just . . . anyway, can I give you her parents' number? I don't think you have it."

"Leave it with my sssecretary." Click, the snake put me on hold giving me an opportunity to browse the paper and learn that common pollutants are disrupting hormones which guide the development of fetuses from conception. A U.S. scientist has evidence that chemicals like dioxins and PCBs (known as endocrine disrupters) cause wrong signals which can change the sexual development and whole course of life of an animal, because the chemicals *mimic the body's own hormones.* She believes that reduced IQs, rising rates of hyperactivity and attention deficit disorder are all due to these chemicals. Our Minister of the Environment says he is taking her thesis "seriously." Oh good.

The snake's secretary never picked up. I had to call back.

Flora's House of Hair Replacement is far away, in the west end. Which is why I chose it, I didn't want to run the risk of meeting an associate or client in my wig quest. I'm not even sure I want a wig. Meryl didn't wear one, just scarf arrangements. But then she wasn't selling real estate. As I intend to keep working, it's kind of crucial that I look reasonably normal.

I was hoping to be greeted by Flora who I imagined to be a kindly, bespectacled, motherly, English lady. Instead a Romanian woman with dyed red hair (obviously her own) and purple eyes accosts me. "How can I help you today?" she demands with a heavy accent. I'm assuming her eyes have been purpled by contact lenses, even so, I feel as though I'm in the presence of an alien.

"Aah . . ." I can't really say I'm just looking because I don't know what I'm looking for. The place is lined with wigs, animal pelts.

She clasps her hands and holds them close to her large and, what I deduce to be, real bosoms. "Are you needing hair replacement?"

"Not right now, but yes, eventually."

"You are losing hair because . . . ?"

"I have cancer."

"I understand. Very difficult."

"Yes."

"My mother had intestine cut out. I know how you feeling." She circles me a couple of times, presumably to assess my hair.

"You have bee-ewtiful hair."

"Thank you." I have weed hair. She's trying to pump me up. I phoned around and found out wigs cost between a hundred and fifty to three hundred and twenty bucks. That's a lot of lattes.

She leans towards me as if to see me better. "You want same image or different?"

"Same." I've always secretly wanted to be a redhead but now is not the time. "As close to my real hair as possible."

"You don't want people to know. I understand."

"I'd like it to be short, low maintenance. I can always look like I've had a haircut."

"Very good. People are saying, 'What is different about her? She changed her hairstyle.'"

"Something like that."

She gestures towards the back of the store. "Please come to fitting room."

"Sure."

It's a cubicle with peach walls and ancient photographs of models wearing wigs. An air freshener has the place stinking of pine.

"Something like this?" the alien inquires, deftly fitting a mop on my head. No pins these days, just adjustable bands. I look up and see a Beatle.

"It's a bit too pageboy," I comment.

She gently brushes it. "Colour's bee-ewtiful though, no?"

"Colour's fine." It isn't, but I want to get out of here. "So is this synthetic hair easy to maintain?"

"Oh yes. Very easy." She pronounces "easy" with two s's. "Cold water. We give you shampoo, conditioner, spray, wig tree. Very eassy to maintain." She fits another one on me. I hate the way they feel, like hats, I've always hated wearing hats.

"These are medical wigs," she explains. "With pad. Otherwise you need nylon cap. This one is bee-ewtiful on you. Very natural." It does look remotely like my hair. I watch as she "styles" it and try to imagine doing this myself daily. I've always been a shower get-up-and-go girl.

"I don't want to have to do much to it."

"No to worry. It is pre-set. You wash, put on tree, that's it. Very eassy."

"How much?" I ask.

"Two hundred and eighty dollars. It is handmade of very good fabric to give more natural look."

I pull it off. "It'll do."

I take the Lake Shore home, drive past seedy motels in which hookers practise their trade, and think only, how could it come to this? As much as I understand that it is impossible to understand, I still persist in trying to understand; find some meaning to it, reason for it. I stop and stare at the lake with the wig beside me. "How are ya?" I ask it. "Seen any good movies lately?"

Healthy people zip by on bikes, blades, Nikes, and I just hate them, hate them for being well. I want to trip them up with piano wire, make them suffer. They who eat ice cream and hot dogs, wear spandex and headphones. They who have no idea how blessed they are.

So were you once. So were you.

Sybil, with blood coursing through her veins, has decided that all the lamps in the house require cleaning. She has them lined up on the kitchen counter, leaving the house in darkness except for the odd overhead that actually has a bulb in it.

"Have you seen Sam?" I ask.

"He left. Didn't like me taking the lights out."

"Well, it is a bit hard to see. You couldn't do them in daylight?"

"You should see the grime I'm getting off these things. They haven't been done in years."

"If ever." I sit, not knowing what else to do. My tooth pain is humming.

"What'd the doctor say?" she asks.

"I'm doing chemo. And tamoxifen. Not right away, the tamoxifen, you're supposed to wait a bit after surgery."

"What's tamoxifen?"

"A hormone blocker." I pull out my prosthesis, toss it into the air and catch it.

"Don't you *need* hormones?"

"It's got to do with my hormone-receptor status. Please don't ask me questions about it, Auntie. I don't really understand it myself."

"You hungry?"

"No."

"Want a drink?"

"Yes."

The front door swings open and in meanders my former he-man.

"There's a bell," I advise him.

"I rang it."

"No you didn't. Did you hear the bell, Sybil?" She shakes her head. "You didn't ring the bell."

"Your door should be locked anyway, why isn't your door locked?"

"I would've locked it if I'd known you were coming."

He looks a little soft around the edges, meaning that he's had a few. Good, we're both enjoying the effects of alcohol. Should make for some fun and games; blood sport.

"I am here," he explains, holding his hand over his heart, "because I wanted to know how you were, and I knew you wouldn't call me to tell me how you were, and whenever I phone the fucking service is on and you never return my calls. Why's it so dark in here?"

The stove light's on, sending out beams of UFO light. "Do you want me to get him out?" Sybil asks me.

"It's okay, Auntie. He has no teeth." I hold up the vodka bottle. "Do you want a bevie?" I ask him.

"Only if you're having one."

"I am." I pour. "How's your mother?"

"Terrible. She claims I said I wished she was dead."

"Did you?"

"Of course not."

"Did you think it?"

"Of course not. Well . . . okay, maybe the thought crossed my mind. In the abstract, of course."

"Of course."

Sybil collects some lamps. "I'm going to bed."

"Night, Auntie, see in you the rosy-fingered dawn."

Jerry looks around like the hunted. "Sam's not here, obviously."

"Nope."

He glugs his vodka. "Anyway, she says I scold her all the time. I can't imagine what she's referring to. I'm just trying to help, granted sometimes I get a little irritated."

"In 'helping' her, you're suggesting that she needs help, your help, meaning she has to do things your way."

"What am I supposed to do? Pretend she's competent? Ignore the gangrenous food in the fridge that will poison her if she eats it? I found a jellied ham in there the other day. It was green."

"Maybe it was lime jelly."

He attempts the I-can't-believe-how-ridiculous-you-are look but, because he's loaded, he can't pull it off. The look dissolves into just plain needy.

"She does okay, Jerr, she's got a few years in her yet. Is Eleni back from Greece?"

"Well, that's part of the problem. She isn't and I've been sleeping there. Sometimes Mum wakes me at four in the morning and asks me if I'd like a cup of tea. She has no concept of time.

She's completely on her own clock." He drinks. "Remember in the summer I set her hose on a timer so she wouldn't have to remember to water? She cut it. And the alarm system? She hates it. Wants me to get the pad removed because she says people are always hitting it by mistake. I don't know what 'people' she can be referring to. Nobody ever visits her. She no longer even speaks to the neighbours. Claims they steal her water, says they use a stick to pull the hose and sprinkler over so it waters their lawns."

I think it's interesting that he came here to find out how I am and yet can do nothing but yak about his own problems. Is this because he's fearful of my condition, or because he's got his head up his butt as usual? I pull the wig out of the box and fit it on my head. "What do you think?"

He stares at me as though I've sprouted horns. "Very nice," he says.

"Really, Jerr?" I ask, trying to sound whiny like Natasha. "Do you *really* think so, do you think people will think it's *natural*?"

"So you've made a decision," he says.

"You got it. Goin' for the big one. The Bonanza. No half measures here."

"Well, I'm glad."

"I'm glad you're glad."

"You're not, obviously."

"I'm trying not to think about it. I'm trying to be an open vessel into which healing energies can flow."

"Good. Makes a nice change."

I look at him, really see him, the dweasel inside the expensive suit, and I want him out. But Sam's locomoting towards the darkened kitchen, oblivious of our presence. I want to warn him, but he's at our feet in seconds. "Not again," he comments on seeing us.

Jerry tries to sit straighter. "I came by to inquire after your mother."

Sam stares at me. "What's on your head?"

"A wig."

"You're going to wear that?"

And I feel as I felt a hundred years ago when Jerry didn't approve of my choice of dress. "You're going to wear that?" he'd ask. Defiant, I'd wear it anyway, but throughout the evening I'd be embarrassed by my attire, even though I didn't know what was wrong with it.

"Of course she's going to wear it," Big Daddy says. "She's going to have chemotherapy, which will make her hair fall out but will probably save her life."

I so badly wanted to have an intimate exchange with Sam on this subject. I wanted to see relief brighten his face as it did when I'd let him stay home from school due to illness. But he's as steely as ever.

"Sit down, stay a while," Jerry tells him.

"You're both canned."

"Are we?" Jerry asks. "That makes us nicer."

"It makes you degenerate." He heads upstairs and slams his door.

"That went well," Jerry comments.

I take off the wig and stuff it in the box. "You should go," I say.

"I know. I will." But he remains sitting. "I don't know what it's going to take to make him talk to me."

I manage to stand, put the vodka away. "You've got a tough climb ahead of you."

"I'm going to have to get me some mighty spiky boots to cling to that mountain."

"Well, you've always liked a challenge. Good night, Jerr."

Interesting how I never look in mirrors anymore. Was a time they were my ally. I'd seek reassuring glances from them. Mirrors were life-affirming. Now they speak of death. I should cover this one. Except I need it to apply my realtor face; nobody wants a pallid agent. In Henry Kissinger's waiting room slumped a patient who wore no makeup, no wig over her patchy hair, and had the absent look of someone who's negotiating with death. Beside her sat her "supportive" friend who was recovering from a divorce and saying things like "thank God we didn't have children," and "even if he hadn't done it, we would've ended up separating." Of course I immediately wanted to know *what* he'd done. She had very large hips and tiny shoulders; a bowling-pin look. I imagined it would be pretty tough to bowl her over. "His maturity was stunted," she kept repeating. "He just stopped evolving." As she expounded upon why, in the modern age, men have ceased to evolve, the cancer patient stared up at the ceiling as though she were waiting for a plane.

"You wouldn't believe what happened to Nancy Looby," Bowling Pin added, "do you remember Nancy Looby?" The cancer patient nodded, eyes still riveted to the ceiling.

"Well," Bowling Pin continued, "she got divorced because her husband, and this is truly unforgivable, couldn't handle it when their five-year-old died. He just fell apart, didn't even spend time with his remaining daughter. Nancy had to look after everything *and* deal with her own grief."

And I felt for the husband, because I don't know how you survive the death of your child. Perhaps the mother was a coper, a fixer, a problem solver, perhaps she was able to soldier onward because she's female and we've been coping with tragedy since time began. But I felt for the man, saw him lost in space, unable to look at the remaining daughter without seeing the other. Unable to speak words that held any meaning in the face of his loss. I saw him standing on the periphery of his wife's coping skills wishing only that *he* could be wiped off the face of this earth.

"She divorced him," Bowling Pin concluded. "I don't think he even sees them anymore."

And I thought about my son. Much better that I die first. Much better.

His light's still on. I knock softly. "Yeah," he mutters.

He's on his bed with his socks at half-mast as usual. *Lady Chatterley's* on the bed beside him. "How's the book?" I ask.

"It's okay. Wordy."

"Yeah, well, words were popular in those days."

"Why's Dad always hanging around here?"

"He's not always hanging around here."

"Is he hoping to fuck you or something? Because some guys are into that—fucking freaks."

I feel as though I've fallen face down in piss.

"I'm sorry," he says. "I don't know why I said that."

"To hurt me."

"I'm sorry." He shakes his head and covers his face with his hands. "I don't know why I said that."

"Because I'm freaky and will get freakier, and that scares you." I sit at the desk I bought for him when he started high school. I remember agonizing over it at IKEA, picturing him huddled over it, getting good grades, living a happy life. "The hair grows back," I say. "The breasts don't, unfortunately."

"Why're you doing it? You said you didn't want to do it."

If I say, Because I want to be with you, he will be hopelessly burdened. "Because I want to live longer."

"You said it doesn't necessarily make you live longer."

"I figured it's worth a shot."

Looking unconvinced, he crosses an ankle over his knee and flaps his sock.

"Anyway, I think your dad's hanging around because he wants to be around you."

"Or Natasha's not sucking him off anymore."

"That may be part of it. My point is, I think he has a sincere interest in you, even though he doesn't show it."

"I'd say he's not with the program."

"Yeah, well, he's . . . he's a bit slow in some ways."

"So when do you start?"

"Tomorrow."

"How long does it take?"

"They say to allow a couple of hours. They have to do blood work before they hook you up. There's probably a fair bit of waiting around, for results and things."

"Are you scared?"

"A little." The wind's picking up outside, batting his window about. Lightning blasts white light into the room.

"There's supposed to be a big storm," he advises me. "There's even tornado warnings up north." He pulls off his socks and drops them on the floor. "I'm glad you're doing it."

"Me too." And this is true, now that the decision has been made.

"Do you want me to go with you?"

This desire to help is so stunning, so uncharacteristic of him. But what will he do there? Sit by his freaky mother, see other cancer patients who may not look too pretty. He'll see who I will become. "I think it'd be boring for you, sweetie. I'll take a book."

"I just wish there was something I could do," he says.

"Make dinner. I can't face another one of Sybil's stews. Macaroni and cheese, you know how to do that."

"Okay."

I get up to pull the window closed. The tarps strapped to our naked roof flap in the wind. We're setting sail, into a storm.

Thirty

It's not that bad, aside from the squinty-eyed nurse taking half an hour to find a suitable vein. "What tiny veins you have," she remarked, while jabbing me repeatedly. "I've never seen such tiny veins." I thought of suggesting that she get glasses but decided this would make me unpopular and there is nothing worse than being an unpopular patient. Experience has taught me that, where nursing staff is concerned, it's best to act mildly retarded at all times. This enables them to feel superior towards you which makes them less likely to ignore you completely. Certainly if you ask for things in a forthright manner, you are doomed. No extra pillows or blankies will come your way; only the wrong food, cold.

There was a burning sensation as the stuff started dripping into me, but that's subsided. Now I just feel alternately hot and chilled. I don't know if this is due to the heavy-metal poisoning, the hospital setting, or my terror. In any case, I'm trying to ignore it, brought a book—a history of London's Soho. William Blake lived and died there. And the interesting thing is that he was one weird kid. His parents labelled him a problem child because he was so sensitive to things: the lowing of cattle in the market's slaughterhouses, the half-buried corpses in a nearby graveyard, brutality in school. He was so "sensitive" in fact that his parents withdrew him from school and let him do exactly what he wanted: draw, wander the streets, and read. He had mystical visions, trees filled with angels and God's face pressing against his window. Later he had prophetic visions which proved to be true, his first employer being hanged, for example. I try to imagine the fate of such a boy in today's world. Doubtless he would be "psychologically assessed" and dosed with Ritalin. If that didn't straighten him out, they'd pump him with anti-psychotics. No end of pharmaceuticals would be spared the nonconforming boy.

"Your first time?" the bloated woman beside me inquires. I've been avoiding her because she's a frightening sight not only because she's hairless, but because her eyes seem to be swollen shut. Swollen eyes is not on my list of side effects.

"Yes," I admit. "Does it show?"

"Hey, we've all been there."

I note movement in the slits of her eyes so presumably she can see.

"It's my last day," she informs me.

"How'd it go?"

"So far so good. It's my third cycle though, so I can't say I'm over the moon about it." She feels her scalp as though checking for hair. "I mean, when I look in the mirror, that's not me. I've gained forty pounds on this shit. It's getting so I can't walk for more than twenty minutes. So now I'm supposed to take tamoxifen for, like, forever, which will make me even fatter."

I don't really want to hear this and try to appear keen to resume reading, but she's the kind of gal who needs a body at which to direct her voice. Unlike Erna, she requires a visible body.

"It's not so bad at the beginning," she offers. "You throw up and all that, blaggablagga. It's when the drugs start building up in your system it gets hard to take. I get all these body aches, like I've got the flu or something. And mouth sores, raw anus, blaggablagga. It's the black stools that totally freaked me out. If you get black stools or you're barfing coffee grounds, tell your doctor, it means your platelets are down. Anyway, just so you know, you get through it, even though it seems like it'll go on forever. I know because my white blood cells dropped to my boots so they had to spread the treatment out longer."

"Well, you must be glad to have it over with." The other patients are ignoring the bloated woman, which is difficult because she has the voice box of an opera singer. Maybe they've heard it all before, maybe when they were "first timers" she updated them on the colour of her stools.

"You know what gets me," she continues, "is how we're supposed to be so cheery about it all the time. My family's like, 'You're doing great blaggablagga.' They don't want to hear about it anymore. It's like we're living with this shit forever, but as long as we're not dead, we're supposed to be celebrating."

"It does seem unreasonable."

"I'm like, 'You get menopause at thirty-eight.' It's like if you have heart surgery, everybody's fine with it. You're sick for a while, but you get better and everybody's comfortable with that. My dad had a triple and talks about it like he's some kind of hero. But if I so much as open my mouth, they all get on my case. 'You're doing really good, Brenda, you should be grateful.' Well, fuck them."

"I agree," I say.

She looks at me, a little surprised that I agree. "Like I'm entitled to feel down."

"You are."

A wigged woman, reading *Cosmopolitan* with a scantily clothed implanted model on it, holds the magazine higher, blocking Brenda and myself from view. Brenda notes me noticing this and whispers, "She's a class-A bitch, goes around saying it's mind over matter. She hasn't gained an ounce and says she does fine on the antinauseants. Mrs. Sweetness and Light. It's in her liver. I bet she'll be dead in a year."

"Has she been here as long as you have?"

"Nobody's been here as long as I have. Guess how old I am?"

"Thirty-eight."

"How'd you know that?"

"You told me."

"Oh. I don't look thirty-eight though."

She looks fifty, but I don't want to say this. "You look tired."

"Tell me about it. I've got these hot flashes, my wazoo's dry, my eyes, my feet hurt, my hands are swollen. It's a fucking nightmare."

The squinty-eyed nurse unhooks the wigged mind-over-matter woman who carefully fits her *Cosmo* into her Louis Vuitton handbag. As she steps by us, she offers a shark's smile. "Good luck to you, Brenda."

"Thank you so much," Brenda says snidely. When the *Cosmo* woman's out of earshot she continues, "One thing I noticed when you get cancer, you see through everything. It's like you got X-ray vision or something."

"I wonder why that is."

"Because you don't give a shit anymore."

"So does that mean that when we were well and did give a shit, we let ourselves be duped?"

"Kind of. Yeah. Like we wanted to believe it."

"Why don't we want to believe it anymore?"

"Don't have the time. It's like who needs these lies, yadda-yaddayadda, it's like shut the fuck up."

"That's a kind of freedom," I suggest.

Brenda doesn't respond, only stares morosely at the drip in her arm.

"If you need to," I ask, "will you do this again?"

She looks at me briefly, snickers, then eyes the red stuff leaking into her. "I have this friend, he's like sixty-something now. Anyway, he had this disease that crippled him, he had too much iron in his blood or something blaggablagga, anyway, they had to cut his legs off and reattach them to plastic hips. Meaning he had to learn to walk all over again. After the first operation he was okay for a while, but then they had to do it again. When I visited him in the hospital the second time 'round, he told me he'd rather die than go through that again. Well, you know what?"

"He went through it again."

"You got it." She sinks her head back in her recliner and closes her swollen eyes. "You never know what you'll do."

I feel all right. I took a cab to the hospital because I didn't know how I'd feel. But I feel all right, and I'm showing a house to the stupefied couple. I had a gut feeling about this listing, and had a long chat with the listing agent who's one of those rare realtors who doesn't fabricate. The reason this house hasn't sold is that it's a one-bedroom house which doesn't suit our breeding, minivan-obsessed population. But my stupefied couple can't have children, have endured the trials of infertility treatment and are still united. A stunning, high-ceilinged, sky-lit, one-bedroom house on a cul-de-sac that backs on a ravine should appeal to them. And by the look on their faces, I'd say it's a bingo. They walk the hardwood floors as though in a trance. She keeps staring out the windows into the woods, disbelieving that there is no toxic waste back there. I say nothing, just giggle inwardly and remember why I don't always despise what I do for a living. It's a long lot, because of the ravine. A solarium at the back of the house is completely shrouded in trees. Their only visible neighbours will be the coons. They stand there, gazing into the green, and reach for each other's hands and I feel myself starting to cry. Because I'm happy for them. And because they care, really care about each other, and I've never felt this, will never feel this—a relationship in which you carefully hold each other's hearts. They turn to me and the wife says quietly, "Greer, we really like this house."

I quickly wipe my eye. "It's well priced."

He clears his throat. "Do you think we should offer them the asking price?"

"I wouldn't go that far."

I find Lyla in her backyard savagely digging up dandelions. This display of energy makes me wonder if she's off her medication. "My father would not tolerate these," she informs me. Her hair has been set in curls and tied with pink ribbon. I suspect that Erna has been transforming her into one of her broken dolls. "And I haven't done anything to his roses. He would be distraught." Her English accent's back. She's definitely off her drugs.

"I'll help you. We'll do it together."

"I don't want your help," she snaps, digging up another one and pitching it into the hedge, then another and another. A shrivelled leaf falls from a tree and nests in her curls. "Quite frankly, I don't know how you can bear to live with him."

"He's my son."

"He's a murderer." She hacks away at a thistle even though she's not wearing gloves.

"He was asleep. He really was, Lyla. He does things in his sleep. Eats, does laundry, digs, I've seen it."

Abruptly, she flops down on the grass, lies back and frowns at the sky. "I feel ill. It's those bloody frozen dinners. There's parasites in prepared food. I've told the silly woman, but she doesn't believe me."

"Do you still think you have parasites?" I ask. She starts twiddling her newly grown hair; soon she'll be half bald again. "Because we all have parasites. That's normal. But I've never heard of them crawling out onto skin."

"What do you think *maggots* are?"

"That's when you're dead." I immediately regret saying this because I know she's imagining her parents infested with maggots.

She pulls her legs into her chest and grips them as though to prevent them from springing away from her. "I can't hear their screams." She shakes her head repeatedly. "I can't. I'm quite certain they screamed." She jumps up to resume her dandelion massacre. "I've tried to forgive your son, I have, but I want him dead."

"I can understand that."

"My parents want me to forgive him, but it's out of the question." She jabs her trowel into the dirt. "I want it like when those racists dragged that black man behind their truck. Chained him and dragged him until his head was torn off."

"It wouldn't bring your parents back."

"What they feared most on earth, *most on earth,* was leaving me alone in the world."

"I feel the same way about Sam."

The back door swings open and Erna hollers, "You girls come in for a cup of tea!"

A doll amputee joins us at the table. I wait for Erna to offer her one of the powdered mini-doughnuts she keeps thrusting at me. "I said, '*Don't* you tell me you can't find a body,' I said, 'get your goddamn dogs out.' I said, 'Are you telling me if the Prime Minister's daughter went missing, you wouldn't find a goddamn body?'"

"Erna," Lyla interjects vehemently, "we don't *know* that she's dead, she might not be dead."

"I said, 'You sons of bitches sit around all day on your arses, collecting your goddamn paycheques . . .'"

Lyla claps her hands over her ears. "Can we *not* talk about the body for five minutes, *please*?"

Erna looks as though she's just noticed her. "Suit yourself." She feels her French twist, readjusts a bobby pin. "Don't she look cute with her hair done nice?" she asks me. "I said, 'Spruce yourself up, girl.' I said, 'You can't go layin' about in your pyjamas all day, what'll the neighbours think?' She's out there diggin' around in her jammies. I said, 'You got a *natural curl*,' I said, 'I know girls would kill to have a wave like yours.' You know what she says to me?"

I shake my head.

"She says it doesn't matter. I said, 'When you start lettin' yourself go, that's when they get ya.'" She winks at me, pulls out a cigarette and lights up. "That's when they get ya."

It's driving back from presenting the offer to the vendors of the solarium house that the nausea begins. I pop more Gravol and try to distract myself with the radio, but every station is rambling about a suicide/murder. A man jumped in front of a subway train, taking his four-year-old son with him. Apparently the boy was devoted to his father, cried daily when he left for work. I can only deduce that the father, in his despair, must've felt he couldn't leave him behind. I'll take him with me and he will be safe.

It's the boy's face I can't lose sight of, even though I've never seen him. The boy's face as he realized that his father, the father he trusted, adored, was dragging him to his death.

And then there's the story of the six children being killed in the minivan by a jackknifing transport truck. Imagine losing your six children in seconds. Cancer's nothing compared to this dose of fate. Nothing.

Sam's wearing my apron, the kitchen's in ruins, the saucepan burned. "What happened?" I ask.

"I forgot it was on. It's okay though, the macaroni, it's in the oven."

"Good. Smells good," I say, but really the smell of burnt cheese is causing my stomach to heave. Sybil trots downstairs, "Want a drink?"

"No thanks, Auntie."

"How was it?"

"It's okay, it's going to be okay." And I see it, finally, relief on my son's face. He has been worrying all day, I realize. What did he think? That I'd quit? One day at it and I'd surrender?

"So it doesn't hurt or anything?" he asks.

"Nope." The vomit is tunnelling through me. "I'll be right back." I hurry upstairs, hide in my bathroom and hurl. Cancer has finally brought me to my knees. I look for coffee grounds in the toilet bowl even though I know my platelets can't be down to my boots yet. After several heaves I feel somewhat better and decide that I must put in an appearance downstairs. I even manage to eat a few mouthfuls and say, "It's yummy." I sit very still and avoid sudden shifts of focus. But even staring at things makes me dizzy. I try to appear interested as Sybil rants about the suicide/murder. "In a crowded world, people do crazy things."

"Sybil," I say finally, "I can't listen to any more of this. Please."

"You want to lie down?" she asks.

"Yes, but I'm dizzy. I need help." And he's there at my side, holding my elbow. I can't believe it. We make slow progress up the stairs. I fear only that I'll puke all over him. Otherwise, the sheer presence of him, feel of him, gives me strength. This will pass, this nausea. My body is designed to reject poison. It needs time to adjust. I'll pop one of Henry Kissinger's prescription antinauseants.

"I don't understand why it's making you dizzy," Sam says as he sits me on my bed.

"I don't really either, my love. It's just, it's potent stuff. There are side effects and I just have to take them as they come." I feel a retch pending and try to dash to the bathroom, but instead trip over my fucking slippers and barf macaroni on one of those carpets woven by blind children. Sam holds his hand over his nose and mouth, probably suppressing a vomit himself. "I'll be okay, sweetie," I tell him. "I'll clean it up."

"Are you crazy?" He gets a cloth from the bathroom and begins mopping up the food he prepared in an effort to "help" his mother. Sybil buzzes about offering flat ginger ale and camomile tea.

"Nothing," I say. "Please. I don't want anything."

"Chicken broth?"

"Are you deaf?" Sam says loudly. "She said she doesn't want anything. You're making her sick talking about it."

"Who are you all of a sudden, Florence Nightingale?"

"No fighting," I say. "Go away, please, both of you."

"I'm not leaving you lying in puke," declares my boy, rinsing the cloth for the third time.

"You need air," Sybil insists, pushing the window open so I can hear the dog. I crawl onto my bed and pull the covers over my head, like Lyla, and hope that the vile taste in my mouth is not permanent, that tomorrow will bring sweet smells and a fresh outlook. Dwell on the positive, I tell myself, you sold a house today, that's good, very good. And your son wants to help which is a cause for celebration in itself. Rejoice in what you have. Think of Eeyore with the busted balloon and the empty honey pot, think that your child did not die in a minivan.

"Mum . . . ?"

"Mmm."

"Are you sleeping in your clothes?"

"I'll get up in a bit."

"You don't want a glass of water or anything?"

"Water would be nice." The thought of water makes my stomach prepare to rocket, but I want him to feel that he's "helping." He sets it on my night table. "Night, sweetie, thanks for the macaroni."

"I'll be around if you need me."

"Okay."

"Dad phoned to ask how it went. It was on the service. He said he'd call again."

"No calls tonight."

"Okay. Night."

"Night."

And I do feel better in the morning but decide not to eat or drink or move except when necessary. I don't know if it's actual nausea or the memory of nausea, but a queasiness lingers. Best to play it safe. I take a cab to the hospital and try to avoid looking at passing cars, people, buildings. I've always found the best way to deal with feeling lousy is to distract yourself from your condition. In this case, the distraction is the Tanzanian cab driver who explains that he drives a cab twelve hours a day, six days a week, so he can send money to his wife and kids back home.

"Are they coming here?" I ask.

"I don't want them to come here. It's not good for children here. North America. Not a good influence."

"But don't you miss them?"

"It's better they are there. Better education. Too much violence here."

What I didn't know until I presented the offer to the vendors of the solarium house was that the wife was hugely pregnant. Her torpedo breasts kept bumping things on the table: coffee cups, pens, papers. I wanted to say, Can't you harness those things? I pitied the infant who would be faced with them. And thought how ironic it was that an infertile couple was buying Mrs. Fecundity's house. And I wanted to ensure that she wouldn't be home during the inspection because her fertile presence might dampen my couple's spirits.

"Saturday night," my cabbie offers, "they try to rob me."

"Who?"

"Thieves. They get in my car. Usually I lock the doors but I'd just let off a fare. They threaten me with a knife."

"What did you do?"

"Stopped in the intersection. Cars honked, people were everywhere. I got out of my car."

"The thieves took off?"

He nods. "Too violent here."

Guess he doesn't recognize the murderer's mother.

I have to walk through a haze of cigarette smoke to enter the hospital. Most of the smokers are wearing hospital garb. Fancy smoking while working in a cancer hospital. The squinty-eyed nurse has even more trouble finding a vein, and the one she lacerated yesterday has become swollen. "You might be better off with a port-o-cath," she advises me.

"A what?"

"They can surgically implant a catheter with a tube that gets hooked up to the IV."

"No thanks," I say.

"You may have to, with your veins being so tiny. We'll see how the swelling goes." Get somebody here with glasses, I want to shout. Beside me, an Irishman is raving about the tax increase on parking permits. "That's thirty percent. Who ever heard of a *thirty percent* increase in one year?" I want to ask, You're sweating about taxes when you could be dead in the not too distant future?

Mrs. Sweetness and Light, with the shark's smile, who I'm sure doesn't require permit parking because she lives in Moore Park with a two-car garage, remarks, "They have to get the money from somewhere."

"From the poor," the Irishman insists. "That's all this blood-sucking government does, feed on the unfortunates. The people who can't fight back."

"We all have to tighten our belts," Mrs. Sweetness and Light says. "Times have changed."

What belt-tightening have you done lately, you silly cow? Only one facial per month? Only an eye job this year, you'll do the jowls the next?

And to my immediate right is a woman too young to have cancer. She's wearing a fisherman's canvas hat, decorated with fishing flies. She seems to be very angry with her "fucking mother" and I wonder if this would qualify as mismanaged emotions in early adulthood which is supposed to cause cancer. Or was it mismanaged emotions in late adulthood? "I didn't want the fucking exercise bike," she explains to her friend who's chewing gum rapidly. "It's my fucking mother wanted the bike. Like I'd rather bike outside. It's her that wants the bike, but she said she got it for me so it'd look like she was giving me a present."

"That sucks," her friend offers.

About now massive nausea hits me, the kind in which you can't even lift your head off the pillow. That's okay, I assure myself, just lie here, go with the flow. I close my eyes because even reading makes me dizzy.

"So I tell her," the young fisherwoman continues, "I'm moving out and I'm taking the bike and she says she'll give me a hundred bucks for it and I'm like, I know that bike's worth more than that. She bought that stairmaster, that cost like, I don't know, five hundred or something. So I tell her I'm taking the bike, even though I don't want it, just because she wants it. Fucking two-faced cunt."

Oh to be so admired by your child. Does the mother know, care, or is she climbing her stairmaster, pummelling her knees in the endless pursuit of cellulite-free thighs? While her daughter curses her in the chemo lounge, is Mommy Dearest cooking up fat-free fries? I did everything I could for that girl, everything, even bought her an exercise bike.

My son does not hate me so. He does not.

I feel as if I'm on one of those spinning rides in amusement parks; you hang on tight enjoying the zooming in your stomach because you know it will be over in minutes and you'll be back to your dull, earthbound life. That's all I want, my dull earthbound life.

The squinty-eyed nurse is shaking me and saying, "Mrs. Pentland, you're done. Mrs. Pentland . . . ?" I look at her and think, Doesn't squinting give you a headache? I try to lift my head but it's out of the question.

"Are you going to be sick?"

"Is there a basin?"

"I can get you one."

The place has cleared out. Only the Irishman remains, clutching the *Sun*, ogling the buxom Sunshine Girl in her teeny-weeny bikini. I start to hurl sans basin and the Irishman says, "You alright, dearie?"

Jerry brought me home. I called his private line, got through to his office-mode voice which quickly softened when I said, "It's me."

"Are you alright?"

"I'm at the hospital," I whimpered, sounding like a lost child. "Can you come and get me?"

"I'll be there in half an hour."

He carried me into the house like a bride. My body conformed to his as it did at the best of times. He smells the same. You'd think once a person who was once a vital part of you has been torn asunder they would smell different, feel different. That smell belonged to you, you're thinking, that intimacy. Go off with the little tramp, but change your smell. Even his shoulder on which my head rested felt exactly the same. His neck felt thicker though, as I wrapped my arms around it. He held me with care even though I stank of vomit. The three of them stand around me with stricken faces and I feel like an actor playing dead in a movie. I've always wondered how the "corpse" resists an urge to peek at the theatrics surrounding him. Is that in the outtakes? Does the corpse corpse when the leading lady, possibly Meryl (with an accent, of course), falls over him and sobs? Does the corpse have to resist an urge to tickle Meryl just to see if she's human?

"Lighten up, guys," I say. But even as I say it I feel about to gag.

"The nurse suggested you stay away from strong odours," my he-man says, "and cold liquids. Just try to get down small amounts of food whenever possible."

"No food," I say.

"You have to drink water," Sam says, "or you'll dehydrate."

"No water. Please." Just looking at them makes my head reel. I close my eyes.

"The nurse said," Jerry adds, "you should be on a stronger antinausea medication."

"I am."

"Obviously you need a stronger one. Do you want me to call your doctor?"

"Just leave me alone, please. I'll get through this, just please, can you get the sales agreement to the Clarefields?" I already asked him to do this in the car. I know they're waiting for it (the stupefied couple). They're waiting for their new life to begin and I want to make it easy for them. The offer was accepted; all they have to do is write a deposit cheque.

Daddyo puts his hands on his hips. "I can't believe you're

thinking about real estate at a time like this."

"It's a commission, Jerry. Money. Legal bills, remember?"

"Fine. I will do it."

"Thank you. The papers are in my case. Go now, please."

"Call me if you need anything."

"Yes." I close my eyes again. "Tell them I've got the flu," I add as he heads downstairs.

Sybil has been remarkably quiet but now she decides it's time to straighten my bed and fluff up my pillows. "Please don't," I tell her.

"What about some mint tea?"

"Leave her alone," Sam says. "She wants to be left alone."

And I don't really. I mean, I don't want him to go. But there's nothing for him here. I can't chain him to my bed just so I can stroke his hair. I try to look at him and smile reassuringly, but another massive, prolonged abdominal contraction squeezes my stomach. I look around for the basin, but of course it's by the sink where I left it after rinsing it out. I lurch towards the bathroom. Sam stands back probably because he's afraid I'll spew on him again. And it's like someone's unplugged a fire hydrant, fluid gushes out of me; no food particles anymore. Afterwards, I rest my head against the toilet seat waiting to feel a little better, at least for a while. But the sick feeling doesn't pass, and for the first time it occurs to me that I might not be able to do this, that it might not be a matter of choice.

Grabbing the edge of the sink, I pull myself up, turn on the taps and rinse my face, my mouth. Not once do I look in the mirror before shuffling back to my room, steadying myself against the wall like the seasick on a storm-swept vessel. I try to think of something to say to him that will offer comfort. But he's gone. Just as well.

Thirty-one

Sybil's slapping my hand in an effort to wake me, but it's not daylight and I resist being brought back to reality. I think I was dreaming about a train I was supposed to be on, going through my basement. I couldn't believe I missed a train that stopped in my basement.

"The police are at the door," Sybil says, patting my face.

"What? Why?"

"They won't tell me. Your car's gone. Somebody must've stolen your car."

"Great." This is all I need, really, thank you so much.

"Hurry up."

"I am hurrying. I'm sick, remember? Let them wait, I hate cops." She grabs my bathrobe and fits me into it. I feel incredibly light-headed, like the merest wind could knock me over. An old stolen car. Fabulous. The insurance company will give me fifty cents for it.

"Mrs. Pentland?" one thug asks. They both look pregnant. I consider inquiring when the babies are due.

"Yes."

"Can we come in?"

"No. How do I know you're real cops?"

"We have badges, ma'am."

"Whoopteydoo, they could be fakes."

"You should let us in, ma'am," the shorter one says.

All I can think is that they strip-searched my son.

"You can tell me whatever you need to tell me here."

"I think you'd prefer it if we came inside," Shorty says.

And then it hits. He's killed someone. I see the blood, hear the screams. "Just what is it?" I almost shout.

The moustached one takes off his hat. "Did you notice your car was missing?"

"Of course not. You woke me up. I didn't know it was stolen when I went to sleep."

"It wasn't stolen, ma'am."

"Oh. Someone borrowed it?"

"Ma'am, your son took the car."

"He doesn't drive."

"Well, he did tonight."

"That's not possible."

"He's in the hospital, ma'am," Shorty says.

"You should come with us."

"What . . . ? Excuse me, you don't understand, my son doesn't drive."

"He did tonight, ma'am."

"That's not possible."

"I'm afraid it is, ma'am," Shorty repeats. "He shouldn't have been on the road, his licence expired."

"So are you going to give him a ticket or something?"

"No, ma'am. We'd like to get you to the hospital as quickly as possible."

Only now am I starting to understand. I feel Sybil behind me, her hand on the small of my back, steadying me. "Let's get you dressed," she says.

I phone Jerry from the cruiser, but he turns his phone down at night because if the twat is woken it's impossible for her to get back to sleep, and she needs her beauty rest. I leave a message. I'm actually quite calm, because he's still alive. That's the important thing. Whatever problems arise, we will deal with. I throw up on the cops' upholstery, which gives me some relief.

The thugs tell me the car crashed into an abutment. They tell me it looked like a suicide attempt. They are morons and should shut the fuck up.

The hospital glare unwinds me. Shorty props me up while

the big guy finds out where we're supposed to go. I completely lose my sense of direction, panic sets in, and I'm actually glad the morons are here to guide me. But of course, unlike on TV, no conscientious doctors are waiting to greet me. Once Shorty and the big guy leave for a doughnut fix, I'm left alone in a "consultation room." Sybil wanted to come, but I wouldn't let her, didn't want to have to worry about her heart. I sit on a vinyl-covered chair and look around. There's not even a *Time* here, we're talking stark. I'm left to my own imaginings. Suicide? What do cops know? Cops know how to takes bribes and consume fast food while driving.

If it were really bad, the men in white would have rushed to meet me saying, "I'm so sorry, Mrs. Pentland, but your son is dead." The fact that they're not here means he's in the O.R., which means they're fixing him.

I should try to drink some fluid, I eyeball the water cooler. Avoid cold fluids, Squinty said. I pour some anyway and warm the little paper cone in my hands. I didn't get a chance to put on my watch and the room is windowless. Doesn't matter, I find it's best to forget about time in the hospital. In the hospital, watched-time stops.

There seems to be some action in the consultation room next door. Folks gathering outside, embracing, sobbing. Not a happy ending. Why are there so many of them, was every relation notified? How helpful can it be to have Aunt Bessy and Uncle Harry, cousin Joey and nephew Jim, hanging around? I'm actually glad Big Daddy is unavailable. He would only get uptight about my treatment of doctors. Like so many, he believes that doctors deserve the utmost respect, simply because they're doctors. Whereas I think the fact that they're doctors makes them suspect. How many good doctors have covered the tracks of incompetent ones to avoid increases in their malpractice premiums? Let's sweep this dead patient under the mat, nobody has to know Dr. I-wouldn't-let-him-operate-on-my-dog screwed up the tracheotomy.

I forgot to ask about the car. Where's my car?

"Mrs. Pentland . . . ?"

"Yup." He has a pointy head. Why can't I ever have a doctor like the ones on TV—forty-something, greying slightly, earnest about saving lives? "We'll do everything we can, no, we'll do more than that, because this hospital is about saving lives."

"We . . . umm . . ." Conehead begins. "Our trauma team has been working extensively on your son. Unfortunately, there was considerable damage to the spinal cord, head and lungs, which means interference with breathing which is . . . is not good. And the . . . umm . . . abdominal organs were also bleeding. We attempted to stop it, but . . . I'm afraid there was just too much damage."

"What are you saying?" He looks twenty, they've got the med student working on my son.

"I'm saying your son is dying."

"What do you mean 'dying'? He can't be dying if he's still breathing, I mean operate on him, that's your job."

"We've done everything medically possible, Mrs. Pentland. At the moment, he's on life-support."

"Meaning what?"

"We've inserted an endotracheal tube that connects him to a ventilator."

"Off it he'll die?"

"I'm afraid so."

I wait to experience a chaotic loss of control. Instead I'm detached, and making quite reasonable deductions. I mean, first of all, how do they know it's Sam? Don't faces get smashed beyond recognition in car crashes? Don't their bodies burn? Aren't dental records required to make identifications? I mean just because some kid stole my car, they're running around claiming he's Sam. This is not possible. Sam doesn't drive. He's probably home in bed asleep.

"Well," I tell Conehead, "obviously I can't take your word for it. I'll need a second opinion. And ID, clothing, something that proves it's him."

"Of course. I'll have Dr. Schnurr speak with you, and locate some personal effects. Umm . . . you should be aware that your son showed organ-donor consent on his health card. He's signed a consent form which is completely voluntary. However, we won't accept the donation if you object."

"Excuse me, did you not hear what I said? Prove to me it's my son."

"You'll be seeing him shortly."

"Fine. Let me see him and then we'll talk. This is crazy. And may I suggest that the 'second opinion' not come from someone involved in transplants." Already the vultures are circling.

He puffs out his little-boy chest. "The medical team that fought to save your son's life is completely different from the team responsible for organ and tissue transplants."

"What do you mean 'fought'? He's not dead yet. And anyway, we don't even know if it's him."

"Would you like to speak with a grief counsellor?"

I want to box this kid's ears. "I really don't want to talk about this anymore until you get what's-his-name in here."

"As soon as Dr. Schnurr's available I'll send him in."

"Good. I'd like to be alone now."

"Of course."

What a crock. I'm supposed to believe these guys? Corrupt cops and organ-thirsty doctors? Sam's home sleeping. I should've checked his bed, nipped this soap opera in the bud. Phone Sybil, she can look in on him. I see him lying there, his mouth slightly open, the furrow gone from his brow, one arm dangling off the bed. But of course, she doesn't pick up before the service clicks in. Once she's out, it takes an avalanche to wake her. Oh well. The show must go on. Honestly, who do they think I am? What do they do with the organs—sell them for cash and install pig's innards into desperate recipients? Oh thank you, doctor for my new heart, oink oink. What a joke.

The surprising thing is I'm managing to drink little sips of water. Sam will be so pleased. I should've picked up my car keys. He can't drive without keys. I know they're there, by the fruit bowl on the kitchen table. He couldn't drive without keys. This is so asinine. These boneheads have me up at whatever hour it is in the morning before they have their facts straight. They're going to find out they made one big boohoo. I should call Muriel, get the name of a lawyer.

"Mrs. Pentland?"

"That's me."

"I'm Dr. Schnurr. I . . . umm . . ."

They all say "umm," what's with the umm? Too early in the morning, is it? Haven't had your cuppa joe, can't think straight, get the words out, the bodies right?

"Dr. Boynton was telling me that you would like a second opinion regarding your son's condition."

"First of all, we don't know that it is my son, so frankly, all deals are off."

"I understand. If you come with me, I can show him to you."

"Fine." Only now do I realize that I'm not wearing my prosthesis and am a single-breasted woman, a Cyclops. I follow Schnurr who looks like an accountant who should be hooked up to the Net showing his willy to his cyber-sex Filipino mistress. We pass by sniffling Aunt Bessie and stoic Uncle Harry. Cousin Joey and nephew Jim speak in hushed tones with eyes cast down. Clear out, I want to tell them, this is no place for a family reunion. God, the smell in here is awful, like a high-school biology lab; pickled frogs and rodents. I don't actually want to arrive at our destination but want to keep travelling in ignorance, bliss. I'm walking on Nerf balls, squooshy, squooshy. And something's pulling my knees to the floor, rubber bands.

But then I see his hair and everything snaps. I fall against something, I don't know what, the accountant. Close my eyes.

"Mrs. Pentland . . . ? Mrs. Pentland, are you alright?"

He isn't smashed or burned, just black and blue, I guess he slammed into the airbag . . . oh my god I can't do this. I can't. I cover my eyes with my hands. He used to do this, clap his pudgy little hands over his eyes when he didn't want to see.

The accountant releases his hold and they're there, my legs, two pegs I can't feel. I can't feel anything.

"I know this is very hard for you . . ." Schnurr says.

I lean over the bed rail. What happened, baby? I touch his forehead, it's cool but not cold, there's life there. What happened, baby? I rest my head beside his and inhale. He still smells like Sam. There's life there. "Why can't you fix him?" I demand.

"We've done everything medically possible. As I think Dr. Boynton explained to you, there were just too many internal injuries."

"He's still alive, what're you talking about? I don't care if he's a fucking quadriplegic, he's still alive."

"He's alive because he's on life-support. Mrs. Pentland, clinical brain death has been confirmed by myself and Dr. Boynton. And we are not involved in transplants."

"Go away," I tell him, like Sam used to tell me when he was three and being a big boy. "Go away, Mummy." I can't go away. How could you do this? Without even saying goodbye? You just get in the car and go? I'm trying, I've been trying, I would do anything for you, anything. I would drive into an abutment for you, cut off my arms, gouge out my eyes, rip out my tongue.

Why are your hands so cold? I'll warm you, we'll stay here, I won't let them have you. I can reach around the crap they've plugged into you and hold you, just hold you, kiss your forehead and just hold my lips there, just hold my lips there. Because I want to go with you, please let me go with you, don't leave me behind, angel, stay with me, sweetie, hold me, there are no bones in my body. I'm falling down, down but it's taking forever, I want to crash into the earth, dissolve into burning lava, without you, there is no reason without you.

But his arms don't reach to catch me, his eyes don't look to see me. What were you doing driving at night?

I've read that soldiers feel no pain, or fear, as they fight on in spite of mortal wounds. They feel nothing but the euphoria of battle until the danger is past. Was it so for you, baby? Did you get in the car with war lust in your blood, I will do this, end this, speedily, cleanly? Did you look at the concrete as you flew into it, or did you clap your hands over your eyes? Did you hear the impact of stone against metal, the shattering of glass, did you feel the engine crush your legs? Or were you somewhere else, free of pain, of yourself?

Or were you asleep?

I will never know if you don't tell me.

"Mrs. Pentland?"

"Go away!"

They've drawn the curtains around us. I caress the sides of your face, your hair, your forehead, I caress you as I never could when you had life.

"Mrs. Pentland . . . ?"

"Go away."

It's a nurse this time. She hands me your watch in a baggie.

"Go away," I repeat and grip it so tightly it hurts my hand. I will never rise from here. I look around for poison. Only what's being dripped into you. The ventilator's too loud, like a robot stuck in a rut. It can't feel good to have this thing shoved down your throat. It can't feel good to have breath forced into you.

I hold my lips against your cheek as I never could when you had life.

Schnurr's back. "As far as the donation is concerned," he advises me, "you can show on the consent form the organs or tissues you do not wish to donate."

"How much time?" I ask.

"Sorry?"

"How much time before his body becomes useless to you?"

"Umm . . . let's just say sooner's better than later. However, let me stress that if you object, that'll be the end of it."

"Do you stitch him back up again? Stuff him with something?"

"He would still look like himself."

"Was he burned?"

"No."

"Did he suffer?"

"I think the impact was sufficient to knock him out."

"Go away."

They will cut you open again, violate you, treat you like so much meat. I can't let them do this. How can you expect me to let them do this. They take your eyeballs, did you know that? Your skin your bones.

Can you feel my tears on your face? When I whisper in your ear, does it tickle? Brain death means it's all gone. Who you are, what you feel, everything, history. I am history because I live inside your head. All the times I wanted to say I love you but didn't because I thought it would sound trivial, corny. Because I thought you would scoff at the word, flinch, run from me. All the times I wanted to hug you, touch you, push the hair out of your face. All the times I wanted to be with you, but wasn't. You can't make up for lost time. It's lost. Nothing but a gaping wound remains, that will never heal; a cancer.

I haven't been sick since I've been with you. Maybe I'm getting better. Sam . . . ? Maybe I'm getting better. Is that what scared you? That I would die and leave you alone? I wouldn't do that. I'm even drinking some water, like you said I should. It's going to be okay. I said it would, remember? I said it would.

When you were a baby I would whisper in your ear like this and you would laugh. You would laugh. And give me that smile reserved for mothers, and only for a short time, because within months the baby has learned to be wary, understands that he is alone in the world and that every action must be calculated to increase his chances of survival.

What were you doing driving at night?

Were you releasing me? Speeding into darkness to free your mother of suffering because you knew, knew that I would never give up as long as you were there? Are you consenting to my release as I must consent to yours? There is serenity in your face, no surprise or terror, not even shock. You've given up, released yourself from this hell. Consciously or unconsciously you are on your way. And I can do nothing but stand on the shore screaming. I can do nothing but allow them to carve out your heart. Because you want to give life after taking it.

People crowd on the other side of the curtain, around another breathing dead man. It's Aunt Bessie, Uncle Harry and family. I'm forced to listen to their conference with Conehead. They have agreed to take their loved one off life-support. He was in a plane, his own, crashed soon after taking flight. Conehead advises them that it will take about a minute for him to die. As he switches off the robot I hear women gasp, then sob. But it takes more than a minute. Conehead remarks on how unusual this is. I have no choice but to listen to the pilot die, actually I can't hear much because of your robot. All the same, it feels wrong that this man's determined heart is being starved of oxygen, that this man's determined heart is being wasted when doubtless there is a lineup miles long of people with defective hearts, people who can't climb stairs or make love or walk to the corner store without fear of excruciating pain and death.

"This is very unusual," Conehead repeats, sounding irritated.

The prim nurse keeps checking on us, as though we might leave town. Her disapproval emanates from her like a fart, not only because I won't let go of you but because she believes it was a conscious act of suicide. And to anyone whose mission is to preserve life at any cost, a teenage suicide must seem a crime.

And maybe, if I didn't know you, I would agree.

Your father phones finally. I become hysterical trying to explain, try to explain what I can't understand. I have to hang up on him, I'm so mad at him, so mad. I need someone to blame. Why wasn't he there? Why couldn't he see? Why couldn't he admit he was wrong, *we* were wrong, should have taken the blinders off our eyes? How long can you live a lie? As long as no one finds you out? Or wants to find you out? You look in the mirror and tell yourself it's not lies that you're living. It's just life, compromise, getting along. Go for a walking/wine tour in Italy, see the happy peasants, stuff your face with olives and buy some pretty crockery to distract you from your lies. Listen to other people's lies knowing that they're lies but *you* won't tell if *they* don't. Go on living impacted in shit because that's what everybody else is doing. Okay maybe there's a few environmentalist wackos out there whining about toxic waste, greenhouse gases, genetic engineering, pesticides, the destruction of wetlands, rain forests, the loss of our water, fretting about honeybees and butterflies, but I mean really, who has the time? I've got a lunch, a two, three, four, five, and six o'clock—oh, and the boss is coming for dinner. Can you play by yourself, honey? Watch a video or something? What about your homework? Is the math tutor helping? I only spoke to him for three seconds, but he seems really nice. Oh, and practise your piano even though you show no talent for it and want to take an axe to it. Sorry I'm so preoccupied at the moment but your father's screwing the neighbour and it's damaged my self-esteem. Oh, are you bleeding? I didn't notice, put a band aid on it. We'll talk about it tonight. Gotta run, honeybun.

It's over. The race. It's someone else's turn. With you inside them they will run, dance, and maybe see, really see, because they've faced death, felt its chill. Every day you give them will be a miracle.

The pilot won't die. Chairs are creaking and folks are coughing. Get on with it, Captain, you're losing your audience. Aunt Bessie needs to pee and Uncle Harry's getting the DTs. Cousin Joey's desperate for a butt and nephew Jim's got a job interview with a ball-bearing manufacturer.

Sybil phones, tells me you're not in your bed. I tell her not to come. She's coming anyway. Do you want me to wait for your father? Do you want his consent, does it matter?

Just let me stay here, close to your ear, with your hair in my eyes.

Please let me stay.

Schnurr's back, acting like he's not itching to slit you open. "Mrs. Pentland, would a grief counsellor help?"

"Shut up about the grief counsellor. I'm waiting for his father."

"I understand."

"Don't you have a body to operate on?"

"Your anger is completely understandable."

"Yaddayaddayadda shut the fuck up!"

He's gone again. I nestle into you. Nobody can see us here. Do you remember at the back of the garden, behind the shed under the lilac, you had a secret place? "This is my secret place," you'd say, "nobody can see me here."

We'll stay here; I'll tell you stories. "The Three Little Pigs," you loved that one, especially when the wolf jumped down the chimney and got his tushy torched.

The pilot's dead. Sighs of relief are audible. The crowd's clearing, not even waiting for the curtain call, probably already divvying up his possessions.

I was supposed to leave you behind.

I'm trying to be strong but the battery's dead. Have you left already? I think you're gone. I'm alone here with your broken body. Sam . . . ? Sweetie . . . ?

"Please don't shake him," the prim nurse tells me.

"Would you quit spying on us?"

"You shouldn't be on the bed."

"Who says?"

"It's unsafe."

"For who? You mean he'll get disconnected and die? Get the fuck out of here." She obeys only because they want you. If you hadn't signed that card they'd sic a security guard on me.

So what am I supposed to do now? Go home? To our house? Sit on the couch that holds your shape and think positive thoughts, watch TV, a movie of the week about a boy who attempts suicide by driving into an abutment but who miraculously lives thanks to extreme medical intervention; lives to tell his mother he loves her, couldn't have done it without her, that he values his life now that he's walked in the valley of death?

"There you are," Jerry says. "They don't want you climbing on the bed."

"If you side with them, I will kill you."

"What good is it doing him?"

Then Sybil's there, it's a fucking party. They both put hands on me.

"Lay off," I say.

"We have to talk," Jerry persists. "We owe it to Sam to fulfil his wishes."

"It's a bit late for that, isn't it, fuckhead? Maybe you should have thought about his wishes fifteen years ago, you fucking asshole."

"That's good, blame me."

"You can't do this to the boy," Sybil interjects, "fight in front of him. He didn't want you to fight. He'd want you to make some kind of peace."

"Just like in the movies," I comment. "Let's join our hands in prayer."

"Greer," your ignorant father says, "you're going to have to settle down. This isn't helping."

"They're fucking cannibals."

"That may be, but time is an element. Sam wanted to donate. Let's not screw this up as well."

"As well as what? His entire life? Yeah, let's not screw up his death. That wouldn't be good parenting. You make me sick. It makes me *sick* to look at you."

He actually looks frightened. I must look insane, am insane. This isn't good, you wouldn't like it; a harridan for a mother clutching at your broken body. Try to be more like Meryl. Assume a role. If I can pretend I'm Meryl, maybe I can get through this. What accent should I use? "Very well," I say.

"Please get off the bed," Jerry says.

If I get off, they won't let me back on. If I get off, that's it, it's over between us. They won't let me back on. Just let me kiss you once more, then I promise I'll be Meryl. I hold my lips here, just hold my lips here. You don't smell of you anymore. You're gone, gone. Is it nice there?

Jerry tries to take my hand. "Greer . . . ?"

I'll caress your face one more time, then I promise, stroke your hair one more time. Is it nice there, angel? Do you have wings? Are you circling above? I'll kiss your eyes one more time, then I'll let them in, I will.

"Greer . . . ?"

You are the noblest, strongest, wisest, bravest person I have ever known. That I brought you into this world gives my life meaning. Without you there is nothingness.

Just once more. Kiss that tiny mole on your earlobe. Will I forget that? I mustn't forget that.

I'm going now, I really am. I'm climbing down, down into a bottomless pit.

Your father and I sit in the consultation room with an ocean between us out of which sea monsters raise their gnarled heads and roar.

They are cutting the life out of you, storing it in coolers before installing it in strangers brimming with hope. Because of you.

You killed strangers. It's only right that you should save them.

I've asked to see you when it is over even though I know you won't be there. I've asked to see you before they wheel you to the morgue because I want to make sure they respect what's left of you. A thick insulation surrounds me, an almost supernal warmth. I'm in a stupor from which I hope never to wake.

I lie in your bed that cradled you, gripping your watch, and the book I gave you. Tick tick tick, time marches on. I can remember choosing it, worrying that you'd prefer digital but not buying digital because I've always hated it. "Cool," you said when you saw it and I felt triumphant. You've worn it every day since, I think. Your sweat is in its leather strap. You've looked at these numbers, over and over again, waited for that little hand to move its butt, waited for your life to begin. Because there's always something, isn't there? We're always waiting for something before our life really begins.

I had to chase your father out just now. He said, "Let me stay with you." I said, "No." He said, "I don't want to leave you like this." I said, "Go home to your wife."

I've behaved reasonably well, pretending to be Meryl. Looking at your corpse drained of blood, tears swelled in my left eye and dribbled quietly down my cheek as hers do. But even as I kissed the stiffening skin of your forehead I did not wail, or tear my hair. You smelled only of chemicals. They'd stuffed you with something, slid marbles under your eyelids. You died with dignity. "See you soon," I said.

I must swallow the remaining Seconal before I lose consciousness. I fear it won't be enough, but it's all I've got. If nothing else, they will free me of thought and pain for a time. And maybe I can see you briefly, standing in the light.

But of course I retch, and must pick the pills out of the vomit to swallow them again. They slip from my fingers. I grovel on the floor in an effort to lick them up. They taste toxic in my mouth and stick in my throat that is flooded with tears.

It is a degenerate end. You wouldn't like it.

Thirty-two

I've won twice at bingo. Arnie's miffed but trying to hide it. I would've missed the first one because, as usual, I became distracted by other things, particularly the peach-haired lady with the Shih-Tzu-excuses-for-dogs she kept trying to stash under the table. But Arnie was keeping an eye on my card and elbowed me hard. "Bingo!" I shouted. What a thrill, eighty bucks. The next time I just won forty, but still got a rush out of it, I was hooked. The problem is it's a bit tricky getting down there now with all my paraphernalia. When I just had the cylinder on wheels it was doable, especially with Arnie's help. What an extraordinary man. Where does it come from, that desire to be kind? I think of all the years I've trusted no one, and here's this guy who looks like Las Vegas Elvis and smells bad, who I trust with my life.

The dog's barking. Right after Sam's death, it stopped for days and I thought oh my god Sam killed it, did that for me, one more merciful act. What did he use, a shovel, a screwdriver? Was he asleep? Was there blood and guts all over their yard? I slept fitfully in and out of doggy horror dreams. But then I heard it again and it no longer disturbed me. Because it reminded me of my son's innocence.

We buried his ashes under my tree. In the spring, I sat with him and watched the Ivory Silk come into bloom. And I've placed a bird feeder there so he is never lonely. When I see monarch butterflies and honeybees, I think of him.

That his heart's beating in someone else's chest offers a kind of comfort. Because hearts are anonymous, interchangeable, once freed of spirit. But his eyes, imagining his eyes seeing out of someone else's skull horrifies me—that crystalline stare belonging to any stranger, child abuser, wife beater. I fear meeting his eyes on the street, in a cruel face, and being unable to accept that they bear no trace of my son. Organs, they're just organs, I tell myself. Doesn't help.

Lyla considers herself responsible for his death because she prayed to God that he would kill him the same way the black man was murdered by the racists. I explained, several times, the circumstances of Sam's death, but she would hear none of it, instead took refuge in the Royals, came by and told me that Charles said to Di, "Am I to be the only Prince of Wales who doesn't have a mistress?" I suggested this was tactless. But Lyla, always loyal, explained that "the poor sod" didn't know any better, being the son of the witch. Lyla still believes that Charles should be king, that the "old stick" should step aside and let Charles be a role model for William. On the surface, she appears to have forgotten about Sam, but I know this is not so. She will suffer unnecessary guilt for the rest of her life, if there is such a thing as necessary guilt. Does guilt provide anything but lead in our shoes? I wanted my son to feel guilt.

Erna's granddaughter's still missing, consequently Erna orbited into another sphere, obsessing over "the body." We tried to convince her that a body had not been found because her granddaughter wasn't dead. "*Don't* you tell me there's no goddamn body, they dig up bodies all the time. They get their dogs out sniffing and—Bob's your uncle—they find a body." She concluded that the police weren't telling her about "the body" because they had no suspects, were never going to have suspects, because her granddaughter wasn't the Prime Minister's daughter.

I understood that Erna needed a body, could no longer stand not knowing, imagining, the fate of her loved one. A body would have meant that the child was at rest, free of suffering. As the months wore on, Erna let herself go, her bleached hair sprung from her head Medusa-style. She smoked steadily and stopped eating, even mini-doughnuts. She accused Lyla of treachery, said she was in "cahoots" with the cops re: "the body." Then she jumped from the Glen Road bridge into a stream of cars, miraculously killing no one but herself. I picture her in mid-air, cigarette held high, gabbing.

It's not so bad an end, really. Quick. She no longer wanted to live.

But Lyla has not taken the loss of her companion well. She's in living hell. She tells me she would rather be dead and I believe her. There is nothing to grasp in her life, except the pills that dull her few bright moments while giving her skin rashes. I finally made the connection between the "parasites" and lithium. When she's manic, the rash recedes as do the "parasites."

I tell her I'll take her with me if she really wants to go. I could do this, have enough assorted drugs. But she looks at me glassily, her conviction waning. Death scares her more than life in hell.

I tell her she did not cause Sam's death. I tell her he didn't want to live with her parents' blood on his hands, didn't want to live when his mother was dying. Didn't want to live in a society that despised and dismissed him, a society unwilling to deconstruct its notions of innocence and wrongdoing. A society immersed in colour, but determined to see only in black and white.

I don't know if this is true. What if he was asleep?

It would mean he unconsciously *chose* suicide. Which means he unconsciously *chose* to kill her parents. Which blurs the line between absolution and accountability. I can't absolve him if he was culpable. All I can do is try to understand, try. And accept that the line can't be easily drawn.

What I do know is we must pay closer attention to our

children, hear their cries, no matter how muted or disguised. What I do know is that I listened too late.

Sometimes I can't remember the sound of his voice. Sometimes I see a boy in the street in the same jeans and baseball cap, and I start to call out.

But I go on, despite the blade continually twisting inside me. At times, I'm numbed to it because I'm preoccupied with other things, breathing for example, just getting around. I keep requiring more and more supplementary oxygen as the space in my lungs gets squeezed out by the tumours. They're secretory and constantly weep. Apparently there's more cell activity in a wet environment (spongy lungs), so I'd say my tumours are happy campers.

But the gasping's uncomfortable, feeling that every breath is taken through a wet facecloth. The shower has offered some relief, which makes no sense as there's less oxygen available in a steamy shower stall.

I've often sat in his room that he forbade me to enter and looked out his window at the patch of sky he used to see. I had to wash his sheets because of the vomit, but otherwise the room remains unchanged. Sybil describes my visitations to his room as morbid. I've tried to explain that I don't have to get over his death like healthy mommies do. And anyway, I don't believe you ever get over the death of your child. Ever.

But you push it aside, push it aside to function, to do the best you can while coping with the little things like nasal prongs that rub your nostrils raw in spite of the lubricant you shove up your nose to prevent drying of your nasal passages. And the strap that fits around your head to keep the apparatus in place that chafes around your ears, making you feel like a horse in harness forever hauling bricks. And the pressure sores on your butt and heels filled with dead and dying tissue, black guck, that smells of rotten meat—sores that can't heal because you must always lie propped up to avoid drowning in tumour tears. You don't actually drown, just feel as if you're drowning. Like you felt when you were a kid and held your head under water until your lungs felt ready to explode. Except then you'd pop up, victorious because once again you'd proved yourself immortal. Now you can't pop up. Now you surface weakened and scared. Drowning is a horrible death.

So these are the little things to think about, besides the big things which I try not to think about. Which I guess I've done all my life.

When I was still on the small cylinder, I would regularly take Arnie to Starbucks for venti lattes. I learned to ignore the stares and just watch the world around me. People always seemed to be discussing relationships or renovations. And I wondered what the connection was there—our relationship is in ruins, let's renovate. I had this picture of the world ending as we ingest cyanide from our toxic waste, nitrogen from our dwindling water supply, emissions from our fossil fuels, while all these people busily renovate. They'll perish slowly, by inches, surrounded by drywall and Scotchgarded carpets. They'll perish with no knowledge of what they'd had and missed because they were so busy talking about relationships and renovations.

Whereas what I had and missed never leaves me. It's become a constant companion. We no longer fight, no more recriminations. A deal has been struck. I won't whine yaddayaddayadda if it will shut the fuck up. Which doesn't mean I've reached this beatific state in which I'm free of hatred, resentment, anger, bitterness, envy, blaggablagga. It's all still there, the hideousness in my makeup, contained in my weeping tumours. When I go, the cancer goes with me, or more specifically, with my corpse. I'll be somewhere else entirely, watching the tumours choke sans blood supply. Ha ha.

So that's one way of looking at it.

I think Sybil figured out things were getting serious when I couldn't blow bubbles anymore. She thought if she could exercise my lungs by forcing me to blow Miracle Bubbles, I would miraculously heal. She's had to go back and see General Norm because she fiddled excessively with her pacemaker, causing slipping and erosion of the skin. Norm sternly advised me that my aunt (he pronounced it "awnt") suffered from "pacemaker twiddle syndrome" and that I *must* restrain her from twiddling. Easier said than done.

Sometimes I ponder Bunny the dead cat and wonder if he's flying around somewhere, gorging on Camembert cheese. My preoccupation with an afterlife is a direct result, I realize, of the pending end of my before-death. Because when my before-death seemed without end, I did not believe in an afterlife. Even now, as I try to believe in it, I get stumped by such details as wouldn't it get awfully crowded over there, what with me and Sam, Bunny and my parents, the pilot, Erna, Linda McCartney, JFK and son, Adolf and Winston, Mussolini strutting about, Elizabeth I shouting "Off with his head"? I mean, talk about overpopulated.

But again, I try not to think about this big thing.

Because I need to believe there is a place beyond. That's all faith is, isn't it, whatever gets you through? Without that "place," I would be unable to plod on hooked up to a tank like a deep-sea diver. The hose is generous in length and gives me enough slack on my good days to toddle downstairs and putter about. The thing is, the stairs are looking more and more like Mount Everest. Currently, a trip to the toilet is a major expedition. Nurse Humourless-but-efficient has placed a commode by my bed, which I ignore like an uninvited guest.

Estelle came by with Laura Secord bargain outlet chocolates and Willy the cat. She proudly demonstrated how he would sit at her command. "Isn't that marvellous?" she kept asking. "A cat? Cat's don't *obey.*" This was some kind of victory for her and got me thinking about our obsession with control. How limiting, stifling it is, controlling ourselves, our cats, each other. Let go, see if you fall. If you do, get up again.

I won't die in debt. I have my affairs in order. Most of it's going to Sybil. Jerry, amazingly, has agreed to let her live in the house for the rest of her life. Sam's trust I'm transferring to Turner, and a lump of cash that will enable Arnie to take him to the Vancouver clinic to try the CP treatment. The tulips I planted came up. "They're tho beautiful," Arnie told me again and again.

I'm leaving nothing of monetary value to Rachel because it would only be snorted by Scientology. She's visited me twice since Sam's death. The second time she'd applied heavy powder to her face to hide bruising. I told her she didn't need to come and see me, not expecting, of course, that she would never come and see me. But that's her life, impacted in shit. Who am I to talk?

I've become quite fearless, except of death, of course, and pain. But what I used to be afraid of—what people would think, say, feel, do if I said, or did so and so—has vapourized and left this clear sky. Clouds occasionally form, but I don't immediately panic and decide that the sky is falling. Really, I don't panic anymore. The loss of my son has changed me in some essential way. Stick me in a cage with a coiled cobra and I would look him in the yellow eyes and say, Okay, what's the deal, let's not beat around the basket.

When I was still mobile with time on my hands, I did a couple of soup-kitchen stints with Sybil. Nobody there talks about relationships or renovating. Mostly they wolf down food. There are those who exude madness, despair, fury, and then there are those who attempt to maintain their pseudo-selves. They behave as though the gathering at the soup kitchen were a social event, a tea party. They exchange niceties about the weather and the quality of sandwiches today. "Not half bad," one comments. "I prefer the tuna," says another while scratching at the lice in his hair.

The only woman in attendance is Hazel dressed in four coats, two hats and shredded boots, who shouts "Fuck a duck!" at regular intervals. She's always accompanied by a shopping cart crammed with plastic bags stuffed with who knows what. She gobbles her sammie in the corner, away from the others. She never completes a meal but stashes leftovers in her cart. Then she begins to rock backwards and forwards in her chair. After several rocks she stops abruptly, pats the back of her head four times, then her forehead four times, resumes rocking, stops, pats the back of her head four times, then her forehead four times. This goes on until the soup kitchen closes.

I don't want this end for Lyla.

Earl Verman sold her house while she was raving and free of parasites. As my son predicted, I invited her to live here, but she prefers the Four Seasons. She'll be broke in no time and, until she threatens bodily harm, will remain at large. Unless she "seeks help" from her snaky shrink who'll only drug her into submission which will bring back the parasites, tremors, weight gain, inability to pee, dry mouth and lethargy. This is not a great alternative to room service at the Four Seasons.

Sybil has promised me that she will watch out for her, but even Sybil can't live forever, I don't think.

Jerry, well, he needs a stiff boot up the ass as usual, but on the whole he's been very good to me. To think of all the times I called him scum-sucking pig-dog. But I should've charged him an hourly fee for our sessions because, really, I didn't need to hear about Gingivitis Girl's latest exploits and Hedley's diminishing personal hygiene. I suspect he was rambling on to distract himself from my reality, a reality he can do nothing about.

A robin nested under the eave outside my window. As I listened to her babies chirp and cheep, a lightness awakened in me, an awe of the nature of things. Mummy Robin was extremely diligent about feeding her young, keeping them alive. Then they flew away from her. The nest is empty.

I don't understand why we make death into this gloomy, punishing dungeon of a place. I mean, it's as natural as birth, and maybe in some cases less painful, that trip down the birth canal can't be easy, and you don't know where that's taking you either. Unable to see, you're squeezed forward into what? You want to turn around, swim back to what you know. But you can't.

How is this different from death?

I've rehearsed with the bag. It's farcical. Finding a plastic bag without a tiny tear in it has proven nearly impossible. Especially a clear bag. I've had to settle for a dollar store version that's made from real plastic instead of the environmentally friendly stuff. How appropriate that I should die in a toxic bag. But it's opaque. Why I want to see in those last seconds mystifies me. One more glance at the rectangle on the wall where the *Iris* used to be? One more glance out the window? Do I want to see in case I change my mind? It must have more to do with claustrophobia. I mean, try putting a bag over your head. It's spooky, you could suffocate in there.

The other challenge has been locating the right-sized rubber band, because it's got to fit snugly around your neck. Many snapped my knuckles before I found the right fit.

I've hidden these tools between my mattress and box spring.

They are my friends.

One of the Starbucks conversations involved two women with muscular thighs and closely cropped hair. One of them, in bicycle shorts, had just broken up with her boyfriend because there were "issues" he wasn't dealing with. The main issue seemed to be that when they went to *The Phantom of the Opera*, he believed that she was letting the man sitting next to her feel her up. She stressed that if it had just been during *Phantom* that he'd thought she was letting men feel her up, she could have coped, but it happened during other shows—and not just musicals—even parties became a problem. The cycling woman sent him to a shrink who referred to his fondling fantasies as "moviemaking." "We'd be somewhere," the cycling woman complained, "and I could tell he was moviemaking."

Don't we all though?

And then, after accusing her of sexual misconduct, he would repent, cry because it was so painful.

"What was?" her friend asked.

"He felt bad that he'd put me through that."

"But then he'd do it again."

Don't we all though, feel bad, then do it again? Where does it stop? Why can't we learn from our mistakes? Why can't we make the movie better?

This part scares me. My hands are shaking, and a cold sweat has oiled my fingers. I have to mix up the powder with the vanilla pudding. Sybil was so thrilled when I asked for pudding. My appetite's been shrinking for weeks as has my body. Pudding signalled revival to her. I can't tell her. I've tried in the note but it's impossible to explain. She'll be angry with me because she believes that "we all must wait our turn." But I can't, Auntie, I can't breathe anymore, don't you see, can't move, can't laugh, even crying feels like asphyxiation. This emaciated body that vomits and shits nothing but the pink syrup of morphine contains only what I want to leave behind. This is no life, Auntie. I am not brave like you. I don't want to see how it turns out. I don't want to be the last one at the party looking at the garbage.

Swallow, wait, sip more vodka. Good thing I took one of Henry Kissinger's antinauseants.

I'll miss my tree. I'll miss sitting beside it, imagining him with me.

What if it's all imagining, moviemaking? What if I'm really never going to see him again? Please don't leave me now, faith, stay with me now, no matter how deluded.

More vodka, try again, all forty have to go down before you pass out or you'll wake up inside your carcass. Get it down. Where's the bag? I had it here, where's the fucking bag? Oh, here.

I'm fading. SWALLOW.

You won't find me here, Auntie, Nurse Humourless-but-efficient will. Please forgive me. I love you so.

No strength left. Get the bag on. O mighty dollar store, deliver me. The plastic clings to my face as I gulp the air inside it. Don't panic, the sky isn't falling. Sing like when you were a child alone in the dark house, sing to keep the demons away. Row, row, row your boat gently down the stream. Merrily, merrily, merrily, merrily, life is but a dream.

I close my eyes and see my son.

Originally published by Thomas Allen Publishers

Published by ECW Press
665 Gerrard Street East
Toronto, ON M4M 1Y2
416-694-3348 / info@ecwpress.com

The author gratefully acknowledges the support of the Canada Council and the Toronto Arts Council.

Library and Archives Canada Cataloguing in Publication

Strube, Cordelia, 1960–, author
The barking dog / Cordelia Strube.

Originally published: Toronto: Thomas Allen Publishers, 2000.
Issued in print and electronic formats.
ISBN 978-1-77041-375-7 (paperback)
ISBN 978-1-77090-951-9 (epub); ISBN 978-1-77090-953-3 (pdf)

I. Title.

PS8587.T72975B37 2016 C813'.54 C2016-905147-1
C2016-902371-0

Editor: Patrick Crean
Cover design: David A. Gee

The publication of *The Barking Dog* has been generously supported by the Canada Council for the Arts which last year invested $153 million to bring the arts to Canadians throughout the country, and by the Government of Canada through the Canada Book Fund. *Nous remercions le Conseil des arts du Canada de son soutien. L'an dernier, le Conseil a investi 153 millions de dollars pour mettre de l'art dans la vie des Canadiennes et des Canadiens de tout le pays. Ce livre est financé en partie par le gouvernement du Canada.* We also acknowledge the Ontario Arts Council (OAC), an agency of the Government of Ontario, which last year funded 1,709 individual artists and 1,078 organizations in 204 communities across Ontario, for a total of $52.1 million, and the contribution of the Government of Ontario through the Ontario Media Development Corporation.

Canada Council for the Arts
Conseil des Arts du Canada

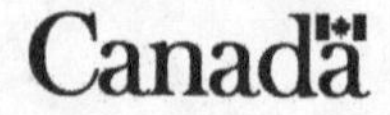